THE HIDDEN MAN

ALSO BY CHARLES CUMMING

Typhoon

The Trinity Six

The Alec Milius Novels

A Spy by Nature

The Spanish Game

The Thomas Kell Novels

A Foreign Country

A Colder War

THE HIDDEN MAN

CHARLES CUMMING

St. Martin's Griffin
New York

This is a work of fiction. All of the characters, organizations, and events portrayed in this novel are either products of the author's imagination or are used fictitiously.

 Printed in the United States of America. For information, address St. Martin's Press, 175 Fifth Avenue, New York, N.Y. 10010.

www.stmartins.com

The Library of Congress Cataloging-in-Publication Data is available upon request.
ISBN 978-0-312-36638-4 (trade paperback)
ISBN 978-1-250-02603-3 (e-book)

Our books may be purchased in bulk for promotional, educational, or business use. Please contact your local bookseller or the Macmillan Corporate and Premium Sales Department at (800) 221-7945, extension 5442, or by e-mail at MacmillanSpecialMarkets@macmillan.com.

First published in Great Britain by Michael Joseph, Penguin Books in 2003

First St. Martin's Griffin Edition: November 2015

10 9 8 7 6 5 4 3 2 1

for my father

AUTHOR'S NOTE

The Hidden Man was my "difficult" second novel, written between 2001 and 2003. For complicated reasons, it is only now being published in the United States, more than ten years after it first appeared in the UK.

For this edition, I have made some minor changes to the text, in an attempt to clarify some of the more obscure elements of the story. Reading the novel again, for the first time in over a decade, I was struck by how much has changed in the intervening years. I began writing *The Hidden Man* before 9/11, at a time when Russian organized crime was on the rise in London and nobody had heard of Vladimir Putin. It is a measure of how much time has passed since 2003 that my characters smoke in pubs, watch movies on video cassettes, and copy sensitive information from computers onto floppy disks. At one point, someone is even heard to ask: "What's Google?"

Thank you to everyone at St. Martin's Press for all their hard work on this belated edition of *The Hidden Man*. I hope you enjoy it.

C.C.

London, 2015

WINTER

1

The Russian is sitting alone on the driver's side of a rented Mercedes-Benz. The key in the ignition has been turned a single click, just enough to power the radio, and it is snowing, wet flakes of soft ice falling like ash in the darkness. A song comes on, an old Sinatra tune the man has not heard in many years: Frank singing live to a room full of screaming Americans hanging off his every note. Sometimes it feels as if his whole life has been lived inside parked cars listening to the radio: sudden movements on side streets; a light snuffing out in a bedroom four floors up; moments of snatched sleep. Cars that smelled of imported cigarettes and the sweat of tired, unwashed men.

A young couple turn the corner into the street ahead of him, walking arm in arm with a jaunty, light-hearted step. Drunk, most probably, coming toward the car and laughing up at the falling snow. They are delighted by it, letting the flakes melt in the palms of up-turned hands, embracing one another as it settles in their hair and on their clothes. He thinks the woman, like so many London girls, is worryingly thin: legs like saplings in high-heeled shoes. He fears that she may topple over on the wet pavement and, if she hurts herself, he will have to get out of the car to help her. Then there will be two witnesses who have seen his face.

The song ends and fades into an advertisement narrated in slang and dialect, words he cannot make out. English is no longer clear to him; somehow, in recent years, the language has changed, it has moved away. The couple skip past the Mercedes and he watches them disappear down the street using the mirror on the passenger side. An old technique. No need even to turn his head.

Now he reaches down to switch off the radio and everything is once again silent. Just a very faint impression of traffic in the distance, the city's constant hum. As an extension of the same movement, the Russian turns the catch on the glove box with his left hand, holds it as the casing falls open, and takes out the gun.

This no longer feels like an act of vengeance. It has been too long for that. It is simply a deep need within himself to attain some level of peace, to sew up the wound of his grief. In this sense his need to go through with it is almost like a lust: he has no control over himself, no way now of turning back.

From the back seat of the car he takes a woolen hat and a pair of leather gloves, items purchased at a shop in Hammersmith three days earlier. They are flimsy, but warm enough to cope with the timid British winter. Then he checks the street one last time and steps out of the car.

The flat is on the fourth floor of a large apartment building at the northeastern end of the street. His legs are stiff and tired as he crosses the road, sore in the knees from waiting so long and tight along the sciatic nerve of his left thigh. Snow falls onto the shoulders of his coat; it flutters into his cheeks like puffs of dandelion. As he is climbing the steps of the building, a woman comes out and, for the first time, the Russian feels a sense of concern. Instinctively, he looks to the ground, taking a bunch of keys from his pocket with the ease and routine of a resident. The woman, mid-forties and slight, is hurried by the snow, muttering under her breath as she springs the catch on an umbrella. The noise of this is like birds breaking for the sky. The two do not look at one another directly, though he knows from experience that this may not be enough to absolve him, that the stranger may have seen his shoes, his trousers, perhaps even caught a glimpse of his face when it first appeared at the door. For an instant he thinks about turning back, but the possibility evaporates in the heat of his obligation. The force of revenge, the lust, carries him through the street door and into the lobby, where a clock on the wall tells him that it is twenty past one.

He has been here before, twice, to premeditate the act, to scout the building for exits, and to get a sense of its layout and design. So he knows that there is a white plastic timer switch inside the front door that will illuminate the stairwell for approximately two minutes, and an old, wrought-iron caged lift on the right-hand side of the lobby, with a staircase leading down to a locked basement and up to seven floors of apartments.

All of his experience has told him to take the stairs, to leave an option should anything go wrong. But he is older now, the fitness ripped from his legs, and has decided to ride the lift to the fifth floor and to walk down a single flight to the fourth as a way of preserving his strength.

The lift is waiting. He slides back the gate and steps inside, pushing a red ceramic button marked 5. The cabin ticks as it passes each floor, slices of red carpet and banister visible through the metal grills of the lift shaft. The aging wheels of the elevator mechanism twist through grease and oil, pulling him up through the building. At the third floor the lights go out on the stairs, sooner than he had anticipated, but a single pearl bulb inside the cabin provides him with enough light to reach into his coat, pull out the gun, and place it in the right-hand pocket of his overcoat.

Now he squints outside, passing level 4, eyes moving quickly left and right to detect any sign of movement. Nothing. The lift continues to climb, halting ten seconds later on the fifth floor with nothing more than a slight jolting bump, like a sprung dance floor. He notices a fresh piece of chewing gum wedged between the roof and the left panel of the cabin. He would like some gum now, something to take the dryness from the inside of his mouth.

Why does he feel nothing? Why, when he is just minutes away from an act that he has envisaged with total clarity and rapture for nearly twenty years, why then has his mind given way to everything but a very basic sense of process and technique? He is trying to convince himself that a moment of catharsis is imminent, but as he pulls back the cabin's metal grill, pushes open the heavy door of the lift with his left hand, reaches into the pocket of his overcoat to release the safety catch on the gun, he is little more than a machine. It is like every other criminal act in his long, corrupted life. Tonight has no special resonance, not yet any sense of joy.

In one of the flats at the end of the corridor, the Russian can hear voices on a television, teenagers shouting at one another, then a screech of tires. A late-night American film. The volume must have been turned up high, because he is able to pick out the noises and his hearing is not what it was. He holds the door of the lift as it swings slowly back on its hinge and then heads for the stairwell, taking each step slowly, keeping his heart rate down. It is very dark and he has to hold on to the banister with a gloved hand, the leather sticking on bumps of dried polish as it slides down the wood. A car sounds its horn on the street just as he reaches the fourth floor.

Simultaneously he feels the first burst of adrenalin, not what it was in his youth, but a quickening nevertheless, lightening his arms and chest. He knows that his heart is beating faster now and has to check his pace moving down the corridor, deliberately slowing as he approaches the door of Apartment 462. Twenty feet away the Russian stops and takes out the set of lockpicks. He sees light glint dully on the metal surface of the keys and finds its source—a fire exit sign at the end of the corridor, bold white lettering within an illuminated green case. Then he pinches the main key between the thumb and forefinger of his left hand and moves toward the door.

With his head pressed to the pale wood, cold against his ears, the Russian listens. No sound inside. Then, way below, there are voices, at least two people, their footsteps clattering on the marble floor of the lobby. Immediately he moves away from the door and walks back to the edge of the stairwell, waiting for the lift to jolt free of the fifth floor and ride back to ground level. But they are walking: when he peers over the banister he can see two heads that stop at the first floor. He assumes—although he can neither see nor hear—that the couple go to an apartment to the right of the staircase, and waits a full minute for silence to re-engulf the building before returning to the door.

Perhaps the distraction has hurried him, for the Russian listens only briefly now before sliding the key, with extraordinary slowness, into the lock. A perfect fit. He pushes open the door, just enough to fit through, and winces as it scrapes on linoleum. Immediately there is the smell of good, fresh coffee; the flat is thick with it. His eyes adjust to the total absence of light in the tiny hall. He knows from a plan of the apartment that the bedroom is beyond the closed door on the other side of the living room. The kitchen is directly ahead of him and it is empty. A Post-it note has been stuck on the frame of the door, and he can just make out the scrawl:

CALL TAPLOE RE: M

The yellow paper moves very slightly as, in these first few seconds, he stands quite still, listening for any indication that the Englishman may be awake.

It is only now that he hears the music. Was it playing as he came in? He has been holding the gun in his right hand all this time and his grip now tightens around the butt. Classical music, a piano, very slow and melancholy. The kind of music a man might listen to if he were having trouble getting to sleep. With his heel the Russian pushes the front door until it is resting against the frame. Then, without needing to look back, he feels for the latch with his hand and closes it very slowly. He waits for the lock to engage and moves one step forward toward the door of the living room, the gun now up and level.

If he is awake, so be it. Let him see me coming.

But there is no other noise or movement as he walks into the sitting room, just the music fractionally louder now and the bathroom door ahead of him, leaking light into a narrow passage. Everything in the sitting room is visible because of it and, out of habit, he takes it all in: the two paperback books lying on the carpet; the empty tumbler on a small three-legged antique table; a framed photograph of a young man and woman on their wedding day hanging unevenly nearby. The room of an untidy, chaotic mind, devoid of a woman's touch.

Another two steps and he is across the room, moving as lightly as he can, cheap deck shoes noiseless against the worn carpet. Still he feels no sense of exhilaration, no impending release for his grief: only a specialist's expertise, an absolute focus on the job in hand. Moving silently between the books on the floor, his eyes fix on the space ahead of him: the narrow, well-lit corridor, the bedroom door to his left. On this he trains the gun, stopping now, his mind a spin of instinct and calculation. For years he has imagined killing the Englishman in his bed, watching him cower and writhe in a corner. It has been planned that way. But he is suddenly uncertain of making that last move into the room, of opening the door into a place where his opponent may hold the upper hand.

The decision is made for him. He hears a single heavy footstep, then the sound of a light switch being pressed and the rattle of the bedroom door handle as it drops through forty-five degrees. Instinctively, the Russian takes two steps backward, hurried now, stripped of control. Light flares briefly into the passage and he blinks rapidly as he looks up, the pale face etched with shock.

The intruder had words to say, a speech prepared, but the first shot punctures the left side of his victim's chest, spinning him to the ground. Blood and tissue and bone shower against the walls and floor of the corridor, one color in the pale bathroom light. But he is still conscious, his blue cotton pyjamas blackened and viscous with blood.

In his own language, the Russian says, "Do you know who I am?"

And the Englishman, propped up by a pale thick arm, shakes his head as the color drains from his eyes.

Again, in Russian: "Do you know who I am? Do you know why I have come?"

But he sees that he is passing out: his neck is suddenly loose and falling. In the moments before the second shot the Russian tries quickly to summon a sense of fulfillment, a closure to the act. He looks directly into a dying man's eyes and tries to feel something beyond the basic violence of what he has done.

The effort is hopeless, and as the second bullet rips into the man's chest, the Russian is already turning, experiencing little more than the basic fear of being discovered. He just wants to be out of this place, to be away from London. And then he will go to the grave in Samarkand and tell Mischa what he has done.

AUTUMN

2

"Don't move. Hold it right there."

The girl stopped immediately, her hand on the nape of her neck.

"Now look up at me." Her eyes met his.

"Without twisting your head."

She moved her chin back toward the mattress. "Good," he said. "Is that comfortable?"

"Yes."

"And you're warm enough?"

"Yes, Ben, yes."

He leaned forward, out of sight now. She heard the itch and whisper of the brush as it moved across the canvas. He said, "Sorry, Jenny, I interrupted you."

"That's OK." She coughed and tucked a loose strand of hair behind her ear. "You said you were six when it happened? When your father walked out?"

Ben took a long drag on his cigarette and said, "Six, yes."

"And your brother?"

"Mark was eight."

"And you haven't seen him since?"

"No."

Outside on the street, three floors down, a distant child was imitating the sound of a diving airplane.

"Why did he leave?"

When Ben did not answer immediately, Jenny thought that she might have offended him. That could happen sometimes, with sudden intimacy. When a model is lying naked in an artist's studio with only a thin white sheet for company, conversation tends toward the candid.

"My father was offered a position in the Foreign Office, in 1976," he said finally. The voice betrayed a controlled resentment, the glimpse, perhaps, of a quick temper. "The idea of it went to his head. The work meant more to him than his family did. So he took off."

Jenny managed a compassionate smile, although there was nothing in her own experience to compare with the concept of a parent abandoning his own child. The thought appalled her. Ben continued to paint, his face very still and concentrated.

"That must have been awful," she said, just to fill the silence. The remark sounded like a platitude and she regretted it. "I mean, it's difficult to recover from something like that. You must find it so hard to trust anyone."

Ben looked up.

"Well, you have to be careful with that one, don't you?"

"What do you mean?"

"Blaming everything on the past, Jenny. We're the therapy generation. An explanation for every antisocial act in our damaged adolescence. Make a mistake and you can always write it off against a shitty childhood."

She smiled. She liked the way he said things like that, the smile that suddenly cracked across his face.

"Is that what you believe?" she asked.

"Not exactly." He stubbed out the cigarette. He was trying to capture the play of light on her body, the darkening hollows of skin. "It's what my brother thinks."

"Mark?"

Ben nodded. "He's a lot more forgiving than I am. Actually works with my father now. Doesn't see it as a problem at all."

"He *works* with him?"

"Yeah."

"How did that happen?"

"Freak coincidence." Ben blew hard on the canvas to free it of dust. He didn't feel much like opening up and telling Jenny all about big brother's dream job running a top London nightclub and flying business class around the world. She was a student, just twenty-one, and would only want to know if he could get her into Libra for free or source her some cheap CDs. "Mark and my dad go on business trips together," he said vaguely. "Have dinners, that kind of thing."

"And you don't mind?"

Ben rubbed his neck. "Nothing to do with me."

"Come on." She rolled over and drew her knees up tight against her chest. A very faint tremor of cellulite appeared on her upper thigh. "Yesterday, you told me you guys were close. Hasn't it affected your relationship?"

Ben decided to kill the subject.

"Are you uncomfortable, Jenny?" he asked. "How come you've moved position?"

She sensed his annoyance, but pressed on, using her body as a decoy. With her legs in the air, cycling for balance as she leaned over the bed, she began looking for a cigarette.

"I just need a break," she said. "Come on. Don't be so mysterious. Tell me."

He was looking at the naked base of her spine. "Tell you what?"

"About your brother. About the way you feel about him."

"The way I feel about him." Ben repeated the phrase quietly under his breath.

"Yes." She was sitting up again now, still without a cigarette. "Tell me how this thing between Mark and your father has affected you."

"This *thing*?"

He was picking at words, escaping her. She knew that he was being clever and shrugged her shoulders in an exaggerated gesture of mock surrender. "Just tell me if you're still as close as you were before."

"Closer," he lied, and looked her right in the eye.

"Good."

Then he paused, adding, "I'm just angry with him."

She seized on this like a piece of gossip. "Angry? About what?"

"For forgiving our father so quickly. For welcoming him back into his life." Ben found that he was sweating and rolled up the sleeves of his shirt. "Mark gives the appearance of being streetwise and cool, but the truth is he's a diplomat, the guy who smooths things over. He hates confrontation or ill-feeling of any kind. So Dad comes back after an absence of twenty-five years and his attitude is conciliatory. Anything for a quiet life. For some reason,

Mark needs to keep everything on an even keel or he gets unsettled."

"Maybe that's how he's learned to deal with hardship in the past," Jenny suggested confidently, and Ben tried to remember if the girls he had known when he was twenty-one had been half as self-assured and insightful as she was.

"Maybe," he said.

"And you?" she asked.

"I'm just the opposite. I don't want simple answers to complicated questions. I don't want to welcome Dad back with open arms and say it didn't matter that he ruined my mother's life. Mark thinks this is stubborn, that I'm locked in the past. He thinks I should let bygones be bygones."

"Well, you have to deal with it in your own way."

"That's what I keep telling him."

Out on the road, the child was now making the noise of a machine gun, swooping up and down the street. Ben's eyes twitched in annoyance and he stood up to close the window. Jenny renewed her search for a cigarette, rummaging around in a handbag among old tissues and bottles of scent. When a pair of sunglasses spilled out onto the wooden floor, he said, "Have one of mine," and threw her a packet from his shirt pocket.

Ben was slightly annoyed, as if she was not seeing his point of view, and went through with an idea. Walking across the studio from the window, he withdrew a scrapbook from the drawer of a cupboard and handed it to her, flicking to the second page before returning to his easel.

"What's this?" she asked.

"Read the cutting."

A wedding announcement from *The Times* had been pasted on the open page.

> The marriage took place on 10 April between Mr Benjamin Graham Keen, youngest son of the late Mrs Carolyn Buchanan, and Alice Lucy McEwan, only daughter of Mr Michael McEwan of Halstead, Essex, and Mrs Susan Mitchell, of Hampstead, London. Mr Mark Keen was best man.

"This is about you and your wife," Jenny said.

"Yes, but you notice the omission?" There was a small note of childish rebellion in Ben's voice that surprised her. "No."

"There's no mention of my father."

"You just left him out?"

"We just left him out."

"Why?"

"Because of what he's done. Because he's *nobody.*" The words were unconvincing, like something Ben had learned by heart many years before. "It's like this," he said. "As far as I'm concerned, the day my father walked out on Mum was the day he ceased to exist."

3

Ian Boyle stood in the vast, air-conditioned barn of Terminal One Arrivals, waiting for the plane. He was cold and tired and wished he was on his way home. Arsenal were playing Champions League at Highbury against a team of third-rate Austrians: there'd be goals and a hatful of chances, one of those easy nights in Europe when you can just sit back and watch the visitors unravel. He'd wanted to have a shower before kickoff, to cook up a curry and sink a couple of pints down the pub. Now it would be a race to get home after the rush-hour M4 trudge, and no time to chat to his daughter or deal with the piles of post.

Two young boys—five and eight, Ian guessed—swarmed past him and ducked into a branch of Sunglass Hut, shrieking with energy and excitement. A woman with a voice not dissimilar to his ex-wife's made a prerecorded security announcement on the public address system, pointless and unheard in the din of the hall. Ian wondered if there were other spooks nearby, angels from fifty services waiting for their man in the stark white light of Heathrow. His own people, working other assignments, would most probably have holed up in Immigration, getting a kick out of the two-way mirrors at Passport Control. But Ian had spent four years working Customs and Excise and was anxious to avoid spending time with old colleagues; a lot of them had grown smug and set in their ways, drunk on the secret power of strip search and eviction. He'd go through only when the plane had touched down, not a moment before, and watch Keen as he came into the hall. It was just that he couldn't stand the looks they gave him, those fat grins over weak cups of tea, the suggestion of pity in their trained, expressionless eyes. When Ian had left for the Service in 1993, he could tell that a lot of his colleagues were pleased. They thought it was a step down; Ian was just about the only one who felt he was moving up.

Finding a seat opposite a branch of The Body Shop, he looked up and checked the flickering arrivals screen for perhaps the ninth or tenth time. The BA flight from Moscow was still delayed by an hour and a half—no extension, thank Christ, but still another twenty-five minutes out of London. Fucking Moscow air-traffic control. Every time they put him on Libra it was the same old story: ice on the runway at Sheremetjevo and the locals too pissed to fix it. He rang Graham outside in the car, told him the bad news, and settled back in his chair with a collapsing sigh. A family of Africans in traditional dress walked past him, two of them pressing handkerchiefs to their eyes as they pushed trolleys piled six feet high with luggage and bags. Ian couldn't tell if they were happy or sad. He lit a cigarette, opened the *Standard,* and waited.

4

Christopher Keen had taken the call personally in his private office. It was a routine inquiry, of the sort he handled every day, from a businessman calling himself Bob Randall with "a minor difficulty in the former Soviet Union."

"I've been informed," Randall explained, "that Russia is your area of expertise."

Keen did not ask who had recommended him for the job. That was simply the way the business worked: by reputation, by word of mouth. Neither did he inquire about the nature of the problem. That was simply common sense when speaking on an open line. Instead, he said, "Yes. I worked in the Eastern Bloc for many years."

"Good." Randall's voice was nasal and bureaucratically flat. He suggested a meeting in forty-eight hours at a location on Shepherd's Bush Road.

"It's a Café Rouge, in the French style. On the corner of Batoum gardens." Randall spelt out "Batoum" very slowly, saying "B for Bertie" and "A for Apple" in a way that tested Keen's patience. "There are tables there which can't be seen from the street. We're not likely to be spotted. Would that be suitable for you, or do you have a specific procedure that you like to follow?"

Keen made a note of the date in his desk diary and smiled: first-time buyers were often like this, jumpy and prone to melodrama, wanting code words and gadgets, chalk marks on walls.

"There is no specific procedure," he said. "I can find the café."

"Good. But how will I recognize you?"

As he asked the question, 'Bob Randall'—whose real name was Stephen Taploe—was sitting in Thames House staring at a JPEG of Keen taken in western Afghanistan in 1983. It was a necessary subterfuge.

"I'm tall," Keen said, switching the phone to his other ear. "I'll be wearing a dark blue suit, most probably. My experience is that in circumstances such as these two people who have never met before very quickly come to recognize one another. Call it one of the riddles of the trade."

"Of course," Randall replied. "Of course. And when shall we say? Perhaps six o'clock?"

"Fine," Keen said. He was already hanging up. "Six o'clock."

Two days later, Taploe arrived at the café on Shepherd's Bush Road half an hour early and picked out a secluded table, his back facing the busy street. At 17:55, he took a call from Ian Boyle, informing him in a jumble of code and doublespeak that Keen's BA flight from Moscow had eventually landed some ninety-five minutes late. Keen had used a public telephone box—not a mobile—after clearing Passport Control, and was now picking up his luggage in the hall. The call had been made to a west London number that was already being traced.

"Understood," he told him. "And was there any sign of Duchev?"

"Nothing."

"Well keep on it, please. And brief Paul Quinn. I'm going to be walking the dog for the next two hours. Contact me again at eight."

At that moment Taploe saw Christopher Keen coming into the café, a striking man in a dark blue suit possessed of a languid self-confidence. Demonstrably public school, he thought, and felt the old prejudice kick in. The photograph at Thames House had not done justice to Keen's well-preserved good looks, nor to his evidently disdainful manner. The two men made eye contact and Taploe gave a thin smile, his moustache lifting slightly to reveal stained yellow teeth.

Keen sensed immediately that there was something unconvincing about his prospective client. The suit was off the peg, and the shirt, bought as white but now grayed by repeated launderings, looked cheap and untailored. This was not a businessman, with "minor difficulties in the former Soviet Union," far less someone who could afford to employ the services of Divisar Corporate Intelligence.

"Mr. Randall," he said, with a handshake that deliberately crushed his knuckles. Keen looked quickly at the ground and registered his shoes. Gray—possibly fake—patent leather, tasseled and scuffed. Further evidence. "How can I help?"

"I'm very pleased to meet you." Taploe was trying to release his hand. "Let me start by getting you a drink."

"That would be very kind, thank you."

"Did you find the café OK?"

"Easily."

Keen placed a black Psion Organiser and a mobile telephone on the table in front of him and sat down. Freeing the trapped vents of his suit jacket, he looked out of the window and tried to ascertain if he was being watched. It was an instinct, no more than that, but something was out of place. A crowd of office workers had gathered at a table on the other side of the window and an elderly man with a limp was walking into the café alone. The traffic heading north toward Shepherd's Bush Green had been slowed by a van double-parked outside a mini-supermarket. Its rear doors were flung open and two young Asian men were unloading boxes from the back.

"It's part of a chain, I believe," Taploe said.

"What's that?"

"The café. Part of a chain."

"I know."

A waitress came and took their order for two beers.

Keen wondered if he would have to stay long.

"So, I very much appreciate your meeting me at such short notice." The businessman had a labored, slightly self-satisfied way of strangling words, an accent located somewhere near Bracknell. "Had you far to come?"

"Not at all. I had a meeting in Chelsea. Caught a fast black."

Taploe's eyes dropped out of character, as if Keen had made a racist remark. "Excuse me?"

"A fast black," he explained. "A *taxi*."

"Oh." In the uneasy silence that followed, the waitress returned and poured lager into his glass.

"So, how long have you worked in your particular field?"

"About seven or eight years."

"And in Russia before that?"

"Among other places, yes." Keen thanked the waitress with a patrician smile and picked up his glass. "I take it you've been there?"

"Not exactly, no."

"And yet you told me on the telephone that you have a problem in the former Soviet Union. Tell me, Mr. Randall, what is it that you think I can do for you?"

Leaning back in his seat, Taploe nodded and swallowed a mouthful of lager. He blinked repeatedly and a small amount of foam evaporated into his moustache. After a momentary pause he said, "Forgive me. It was necessary to employ a little subterfuge to prevent your employers becoming suspicious. My name is not Bob Randall, as perhaps you may have guessed. It is Stephen Taploe. I work across the river from your former Friends."

Keen folded his arms and muttered, "You don't say," as Taploe pushed his tongue into the side of his cheek. His feet moved involuntarily under the table. "And you think that I can help you with something in Moscow?"

"I'm afraid it's a good deal more complicated than that," he said. "To come straight to the point, Mr. Keen, this has become something of a family matter."

5

"It's possible, Jenny, that one day you'll walk into a public art gallery and look at nothing at all. A total absence. Something with no texture, no shape, no solidity. No materials will have been used up in its construction, not even light or sound. Just a room full of nothing. That will be the exhibit, the gimmick, the thing you're encouraged to look at and talk about over cranberry juice at Soho House. Emptiness. Actually, the *opposite* of art."

Jenny was glad that Ben wasn't talking about his father anymore. She preferred it when his mood was less anxious and abrasive. It was another side to him, more relaxed and quick-witted; she wondered if it was even flirtatious. But Ben looked like the faithful type: he was only thirty-two, after all, and there were pictures of his wife all over the studio walls, nudes and portraits of a quality that had persuaded her to sit for him in the first place.

"Have you lived here long?" she asked, and began gathering up her clothes. Ben was cleaning his brushes at the sink, wrapping the bristles in rubber bands and covering any exposed paint with small wraps of cling film.

"Since we got engaged," he said. "About three years."

"It's such a great house." Jenny's stomach flattened out as she stretched into a thick woolen polo neck, her head disappearing in the struggle to find sleeves. "Alice's father bought it cheap in the late seventies. Thought it would make a good investment."

The head popped out, like somebody breaking free of a strait-jacket.

"Well, he thought right," she said, shaking out her hair. "And it's useful for you to be able to work from home."

"It is," Ben said. "It is. It's a great space. I'm very lucky."

"A lot of artists have to rent studios."

"I know that."

She was oblivious to it, but talking about the house always made Ben feel edgy. Three storeys of prime Notting Hill real estate and not a brick of it his. When Carolyn, his mother, had died seven years before, she had left her two sons a few hundred pounds and a small flat in Clapham that they rented out to unreliable tenants. Alice's father, by contrast, was wealthy: on top of her basic salary as a journalist she had access to a substantial trust, and the house had been purchased in her name.

"So what are you cooking for your brother?"

Ben was glad of the change of subject. Turning round, he said, "Something Thai, maybe a green curry."

"Oh. Bit of a dab hand in the kitchen, are we?"

"Well, not bad. I find it relaxing after a day in the studio. And Alice can't boil an egg. So it's either that or we eat out every night."

"What about Mark? Can he cook?"

Ben laughed, as if she had asked a stupid question. "Mark doesn't know one end of a kitchen from the other. He's always out at night, with clients or away at the club. Spends a lot of his time traveling overseas. He doesn't get much chance to be at home."

"Really?" Jenny was putting on her shoes. "What time's he due back?"

She's interested, he thought. *They always are.* They see photos of Mark in the hall and they want a chance to meet him.

"I'm not sure. He just called on the phone from Heathrow."

"Right."

From her reaction, it was clear that Jenny would not have time to stay. Picking up her bag, she soon made for the stairs and it remained only to pay her. Ben had thirty pounds in his wallet, six five-pound notes, which he pressed into her hand. They were walking toward the front door when he heard the scratch of a key in the lock. The door opened and Alice walked in, talking rapidly into her mobile phone. She did a double take when she saw Ben standing at the foot of the staircase beside a tall, slightly flushed pretty girl, and he raised his eyebrows as a way of saying "hello." Jenny took a step back inside.

"That's not the *point*," Alice was saying. Her voice was raised to a pitch just below outright aggression. "I told her she'd have a chance to read through the piece. To check it. That was a promise I made." Jenny found herself standing awkwardly between them, like an actor waiting to go onstage. "So if you go ahead and print it, her whole family, who I've known since I was six fucking years old, are going to go . . ."

Ben smiled uneasily and felt the dread of the phone call's aftermath, another work crisis the dutiful husband would have to resolve. "Thanks, then," Jenny whispered to him, moving toward the door. "Same time tomorrow?"

"Same time," he said.

"About midday?"

"Midday."

"Your wife's *lovely*," she mouthed, standing below him on the threshold. "Really *pretty*."

Ben merely nodded and watched as Jenny turned toward Ladbroke Grove. Only when she was out of sight did he close the door.

"But that's exactly what I'm *saying*, Andy." Alice had kicked off her shoes and was now stretched out on the sofa. A great part of her lived for arguments of this kind, for the adrenalin surge of conflict. "If the article appears as it is . . ." She pulled the phone away from her ear. "*Fuck*, I got cut off."

"What's happened?"

Ben came over and sat beside her. Her cheek as he kissed it was cold. She smelled of moisturizer and cigarettes.

"You remember that piece I wrote about my friend from school, the girl who was arrested for drug smuggling?" Alice was redialing Andy's number as she spoke. Ben vaguely remembered the story. "It was supposed to be a feature but the news desk got hold of it. Now they've gone and made the girl out to be some kind of wild child who should have known better, exactly what I promised Jane we wouldn't do." She stared at the readout on her mobile phone. "Great. And now Andy's switched his phone off."

"Her name is Jane?" The observation was a non sequitur, but Alice didn't seem to notice.

"She came to me because she knew the press would be on to her sooner or later. She thought she could trust me to tell her side of the story. I'm the only journalist her family knows."

"And now it's been taken out of your hands?"

He was trying to appear interested, trying to say the right things, but he knew that Alice was most probably lying to him. She would have leaked the story to the news desk in the hope of winning their approval. Alice was ambitious to move from features into news; the more scoops she could push their way, the better would be her chances of promotion.

"That's right. Which explains why Andy isn't returning my calls."

"And how did Andy get hold of the story?"

Her answer here would prove interesting. Would she confess to showing the interview to a news reporter, or claim that it was taken from her desk? Each time there was a crisis of this kind, Alice inevitably found someone else to blame.

"I just mentioned it to a colleague over lunch," she said, as if this small detail did not in itself imply a breach of trust. "Next thing I know, the news editor is demanding that I hand over the interview so that he can farm it for quotes."

Ben noticed that she had stopped trying to reach Andy's mobile phone.

"So why didn't you just refuse?" he asked. "Why didn't you just tell him you'd made a deal with the girl?"

"It doesn't work like that."

Of course it doesn't. "Why not?" he said.

"Look, if you're just going to be difficult about this we might as well—"

"Why am I being difficult? I'm just trying to find out—"

"Did you pick up my dry cleaning for the party?" The inevitable change of subject.

"Did I *what*?"

"Did you pick up my dry cleaning for the party?"

"Alice, I'm not your fucking PA. I've been busy in the studio all day. If I have time, I'll get it tomorrow."

"Great." And she was on her feet, sighing. "Too busy doing what? To walk five hundred meters to the main road?"

"No. Too busy working."

"*Working*?"

"Is that where we're going with this?" Ben pointed toward the attic. "Painting isn't work? There's no such thing as a busy day when you're an artist?"

Alice took off her earrings and put them on a table. "Was that her?" she asked, trying a different tack. "The one at the bottom of the stairs?"

"Jenny? Yes, when you came in. Of course it was."

"And is she nice?"

"*Nice*?"

"Do you get on with her?"

A pause.

"We get on fine, yes. She just lies down and I start painting. It's not really about 'getting on.'"

"What *is* it about then?"

"So you're now picking a fight with me about a model?"

Alice turned her back on him.

"It's just that I thought you were painting older people nowadays. Isn't that the idea for the new show?"

"No. Why would you think that? It's just nudes. Age doesn't come into it."

"So you still hire a girl purely on the basis of looks?"

Ben stood up from the sofa and decided to get away. He would go back upstairs to the studio, put on a record, and wait until Alice had calmed down.

"Look," he said, "you've had a bad day at work. Somebody fucked you over. Try not to take it out on everyone else." Alice stubbed out her cigarette and said nothing. “Why don’t we start again later? Mark’s arriving in less than an hour. Have a bath and chill out.”

“Don’t tell me to ‘chill out.’ Just give me a straight answer to my question.”

Ben had to stop and turn. “To what question?”

Alice reacted as if he were deliberately concealing something.

“Fine,” she said, pointedly looking at her watch. “What time does the dry cleaner close?”

“How the fuck should I know?”

“Well, I’m just wondering what I’m going to wear to this party tomorrow night, now that you haven’t picked up my dress.”

“So go and get it. You’re a big girl.”

“Well, I don’t have much choice, do I?”

Ben was halfway upstairs, heading back to the studio, when he heard the front door slam behind him.

6

Stephen Taploe called the waitress over with an impatient wave of his hand and asked for the bill. It had become necessary to conduct the rest of the conversation outside the café, because there were now three men standing idly behind Keen's chair, sucking on bottles of Mexican lager. The bill came to a little under nine pounds and Taploe put the receipt carefully in his wallet. He was very exact when it came to filing for expenses.

The two men crossed the road and turned toward Brook Green, a steady head-on wind blowing dried leaves and litter along the pavement. Choosing his moment with care, Taploe said, "What do you know about a man called Sebastian Roth?"

The question took Keen by surprise. His first thought was that someone inside Divisar had breached client confidentiality.

"Why don't you tell me what *you* know about a man called Sebastian Roth and I'll see if I can be of any assistance?" he said. "Sort of fill in the blanks."

Taploe had anticipated that Keen would be evasive; it would buy him time.

"I know what any person can read in the papers. Roth is thirty-six years old, an entrepreneur, very well connected with the present Labour government, the only son of a Tory peer. He went to Eton, where he was neither particularly successful nor popular, and dropped out of Oxford after less than a year. After a stint in the City, he opened the original Libra nightclub about six months before Ministry of Sound and at least a year before Cream first took off in Liverpool. Those three are still the nightclubs of choice for the younger generation, though it's mostly compact discs now, isn't it? That's how they make their money." Keen remained silent. "Judging from the photographs in certain magazines—*Tatler*, *Harpers & Queen*, and so on—Roth looks to have a new girlfriend on his arm every week, although we think he's something of a loner. Very little contact with his family, no relationship at all with either of his two siblings. Libra is his passion, extending the brand, controlling the business. Roth spends a lot of time overseas, collects art, and has recently finished conversion on a house in Pimlico valued at over two million pounds. I also happen to know that one of his representatives came to your company some months ago asking for assistance."

Keen slowed his pace.

"You know that I can't discuss that," he said.

"Then allow me to discuss it for you." It was all going very well for Stephen Taploe, the one-upmanship, the gradual trap. He flattened down his moustache and coughed lightly. "Roth has a lawyer friend, an individual by the name of Thomas Macklin. Helped him build the Libra empire, the Paris and New York sites, the merchandizing arm in particular. I believe you've made his acquaintance?"

"Go on." The hard soles of Keen's brogues clipped on the pavement as they turned left into Sterndale Road.

"In the past four months, Macklin has made eight separate trips to Russia. On three of those journeys he took internal flights from St. Petersburg to Moscow, where he remained for several days."

"May I ask why he was being followed?"

To encourage a greater openness in Keen, Taploe opted to be as candid as the situation would allow.

"He wasn't being *followed*, exactly. At least, not at first. But on Macklin's third visit to the Russian capital he was observed by local law enforcement officials talking to a known member of the Kukushkin crime syndicate under observation in a separate case. Nothing unusual there, you might think, but the meetings then occurred again, on trips four, five, and six. Each time with the same man, albeit in a different location."

"What was the contact's name?"

"Malere," Taploe replied. "Kristin Malere. A Lithuanian, originally out of Vilnius. Anyway, as you may or may not be aware, my organization has been developing increasingly strong links with the organized crime division of Russian Internal Affairs. Because Macklin is a British citizen, these meetings were brought to our attention and my team began looking into it."

"On the basis of a few meetings with a low-level Baltic hoodlum?"

Taploe sniffed. He did not enjoy having his judgment brought into question by anyone, least of all a disdainful MI6 toff eight years in the private sector.

"Ordinarily, of course, this would not have aroused our suspicion." He wanted Keen to know his place, to feel like an outsider.

"After all, Mr. Macklin was only representing the interests of his employer. As you will be aware, it is often necessary in the present climate to climb into bed with what I like to call some of the unsavory characters on the Russian landscape."

Keen looked at his watch.

"We have reason to believe that Viktor Kukushkin is presently trying to consolidate his position in the UK," Taploe wasn't going to be rushed. "Simply as a precaution, we put surveillance on Macklin when he returned home. So imagine our surprise when, just days after arriving back from one of his trips to Russia, he met one of Kukushkin's London representatives at a hotel in Sussex Gardens. Another unsavory character by the name of Juris Duchev." The corners of Keen's mouth twitched. "These meetings started to happen at other hotels in the greater London area on a fairly regular basis. On at least four occasions we suspect Macklin left with cash sums in excess of eighty thousand pounds. To my knowledge he also banked two six-figure dollar sums in a legitimate, Cypriot-registered shell company named Pentagon Investments."

Taploe took a long, deep breath, as if the effort of summing up the Libra case with such clarity and precision had left him briefly exhausted. He was on the point of elaborating further when a squat, thickset man wearing a pin-striped suit emerged from a nearby house and turned toward them. He was well within earshot and Taploe immediately assumed cover.

"So you'll be away all weekend?" he said quickly. "Why don't you leave me your number and I'll try to get hold of you then."

The switch, a very basic precaution, was also second nature to Keen. Given that many of Divisar's employees were drawn from the secret world, the company operated on much the same basis as the intelligence services. If, for example, Keen happened to be discussing an operation at headquarters and was interrupted by another member of staff entering the room, he would quickly drop into small talk until that person had left the area. There were pockets of expertise within the company, and very little crossover due to the requirements of secrecy; many employees were strangers to one another. Nevertheless, he felt that Taploe had overreacted, and enjoyed delaying his response for as long as possible.

"Or you could just call my mobile," he replied slowly. "Do you have the number?" His voice was deliberately provocative. "It's printed on my card."

The man was now thirty meters behind them, standing beside a two-door BMW. Keen heard the double sonics of central locking and registered amber hazard lights flaring briefly in the back window of a nearby van. Then he heard the driver's door clunk shut as the man climbed inside.

"The answer to your question, Mr. Taploe, is that I cannot tell you very much." Keen sounded assured, imperial. "I have neither seen nor spoken to Thomas Macklin in over two months. Whom he chooses to hold meetings with in Moscow, London, or Timbuktu is his business, not mine. Ditto any strange bank accounts. Obviously you suspect money laundering . . ."

"Obviously," Taploe said quickly. "The thing is, we can't make an arrest until we know the source of the cash. Macklin could realistically claim that he had no knowledge of handling dirty money, or say that he was acting as a lawyer for Viktor Kukushkin and planned to use the funds to buy real estate. But we'd be interested in what you could tell us about your early contact with Libra."

Keen noted the use of the plural pronoun: making it a point of honor, a duty to the old firm. However, rather than answer immediately, he asked a question of his own.

"How did you find me?"

Taploe was looking down Augustine Road toward Brook Green. He rubbed his cheek.

"Your name was recognized when it came up during preliminary research into Divisar."

Keen sounded a sarcastic note.

"So—what?—you found out I'd been in the Office, thought it was your lucky day, and ran me as a trace request through the ND? Is that how it still works over there?"

Taploe hesitated. "Something like that."

"Was there anything recorded Against?" Keen asked, employing the Service euphemism. "I'd love to know."

Taploe ignored the question.

"Why don't we just talk about your initial contact with Libra?"

Keen sighed, loathing the dryness of bureaucracy. "Very well. This is what I know, although I can't think why it will be of any use to you. Thomas Macklin approached Divisar about six months ago. I'd have to check the file to be more precise. He was sharp and efficient and he came as Roth's representative, which is often the way in our business. If push comes to shove, those boys want as much distance between us and them as they can manage. It was a simple job, of the sort I do all the time. Libra were interested in setting up operations in Russia and Macklin had a lot of very sensible questions that needed answering. Due diligence on real estate and freeholders. Wanted to know how to go about recruiting staff, finding suppliers, who Libra's competitors would be, and so forth. I remember he was slightly obsessive about the tax and licensing position. Above all, he needed to know about the roof. What palms needed to be crossed and how much silver." To amuse himself, Keen added, "You know what a roof is, don't you, Mr. Taploe?"

"I've been working organized crime for two years," he replied. "Of course I know about the roof." It irritated Taploe that Keen was not as concerned by his line of questioning as he might have been; but then that was the birthright of the upper classes, the lizard-thick skin of the FCO. "So did Divisar put Libra in touch with the appropriate organizations?" he asked.

"That's not how it works. Kukushkin would have come to them. He's one of the new-style mobsters, the *avtoritet*. Less regard for tradition than the older *vors* and a lot more unpredictable when it comes to things like chopping people's fingers off. But, yes, I pointed them in the right direction, told Macklin who the main players were. Divisar did what we were paid to do."

Taploe listened to this and decided that it was time to play his trump card.

"And how long was it before you realized that your eldest son was a senior executive at Libra?"

Keen had known that the question was coming; Taploe had been deliberately withholding it as a tactic to arouse his suspicion. Nevertheless, he felt squeezed by it, cornered into obfuscation. His immediate response was defensive.

"Now what does that have to do with anything?"

Taploe stopped walking and turned to face him. Keen was a good six inches taller and considerably better built, with narrow blue eyes that he used as tools of concealment, to frighten and charm in equal measure. Taploe tried as best he could to look through them.

"Perhaps you could just answer the question," he said. "We have no wish to pry into your personal life. It is simply our understanding that since Libra's first approach you have been able to form some sort of a relationship with your eldest son after . . . how should I put it? . . . an *absence* of almost thirty years."

"You're clearly very well informed."

"Not as well informed as I'd like to be. Did you know that Mark was working at Libra when Divisar took them on as clients?"

Keen waited. He could feel frustration, even anger, beginning to undermine his better judgment. All that residual guilt over Carolyn and the boys rising up in him like a sickness.

"As I recall," he said firmly, "there were two preliminary meetings between Macklin and one of my colleagues before I was brought on board. During that time, Mark found out that I worked for the company and telephoned me with a view to getting together."

"And what was your reaction?"

"Is that relevant? I wasn't aware that I was talking to a psychiatrist."

Taploe had pushed too far. He was annoyed with himself and felt the heat of unease flush through his cheeks. He would have to back down, if only for the sake of the pitch.

"You're right," he said. "It's not my business. I am simply interested in Mark's role in all of this."

"Then at last we have something in common."

"I can tell you that there's no evidence to suggest your son knows what Macklin is up to," Taploe offered. "He didn't accompany him to Russia on his last two visits, nor has he been seen with any of Kukushkin's representatives in either Moscow or London."

"So why am I here this evening?" Keen asked. "What on earth do you need me for?"

It was a question to which he already knew the answer. Taploe was simply priming himself.

"Just an act of kindness," he said quietly, "a favor, for want of a better description."

"A favor." Keen paused and then repeated the word under his breath, killing its implications, the nuance. "Tell me," he said. "What is it about people in our business that they can never say exactly what they *mean*?"

7

The dummy London cab that had tailed Mark Keen's taxi from Heathrow stopped a hundred and fifty meters down Elgin Crescent, engine idling. They had made good time from Terminal One, almost slipstreaming Keen in the outer M4 lane denied to cars.

"So this is where the brother lives?" Graham asked.

Ian Boyle cleared his throat and said, "Yeah, house up on the left."

They saw Mark step out of the taxi, pay the driver, and make his way toward the front door carrying a large overnight holdall and several plastic bags. He was broadly built and did not appear to struggle with the weight.

"Nice fucking place," Graham muttered, tilting his head to one side to get a better look at the house. "What does the brother do for a living? Stockbroker? Investment banker? Dot-com millionaire?"

"None of the above." Ian dialed a number in Euston on his mobile phone and held it up to his ear. "Our Benjamin's an artist. Farts around all day in oils and charcoal, struggling with the impossibility of the authentic artistic act."

"I thought that sort of behavior was out of fashion?"

The number wasn't answering and Ian hung up. "Not so," he said.

"What does the wife do?" Graham was new on the Kukushkin case and still a bit sketchy on details. He looked upon Ian as a mentor, an older hand he wanted to learn from and impress.

"Journalist," Ian said. "Writes about canapés and boy bands for the *Evening Standard*. One of your gorgeous, pouting, twenty-something hackettes, arse so firm you could crack an egg on it. Drive up and we might get a look at her."

Graham flicked on the headlights, moved back out into the road, and took the cab past the house. They saw Alice open the front door and fling her arms around Mark's neck, her smile a flash in the darkness.

"Fuckin' hell," Graham muttered. "Wouldn't mind one of them in my Christmas stocking." He pulled up another fifty meters farther along the street and peered back over his shoulder. "How long they been married?"

"Couple of years; three, maybe. Daddy threw eighty grand at the wedding. Nice of him, wouldn't you say?"

"All things considered." Graham couldn't keep his eyes off her. "Does the gaffer have ears in there?"

"Not yet. Only at Mark's place. And the lawyer, Macklin. We don't reckon young Benjamin's involved."

"Right."

"So what time's Michael taking over?" Ian scratched his armpit. "I wanna get the Arsenal score, find a pub with ITV."

"Search me," Graham replied. "The way I heard it, I thought we was on all night."

8

A man of sixty looks back on his working life and feels, what? A sense of regret at opportunities lost? Shame over badly handled investments, businesses that might have turned sour, a colleague treated with contempt by the board after forty years' loyal service to the firm? Keen simply did not know. He had lived his life in a separate world of deliberate masquerade, a state servant with carte blanche for deceit. Waiting for Mark in his son's favorite, if over-priced, Chinese restaurant at the south end of Queensway, Keen had the odd, even amusing sensation that most of his professional life had been comprised of *social occasions*: Foreign Office dinners, embassy cocktail parties, glasses of stewed tea and mugs of instant coffee shared with journalists, traitors, disgruntled civil servants, ideologues, and bankrupts, the long list of contacts and informants that make up a spy's acquaintance. Indeed it occurred to him—over his second glass of surprisingly decent Sancerre—that he was a scholar of the long, boozy lunch, of lulling strangers into mistaken beliefs, of plying dining companions with drink and sympathy and then sucking them dry of secrets. It was his talent, after all, the knack they had spotted at Oxford, and the reason now, more than thirty years later, that Keen could charge Divisar £450 a day for his old-style flair and expertise. But to use those skills on his own son? To do that, if he looked at it for too long, would seem horrific. But Christopher Keen never looked at anything for too long.

Mark was late by half an hour, a mirror image of Keen's own father at thirty-five, coming into the restaurant at a brisk walk mouthing, "Sorry, Dad," from fifty feet. Keen thought he looked tired and preoccupied, but that might have been his paranoia over Taploe.

The Service would like your assistance in clearing up Libra's position, in revealing the exact nature of their relationship with Kukushkin. We just need you to pick your son's brains, find out what he knows.

"Where the hell have you been?"

He said it without anger, because Mark looked genuinely contrite.

"I'm really, really sorry." He placed a hand on his father's shoulder. "Meetings. All morning. Fucked electrics at the club and a tabloid hack giving me gyp."

He was wearing a dark blue corduroy suit and, for want of something better to say, Keen remarked on it.

"Bespoke?" he asked.

"Thought you might notice that." It was a shared passion between them, the luxury of fine clothes. Mark sat down and flapped a napkin into his lap. "This here is a Doug Hayward original in navy corduroy, a sympathetic cloth flexible enough to accommodate today's retro styling." He was beginning to relax. "The jacket has high lapels, as you can see, with long double vents and three buttons at the front. Furthermore, if I stood up you'd notice an immaculately tailored flat-fronted trouser with straight legs that flare just above the tongue of the shoe."

"Ho ho," Keen said, enjoying Mark's charm. He poured both of them a glass of Sancerre and ordered another bottle from the waiter. "What's in the bag?"

Mark said, "Oh, yes," and leaned over to retrieve two bottles of vodka from a duty-free bag he had carried into the restaurant. Three liters of Youri Dolgoruki, his father's favorite brand.

"Present for you," he said. "Picked them up in Moscow three days ago. Know how you prefer the real thing."

"That was immensely kind of you." Keen put the bottles on the floor beside his chair and wondered if they would clink in his briefcase. "You shouldn't have bought me anything at all."

"For all the birthdays I missed," Mark replied lightly, as if the observation held no resonance. Then he opened his menu.

Keen had noticed this about Mark before: the way he gave presents to people at Libra and Divisar, little surprises to lighten their day. The cynic in him had decided that this was an unconscious way of keeping colleagues onside, of buying their trust and loyalty. It was the same with his memory: months after meeting them, Mark could recall the names of personal assistants who had brought him cups of coffee during fifteen-minute meetings in downtown Moscow.

"How do you *do* that?" he asked.

"Eh?"

Mark was staring at him and Keen realized he had been thinking aloud.

"Sorry, I was just mulling something over. Your ability to remember names. I was thinking about it while you were late."

Mark clumped the menu shut.

"Trick I was taught by Seb," he said frankly, and put his jacket on the back of the chair. "Remember someone's name and it makes them feel special. Tack on a fact or two about their lives and they'll practically offer themselves up. It's all vanity, isn't it? We all want to feel cherished. Bloke comes to work to fix the sound system and I remember he's got a ten-year-old kid who supports West Ham, he's gonna be touched that I brought it up. Good business, isn't it? How to win friends and influence people."

Keen nodded and could only agree. At a table nearby, a decent-looking woman in a Chanel suit was eating lunch with her husband and giving him the occasional eye. Mutton dressed as lamb, Keen thought, and wished she were ten years younger.

"Will you order for me?" Mark said. "My brain's gone numb."

Lacquer-black walls and a low oppressive ceiling patterned with dimmed halogen bulbs lent the interior of the restaurant the atmosphere of a mediocre seventies nightclub. Mark was always impressed by his father's knowledge of the more obscure dishes on a menu—in this case, preserved pork knuckle, fragrant yam duck, a soup of mustard leaf with salted egg and sliced beef. He even ordered them in an accent that sounded authentically Chinese.

"You spend time in Beijing?" he asked. "In Shanghai, Hong Kong?"

"Not really." Keen refilled Mark's glass with the new bottle. "A fortnight in Taiwan in the seventies. Overnight stop in Kowloon harbor a few years ago. Rather a lovely ketch, if I recall, French owner. Otherwise just homogeneous Chinese restaurants the world over. Anxious-looking fish in outsized tanks, ducks flying anti-clockwise around the walls."

Mark listened intently. He was good at that. Keen wondered if he had an image, in technicolor, of his father calmly going about the Queen's business, standing on the prow of a luxury yacht wearing a battered Panama hat.

"Why does everyone insist on calling it 'Beijing' nowadays?" he asked. "You don't say 'Roma,' do you? You don't talk about 'Milano' or 'München'?"

"It's just the fashion," Mark replied.

"Ah yes, the fashion." Keen sighed and let his eyes drift toward the ceiling. He enjoyed playing the fuddy-duddy with Mark, assumed that it was a part of his paternal role. "I sometimes think that everything these days is about fashion, about not doing or saying the wrong thing. Common sense has gone right out of the window."

"I guess."

A smooth-skinned waiter, working in tandem with a pretty Chinese girl wearing a sky-blue silk qipao, ferried plates of dim sum and steamed rice to their table. They were on to their third bottle of wine—a characterless Ribera del Duero—by the time Keen got round to Taploe's business.

"Oh, by the way," he said. "I had a call from Thomas Macklin while you were away."

"Oh yeah? Tom? What did he want?"

"Just a couple of routine questions. Divisar business. Tell me about him. How do you two get on?"

Mark was swallowing a mouthful of prawn satay and for some time was able only to nod and raise his eyebrows in response.

"Why do you want to know?" he asked eventually, wiping a napkin over his bottom lip.

"He intrigued me. As you can imagine, we get a lot of lawyers coming into the firm. He's still relatively young, highly competent, somebody whom I imagine would be an asset to Libra."

"Tom's all right. A bit flash, bit lippy. Good lawyer, though."

"Does your work dovetail?"

Mark could not hear the question over the noise of the restaurant and he cocked his head to one side to encourage his father to repeat it. Keen leaned in.

"I said, does your work dovetail? How much of him do you see, apart from when you're both abroad together?"

"I was out with him last night, matter of fact. Tom's a big drinker, likes to whip out the company credit card. If there's a new secretary in the office he's always the one who asks her out. Champagne and oysters, loves all that shit. Never has any luck with the birds, mind, but you'll have a good time if you tag along."

Whenever Mark discussed Libra business, his voice unconsciously dropped into a mannered sub-Cockney that cloaked its true origins in private education. This work accent, this music-industry drawl, deliberately shaved off consonants and slackened vowels. It was an affectation that irritated Keen, though he had never mentioned it.

"And what happens when you go on these trips?" he asked, pouring himself a glass of water. The woman with whom he had briefly flirted rose from her table and managed a final seductive glance. Keen ignored her. "You must get sick of the sight of one another."

"Not necessarily." Mark was using a pair of chopsticks to pick up a pork dumpling. He held it in the air for some time, like a jeweler examining a gem for flaws. "I like the company, to be honest." He popped the food into his mouth and began chewing it vigorously, smiling as he ate.

All of this was of interest to Keen. *Is Viktor Kukushkin's syndicate providing Libra with protection in Russia, or is there a larger conspiracy evolving here in London?* Taploe had almost whispered his requests, eyes glued to Keen's lapel. *Mark could prove vital in giving us a clear picture of Roth's and Macklin's activities. We'd like to know everything you can find out.* But Mark did not appear unsettled by the line of questioning: on the contrary, he seemed comfortable and relaxed, just chatting and enjoying his lunch.

"Good, these, aren't they?" he said, and picked up another dumpling.

"Yes," Keen nodded. "I must say I was impressed by all of your people. Sebastian, of course, though we met only briefly. The two marketing girls as well. And that Frenchman you brought in last time, Philippe d'Erlanger."

"Philippe, yeah. He's Belgian, actually." Keen acknowledged the mistake.

"But Macklin stood out. Very bright, very capable. During our initial meetings he impressed me a great deal. I acted only as a conduit, as you know, so I have no idea how he's behaved latterly. But he was very well informed, seemed to know his stuff. A bit pushy, clearly, not necessarily someone one would want to buy a used car from. Do you trust him?"

"No," Mark replied, swallowing. "But I wouldn't have thought he trusts me, either."

"Now why do you say that?"

"Best policy, isn't it? Rule of thumb. Never trust the people at the top. Don't put yourself in a position where you have to rely on anyone. That way you won't be too disappointed when they fuck you over."

Keen's eyes narrowed. He wondered if the sentiment had its origins in Mark's childhood.

"Do you think he's capable of that?" But he had pushed too hard.

"Why are you so interested in Tom?" Mark asked. "Have Divisar had trouble with him? Has he not been paying our bills?"

"No, no. I'm just fascinated by the way your partnership works. He obviously has the ear of Roth, so where does that leave you?"

"Well, I'm not a lawyer, am I? That's not my area of expertise. So the relationship he has with Seb is different from the one he has with me. More personal, if you like. Those two share a lot of secrets which nobody else is privy to."

Perhaps there was something here for Taploe. "What kind of secrets?" Keen asked.

"Well, they wouldn't be secrets if I knew, would they? Financial stuff, I guess; plans for the future. That sort of thing."

"I see." Mark looked vaguely bored, but Keen was anxious to probe further. "Just while we're on the subject," he said, "were there any developments on your trip that I should know about? The position on the roof, for example?"

"No. Tom's handling it. He deals with those boys."

"So you've had no contact with the gangs?"

"I wouldn't say *no* contact." The waitress picked up two plates from the table, smiled at Mark, and walked off. "They're everywhere out there. Hotel foyers, restaurants, sitting in their shiny four-by-fours on Novy Arbat. You can hardly move without bumping into some wanker in a cheap leather jacket who thinks he's Chechnya's answer to Al Pacino. Mack's all for it, of course, loves hanging out with them. Acts like he's landed a walk-on part in *The Sopranos*. But they're not for me. Far as I'm concerned, the mafia makes a living out of other people's misery and that's not a good reason to go drinking with them."

Keen registered this last remark: at SIS he had been trained to be wary of the man who declares his innocence unprompted. It was usually the case that those who made a frequent expression of their moral outrage were most often the ones who turned out to be unscrupulous.

"Surely Macklin's just doing his job, just trying to get the best deal for Libra?" he suggested. "I would have thought it was important to keep them onside."

Mark smirked.

"What's so funny?"

"He keeps them onside, all right."

"What do you mean?"

"Whenever we're in Moscow, Tom makes sure to get a hooker up to his suite. Her twin sister as well, if he's feeling perky. He'd like to call that 'keeping them onside.' That way he could run it through expenses."

Keen frowned.

"He's got sucked into that, has he?"

"Well, let's face it, no one else is going to sleep with him."

Keen duly grinned but the conversation appeared to have exhausted itself. As he had both hoped and expected, there had been nothing of any content to unsettle him, nothing he would feel obliged to reveal to Taploe. He felt an odd, protective urge to tell Mark that his flat was most probably wired, that the grass skirts had eyes and ears in the homes of every one of the senior employees at Libra. Yet he was bound by an older loyalty, barred even from advising caution. He placed his chopsticks to one side, put his napkin on the table, and was quiet.

"You look worried about something." Mark had also finished eating.

"I do?"

"Yeah."

Keen frowned and said, "No, I'm fine. Just digesting."

"Is it Ben?"

The question took him by surprise, if only because, for once in Mark's company, Keen had *not* been thinking about Ben. It was a rare occasion on which the two failed to discuss the possibility of reconciliation. Their last two meetings, for example, had descended into an awkward row about Ben's stubborn refusal to put the past behind him. Mark had been sympathetic to his father's position, but his first loyalty was to his brother.

"Have you thought any more about that?" If this was an opportunity to reopen the subject, then Keen would grasp it.

"Not much," Mark said.

"I see."

"But you're still eager to make amends, to tell him how sorry you are?"

"Something like that." Keen wondered if Mark had a plan, but his manner seemed dismissive and offhand. "Have you seen him lately?"

"Matter of fact, I have." Mark finished off the last of the wine. "Had dinner with him the night I got back. Brother cooked up a green curry and spent most of the evening arguing with Alice."

"That seems to happen a lot."

"All the time lately."

"Are they unhappy?"

Mark breathed in deeply and puffed out his cheeks. "Who

knows?" he said. "Sometimes I wonder what he sees in her, beyond the looks, the lifestyle."

"Yes, you've said that before. But Alice was very helpful to Ben when your mother died, wasn't she? Isn't that the case?"

"That was the case." Mark paused briefly. He was reluctant to betray Ben's confidence, but the wine had got the better of him. "But there's more to it than that," he said.

"Expand."

A waiter placed two steaming napkins on a plate in front of them. Mark turned his hands heavily through the cloth and then wiped his mouth.

"It's like this," he said. "They've been together a long time. Brother helped to get her career started and Alice supported him when he wanted to get into painting. Far as I can tell they have great sex, you know, so that helps when things turn nasty. And besides, a part of me reckons they love all the arguments, that they feed off the aggro and tension."

Keen leaned back in his chair.

"Interesting," he said, with apparent empathy. "So you don't suppose he's any closer to the idea of meeting up?" He was aware that the question was cack-handed, yet determined to make an approach. "You don't think he'd be amenable to, say, a drink or perhaps dinner?"

Mark laughed and stared at the ceiling.

"Is that what this is about?" he said. "You want to have this conversation every time we meet up?"

"Until he's prepared to forgive and forget, yes."

Keen had not intended to sound angry, but his words had a remarkable effect. Mark, ever the conciliator, resolved to calm his father down.

"All right, all right," he said. "You just have to understand that Ben is stubborn, that he's very set in his ways. For him to agree even to talk to you would mean a betrayal of Mum. That's how he feels about things. We've spoken about this. In his mind, it's either you or her."

Keen managed to look appropriately dismayed, but he had been taken with a sharp, persuasive idea. Earlier in the day, he had collected a signet ring from a jeweler in Paddington who had reset the bloodstone. The box was in his briefcase. He could use this as a lever, something to play on Mark's sense of decency.

"I had your photograph framed," he said.

"My photograph?"

"Of Ben's wedding. It's hanging in the flat." Two weeks earlier, Mark had given him a photograph of Ben's wedding day, taken moments after he had first emerged from the church with Alice at his side. Keen had had the picture enlarged and framed and it now hung in the sitting room of his London flat. "I thought that I might give you something in return."

"Oh yeah?"

Keen was quickly into the briefcase, leaning down beside his chair. The box was covered in a thin mock-velvet cover and he handed it to Mark.

"Are we getting married?"

"Just open it. Have a look."

"What is this?"

"Call it a present. Of a family nature. More accurately described as an heirloom."

Inside, Mark found the gold-banded signet ring, set with an engraved bloodstone.

"This is for me?"

"I've wanted you to have it for some time. It was your grandfather's."

Mark was oblivious to any deception. Prising the ring from its box he began turning it in his fingers. A small smudge of grease formed on the gold and he wiped it away with his napkin.

"This is really kind of you," he said, finding that he was actually blushing. "You sure about this, Dad?"

"Of course I'm sure. Why don't you put it on?" Mark looked briefly around the restaurant, as if conscious of being watched. Then he placed the ring on the fourth finger of his left hand and held it up for inspection.

"That's where it's supposed to go, right? The 'pinky'? Is that what it's called?"

"I believe so." Keen cleared his throat. "I don't suppose they're really the fashion these days among the nightclub classes, but you can always give it a go."

"I'm really touched. Thank you."

And now he played the ace.

"I wonder how Ben would feel if I were to do the same for him."

From the direction of the kitchen there was the sound of a plate smashing on stone. Silence briefly engulfed the restaurant before conversations resumed.

"I'm not following you." Mark looked slightly worried.

"There are two signet rings in the family," Keen explained. "One belonged to your grandfather, the other to his brother. As you may know, Bobby died without producing any children. I've always thought his ring should be passed on . . ."

"So you thought you'd wait twenty-five years and get me to do it for you?"

Keen acknowledged the slight with just a tilt of his head. He was determined that the plan should succeed. "Point taken," he said. "But would you be prepared to have a word with your brother, to perhaps sound him out?"

Mark ground his chair a foot back from the table. "Haven't we just had this discussion?"

"It's just that I feel we've never really given Benjamin a chance to come forward, to give his side of the story."

"To come *forward*?"

Keen pushed his glass to one side, as if making a clear channel through which any request could not realistically be turned down.

"I apologize," he said. "I'm obviously not making myself clear. Call it a symptom of my frustration. You have always presented Ben's reluctance to talk to me as a fait accompli. The idea that he might change his mind has simply never been tabled. Well, I propose that we should give it a shot, ask him straight out what exactly it is that he's afraid of."

"Brother's not afraid of anything. I've told you that . . ."

"Then let's at least clear the air. I would rather have the opportunity of being castigated face-to-face than endure this rather childish stand off."

"Well, you see, that's just the problem. Ben doesn't really care what you think."

Mark's candor had the effect of silencing his father. Like a man who has suffered a losing hand at poker, he fell back in his chair, as if conscious of the hopelessness of his position. It was the first time that Mark had ever observed any trace of defeat in his father's face. And it worked.

"Look, I'll see what I can do," he said.

"Would you really?" Keen's eyes lit up with hope. "I think it would be in everyone's best interests. Imagine if we could all just get along, make a fresh start. You, me, Benjamin, Alice. I'd like to get to know her, too."

"I'm sure you would," Mark muttered.

"I mean, wouldn't it be wonderful if we could get this thing knocked on the head by Christmas?"

Mark was simply amazed by his attitude. It was as if his father had an assumed right of access, an inherent belief that the past should be ignored in the interests of his own peace of mind. Nevertheless, he felt a duty at least to make an effort.

"Leave it to me," he said. "I'll talk to him and see what I can do."

And that was enough to satisfy Keen. His work done, he closed the briefcase, cleaned his hands with the napkin, and within moments had asked for the bill.

9

Stephen Taploe moved gradually along the aisles, filling his trolley with foods. It was a nothing moment. Once a week, he ventured to the Clapham Junction branch of Asda and bought enough provisions to last him for exactly seven days. Taploe was frugal, although, as a single man earning £41,500 a year, he did not have to be. Armed with reward points and a fistful of vouchers, he would attempt to check out for less than twenty-five pounds, but it was difficult with London prices and sometimes he would treat himself to an extra bottle of medium-dry white wine, or a tub of ice cream in his favorite flavor, vanilla. Taploe lived alone and had, on average, eight meals to cater for each week: two lunches (Saturday and Sunday), as well as six evenings at home. On Thursdays he was always sure to join his colleagues at a tapas bar in Victoria that was popular with D-Branch personnel: promotion, he assumed, would come quicker if he could develop and sustain relationships with senior management outside of office hours.

The supermarket was noticeably less salubrious than the branch of Marks & Spencer in nearby St. John's Road, and lacked the international range and flair of products available at Sainsbury's. Nevertheless, Taploe preferred Asda, largely because it was cheaper and closer to home. He eschewed fancy microwave meals, preferring to cook from scratch; indeed, he would derive a certain satisfaction from making a single item last for several days. He could, for example, let a medium-sized battery chicken suffice for three meals: roasted first, then curried, and finally cold. Every week he bought a packet of six Porkinson's sausages (two meals), three fillets of salmon (one of which he would habitually freeze) and a ribeye steak with oven chips for Sunday lunch. He ignored the aisles given over to juices and did not buy food in tins. For something sweet, Taploe allowed himself ice cream, a single packet of Penguins, and a punnet of Elsanta strawberries.

It was a Friday evening, the pre-weekend crowd, precious few children screaming at the hips of single mothers. Week after week Taploe watched them bumping trolleys into shelves and walls, spilling bottles of Sunny Delight in egg-yolk pools on the floor. But he could move with comparative ease tonight, through fruit and veg to wines, and would be home within ten or fifteen minutes, depending on the queue at the tills.

Just before seven thirty his mobile rang. "Mr. Taploe?"

It was Katy, a low-level researcher less than six months out of college with a degree in media studies from Exeter University. He liked the fact that she sounded nervous on the phone and made a point of calling him "Mr. Taploe."

"Yes, what is it?"

"Well, I've been looking into Juris Duchev as you instructed, sir, and I've been advised by Paul Quinn to contact you directly with some information that I think you might find of interest."

Taploe was standing beside a bored shelf-stacker. He moved toward the tills.

"Go on."

"Interpol suspect that Duchev has been involved in at least two recent incidents still under investigation by the relevant law-enforcement authorities in those areas. The first was in Monaco three years ago, the shooting of a French investment banker with links to the Kukushkin organization. He was shot in his car waiting at traffic lights on the lower of the connecting roads between Monaco and Nice. The second took place in a Moscow suburb back in 1995." Katy breathed in quickly. It sounded as though she was searching through notes. "Again, that was a motorcyclist with a passenger riding pillion shooting directly into a vehicle. We suspect that if there's *razborka*—the Russian term for the settling of a mafia dispute—then Juris Duchev is the individual who would carry it out on the mainland on behalf of the Kukushkin syndicate."

Taploe didn't say "Thank you" or "Well done," simply: "Is there any record of arrest?"

"None, sir. Not on the files. And nothing from RIA."

"So your point is?"

It was the bully in him, the small man.

"Well, what we didn't know, sir, is that Duchev has a UK right of residence. It just came up. At the moment, he can come and go as he pleases."

Taploe reached the end of aisle 14 and stopped.

"I see." The news irritated him, though he maintained a level tone of voice. "Well, thank you for passing on that information. I'll come in to see you after the weekend and we can discuss it further."

"Very well. Thank you, sir."

"And Katy?"

"Yes, sir?"

"I know full well what *razborka* is. There was no need to enlighten me."

"Yes, sir. Sorry, sir."

"Good-bye."

As he replaced the phone in his pocket, the back wheel of Taploe's trolley caught on a sticky ball of waxed paper. He had to bend down to free it and missed a slot in the queue. *Duchev*, he thought. We let men like that live here, let them enter and leave at will. The British, in the name of decency and fair play, wave their enemies through the gates without so much as a glance. Tends to make my job harder, he mused, pushing toward the tills.

10

From: alicelucy1212@aol.com
To: mkeen@clublibra.net
Subject: Ben drink

Mark sweetheart

Very very busy here. On deadline. Yes, we talked about it last night. Basically he's still very pissed off, obstinate, the usual thing, but I get the impression it's not totally a lost cause. I mean how long can he keep going like this?

It's like he's making a point not just to his father, but to you, to me, to anybody he comes across. And of course to your mum. You know what B's like when he makes his mind up.

If you think it's a good idea then I would give it a try but I'm not sure how much luck you'll have. I didn't push it last night. I don't want him to think I'm turning against him, and I didn't say anything about you asking me, of course.

We've already arranged to meet in the Scarsdale pub at the back of the cinema on Ken High St.—the place you came to before we went to the Doves concert. Can you be there by maybe half-past seven? There might be some people from work so be warned.

Lovely to see you the other night. Thanks for the vodka—weird bottle!

lol

Als

x

From: Mark Keen
To: alicelucy1212@aol.com
Subject: Re: Ben drink

That sounds good. I'll be there at 7:30 at the latest. Don't mention anything to him about it, OK? I don't want him to feel like we're setting a trap or something.

Thanks for this Alice—I appreciate it a lot. Mark

Mark hit "Send" and wondered if this was a good idea; he doubted whether Alice would be able to keep their arrangement a secret. Sometimes, in fact, he couldn't even remember why he was doing his father the favor.

11

Taploe waited for Keen in the downstairs seating area of a Baker Street coffee shop. American-owned, the chain was populated by a preppy clientele drinking foam-laden lattes at Internet terminals. Bewildered by the range of drinks on offer, it had taken Taploe more than three minutes to explain to the South African girl working behind the counter that he simply wanted a black coffee, nothing more, nothing less.

"You want an espresso, then?"

"No. Just a black coffee. A normal black coffee. In a mug."

"Do you want me to make it a double? That's longer."

"No. I find espresso too strong. Look—"

He scanned the menu board for the appropriate description. Latte. Mocha. Espresso. Ristretto. Mochaccino. Cappuccino. Iced Mochachino Latte . . .

"It must be Americano," he said eventually. "That looks the closest."

"Americano!" the girl shouted to her colleague and, given that there were four or five people queueing up behind him, Taploe felt that he could not now change his order.

"Is that a shot of espresso with plenty of boiling water?" he asked.

"That's right, sir," she said, pointing to the counter on her left. "Your order'll be ready in a few minutes. Can I help anyone, please?"

Taploe had found a small round table at the rear of the basement where any conversation would be drowned out by the tapping of computer keyboards, the quack and beep of the World Wide Web. Twenty or thirty people, mostly students, were crowding up the seating area.

Taploe sensed Keen before he saw him, a sudden intimation of good taste and disdain moving through the room. He was wearing a long, dark overcoat and carrying a small white cup of espresso in his right hand. Taploe was reminded of a Tory grandee.

"Christopher," he said.

"Stephen." Taploe's view of his joe was already colored by the basic antipathy that existed between the organizations to which both men had dedicated the bulk of their working lives. But the sense Keen gave off of living in an infallible bubble of privilege added a particular hostility to his contempt.

"Did you find the place all right?" he asked.

"No problem at all. But it's bloody cold outside. They say it might snow."

"Well, thank you for agreeing to the meeting at such short notice." Taploe sipped at his coffee but found that it was still too hot to drink. "I hope we didn't put you out."

"Not at all. I have a dinner engagement in the West End at nine o'clock. The timing was rather convenient."

Slowly, Taploe drew the tips of his fingers across the wooden surface of the table. It was an unconscious manifestation of his anxiety, and he was irritated with himself for showing it.

"Can I get you anything from upstairs?"

Taploe could not think why he had asked the question. Keen simply lowered his eyes and indicated his espresso with a downward nod of the head.

"Oh yes, of course."

There was an embarrassed silence that Taploe eventually broke.

"This shouldn't take long," he said. "It was just to find out about your inquiries."

Keen could see a Japanese student poring over notes held in a loose-leaf folder to the right of his chair. If Taploe considered this a secure environment in which to talk, he would take that on trust, but keep his remarks general to the point of being obtuse. Christian names. No specifics. Operational shorthands.

"My view is very straightforward," he said. "If the lawyer is involved to any extent with the Russian organization then my son knows nothing about it. That would indicate to me that this is something that is happening only at the very highest level within the company. That is to say, only Thomas and perhaps Sebastian know anything about it."

"What makes you so sure?"

"Body language. A certain openness about the way he answered my questions. No obvious nerves. As our American friends might put it, Mark is out of the loop."

By his expression, Taploe seemed unconvinced. "What did he say about the lawyer?" he asked.

"Nothing that you won't already know. Bit of a chancer, man

about town. Taste for what certain people regard as the finer things in life. Champagne, oysters, *bliads*."

Keen assumed correctly that Taploe would recognize the Russian slang for prostitute.

"Is that right?" He pursed out his lips. "To what extent is he involved in that when he's in Russia?"

"Happens mostly in Moscow, by the sound of it. You know the form. They hang around the hotel lobbies and mezzanine floors, looking for businessmen with a wedding ring . . ."

Taploe essayed an exaggerated frown, as if the moral implications of Macklin's behavior had briefly overwhelmed him. He looked visibly disappointed.

"And is Mark involved with them as well?"

"Good god, no."

Keen's reply was abrupt and Taploe wondered if he might have offended him. He found himself saying, "Of course, sorry," and then again resented his own awkwardness. A clatter of schoolgirls came down into the basement bearing tall beakers of coffee. One had a lit cigarette in her hand and was smoking it without skill, like someone sucking on the end of a pencil.

"Is that an area you're investigating?" Keen asked. "Women being trafficked from eastern Europe, Russia, and so on?"

Taploe's eyes flicked across to the Japanese student who was still engrossed in his notes. Next to him, about three feet away, sat a vast man in his late thirties dressed head to toe in Reebok sportswear. He was slowly typing an email using only the index finger of his left hand.

"It's certainly a possibility," he said, and swallowed a long intake of still-hot coffee. The roof of his mouth throbbed. "Did Mark add anything else in connection to that?"

"Only that Thomas fools around with them in his hotel room. Perhaps he gets a discount."

Taploe did not smile.

"The impression I was given," Keen continued, "is that our lawyer friend is somewhat overwhelmed by the glamour of the way things work over there, the influence those boys wield. Unchecked power and unlimited violence. Excessive privilege for the select few. Free access to money, girls, narcotics, fast cars, restaurants; he's in thrall to it all. The adrenalin, you see? Nothing like it over here, back in the old country."

"Yes," was all that Taploe managed to say, though everything that Keen was telling him fitted the emerging profile of Thomas Macklin. London surveillance had revealed nothing out of the ordinary: an on–off girlfriend (a receptionist in the City), the occasional escort, no tendency to gamble, a mild, recreational cocaine habit. He had an enthusiasm for lap-dances and expensive clothes, few close friends, and a tendency to become aggressive when drunk. Macklin paid his bills regularly, but at any one time his major credit card—Visa—was never less than two or three thousand pounds in the red. He had sufficient funds in other bank accounts to pay the debt off, but for some reason failed to do so; Paul Quinn, Taploe's closest associate on the case, had put this down to little more than negligence. There was nothing unusual about Macklin's phone records, either at work, from home, or on his mobile, save for the fact that he always called his Kukushkin contact in London from public telephone boxes, from which the calls were harder to trace. That, at the very least, hinted at a degree of concealment. The Internet, thus far, had revealed little that Quinn and Taploe did not already know: Macklin used email frequently, but only to stay in touch with developments within Libra worldwide. There had been nothing of any consequence to the ongoing investigation in the analysis of his Internet traffic, only incidents that colored the psychological profile.

"And Mark? That sort of lifestyle doesn't appeal to him?" Taploe asked.

Keen swallowed his espresso in a single controlled gulp. "I've told you," he said. "He's more sensible, more down to earth. Like his father."

Taploe did not acknowledge the joke. He thought that this would help him to make up some ground.

"But you've spent a lot of time in that part of the world," he said, deciding to take a risk. "You can understand why Thomas might be tempted by the high life?"

Keen looked at him very quickly. His eyes appeared to blacken at the implication.

"Thomas is a very different animal, Stephen, I can assure you. The lawyer's a barrow boy, a bright entrepreneur out for whatever he can get. His sort usually run into trouble."

A braver part of Taploe wanted to embarrass Keen into an explanation of the term "barrow boy," but he let it go.

"And the boss?" he said. "How does Sebastian fit into the picture? How does he benefit from the Russian organization?"

Keen shifted slowly in his chair.

"Look," he said, "there's absolutely no point in asking me about Roth." The use of his surname was a slip. "I should have thought that these were the sort of questions to which you might already have answers. As I told you at our previous meeting, my organization doesn't tend to meet the chaps at the top of the tree. They send their underlings, their lawyers. Mr. Ro—" This time he checked himself. "Sebastian is a man about whom I know very little. I take it as read that he is greedy. I take it as read that he is unscrupulous. So many of us are, Stephen. But why would he be stupid enough to get involved with the Thieves? He must understand the power they exert in Russia? He'd be in over his head, could very quickly lose control of all his investments. It simply doesn't make sense."

"And did Divisar warn him about that?"

"Of course we did. Unfortunately, Thomas ignored our advice to get a Russian partner on board whose contacts would have facilitated the company's expansion. Nor were they interested in franchising the name to local entrepreneurs. I advised them to become active in establishing relationships with senior government officials in the Ministry of Interior, men who might have offered them protection from organized crime, even if that meant paying off government bureaucrats instead. But Sebastian wanted total control. Apparently that was how he had built up the company and that was how he knew how to operate."

The schoolgirls, gathered in a chattering huddle around one of the larger sofas, began giggling at a photograph in a magazine. Taploe looked across at them, absorbing Keen's remarks and then running them through his mind like a filter. Eventually he said, "Does your son trust Thomas?"

Keen did not know how to answer the question beyond a simple, one-word response.

"No."

"But they're friends? They rely on each other."

"If that is your impression, then yes," he replied unhelpfully. He recalled asking Mark a similar question in the Chinese restaurant.

"But what's your impression?" Taploe had begun to feel hemmed in by the crowded basement, the black coffee working through him to a flushed sweat. It was not even a question to which he required an answer, but he had been flustered from the moment he walked into the coffee house.

"My impression?" Keen ran the dark blue silk of his tie between the thumb and index finger of his left hand, smoothing it before letting it come to rest on the soft folds of his cream shirt. "My impression is merely common sense. That they may rely on one another, but that there is a world of difference between reliance and trust. If there weren't, after all, men like you and me would be out of a job. Loyalty within the world of business is a fiction. When push comes to shove, Thomas will no more look after my son's interests than he would cut off his own hand."

"And vice versa?" Keen moved forward.

"You appear to be laboring under a misconception. Mark may have made several trips with Thomas, but they spent a lot of that time apart. What he gets up to in my son's absence remains a mystery. You seem to think they're some sort of double act, Libra's answer to Morecambe and Wise."

Taploe frowned, angered that Keen had mentioned the company by name.

"You can understand that he's our best lead," he said.

"Well, what about the French chap?" Keen asked. "If you want someone on the inside, why don't you run him?"

"French chap?" Taploe said.

"Philippe, I think his name is."

"D'Erlanger? He's Belgian," Taploe corrected. "Anyway, he left the company to run a restaurant."

"Well, I was merely trying to help."

"Of course."

"So call Mark yourself," Keen suggested. "It's obviously the next step." He felt no ordinary moral reason why he should not hand his son over to MI5. He was anxious to leave for dinner, and Mark would at least be able to help with the investigation. "To be honest, I've become bored playing the middleman," he said. "There's something rather demeaning about it."

12

Why had he bothered coming?

The pub in Edwardes Square stank generally of sweat and spilled pints, and specifically of stale sick in the area where Ben was sitting. He was halfway through a pint of Guinness, talking to an earnest financial journalist from the *Evening Standard* who wanted to know how he found the motivation to get up every morning and paint in his studio and, "Wasn't there a temptation when you're working from home just to fuck off and spend the whole afternoon in the cinema?"

"Sometimes," Ben told him.

"Well, I really admire you, man," he said. "No, I really do."

Alice was at the bar, surrounded by five drooling male colleagues making wisecracks and pulling rank. She had phoned at the last moment and all but demanded that Ben join her for a drink. *Come on. We never see each other. You never want to meet my friends.* He had been forced to abandon work on the picture of Jenny, but now that he was here Alice was scarcely giving him the time of day. Ben was thinking about leaving as soon as he had finished his pint and going back to work in the studio.

"So how much do you charge for a portrait?" the journalist was asking.

"What's that?" Ben had heard the question, but wanted to suggest with his eyes that he thought it was none of his business.

"I said how much do you—"

"It depends."

"Oh, right. What on? I mean, how do you rate it? By the hour?"

The conversation went on like this for fifteen minutes. *But can you make any real money as a painter? Don't you get bored and lonely?* Ben couldn't get away. The constant opening and closing of the street door fed muffled traffic noise into the pub. Ben found himself explaining why he hated the cocktail-party circuit of art exhibitions and gallery openings, all that air-kissing and people with too much money buying paintings just to match a sofa. The journalist was laughing, agreeing with everything Ben said, even offering to buy him a pint and introduce him to a City financier who was collecting art and "really knew what was right and wrong."

"You know, man. Not shark tanks and elephant shit. *Paintings.* He really likes oils and watercolors. Give me your number and I'll text you his details."

That was when Mark walked into the pub.

He was stopped by Alice almost immediately among the jam of bodies at the bar. She squealed and put her arms around his waist, looking over in Ben's direction. Was this more than coincidence? Ben was so pleased to see him that he dismissed the thought immediately. He stood up, said, "Back in a moment," and walked toward the bar.

"What the fuck are you doing here?"

"Hello, brother. Had a meeting next door. Just popped in for a pint."

"Isn't it amazing?" Alice was saying, putting her hand on Mark's back. "Of all the places."

There were introductions, rounds of drinks. For half an hour they talked at the bar, Mark telling stories about Libra and Moscow, Alice involving everybody in the conversation and making sure to laugh at the news editor's jokes. A frustrating evening became suddenly enjoyable for Ben, the easy slip of Guinness and close family. And as Alice's colleagues left the pub one by one, it was easy for Mark to pull him away into a private huddle and to deal with the task in hand.

"Listen," he said, putting a grip on Ben's arm. "It's good we've run into each other. I need to have a chat with you about something. Something important."

Ben was smoking and pointed to the fourth finger of Mark's right hand with his cigarette. "Is it about that?" he asked.

Mark looked down. "What? The ring?"

"The ring." A bad start.

"Not exactly, no."

"Something else, then?" Ben said, and sat down at a free table.

Mark was slow to follow, as if assembling his thoughts. He was always apprehensive when it came to talking to Ben. A desire to protect and assist his younger brother coexisted with an older insecurity, rooted in childhood squabbles and fights—a feeling that Ben could outsmart him. At Libra, Mark was superefficient, the man Roth relied on to charm and cajole, an executive ten years in the business and never a foot put wrong. But when it came to Ben, those talents were compromised by sheer familiarity. He hooked his suit jacket on the back of a beer-stained tartan chair and wondered how he was ever going to bring him round.

"You OK?" Ben asked.

"Oh, sure."

Mark must have looked tired and distracted, some sort of apology already evident in his eyes, because right away Ben said, "It's about Christopher, isn't it?"

And Mark nodded, hunching forward with an awkward smile.

"'Fraid so," he said. "Had lunch with him last week, before I went back to Moscow. That was when he gave me the signet ring. It belonged to . . ."

Ben immediately raised his hand and a column of ash fell free of the cigarette, drifting in scatters toward the carpet.

"Forget it," he said. His attitude was not aggressive or unfeeling, merely a relaxed, clear assessment of his position. "I don't care where it came from, why he gave it to you, or which one of the Keen great-great-grandfathers wore it during the Crimean War. That stuff is between you and him. I don't want any part of it."

At the bar a soft-drinks gun coughed.

"Fair do's," Mark muttered. "Fair do's. I just wanted to let you know, so there was no big mystery or anything."

"Well, I appreciate it."

There was hefty silence. Mark instinctively felt that the timing was all wrong; both of them a little drunk, Alice only ten feet away, and their father on the other side of London. Why had he agreed to do Keen's dirty work? What was in it for *him*?

"But it's connected to what I wanted to talk about," he said.

"What's connected to what you wanted to talk about?"

"The ring. The dinner," Mark replied.

"Oh. Right."

Ben actually looked quite bored.

"The other night, when I came round for dinner and you and Alice were going at it . . ."

This seemed to galvanize Ben briefly. He looked up and gave a quick response.

"Yeah, I'm sorry about that. Alice has been a bit stressed lately. Both of us, in fact. Work stuff, marriage. We haven't been getting on and it's just been one argument after another . . ."

"No, that's not what I mean."

Ben cocked his head to one side.

"What then?"

"Look, why don't I just spell it out?" Mark moved uneasily in his chair. It was like breaking bad news, waiting for the right moment. "I think things have changed between me and you, brother. Not as easy as they were. You follow?"

Ben shook his head. On the way to the pub Mark had sketched out the basics of a speech in his mind, but he was moving on to it too quickly.

"It's like this. The last six months, however long it's been since Dad and I started meeting up, it's as if you've gone into yourself, moved away."

To illustrate his point, Mark spread his arms outward like a cross and nearly knocked half a pint of cider out of the hand of a passing customer. Across the pub, a man was slamming his fist against the hard plastic casing of a fruit machine, spitting the single word "Fuck."

"It's just that we've never really chatted about any of it." Mark was rubbing his jaw, words coming out before he had time to contemplate their impact. "It's just been swept under the carpet.

I'm abroad a lot, you're with Alice, it's not easy finding the time. But we need to clear the air. Your opinion matters to me. Now talk to me about what's going on."

Ben looked completely taken aback. "Where's this coming from?" he said.

"It's something I've been thinking about for a long time. Just seeing you tonight made me want to talk about it."

Ben's hand went up to his forehead, almost pulling the skin back from his eyes. He looked bloodshot and tense.

"So OK, we'll talk about it." He tipped his face up to the light and exhaled in a gasp. "It's like this." Mark was listening very carefully. "I don't *allow* myself to think about him. There are hard certainties in my life. There's you. There's Alice. I have my painting and my good friends. That's how things stay under control. That's how I manage to get by." The answer was so characteristic of his brother that Mark felt there was almost no point in going on. When Ben got an idea into his head it was impossible to change his mind. Only a basic desire not to let his father down led him to say, "Is that good for you? Thinking about things in that way? Breaking them down?"

"It's just how I've learned to cope." Across the room, somebody had paid fifty pence to hear a bad cover version of "Like a Rolling Stone" on the jukebox. The song was forced and loud and Ben had to speak up. "And now that Alice and I are married I have to deal with that. She needs my support. I want to look after her, to make things right. You know all this. Why the fuck are you bringing it up now? Let's get back to the bar and relax."

Yeah, let's, Mark thought, and hated what he was doing. He genuinely believed that the standoff between his brother and Keen was unhealthy, a running sore in the family, yet there was nothing, surely, that could be done about it. He was manipulating Ben for his father's benefit, pure and simple. They had set a trap for him, pushing Ben toward something that he wanted no part of. And where was Alice? Laughing at the bar, oblivious to what was going on, facilitating her career while Mark was risking everything. Why didn't she come over, why didn't she think of someone else for a change? He felt heavy with sweat and drink. A woman at the bar was hanging her arm around the neck of a fat, bald Irishman mouthing the lyrics "How does it *feel*?" over and over again.

"What does Alice think about it?" Mark found himself asking. "What does she reckon you should do?"

"We haven't talked about it much," Ben replied. "Why? Has she said anything?"

And suddenly Mark had a chance to force the issue. He remembered that Keen had asked an almost identical question as they were leaving the restaurant in Queensway.

"What's Alice's view?" his father had said. "Does she think Ben's right about this? Right not to want to meet me?"

Mark had hesitated briefly, but the wine at lunch had led him to betray a confidence.

"She's just got used to the idea. Ever since she's known Ben, she's known about you and your situation. And if you want my honest opinion I reckon she thinks Ben's being narrow-minded. In fact, she's told me as much."

If Mark could have retracted that statement, he would have done so in an instant. Keen's eyes had lit up.

"You could use that," he said, and the inference was appalling.

"*Use* that? What do you mean?"

"Tell Ben that you and Alice are in agreement. Tell him that it's time he reconsidered. It's the truth, isn't it?"

". . . Mark?"

Ben was trying to attract his attention. "Yeah. Sorry. I wandered off."

"I asked you a question. I said, has Alice said anything about this?"

"Well, maybe you should ask her." Mark had not intended to sound mysterious.

"What's that supposed to mean? Does she know about this? Does she know that we're having this conversation?"

And at that moment Alice looked over, sensing the note-change in the tenor of her husband's voice. Ben saw the setup instantly.

"Jesus. You're not here by coincidence, are you?"

Mark wasn't sure whether Ben was touched or angry; his face was momentarily unreadable. As a consequence he did not bother to lie in response. Shaking his head and even smiling at the stupidity of Keen's plan, Mark said, "I'm not here by coincidence, no."

And Ben was out of the pub in seconds.

13

Ben knew that it was not a good idea for a man of thirty-two to walk out of a crowded London pub after telling his older brother to fuck off. Not in Kensington and Chelsea, at any rate. And not in front of half a dozen of his wife's colleagues, most of whom would now be on their mobile phones telling anyone from the *Standard* not fortunate enough to have been there in person just exactly what happened in the lounge bar of the Scarsdale at 8:28 p.m.

Mark had followed him outside, and Ben had heard Alice calling his name as he turned onto Kensington High Street, but they had both decided to let him go and were probably still waiting back in the pub. There was no sense, after all, in going after Ben when the red mist descended. They both would have known that from long experience.

He walked in the direction of Hyde Park, turning back on himself at the gates to Kensington Palace and returning along the opposite side of the street. Alice tried calling him on his mobile phone but he switched it off. It took about ten minutes for Ben to calm down and another five for embarrassment to set in. So much of his anger, he knew, was just a pose, a melodramatized statement of his long-term refusal to change. Whatever arrangement, whatever trap had been set by Alice and Mark, angered him only because he had been kept out of the loop, treated like a child by his wife and brother, and finally cornered in a place from which there was no realistic escape. It had occurred to him many times that he was clinging to old ideas simply because they shielded him from facing harder choices; in a very dangerous sense, Ben was defined by an attitude toward his father that he had formed as a teenager. To abandon that principled stand would mean the dismantling of an entire way of thinking. How would people react to him? How would he square it with what had happened to Mum? Ben wished to honor her memory, and yet that was the easy position. Far more difficult, surely, to do what Mark had done, to let bygones be bygones and to open himself up to chance.

He was heading back to the pub via a street at the western end of Edwardes Square when he heard a voice behind him.

"Ben?"

He turned and saw that Mark was following him. He looked shattered. With the club opening in Moscow, he was probably only sleeping five hours a night and this was the last thing he needed.

"Look, I'm sorry. It's my fault. Don't blame Alice. I asked her to help me out and she was just being loyal."

Ben said nothing.

"I'm sorry if I took you by surprise. I'm sorry if I embarrassed you. We just . . ." Mark stalled on the words.

He had obviously rehearsed something and was determined to get it right. "All I was trying to say was this. More and more I've been thinking about the future, you know? Where are we gonna be ten years down the line? You and Alice have kids, Dad's their grandfather, but because of all this shit that's thirty years in the past his name can't be mentioned at the dinner table. Meanwhile, he and I are getting on better than ever, but we're still having to creep around behind your back. How long's it gonna last?"

"So you want me to meet him just so that you can have a better time of it when you're fifty-five?"

Ben regretted saying that, but for the sake of fraternal pride did not want to concede too early.

"I'm just saying that you should think about giving him a chance. Not tonight. Tonight is fucked into a hat. But soon, Ben, soon. Otherwise, he's just going to be this barrier between us, a bridge we can't cross."

Ben smirked and looked up at the night sky.

"I knew this was going to happen," he said. "Something like tonight."

"It was inevitable," Mark said.

"Yes, it was. And you know why? Because he's talked you into it. You're too soft on him, brother. You always want to do what's right so that no one gets upset. Well, *I'm* upset. I got *very* upset in there. I embarrassed myself, I embarrassed you, and I embarrassed my wife in front of everybody she works for. How does *that* feel?"

Mark did not respond. It looked as if he wanted to, but was holding back for fear of making things worse.

"You want my truthful opinion?" Ben was not surprised to feel that there was still resentment inside him. Most of it was a desire not to lose face, and he knew that he was prepared to make a later concession. "I think the relationship Dad has with you gives him what he wants—an opportunity to absolve himself of guilt." From his jacket pocket he took out a packet of cigarettes and watched his brother's face for a register of annoyance. "Now he wants to complete that process, supposedly to convince me of his worth as a father. But that's not motivated by a genuine concern for my welfare, or Alice's, or anyone else. It's just a selfish desire to convince himself of his blamelessness in respect of the past. He's a *spy*, for Christ's sake. All his relationships are games, little intrigues and power struggles. Look how he's manipulated you. For most of his adult life Christopher Keen has been making a living out of an ability to convince people that he is something other than the person he appears to be. *Think* about it, Mark. If he could do it to Mum when they were married, if he could do it to us when we were kids, what's to stop him doing it now?"

"Thanks," Mark said, his face tightening. "You think I'm that much of a mug?"

Ben didn't answer. He started walking toward the metal fence that ran along the western edge of the square. He had to move between parked cars.

"You've got him all wrong," Mark said, following behind. "He's not some puppet master pulling the strings. Don't you think people change? Don't you think it's possible that he might want to say sorry?"

Ben stopped and turned. "Has he said sorry to you?"

Mark could not give the answer he needed to without lying.

"That's not his style," he said, fudging it. They were now standing together on the pavement. "Dad just wants to make his peace."

"Well, maybe he does," Ben conceded. "But he can make it somewhere else."

There were lights on in several of the houses on Edwardes Square, oil paintings and chintz, Peter Sissons reading the news. Ben saw a man enter a yellow-wallpapered drawing room wearing bottle-green corduroy trousers and a bright red sweater. The man was carrying a tray of food and talking to someone in another room.

"You don't believe that," Mark said.

"Don't I?" Ben stared hard into his eyes. "He's doing what I always thought he'd do. Crawling back, midlife crisis, wanting us both to pat him on the head and tell him everything's OK. Well, it's not OK. He doesn't meet me, he doesn't meet Alice. End of story."

"Is that how *she* feels?"

"Why don't you ask her?" Ben turned again. "You two seem to be very close."

"I don't need to ask her." Mark was angry now. He couldn't keep it in. "She knows what I know. She knows what you *should* know if you weren't so fucking pigheaded. She knows that you're *fascinated* by Dad. She knows that you can't *wait* to meet him."

Until that moment, Ben had thought that he was in control, bending Mark to his will. But this last remark caught him off guard. He ran through every one of his recent conversations with Alice, every argument, every lie, every quiet chat in the house, but he could not recall even hinting at what Mark had just suggested.

"Is that what she told you?" he asked.

"She doesn't need to tell me."

Ben frowned.

"Look," Mark said. "Don't you even want to know what he looks like? How his character is different from yours? Don't you want to know if he's boring or vain or funny or rich? Doesn't any of that interest you? Don't you wonder what sort of a person he is, the hidden man?"

"We have nothing in common," Ben said, but the statement

lacked conviction. He blew a column of smoke at the railings. "Anyway, I'm not interested in any of that at all."

But Mark was on to him.

"I don't buy it. You have nothing *but* interest in that. Listen, if you turn around now and agree to meet him, Alice is not going to think badly of you. Your friends won't think you've sold out. *I* won't think you've sold out." Mark touched his chest. "Is that all that's stopping you? What other people might think?"

Ben was stunned by how well they both knew him. He thought that he had concealed his feelings, maintained a privacy, but his thoughts had been preempted. It was as if he were listening to his entire personality being pulled inside-out. He managed to say "No," but the word was meaningless. Mark was whispering.

"And it's not disloyal to Mum. I know that's always been on your conscience, but she wanted us to be happy."

"Does Alice think I'm stubborn?" It was a question to which Ben already knew the answer. Somebody walked past them, whistling on two notes. "Does Alice think I'm too proud to face facts, that I'm stuck in the past?"

"No."

"And what about you?"

"Ben, it doesn't *matter* what I think. It doesn't matter what *anyone* thinks. If you feel the way you feel, then it sounds like we're all wasting our time. It sounds like there's nothing more to be said."

Ben waited. He was ready now. It was the right moment. He knew that Mark was being shrewd and not forcing the issue.

"Nobody should make you do something that you don't want to do," he said. "At the end of the day, just because I've started seeing Dad doesn't mean that you should too."

"I know that . . ."

"But I think it would do you good to meet him. I think it's something that you need to do. Even if it's just to let off steam, to have it out with him. That's why we set this thing up tonight, this disastrous fucking drink in this disastrous fucking boozer." Mark nodded his head in the direction of the pub. "But to know that he's here in London and not do anything about that is just going to eat away at you. It's bad for you, it's bad for me, and it's bad for your marriage."

And, finally, he had said enough. For a moment Ben allowed the silence of the square to envelop them, then he extinguished his cigarette on the black painted spike of a gate.

"I'm right, you know," Mark said.

"I know you are."

"So you'll do it?"

Ben stared, taking his time.

"I'll think about it," he said.

14

There was something almost mundane about the hour that preceded their reunion. Ben simply showered, put on a clean shirt and a suit, placed a tie in one of the pockets of his jacket, and drank a single gulp of vodka from a bottle of Stolichnaya he kept in the fridge. The spirit burned in his throat, spreading like linctus across his chest. Then he walked outside onto Elgin Crescent and began looking around for a cab.

It was a quarter to eight on a Thursday night. Alice was still at work, Mark already back in Moscow having acted as the intermediary in setting up the reunion. Ben found a taxi on Ladbroke Grove and settled into the back seat, wearily informed by the driver that pre-Christmas traffic had jammed up throughout London and that it might take as much as an hour to reach the Savoy. Ben was already late and wondered how long his father would wait before giving up and going home. Twenty minutes? Half an hour? What would be an appropriate span of time for a man who had not seen his son in twenty-five years? At eight thirty, still five hundred meters short on the Strand, Ben decided to walk and paid off the driver with a twenty-pound note. He resented the cost of the journey.

A small group of European tourists wearing brand-new Burberry raincoats were clustered in the art deco forecourt of the Savoy: tanned men with immaculately coiffed hair, their wives balanced precariously on high-heeled shoes. A doorman dressed in full morning suit scoped Ben briefly, saw that he looked respectable, and stepped aside to allow him through the revolving doors.

Polished wood paneling. Squares of black and white stone set into the floor like a chessboard. The lobby resembled the set of some prewar costume drama. Sheer nervous momentum carried Ben through the lobby, past whispering guests on sofas and a pretty receptionist who caught his eye. He found himself heading toward the source of some music, piano notes played lightly on the black keys, coming through a wide drawing-room area packed with tables and chairs. Everything to Ben's eyes looked green and peach: the flecked, avocado-colored carpet, the Doric-order columns finished in tangerine marble. More men in morning coats were moving soundlessly around the room, collecting trays of empty cups and spreading linen cloths reverently across tables. The white-tied pianist was playing on a raised platform at the center of the room. Ben thought that he recognized "I Get a Kick out of You," but the melody was lost, chopped up into shapeless bursts of modern jazz.

Ahead of him, behind a glass partition, he could see people seated for dinner in the restaurant. Some of the tables looked out over the Thames. A group of waiters, many with gray hair, had gathered near what appeared to be a lectern at the entrance to the restaurant. The oldest of them, whom Ben took to be the manager, broke away to greet him.

"Can I help at all, sir?" he asked in a thick East End accent. The man was almost entirely bald, with a dry, ridged complexion like the surface of a golf ball.

"I'm having dinner with my father," Ben told him. "He should be here."

"The name, sir?"

"His name is Keen. Christopher Keen. It was for eight fifteen."

The waiter turned to consult his reservations book. Ben was almost too afraid to scan the tables beyond the glass in case he should catch sight of his father.

"We don't seem to have a booking for that name, sir."

The waiter's tone suggested that Ben had wasted his time.

"Are you sure?"

He felt tricked, gripped by the sure thought that his father had bottled out.

"Quite sure, sir. Of course, it's possible that you're dining with us in the grill room."

"The grill room?"

"Our other restaurant, sir. You would have passed it on the way in. Just go back to the main door. You'll find it on the right of reception, top of the stairs."

Muttering an embarrassed "Thank you," Ben turned and walked back toward the foyer. He felt rushed now, no longer in control. A slim Frenchwoman introduced herself at the entrance to the Grill and took his name with a smile. He was surely on the brink of it now, his father only seconds away. She was conferring with one of her colleagues, pointing out into the room, and when Ben looked up to take in the quiet formality of his surroundings he saw his father at the far end of the restaurant, seated at a table backed up against the wall. Their eyes met and Keen nodded, rising to his feet, a man of sixty who seemed never to have aged. A very broad, effortful smile and that steady, unreadable gaze that Ben remembered even as a child. His breathing doubled back on itself as he moved toward the table. Ben tried to set his face but the effort was hopeless.

"Benjamin."

"Hello."

A firm handshake, a contact of skin, examining his father's face for the bits that looked like him.

"It's so wonderful to see you. So wonderful. Do come and sit down."

Some men of Keen's generation had faces weakened by experience, eyes and mouths rendered timid by the failures of age. But his father looked capable, renewed, not someone whom a younger man might profitably challenge. Ben was amazed by the preservation of his good looks; his father had the vigor and apparent fitness of a man half his age. He was, against all expectation, impressed by him.

"Will you have a glass of something?" he asked, and Ben nodded at the waiter, dryly requesting water as he sat down.

"Nothing a little stronger?"

The question, quite unintentionally, came off sounding like a test of Ben's masculinity. He felt automatically obliged to order a vodka and tonic. Already, so soon, he had been undermined by something like the force of his father's personality.

"I'll have one too, Gerard," Keen said to the waiter, who deposited two menus and a wine list on the table. *He even knows the waiter's name.* Sweat collected across the upper part of Ben's back, the shoulders of his suit jacket now tropically hot.

"And some water as well," Keen added, fixing blue eyes on his son. "Gas or no gas?"

It was another question to which he must find a quick answer. Ben wanted to say that he didn't care, but muttered, "Without gas, please," in a low voice. Then the waiter moved off.

Before he was out of earshot Keen said, "I wanted to thank you right away for agreeing to meet me."

"Not at all," Ben replied, responding with a smile, and he was immediately frustrated with himself for adhering to decorum. He had badly wanted to make things difficult at this early stage, to find some dark expression of his contempt, but instead was playing the genial, even-tempered son.

"I went the wrong way when I came in," he said, just to fill the silence. "Didn't realize they had two restaurants."

"No," his father replied, and he might almost have been bored. Why had Ben expected it to be one-way traffic? Why had he thought that the evening would see Keen on bended knee, uttering a groveling apology? There was no sign of that at all.

"So why did you want to see me?" he asked, and it was the first question he had set that carried any kind of weight. Keen leaned forward as if to draw the sting out of it, to envelop Ben in goodwill.

"Well, it's been too long," he said. "Too much time has gone by and I am responsible for that."

"Yes, you are."

That's better. Put him on the back foot. Claw back some ground.

"Ah. Our drinks."

Gerard was returning with two tall glasses of vodka and tonic, balanced on a chrome tray. The moment was lost.

"Thanks," Ben said, taking a mouthful straightaway.

"Have they made it strong enough?"

"It's fine, thank you, fine."

"I never think us Brits put enough booze in. Tend to hold back on the vodka, don't you think?"

"Really, it's OK."

The restaurant's decor was a time warp of imperial England: more wood paneling, lamps with hexagonal shades bolted to the walls, even slices of Melba toast like dried skin racked on a plate at the table.

"This a place where you eat a lot?" Ben asked.

Why hadn't he at least let the silence linger? Why had he felt the need to rescue the situation?

"You mean, do I come here often?"

"I suppose I do."

"Not infrequently," Keen lied.

Another waiter was standing stiffly beside his chair. "Are you ready to order, gentlemen?"

"I haven't had a moment to look at what's on offer," Keen said, idly picking up his menu. "Can you give us five minutes, Philippe?"

"Of course, sir. I'll come back later." And he cleared his throat.

"Let's have a look, shall we?"

The simple act of opening the menus swamped the table in silence. Keen seemed oblivious to it, entirely at ease, but Ben was beginning to feel like a young boy on a day out from school. He spent thirty or forty seconds staring at the stiff cream card without registering a single one of the dishes on offer. Pumpkin Bisque with Ricotta £7.50. Sole Veronique £18.00. Pan-Fried Sea Bass with Confit Fennel and Chorizo £23.00. Breast of Chicken with Celeriac Fondant and Wild Mushroom Ravioli £24.00. Trying to imagine what each of the dishes would entail was simply impossible: they were just words on a page, a blur of text. Calf's Liver on Sweet Onion Tarte Tatin with Sage Beignet £18.50. Cannon of Lamb with Ratatouille and Basil Cream £23.50. Even by London standards, Ben was astonished by how high the prices were.

Keen closed his menu with what was almost a snap.

"Have you decided?"

"There's such a lot to choose from." It was another remark Ben regretted instantly: his voice sounded childish and flustered. He looked back at the menu and simply went for the first dish that his eyes settled on. "I'll have the Tournedos of Beef."

"But nothing to start with?"

"Vichyssoise," Ben replied, vaguely recalling its presence on the menu. The words were out of his mouth when he remembered that Vichyssoise was chilled. He hated cold soup.

"I believe it's very good here."

Keen ordered—he would have the pumpkin bisque and the cannon of lamb—adding petit pois and roast parsnips as vegetables for both of them. He then turned his attention to the wine list.

"Do you prefer red or white?" he asked.

Ben knew enough by now to express a preference and said "Red" very firmly. So Keen passed the list across the table.

"Have a look," he said.

"Oh, I'm no expert," Ben told him, scanning the selection. The list must have run to ten or twelve pages, bound in a cumbersome leather case so heavy he had to rest it in his lap. "What about the Beaune Clos des Marconnets?"

He had simply skipped the cheapest four bottles and opted for the first red Burgundy on the page.

"Very good," Keen said. "Very good." He adjusted his tie and nodded. "What year is it?"

Ben had to look again. "Nineteen ninety-five."

"Perfect. A bottle of Clos des Marconnets it is."

"And then I should head off and maybe wash my hands. Where would I find the bathroom?"

The act of splashing cold water on his face felt oddly self-conscious. Ben stared at his reflection in the mirror and exhaled heavily. He was alone in a gleaming bathroom with only an aging attendant for company. The man, as old as the Savoy itself, came forward to offer a small white towel.

"Is everything all right, sir?" he asked.

"Oh, everything's fine," Ben replied, drying water on the back of his neck. He pummeled his face with the towel as if it would somehow rub the anxiety out from under his skin. "Just a bit tired."

This is what it feels like to be drunk, he thought. *Just can't seem to get it together at all.*

The attendant proffered a small bottle of cologne, which Ben declined. At waist level he caught sight of a small copper plate scattered with pound coins and reached into his pocket for a tip.

"You work here all night?" he asked, palming the man a clutch of twenty-pence pieces.

"Oh, no, sir." The attendant sounded surprised, as if no guest had bothered to talk to him in over forty years. "Just a few hours at a time."

"I see."

"And are you dining with us this evening, sir?"

"I am, yes," Ben said, moving toward the door.

"Well, do enjoy yourself, won't you?" he said, wiping a towel across the sinks. The man moved with an arthritic slowness, the skin on his hands mottled by age.

"Deference" was the word in Ben's head as he headed back across the lobby. He was beginning to realize why Keen had wanted to meet in such a place. The hot, formal atmosphere of the Savoy, the buzz and fuss of waiters, the businessmen whispering confidences at nearby tables; there was little chance of having a frank and revealing discussion in such an atmosphere. He felt that he had been tricked, and experienced a renewed determination not to be finessed by Keen.

"Bit formal here, isn't it?" he said as he sat back down. He immediately took his jacket off and felt looser, more at ease.

"What do you mean?"

"Very old school." Ben looked back toward the foyer. "I just met Neville Chamberlain in the gents."

Keen smiled encouragingly and rotated his glass through the air, advising Ben to try the wine.

"You chose very well," he said. "It was a bottle I might have ordered myself. I actually prefer Burgundies to Bordeaux."

Ben did not reply. He was learning how to cultivate the silences.

"A friend of mine from Russian days says much the same thing. Mark may have mentioned him to you. Jock McCreery. The three of us had dinner one evening in London . . ."

Again Ben said nothing. *Let him make the running.*

"So tell me about your work." Keen seemed anxious to keep the conversation ticking over.

"No. Let's talk about you first."

"Fine."

"You worked in the Foreign Office for a long time."

"That's right, yes."

"Which was why you left us, of course. In the first place."

His father's expression tightened. "I . . ."

"Brother says you were in MI6."

Keen had not expected this. Any rapport that might have built up between them was quickly dissipating. He glanced at a nearby table and muttered, "Well, of course, that's a side of things one is encouraged to keep quiet about. You never know who may be listening."

"But you've retired now?"

"Of course."

"So what's the problem?"

"The problem is quite straightforward." Keen was still smiling, though with less conviction. "One is not supposed to talk about the Office. I'm sure you understand."

"So why did you tell Mark about it?"

"I'm sorry?"

"Why did you tell Mark? To impress him?"

"You've suddenly become rather confrontational, Benjamin. Did something happen while you were away? Is everything all right?"

"Everything's fine. And it's 'Ben.' I'm simply looking for an answer to my question. Did you think he'd be impressed by what you've done with your life?"

"I don't quite understand."

"I mean, is that the vanity of the spy? Not enough adulation on the job? Nobody saying, 'Well done, Christopher, and keep up the good work'?"

And suddenly they were on the edge of an argument. Keen was desperate to preserve the dignity of the occasion and astonished by how quickly the evening had disintegrated into spite and ill-feeling. Unconsciously chewing his upper lip, he began looking around for a waiter. A two-deck sweet trolley was wheeled past and he followed it with his eyes, eventually settling them somewhere around Ben's midriff.

"Why don't I ask you a question instead?" he suggested. "Far more interesting, I would have thought. Mark's been rather vague about your painting."

"My painting," Ben replied flatly, as if Keen thought of it as no more than a hobby. He was now enjoyably committed to making the meal as difficult as possible.

"Yes. Your painting."

"Vague?"

"Vague."

He feigned disinterest.

"Well, brother can be a bit philistine when it comes to art. Might take a girl to the Turner Prize, but that's about it."

Keen laughed self-consciously, as if they had shared a private joke, but he felt increasingly undermined, his plan unraveling. Why had they arranged to meet in the Savoy? What had he been thinking? That a surfeit of Italian marble and silver service would somehow paper over the cracks of his past mistakes? Ben had been nervous at first, of course, but he was settled now, and itching for the fight. His temperament was exactly as Mark had described it: wounded, blunt, argumentative.

"What sort of stuff do you paint?" he asked, and felt that the question might be his last opportunity to maintain a civilized air of polite inquiry.

"Do you really care?" Ben replied. "Or are we just making small talk?"

For the first time he managed to hold his father's gaze. One beat, two. Keen, now visibly unsettled, put his glass down and frowned.

"Perhaps this was a bad idea," he said.

"You think?"

"I really don't understand what's brought this on." An elderly man at a nearby table cast Keen a disapproving look, alerted by the suddenly aggressive tone of their conversation.

"Just traditional stuff," Ben said, and it was a moment before Keen realized that he was talking about painting. He felt almost ridiculed, toyed with. "Watercolors. Sketches. Oil paintings. The sort of work that's out of fashion nowadays."

Two more waiters appeared and began ladling soup into bowls at a serving table beside them. For some time nothing was said except a very quiet "Thank you" from Keen as his bisque was placed in front of him. Then they ate in silence for as much as two or three minutes. Ben's pulse was a drum of adrenalin as Keen's consternation settled. Eventually, he found a fresh subject and tested new ground.

"So you're married," he asked.

Ben nodded.

"How long ago, if I may ask?"

"A couple of years."

"And you met here in London?"

These were questions to which he already knew the answer, and the curt manner of Ben's reply implied as much.

"That's right," he said.

"She's very pretty."

"Is that a statement or a question?"

Keen took a deep breath.

"A statement."

"Who told you? Brother?"

"Mark, yes."

Ben wondered what else he had revealed about their relationship. *Alice is tricky. Alice is ambitious and manipulating.* He knew that Mark had his reservations about her, however well he tried to disguise them. Odd that they should be so close and yet labor under such an obvious pretence. Perhaps Mark had also mentioned something about the constant arguments, the money, a marriage turning sour.

"So what else did he say about her?"

"That she's a writer. A journalist of sorts."

"For the *Standard*, yes."

"Actually, he gave me a photograph of your wedding day."

The revelation hit Ben with the full force of betrayal. He was not even conscious of the speed with which his temper flared.

"He did *what*?"

Keen realized instantly that he had made a mistake. "I have it hanging in my flat," he said, feigning innocence. "You didn't know?"

"You had no right to take that."

"It was a present."

"It was an invasion of our privacy."

"Well, I think you're overreacting. It looked like the most wonderful day. There's really no need to be upset."

Several heads now turned to look at Ben, yet he was aware of nothing but his own anger. Every promise he had made to Mark and Alice, every private undertaking to give his father a second chance, had evaporated.

"You think you have any right to *tell* me that?"

"Mark informed me that he'd asked your permission."

"Oh, come off it. You trying to play us off against each other? Is that how this works? Divide and rule? You think that by making me angry with Mark I'll somehow come over to your side?"

The thought had occurred to Keen, but he said, "Of course not, don't be ridiculous," with as much credibility as he could muster. Flushed now with the awkwardness of a very public row, he searched for a means of salvaging what was in all probability a lost cause. Mark had been biddable and eager to please, as accommodating and straightforward as his mother. But Ben was a different proposition. Looking across the table at his son, Keen might almost have been faced with himself.

"I don't know what exactly it was that you were expecting from me this evening."

Ben looked at him, almost breathless in the wake of his outburst, and realized that he did not know either. He was sure only that their reconciliation had come too soon, or that Mark should have accompanied him to dilute the awful sense of occasion. He wanted very much to leave, to go back to his old life, to the simplicity of the abandoned child. And yet in the square just a few nights before he had been so sure, and really only waiting for Mark to provide him with the excuse he needed to reach out and take the step. His mind was a crosshatch of contradictory emotions: of loyalty to Carolyn; of anger at himself for lacking the maturity and good sense merely to sit the evening out; of frustration at Mark for betraying his trust. Most oddly, perhaps, he felt affection toward Keen for craving a simple photograph of his wedding day. There was love contained in such a gesture: perhaps that, above all, was what had upset him.

For five minutes, they ate their soup without saying a word, until Ben could no longer stomach the awful metal silence of cutlery and glass. With the conviction of a man seemingly faced with no other choice, he pushed his bowl to one side and cleared his throat.

"You know, I just think I'm going to go," he said, and Keen seemed to have expected it.

Calmly, he picked up his napkin, wiped the corners of his mouth, and with a slow, physical deliberation said, "Fine, yes, I think that's a good idea. I can understand that this has been very difficult for you. I invited you here this evening because I hoped that . . ."

But Ben did not even hear him finish. He rose from the table, took his jacket from the chair, and walked the short distance to the lobby. Eyes followed him; there were murmured expressions of surprise. His entire body felt hot with shame and regret as he pushed through the revolving doors and went out onto the street.

15

Mark was lying on the hard, starched bed of his Moscow hotel room, nursing a stomach cramp brought on by two days of cheap Georgian wine and deep-fried meats. Thomas Macklin was downstairs in the lobby cracking jokes with an entourage of deal-hungry Russians wearing badly cut suits and explosive aftershave. Neither of them had any idea of the whereabouts of Sebastian Roth.

Ben telephoned him from a booth outside Charing Cross Station. At first Mark thought about ignoring the call, but he had given his number to a good-looking French television journalist whose eyes had worked him over at a bar on Tverskaya. There was just the faint possibility that it might be her, bored and lonely on another cold night in Moscow. He cleared his voice by saying, "Telephone" into the room and moved off the bed. His body felt slow and lumpen, a searing pain across his abdomen when his feet touched the floor.

"Yes? Hello?"

"I fucked up."

His brother's voice was so clear he might have been speaking from the next room.

"Ben?"

"I couldn't do it. Couldn't sit there and listen to his bullshit. I didn't have the patience just to ride it out and let everything take its course."

Mark rubbed his face.

"What happened? You went to the dinner?"

"Yeah. Lost my rag. Flew at him. Why'd you give him the photograph, brother? Why'd you do that?"

Dissembled by fatigue, Mark rubbed his head and said, "He told you about that?"

"Yeah."

"It was just a present, a way of showing him . . ."

He heard Ben sigh deeply, then the noise of passengers going into the station.

"Fuck it," he said. "Look, don't worry. It's not important. I just needed to talk to you. I think I would have walked out whatever."

"What happened?" Mark asked again.

"Nothing. Everything. He was confident, tricky. I never felt comfortable. So I got upset, started asking awkward questions, putting him on the spot. I don't know why I did it, Mark. I never felt comfortable letting Mum down."

"Sure. Sure."

"It was like I was just looking for an excuse to lose my temper. You know how I can do that?"

"I know how you can do that," Mark said softly.

"I mean, I'm not looking for a fight, but sometimes . . ."

"I know. I know."

Ben stopped talking. He was aware of the piss and grime of Charing Cross Station. He fed the last of his coins into the payphone and said, “Look, I’m almost out of money. How’s Moscow?”

“Don’t worry about Moscow. Just go home. Is Alice there? We can talk from your house.”

“No. In the morning.” A woman walked past Ben with snow on the shoulders of her coat. “Call me when we both know what we’re saying. It sounds like you were asleep anyway. I didn’t mean to wake you up.”

Mark rolled his neck until it clicked.

“You didn’t wake me up,” he said. “I was just lying here. It’s been a long day. Look, I’m sorry it didn’t work out. Maybe we shouldn’t have forced you into it. It just seemed the best thing to do.”

“It was the best thing to do,” Ben said. “I’ll speak to you tomorrow.”

16

Christopher Keen emerged from the Savoy and squeezed a smile at the doorman as snow began twisting into the forecourt. A cab pulled up and he stepped inside, instructing the driver to take him to his flat in Paddington. It was not yet ten o'clock but he felt dejected and worn out.

The driver said, "Enjoyable evening, sir?"

"Not particularly."

"Oh, I'm sorry to hear that. Dodgy meal, was it? I have heard, sir, that the Grill is not quite what it used to be. You know, in the old days."

"It wasn't the food," Keen replied.

It took more than half an hour to reach Paddington, thirty minutes of regret and silent reflection. The snow began falling more heavily, coating the streets in a thin viscous film of gray slush. Keen was still surprised by how much of the basic geography of London he recalled: shortcuts, obscure streets, the façade of a fondly remembered building. Nothing about England ever changes, he thought. There are just more cars on the roads, more people, more litter in the streets. He considered stopping off at his club in St. James's, but his mood was too bleak and forlorn. When the driver reached the entrance to his apartment, Keen tipped him three pounds and grimaced at the freezing wind. Tightening his scarf, he walked up the steps to the foyer and rode the lift to the fourth floor.

Inside the flat, he noted the packet of coffee that he had spilled in the kitchen that morning and decided to leave it for another day. He was still hungry from not eating and cut himself a slice of cheese, taking several cubes of ice from the freezer and dropping them into a tumbler of whisky. In the small sitting room next door, he sat down in his favorite armchair and rested the glass on a low antique table. There, on the wall, was the photograph of Ben's wedding, and Keen thought for a moment about smashing it on the floor, a crude, adolescent gesture against everything that had gone wrong. Instead he would drink his whisky, perhaps watch television, and then try to get some sleep. Mark might even telephone from Moscow to find out how things had gone. Keen did not have the will to call him of his own volition, but the thought reminded him to contact Taploe. Going back into the kitchen he pulled a pad of Post-it notes from a drawer and scrawled *Call Taploe re: M* across the top copy. Then, having fixed it to the frame of the door, he returned to the sitting room and switched on the television news.

17

When the policewoman came to Ben's house, six hours later, it was after four o'clock in the morning and yet he was still awake, sitting at the kitchen table reading an article Alice had written for that evening's edition of the *Standard*.

She had been asleep since midnight or thereabouts, tired out by work and conversation. For a while Ben had lain beside her, trying to let the day slip past him, but his mind kept turning over the events at the Savoy and after an hour he had given up, dressed again, and come downstairs.

His insomnia was not infrequent. Ben and Alice kept different hours and he had begun to feel separated from her when they were in bed together. When the lights went out, all the cuddled intimacy of their first years had been somehow lost; to careers, to age, to some misplaced idea of how a marriage should be. And yet he liked the anonymity afforded by night; so much of his life was given over to the idea of making Alice happy that Ben was glad to have just a few hours to himself. Often, he would read a book or watch a film on television, sometimes go for a drive or seek out a late-night bar.

It balanced things out: those quiet hours when Alice was asleep belonged to him and to him alone. Ben had no office to go to in the morning, no responsibility to anyone but himself: he could wake up with a hangover at eleven in the morning and still put in a good day's work in the studio.

He was nearing the end of the article when the doorbell rang, the sound of it shaking him out of an almost hypnotic concentration. Ben stood up and the newspaper fell to the floor. He assumed that it was one of his friends leaving drunk from a club, coked up to the eyeballs and coming round for a nightcap. As long as they didn't ring the bell again, there was a chance that Alice would not wake up.

"Who is it?" he asked as he reached the door, keeping his voice deliberately low. It occurred to him that somebody might have simply pressed the bell as a prank and then run away.

"The police, sir." It was a woman's voice, measured and serious. "Could I come in?"

Ben's first thought was that something had happened to Mark. A car accident in Moscow. A mugging. And, as he quickly unhooked the chain, he saw that the face of the woman on the other side of the door had prepared itself for delivering bad news. Her hair was tied up under a flat hat and her eyes seemed robbed of color.

She said, "I'm sorry to come round so late, sir."

"Is everything all right?"

Please. Not Mark. Just tell me that Mark's OK.

"I have to ask, sir. Does a Mr. Benjamin Keen live here?"

"I'm Benjamin Keen," Ben said quickly. "Is it Mark? Has something happened to my brother?"

"No. It's not your brother, sir. We couldn't find him."

He felt a wave of relief that was short lived. *Couldn't find him?* So was it a friend, somebody close to the family who had been hurt, even killed? Ben ran through a checklist of names: Alice's parents; Joe or Natalie; his oldest friend, Alex, who was on holiday in Spain. At no point did it occur to him that something might have happened to his father.

The policewoman asked again if she could come in and they went inside to the kitchen. She was wearing a fluorescent waterproof jacket that rustled as she sat down. Away from the flared light of the doorstep her face looked darker, prettier, but no less disconcerted. Ben saw that she was younger than he was by at least four years and that whatever it was she had been asked to tell him, she had never had to do it before.

"You said that you couldn't find Mark."

"That's right." Her voice was very quiet and she could barely look at him.

Ben began to ask another question, as if that would hold off the bad news, but she interrupted him.

"There's no easy way for me to tell you this, so I'm just going to come out and say it . . ."

"Yes . . ."

"I'm afraid it's some news about your father, Benjamin." When she used his first name he felt that he was going to be sick. "He's been involved in an incident. He was found dead at his flat two hours ago."

The news was simply a freak, a sick joke. Ben took several seconds to clear his head of what seemed like a wall of noise.

"My father? But I had dinner with him tonight."

For a moment the policewoman did not respond, but in time she said simply, "I am so sorry."

Six months before, three weeks even, she could have walked in here and given him this news and his reaction would have been quite different. Not dismissive exactly, not unfeeling, but certainly less traumatized. Anything she might have told Ben would have been prior to his new experience: the reunion, the first failed steps toward reconciliation. But he was now locked into a new set of feelings toward his father, forever altered by the events of just a few hours before.

"Are you sure about this?" he said, and felt foolish for asking. "I just don't understand. I had dinner with him tonight for the first time in twenty-five years. At the Savoy. *Tonight.*"

"You hadn't seen your father for that long?"

"For the first time, yes. This is just ridiculous . . ."

"I can understand how difficult it must be for you . . ."

"You said you couldn't find Mark? I spoke to him after dinner on the phone. He's in Moscow. What happened? You said there was an 'incident.' What does that mean?"

They were the first questions that had come into his mind, panicked sentences emerging from an absolute confusion. Ben had a sense that he had been robbed at a critical moment. When his mother was dying, in his early twenties, his whole life had seemed scarred by absurd bad luck; that feeling was suddenly apparent all over again.

"We're not very sure at this juncture, Benjamin." She kept using his first name. Was that what they were trained to do? "There appears to have been an intruder at your father's flat."

"He was killed?"

The policewoman brought the sleeve of the waterproof jacket

close to her face. That sound again. The whistle of the material. Then she was nodding slowly, eyes shuttling from one corner of the room to the other.

"I have to tell you that he was shot."

Ben appeared to freeze. The policewoman could think of nothing to say. He merely repeated the word "Shot?" as his mouth slackened with dismay.

"What I can do is arrange to come and pick you up in the morning and we can . . ."

But Ben was not hearing her. He had some basic sense of how hard it must have been to come to his house, to break news of this kind, a thing she would have to live with for the rest of her career. But he was now completely alone with his brother, orphaned, and that sudden realization consumed him.

". . . One of the things we do is to appoint a Family Liaison Officer who can provide a designated point of contact with—"

Ben raised his hand. He was shaking his head. He looked across the table. The policewoman's lips were pushed out and creased and she was speaking as if from a handbook. Yet her sympathetic expression was more than mere professional courtesy: she seemed genuinely upset.

"Would you like someone to stay with you?" she asked.

"I have my wife upstairs," Ben said, and for the first time felt that he was on the verge of tears. "I see."

She hesitated. There was something else she was obliged to add.

"Yes?" he said.

"I'm afraid we will need somebody to identify the body. As soon as possible. In your brother's absence, Benjamin, it's my understanding that you would be the next of kin. Do you think . . . ?"

"Of course," he said. "Do you want me to come now?" Again she paused. Edging round his confusion.

"It would probably be better if you stayed away from the scene for the time being . . ."

"I don't even know where he lives." She looked astonished by this.

"Mark knows. I hadn't met my father until . . ."

"Yes." The policewoman's voice was quiet. She told him that he had lived near Paddington Station and wrote down the address.

"So why don't you try to get some sleep?" she suggested. "Or perhaps let your wife know."

"Yes."

She began to stand up. He could sense her relief at leaving.

"I think it's best that I go," she said. "Will you be all right?"

And Ben nodded.

"We can send a car for both of you in the morning."

"That sounds fine." His mind was adrift with consequence. He was thinking about breaking the news to Mark, to Alice, and heard the policewoman say, "Sorry" as she walked down the steps. When she was no longer visible on the road he closed the front door and then climbed the stairs.

Their bedroom was stuffy, a smell of stale air and cigarette smoke woven into fabrics. He picked up the hot, sweet drift of Alice asleep, a curious blend of perfumes and sweat. Ben crossed the room and opened a window onto the street. Birdsong. Behind him, he heard Alice moan, an impatient sound. She turned over onto her side, exhaling heavily, and he felt reprimanded even from the depths of her sleep. He had been on the point of shaking her awake, but something about her impatience made him hesitate. Why do it? Instinctively, he did not want Alice to have any part in this. If he woke her, she would complain; as he told her, she would become confused. To involve her now would only complicate matters. He would have to take her feelings into account and, for once, he wanted to act without interference. Ben felt that she might even appropriate the grief for herself, that his father's murder might become something that he would have to comfort *her* over, rather than the other way round. She had a habit of doing that, of switching things, of giving them a cynical emphasis. It was a part of her selfishness.

The room was much cooler now, fresh air from the open window. Ben went back out onto the landing, closed the door, and felt for the car key in his pocket.

18

He should not have driven.

At the Savoy, Ben had drunk the better part of a bottle of wine and a double vodka and tonic. Back home, he had finished off a can of lager and then poured himself a whisky when he couldn't get to sleep. There had been wine with Alice at eleven and that shot of vodka at eight. As he turned the key in the ignition, he wondered if the police would let him off if they stopped him on the way to Paddington.

The journey touched on the absurd: four times he took wrong turnings, four times he had to pull over and consult an *A to Z*. Slush fizzed under the tires of his car. Ben became lost in one-way systems, pulled down side streets that led him farther and farther from the flat. With the heating on and the chill air outside, the interior of the car quickly fogged up and he was constantly having to wipe the windscreen with the sleeve of his coat. At times he had to crouch close to the wheel and try to peer through the steamed-up glass; then his eyes would be dazzled by lights catching on the slick surface of the road and he feared losing control altogether. As his mind became numbed by the thick, drumming heat in the car, only the sure conviction that he wanted to witness the crime scene for himself, to get as close to his father as he could, drove Ben on.

He parked just after five thirty and had to walk two blocks toward the building where Keen had lived. An entire stretch of street had been cordoned off by the police with lengths of blue-and-white tape slung across the road. Three men wearing boiler suits and heavy overshoes were coming out of the entrance to the apartment building. Ben thought he heard one of them laugh. A single light flashed blue in the road, strobing against London brick.

It was as if he were being controlled by forces outside of himself, a bank of instincts making decisions on his behalf. Ben ducked under the police tape and made his way toward a uniformed officer standing near the entrance. The presence of a stranger had unsettled them: Ben could hear the fractious static of voices breaking up on a radio concealed somewhere on the policeman's uniform.

"I'm sorry, sir, you can't go into the building."

He put a hand on Ben's shoulder. It felt heavy, capable. The two men looked at one another.

"I'm Benjamin Keen," Ben said. "I was his son."

The policeman withdrew his arm like a static shock and took a step back toward the door.

"The son," he replied, as if in the presence of something cursed. "I understood that one of my colleagues visited you at your house this evening."

"That's right."

"We didn't anticipate that you would come here."

The policeman—Ben saw that his name was Marchant—stared across the street as if in need of assistance. Without looking directly at Ben he added, "Can I just say, sir, on behalf of all of us, how very sorry I am . . ."

"That's kind. Thank you. Look . . ." Ben's voice was impatient as he asked: "Is there any way that I could just go up? I need to see my father. I need to find out what happened."

"I'm sorry, but we can't allow ordinary members of the public . . ." Marchant checked himself. ". . . even close relatives such as yourself, access to the scene until the forensic examination has been completed. I'm sure you understand."

A woman wearing a white boiler suit, holding a flash-mounted Nikon camera and a black Hi-8 video, came out of the building and walked across the street. Immediately behind her Ben noticed a man with a moustache dressed in civilian clothing, his dark hair cut short and neat to the scalp.

Stephen Taploe looked to his left and found himself staring directly into the eyes of Benjamin Keen. Already drained by shock, by the shame of losing a joe, he flinched and turned away.

"That guy," Ben said. "He's not part of the forensics. He's wearing ordinary plain clothes. How come he's allowed in?"

"That's one of our investigating officers," the policeman lied. He had first set eyes on Taploe just thirty minutes before, nodding him through under orders. Uppity, dismissive, shrewd. Your classic grass skirt.

"Why all the police?" Ben was asking. "How come there are so many people?"

It was a question to which Marchant himself would have liked an answer. When the call had gone out about Christopher Keen, it seemed as if half of London had climbed out of bed.

"Why don't I take you over to our vehicle?" he suggested, trying to deflect Ben's question. "We can sit down there and I can introduce you to some of my colleagues."

Ben nodded, as if gradually acknowledging the hopelessness of his situation. He spent the next thirty minutes inside a white police Transit van, sipping heavily sugared tea from a polystyrene cup. An older officer, rank of DCI, explained how a neighbor coming back from a party had noticed that his father's door had been left ajar. He had discovered the body and immediately telephoned the police. No, they had no idea of a suspect: they were still at a very early stage in their inquiries. Yes, they would keep him apprised of any developments. Ben would be asked to identify the body in a few hours' time and given the chance to answer any questions that might help to piece together his father's last movements.

"And may I add my sincere condolences, Benjamin," the DCI said. "This must be a very difficult time for you. Why don't I have one of my colleagues take you home so you can have a shower or something before we take you up to the station?"

Almost as if somebody had been listening from outside, the back of the van opened up and Ben was introduced to a black policewoman whose thick leather gloves felt damp as he shook her hand.

"Will you escort Mr. Keen back to his house, Kathy?"

"Of course, sir."

"We'll arrange for a car to come and pick you up at around ten."

"Fine," Ben said, now exhausted to the point of collapse. He wondered when he would ever sleep again. "Thanks for the tea," he said, and stepped down onto the road.

The street was a trench of stunned activity. Ben experienced a strange kind of amazement that a new day was beginning, the City oblivious to his loss. Residents were emerging from nearby buildings, asking questions of uniformed officials, walking backward as they stared up at the windows of the fourth floor, like boxers on the ropes. Marchant was still standing on the door, taking the names of everybody who entered or came out of the building.

Standing fifty meters away, beside a battered telephone box, Taploe watched Ben emerge from the van looking lost and broken. The policewoman ushered him down the street, under the taped cordon, and, finally, to a car parked two blocks away that was just a shadow in the distance. Minutes later, Keen's body was brought downstairs on a stretcher and placed in the back of an ambulance, which drove slowly away in the direction of Edgware Road. Taploe watched this, listening to the appalled murmurings of the crowd, and wondered if he was witnessing the final act in his long and as yet undistinguished career.

Nevertheless, he sensed the remote possibility of second chance. *Clear the trail*, he told himself. *Distance yourself from the victim.* From his coat pocket, Taploe extracted the Post-it note he had removed from the doorframe. Tearing it into six separate pieces, he dropped the shreds into a storm drain and went in search of a cab.

19

When they had buried Carolyn, seven years before, Ben and Mark had floated through the funeral in a trance of grief. Mourners had drifted in and out of focus, approaching them tentatively, offering their whispered condolences. Now and again one of his mother's friends would take Ben to one side, her eyes swelled and puffy with tears, and attempt to make sense of what had happened. These conversations were all eerily similar: the friend would do most of the talking, invariably relating an anecdote that conveyed Carolyn in a good light, touching on her bravery throughout the long illness, her sense of humor, or the loyalty she showed to close friends. Ben was not cynical about this; he realized that it was a necessary and inevitable part of what the second-rate shrink he had briefly visited described as "the grieving process." But on each occasion he had the distinct impression that he was being taken aside not to be consoled but rather, by his sheer presence, to offer consolation to his mother's friends. The entire afternoon was like a dumb show of the English stiff upper lip: Ben said and did all the right things, kept his emotions in check for the good of the crowd, and felt a strong determination not to let anyone down.

A few days after the service he had had dinner with a friend whose mother had also died of cancer. They agreed that funerals benefited only the deceased's acquaintances and distant relatives, providing them with an opportunity to make a public display of grief and respect before returning home, where the sadness, in most cases, would quickly dissipate. For closer relatives—husbands, wives, sons, daughters—the sense of loss took far longer to kick in. Ben and Mark, who had watched in hospital as the life literally drained out of their mother, had mentally prepared themselves for a funeral. The hard part was to follow, pain like a slow puncture lasting months, years.

Yet their father's funeral was quite different. At the service to commemorate the life of Christopher Keen, Ben felt like a stranger.

More than seventy people came to the crematorium outside Guildford, not one of whom he recognized. Ben met his uncle—Keen's younger brother—for the first time since he had been a pageboy at his wedding in 1974. There were work colleagues from Divisar, old Foreign Office hands, distant cousins with second wives huddled in impenetrable groups. A man in his early sixties wearing spit-polished brogues and a Life Guards tie introduced himself to Ben as Mark's godfather, an "old university chum" of Keen's.

"I haven't been all that good at keeping up," he explained, as if the broad, gutless smile that accompanied the remark would in some way make up for this. "Rather abnegated my godfatherly responsibilities, I'm afraid."

The service had been arranged jointly by Jock McCreery, his father's oldest friend from his days in MI6, and Mark, who had flown back from Moscow immediately. Ben had had no input: he had been too busy dealing with the police. This had left him with little opportunity to talk to his brother, and the two hours that it took them to drive against the morning rush hour to Guildford was the longest period of time they had spent together since Keen's murder.

Alice sat in the back seat, fielding calls from the features desk on her mobile phone. To every member of staff she said the same thing—"I have to go to a funeral. Don't worry. I'm meeting him this evening. I'll ring you as soon as I get back"—until Mark's patience finally snapped and he told her to switch it off. For days they had existed in an atmosphere of stunned upheaval. In the hours leading up to Carolyn's burial an odd kind of order had asserted itself, an innate knowledge of how to proceed. But this was quite different: there was no template for their situation.

The crematorium car park was already full, with only two or three spaces remaining by the time Mark pulled in. An elderly man and woman, dressed in what looked like their Sunday best, were eating sandwiches from the open boot of a Vauxhall Astra, blue plastic mugs of tea resting on the bumper. Ben held Alice's hand as they walked slowly toward a low building with an emerald-green roof surrounded by carefully tended lawns. McCreery, his black tie whipped up over his shoulder by a strong winter wind, strode out to meet them at a military clip.

"Mark," he said, pumping his hand. He had an instantly forgettable face. "And you must be Benjamin. I'm so sorry about what's happened. And Alice. How good to see you. They say it'll just be a few minutes."

There were two small waiting rooms on either side of the entrance to the main chapel building. Both were crammed with people, separate groups of mourners attending different services. Keen's relatives and friends had gathered in the left-hand area in a room no bigger than a badminton court. Facing them, down a narrow corridor, a cluster of men and women, many of whom were weeping, were being spoken to in hushed tones by an undertaker with a practiced face of condolence.

It was winter, but the waiting area was very hot. A service was being held in the chapel and the quiet melody of "Abide with Me" fed into the narrow corridor, barely accompanied by singing. Two of Ben's friends—Joe and Natalie—had offered to come with him as a gesture of support, and he regretted now that he had told them not to bother. Just to have someone to talk to, a familiar face other than Mark or Alice, would have consoled him slightly, given him someone to rely on.

"May I introduce Christopher's sons, Benjamin and Mark?" McCreery was saying. His demeanor managed to combine an almost stately dignity with a concealed sense that he had more pressing matters at hand. "And Benjamin's wife, Alice."

McCreery had led them toward a group of five men, all of whom were in late middle age and seemed, by their relaxed and close proximity, to have known one another for some time. Ben assumed they were Foreign Office, probably SIS, and felt an immediate antipathy toward all of them. As the handshakes flowed he noticed the tallest of the five men staring too long at Alice, his eyes drifting steadily toward her breasts, and almost lashed out in frustration. He had experienced this so many times before, just walking beside her on the street or at parties for the *Standard*, men with tired marriages and Alice that friend of their daughter's they'd always wanted to fuck. But at a *funeral*? Doesn't it stop even *then*? Instead, he deliberately caught the man's eye and stared him down.

Beside him someone with a beard was saying, "I knew your father for many years. Liked him a lot. I'm so sorry for what's happened."

"Thank you," Mark told him.

Someone else asked, "Have there been any developments with the police?" as if he were inquiring after the time.

"Not really," Mark said. "There was nothing stolen from the flat, so they're assuming it was premeditated. None of the neighbors have been able to come up with anything. Ben knows more about it than I do. He's been under a lot of pressure."

Five pairs of eyes settled on Mark's disheveled, self-evidently artistic younger brother as if to weigh up the veracity of this observation. The man standing nearest him said, "I'm sure," a remark that sounded unconvincing. Ben felt an obligation to say something, but was sapped of will. Then the tall man who had eyeballed Alice moved fractionally forward, smoothed down his hair, and said, "Have you found the police helpful?" His voice was candid and precise. "We were all of us in the Foreign Office, you know. I'd be only too glad to put you in touch with various people who might be able to give you a clearer picture of what steps are being taken to—"

"No," Ben told him, staring at the ground. He wanted to pull away the mask of their feigned concern. "The police have been fine. They're just doing their job. We have a Family Liaison Officer assigned to the case . . ." He nearly lost his train of thought. ". . . and she acts as our contact with the police. That's all working out as well as we could have hoped."

Then, to his relief, the doors of the chapel opened and around a dozen mourners emerged into the corridor, some dabbing their eyes with handkerchiefs, others supporting them as they walked outside into the dull light of late morning. Undertakers moved silently between the rooms, holding doors and nodding humbly as torpid organ music held in the air.

"I think we're next," Mark said, and Ben squeezed the slight bones of Alice's hand. He had a feeling in his stomach like a stone resting on his soul.

"Yes," said one of the men, touching the knot of his tie. "The service was scheduled to begin fifteen minutes ago."

You got something else you'd rather be doing? Ben was on the point of erupting, but checked his temper and glanced at Mark. His brother looked suddenly buckled by grief, his back slumped like an old man. McCreery appeared beside him.

"You all right, fella?" he asked, a consoling arm on Mark's shoulder.

"Oh, sure," Mark told him, straightening up. He could put on a good show when he needed to. "Sorry, Jock," he said. "I just wandered off there for a second."

"No problem," McCreery said. "No problem," and they moved toward the chapel.

Two undertakers were handing out service sheets on the door, their heads deferentially bowed. Ahead of them, to one side of the altar and resting on a raised platform at the mouth of what Ben took to be an incinerator, lay Keen's coffin. Mark had picked it out, without asking for Ben's approval, but he saw that he had made a good choice. Simple pale wood with a single bouquet of flowers resting on the lid. Yet the sight of it appalled him, bringing home all the finality of the act. His father's contradictions, all the pain that he had caused, an unknown life just lying sealed up in a box.

"You OK?" Alice whispered, and he was grateful for her, for the simple beauty of her face and the comfort that it gave.

"Sure," he replied. "We should just keep an eye on brother."

They took their seats in the front row. Everything was moving smoothly. Ben heard the door closing quietly behind them, sealing in the chapel's disinfectant smell. He leaned forward at the pew and pretended to pray.

20

Jock McCreery's house was situated fifteen miles south of the crematorium along a narrow country lane. A faint drizzle had begun falling by the time Ben and Alice arrived. The gravel drive leading up to the house was already packed with cars, some banked up onto the edges of a damp lawn churned with mud and leaves, others parked in a small courtyard at the back of the property. Mark had offered to go in a separate car with three of Keen's colleagues from Divisar, in order to show them the way.

Sandwiches cut into white, crustless triangles had been laid out on a table in the sitting room alongside bottles of wine, malt whisky, and mineral water. McCreery's wife, Gillian, a rotund woman in her late fifties wearing a baggy skirt and a necklace of fat artificial pearls, made a point of introducing Ben, Mark, and Alice to a constant stream of guests whose names they instantly forgot. The atmosphere in the house was one of nervous civility: guests were crammed into every room, even gathering on the stairs, but their conversations seemed muffled out of respect for Keen. Smoking was forbidden inside the house ("We just find that the smell gets into everything," Gillian explained, "the curtains, one's clothes, you understand.") and Ben longed for a cigarette. He was relieved to be free of the oppressive mood of the crematorium and had become quickly drunk on cheap red wine, but his attempts to go outside were blocked at every turn by guests approaching to offer their sympathy.

Sebastian Roth arrived just before two o'clock. Alice noticed him first, like the scent of a good story, holding himself at the edge of the room in a manner characteristic of someone who was used to being noticed. She felt, from a distance, that Roth was interesting to look at rather than handsome, exuding a sense of power worn comfortably. Only his carefully tended hair, thick and lustrous, betrayed a probable vanity. Ben was standing beside her, watching McCreery's black Labrador flick its wet tail against a Colefax & Fowler sofa as he drank wine from a plastic cup.

"Look who's here," she whispered, touching his arm. Alice had waited more than three years for a chance to meet Roth; that the opportunity should arise at her father-in-law's funeral was merely an inconvenience.

Ben raised his eyebrows, glancing in Roth's direction. "The boss," he murmured.

"He doesn't look like someone who runs a nightclub."

"What were you expecting?"

"I don't know. More glamour. Not such a nice suit. He's so . . ." She reached for the word. "Groomed."

"Roth's a businessman, just another free marketer."

Ben put his cup down as the Labrador wandered out into the kitchen. "Ask him about the retail price index and he'll talk to you for five hours. Try to find out whether he prefers trip-hop to speed garage and he'll defer to his agent. Nightclubs, pharmaceuticals, junk bonds, makes no difference to guys like that. Libra is just another way of making money."

Roth had made his way across the room to where Mark was standing, talking to the genial, chalk-haired American who had read from Keats at the service in Guildford. Handshakes. Mutual smiles. Alice noticed a slight air of deference come over Ben's brother, his body language becoming more animated, a widening of the eyes.

"You've never met him, have you?"

Ben said, "Who? Roth?"

"Roth."

"Never. Only seen him on TV. BBC film about the club when it was expanding into the States. Otherwise, just gossip columns, titbits in the papers."

"I saw him at a book launch once." Alice was speaking very quietly. "I think he's the kind of guy who likes to be seen with beautiful women. You know the type. Fake tits, lots of Versace, and no conversation."

Ben smiled as a secretary from Divisar, her eyes bruised from crying, introduced herself, said how sorry she was, and walked back toward the hall. Moments later Mark was ushering Roth across the room toward them. Ben had been on the point of going outside for a cigarette and was frustrated once again to have to endure the wake's miserable platitudes.

"Sebastian Roth. I just wanted to pay my respects." Up close, Roth's skin was smooth and implausibly tanned. He was shorter than most of the men in the room and had not yet looked at Alice. "Your father was somebody we'd been working very closely with. His experience was invaluable to us in Russia. It goes without saying that we'll all miss him a great deal."

"Thank you."

It was a conversation Ben had been having all day. What to say next? How to follow it up?

"Did Mack not come with you?" Mark asked, rescuing him.

"My lawyer, Thomas Macklin," Roth explained. He was still ignoring Alice, perhaps deliberately, training his eyes solely on Ben. McCreery appeared beside them and pulled Mark away into a separate conversation. "He's in Moscow at the moment. You've met, haven't you?"

Ben nodded.

"Mack also worked alongside your father, as you know. He wanted to be here, but it just wasn't possible. Asked me to pass on his condolences. And I'm sorry that I wasn't able to make it to the funeral in person. I've also been away for the past few days."

"It's really OK."

There was a prolonged silence. Alice eventually edged forward and Ben took the hint.

"Oh, sorry." It was as if he had been locked off in a meditation. "Sebastian, this is my wife, Alice. Alice, this is Mark's boss, Sebastian."

What followed was a textbook first encounter of instant chemistry, a series of split-second subconscious acts. Alice touched her necklace, her skirt, reached out to shake Roth's hand, and then ducked her eyes to the floor. Roth, attempting to hold her gaze, absorbed Alice's physical beauty in an instant, registering it as a challenge. The least significant part of their exchange were the words they used to greet one another. Roth said, "It's a pleasure to meet you," and Alice replied, "You too."

For the next few minutes, she allowed Roth to talk. *Mark told me it was a wonderful service. Very sad, very moving.* His voice was like a well-oiled machine, dipped in self-love. On reputation, Alice wanted him to find her attractive, and she waited for the secret glance, the shared indiscretion.

"You must be exhausted," he said to Ben, who paused before replying with a candor that surprised both of them.

"Actually I found the service pretty unaffecting," he said. "It's been very difficult to get a clear perspective on things in the last few days. Jock spoke for about ten minutes, did the eulogy thing, but it was frustrating and incomplete, like he was holding back information about my father's life just to protect state secrecy."

Roth coughed nervously and said, "I see."

"And then the local priest stands up and tries to say a few words, but it's just embarrassing. My father wasn't a spiritual man, a Christian. The vicar had probably only met him a handful of times. He was just someone whose hand he might have shaken on Christmas Day."

Alice put her arm around Ben and said, "You OK?" but he was already pulling away. Something about Roth's overdeveloped charm had annoyed him and he wanted to be outside.

"Listen, Mr. Roth . . ."

"Sebastian, please," he said instantly.

"I was just on my way outside to have a cigarette. Do you mind if I leave you two alone? It's been difficult to get away."

"Of course not."

"It was really a pleasure to meet you. I'll only be gone five minutes."

If Roth was surprised by Ben's attitude, Alice was more sanguine.

"Sorry," she said, as Ben walked off into the kitchen. "He's been like that since it happened. Off in his own world."

"I'm not surprised. This must be a very difficult time for him."

"Very."

"I've never lost a parent. You?"

"No," Alice said.

"The most awful feeling of emptiness, I should imagine. A complete void. Ben must be devastated."

"I think they both are." For the third time that day, Alice found herself saying, "In a sense it's worse for Mark because he'd built up a relationship with his father and now all that's been taken away from him."

"Yes. And just as they were getting started." Roth was making what felt like a very concentrated effort to look Alice in the eye, as if someone had once told him that there was an advantage to be gained in making a woman feel like the only person in a room. "But I imagine Ben is in this awful limbo. He has no specific memories to draw on, just one all too brief encounter over dinner. It's horrific. I wish there was more one could do."

Alice needlessly straightened the collar of her shirt, but did not reply.

"And what about you?" he asked her. "I imagine it's very hard being in your position. Not knowing what to do. Not knowing what to say to Ben. I often think these things are just as painful for the partner of someone who's grieving."

This was her first proper glimpse of Roth's reputation, of the cad's talent for empathy. Alice could see how it might work; his manner was not overtly flirtatious, but thoughtfulness and self-confidence were always attractive in a man.

"Well, we haven't really had much of a chance to talk," she told him. "Ben's been so involved with the police, you know?

They've interviewed him, gone through every last detail of what happened . . ."

"And they're no closer to a suspect?"

"No closer. A couple in the street remembered seeing a man sitting in a Mercedes about half an hour before the shooting, but they didn't get a number plate. There weren't any security cameras outside the apartment or in the foyer. The police have hairs for DNA, but they could be anyone's. It's a lottery."

"Yes. Locard's Principle."

"Locard's Principle?"

Roth looked pleased to have sparked her interest. "A technique of forensics," he explained. "Everything leaves a trace."

Calmly, he reached out and took hold of the sleeve of Alice's shirt. She let her arm fall loose, but did not dislike the presumption of being touched. "If I come into contact with your clothes—even for a fraction of a second—I leave a mark, a record of myself." Roth released her, briefly taking the weight of her arm as it dropped. "It's the same with footprints, or tiny fragments of skin."

Alice took a quarter-step backward. "That's fascinating."

"And have Divisar been able to help?" he continued, as if nothing had passed between them. "Do the police think it may be connected to his job?"

"I really don't know. Ben's dad was in MI6 before working there. They're looking into that."

"I see."

Roth appeared to be on the point of asking a further question when his expression stiffened considerably. A guest had caught his eye, someone he had clearly not been expecting to see. For the first time his focus on Alice appeared to waver, like an actor forgetting a line. To trace the source of this sudden change, Alice turned round. A slim, blond woman—thirty-five going on forty—was approaching from the door, a knowing smile set across her face. She walked with a striding, authoritative self-confidence and Alice scoped her, head to toe: expensive if conservative hair; a decent black suit; striking, intelligent eyes; a handbag three seasons out of date.

"Isn't it extraordinary who you bump into at these things?" the woman said. Alice disliked her on sight.

"Elizabeth," Roth said, still noticeably unsettled. "It's wonderful to see you. I thought you were in Moscow."

"Not so, not so," she said, and gazed distractedly around the room. She looked at Alice with a short glance that somehow managed to mix civility with a clear and unambiguous contempt.

"Elizabeth Dulong," she said, proferring an iron handshake. She was wearing Chanel No. 19 and her accent bore the faintest trace of a Scottish burr. "I'm an old friend of Sebastian's. And you are . . . ?"

"Alice," Alice replied. "Alice Keen . . ."

"Christopher's daughter-in-law," Roth explained, tilting his head for emphasis.

"Oh. Is that so?"

Dulong gave Alice a brief second look but maintained a chill composure.

"When did you arrive?" Roth asked her, pushing a hand through his hair. All the easy assertiveness of his manner had disappeared. There was a clear connection between them, yet Alice assumed it was not sexual. Dulong was neither glamorous nor young enough to be Roth's type, and she was wearing an engagement ring on her left hand.

"Just arrived," she replied. She was exactly the sort of career woman—chippy, contemptuous of prettier girls—with whom Alice routinely fell out at the *Standard*. "I came down from London with Giles."

"Giles."

It was like a conversation in a bus queue. For several minutes they made stilted small talk until McCreery interrupted to ask where he could find Ben. In that time Alice was able to discover only that Elizabeth Dulong worked for an obscure section of the Ministry of Defence, and that she had met Roth at a cocktail party in Moscow hosted by the Russian Minister of Transport. Drinking sparkling mineral water, Dulong told a dull, clearly thirdhand story about Boris Yeltsin before bombarding Alice with curt questions about the *Standard*, all of which conveyed her obvious contempt for journalists of every persuasion.

"I'll go and get him for you," she told McCreery, pleased to have an excuse to leave, and with a deliberately seductive glance at Roth, Alice slipped outside.

Ben was wearing a pair of polished, hundred-pound brogues that he had owned for a decade but barely worn. Shoes for weddings, funeral shoes. McCreery's garden was soaked with rain, the lawn a catastrophe of molehills and weeds, and to avoid ruining them Ben had been forced to smoke his cigarette while walking up and down the drive. He began to feel self-conscious as cars left the wake and headed down the road. There he was, right in front of them, the bereaved younger son smoking alone in the gloom. When they saw Ben, one or two guests braked to a crawl and waved tentative good-byes, but the majority were too embarrassed to stop, and accelerated toward Guildford evidently hoping that he hadn't seen them. He wished that he had gone out of the back of the house, where there might have been a shed or shelter of some kind. Just to be alone for five minutes, away from the prying eyes of strangers.

He was taking a final drag on his second cigarette when a Mercedes pulled up beside him on the road. Through a misted window he recognized the American who had read from Keats at the funeral. His name had been printed on the service sheet. Something literal, he remembered. Something like Kite or Judge.

"It's Benjamin, isn't it?" the American said. He had switched off his engine. "My name is Robert Bone. We haven't met. This is my wife, Silvia."

Ben ducked down and saw a pale-looking woman wearing a headscarf poring over a map in the passenger seat. *Post-chemotherapy*, he thought; she had the same exhausted features that had characterized his mother's face in the final months of her life. Unlike Bone, she was not stepping out of the car.

The American was six foot four with a handshake as firm and sympathetic as any Ben had known all week. Compassionate, judicious eyes glowed beneath a disheveled mop of white hair. It was a face Ben would have liked to paint: wearied by experience yet possessed of a certain benevolence. For the first time, against his expectations, he instinctively felt that he had come into contact with somebody who had been deeply affected by his father's death, a friend for whom the loss of Keen would mean more than simply a twenty-minute funeral service and a glass of lukewarm wine. At first he put this feeling down to sheer melancholia.

"You read at the service," he said. "*Endymion*, wasn't it?"

"That's right. A beautiful piece. One of your dad's favorites. But I guess you wouldn't know that?" Bone settled a hand on Ben's shoulder. "It's too bad, son. Really, it's just too bad."

A bird flew low over their heads and Ben followed it across the sky.

"How did you know my father?" he asked.

The American paused momentarily and seemed quickly to sweep aside considerations of tact or secrecy. "I used to work for the Central Intelligence Agency," he said. "Your father and I did time together in Afghanistan. I'm just sorry I didn't catch up with you back there." He nodded toward McCreery's house, the light winter drizzle now obliterating all color in the garden. "I spoke to your brother quite a bit, and to your wife, Alice, about her journalism career and so forth. She seems a fine, ambitious person. She's obviously gonna be very successful. But every time I looked over toward you, you seemed busy talking to somebody else."

"Yeah, it was hard getting away."

"No problem. Listen, I got a plane to catch back to the States. My wife hasn't been well and . . ."

"I'm sorry to hear that . . ."

"But I'm gonna write you . . ."

Ben shook his head. "Please, there's no need."

"No, not that kind of letter." Bone's hand was still resting on his shoulder, as if by leaving it there he was fulfilling a promise to Keen. "There are things I need to tell you. Things your dad would have wanted you and Mark and Alice to know. He talked about you kids the whole time. I know that's gotta be hard for you to hear right now, but Christopher always had a hard time"—he paused—"*communicating.* He was a stubborn sonofabitch, a goddam snob, too. But your old man was my best friend, Benjamin, and I wanna make sure you boys are OK."

The American's plain-speaking, unironic good-naturedness appealed to Ben in his despondent mood. Bone was a good man wounded by a friend's violent death; he was trying to reach out, trying to do the right thing. The opposite, in fact, of all those refined, carefully worded Foreign Office snakes who took the world for idiots and betrayed everything but their own good name.

"Do you have any idea who could have done this?" Ben asked. He had trusted Bone immediately, fallen straight into his decency.

"Later, son," the American replied. "Later." And finally, he took his hand from Ben's shoulder. A car had pulled up behind them. "I better go, not block these people in. Mark gave me your address in London. I'll be sure to write you both just as soon as I get back home."

21

"I know what's needed, Keeno. We need to get you out, mate. A night on the tiles. Something to relax you."

Thomas Macklin was hunched forward at his desk, rubbing his hands vigorously together. His cheeks were puffy and flushed red, eyes like sockets of concentrated ambition. Roth's lawyer, his confidant and right-hand man, was wearing a dark, single-breasted moleskin suit, a blue silk shirt, and an off-gold cashmere tie. Enough money invested in designer clothes to make an unattractive man look passably stylish.

"I don't mean to sound insensitive, mate, but fuck it, where's the harm? It's good to see you back in the office. What's it been, three weeks? Everyone admires the way you've handled this thing. But I wanna see a smile back on Keeno's face. There's this new place we've been going, lap-dancers that can't get enough of you. Cocktails, music, stage acts, the lot. Couple of birds there you wouldn't believe. Tits like mangoes and Happy New Year. We can take one of the Russian crowd along, write it off on expenses. Mr.-Sebastian-Roth-does-not-have-to-know. If Seb wants to spend his nights hobnobbing in art galleries with New Labour while his mates are out having a good time, well, that's his prerogative. You and me are gonna have some *fun*."

Mark smiled. There was something touching about Macklin's fantastic insensitivity. The last time they had been to a lap-dancing club was in New York two years before, while overseeing the opening of the club's site in Manhattan. Five executives on the company credit card and Mark the only one not drunk and groping girls. One of the dancers, a Costa Rican, had kept giving him the eye; she had asked Mark more than once if he wanted her to dance for him and, even when he had said no, stayed beside him at the table, just talking. Meanwhile Macklin and his friends had stuffed fifty-dollar bills into her g-string and begged her to come back to their hotel. At the end of the night she had slipped Mark her number and they had got together a couple of times before he flew back to London.

"Sure," Mark said. "It's a nice idea."

"Fuckin' right it's a nice idea." Macklin stood up, backing away from his desk. He was heavily built and in the grip of a big idea. "Tell you what, we should get your brother along. How does young Benjamin feel about topless birds nibbling his earlobes?"

"Not really his cuppa tea," Mark replied. His accent had assumed the work Cockney.

"No," Macklin muttered quickly. Against the gray London sky visible through the closed window of his office, he looked colorful, even vibrant. "I suppose he wouldn't go in for that, would he? Can't imagine his wife being all that chuffed. Tends to make herself heard, doesn't she? What's her name again?"

"Alice," Mark said quietly.

"That's right. Lovely-looking girl. He's done well there, your bro. Real ballbreaker, though, isn't she? They always are, the fit ones."

Mark nodded awkwardly and looked down onto the street. A Bangkok cycle-taxi was passing below the window, ringing its bell. "Yeah, I suppose Alice can be a bit tricky," he conceded, talking into the glass so that it steamed up with his breath.

He might have added that he felt Ben had settled for the first girl that had fallen in love with him, out of an understandable desire for the stability of marriage. He might have said that he feared Alice would one day up and leave, lured by the connections and money of a less troubled man. He might have said that Ben had not spoken to him since the reading of the will, in which it had been revealed that Keen had left everything to Mark: the flat, the money, the car. But he was not a person given to discussing family issues at work. Instead he hummed a tune under his breath until Macklin said, "What was that?"

"Nothing."

"Right." Macklin stretched until a bone cracked in his arm. "Anyway, it was just an idea. I'll give Vladimir a call, see if he wants to join in."

"Who's Vladimir?"

Very quickly Macklin said, "One of the crew from Moscow. Vlad Tamarov. Big fucker. Rolex and leather. He's handling a few things for Seb on the legal side."

"He's a lawyer?"

"You could say that, yeah. More of a specialist in our line of work. Helping out with contracts, security, that kind of thing. He's come over for a few days, see how we operate."

"Is he mafia?"

Macklin made a loud snorting noise and dismissed the question with a shrug.

"Well, who is and who isn't out there, eh, Keeno? Half the time I don't even know myself."

"So how come you didn't mention it?"

"Well, you've been out of the loop, haven't you, mate? Had a shite few weeks. Didn't think it was necessary to fill you in." Macklin had slapped his hand onto Mark's back and was rubbing it in abrupt circles. "Now old Tom wants to help you out, see? Wants to put a smile back on his mate's face. So are you on for this thing or you after doing something else?"

"It all sounds fine." Mark picked up a copy of *GQ* from a low, glass-surfaced table at the edge of the room. He began flicking backward through the pages, male models and sports cars, taking none of it in. "There's just something I have to do beforehand. Some stuff I have to collect from Dad's flat."

"Course you have," Macklin told him. "Course you gotta do stuff like that. So when will you want to leave?"

"Just tell me where it is and I'll meet you there." Mark put the magazine down. "I don't know how long I'm going to be."

Macklin wrote down the address. "I might bring Philippe along as well," he added, apparently as an afterthought.

"Club Philippe?"

"The very same. Night off from running his beloved ristorante. We're having a pint after work."

"Oh."

"So," Macklin said, "around ten suit you?"

"Around ten sounds fine."

It was the last thing he felt like doing. A night out with Macklin, d'Erlanger, and a Russian Mr. Fixit, characterized by Macklin's gradually deteriorating behavior, the four of them just another set of suits in early middle age ogling girls and stinking of booze and fags. Vladimir probably wouldn't speak much English, so the evening would consist of shouted, stop-start conversations about "Manchester United" and "Mr. Winston Churchill." Slowly, Macklin would lose what few moral scruples he possessed and demonstrate the full range of his aggressive sexism, culminating in their inevitable ejection from the club at two or three in the morning. Then one of them—Macklin, most probably—would pass out on the street before Mark had a chance to put him in a cab. Why had he agreed to go? So that Tom wouldn't think he was *boring*? It was something to do with the aftermath of his father's death; Mark just didn't have time for this kind of thing anymore.

He took a taxi to the Paddington flat. The heating was on high in the back of the cab and when Mark stepped out to pay the driver a January wind caught him like a blast of ice in the face. He took out a set of keys—the ones his father had used—and opened the door to the lobby.

Gray, bleak light was leaking in from the street. Ahead of him, Mark could barely make out the stairwell or the entrance to the lift. He pressed the white plastic timer switch on the wall beside the door, blinking as the foyer lights came on. It seemed odd, but he could sense his father's presence here, his routine of checking the mail, that stubborn habit he had of taking the stairs and not the lift. *Got to keep fit at my age*, he would say. *Got to look after the old lungs.* One time they had come back for a whisky after eating dinner in Islington and Keen had spent five minutes standing at the foot of the stairs talking to a widower named Max who lived on the first floor. Where was Max now? Maybe Mark should knock on his door and talk to him about what had happened, ask if he had heard or seen anything on the night of the murder. He would rather do that, rather be with someone who had known his father, than spend five hours with Macklin and an anonymous Russian lawyer in a lap-dancing club in the West End. But the police would have already talked to him. No doubt, like everybody else in the building, Max hadn't seen or heard a thing.

He rode the lift to the fourth floor. The police still weren't certain whether his father's killer had reached the flat that way, or via the stairs. There were so few clues, so little evidence around which to base even a theory.

A teenager wearing baggy denims and a black puffa jacket passed him in the corridor as he came out of the lift and made his way to Apartment 462. Mark was just a few meters away from the door when he saw that it was already open. There were lights on inside and he stopped in his tracks. A faint shadow fell slowly across the floor, and then the door abruptly closed. There were no voices, no clues as to the identity of the intruder. Kathy, the Family Liaison Officer, had told Mark that the police had long ago finished their investigation. He moved forward, inhaled deeply, and pressed his ear to the door.

Nothing. Not a sound. Whoever was inside was alone and remaining deliberately quiet. The wild thought occurred to him that the killer had returned to the scene of the crime. Again, Mark breathed deeply and slid his key into the lock, banking on an element of surprise. Then, with great speed and no thought to his own safety, he opened the door.

Ben was standing in the kitchen, looking out of the window.

"Brother. Jesus. What are you doing here?"

Ben turned round. He looked to be in a trance.

"Hi," he said very quietly, unfazed by the sudden intrusion. He looked back at the window. "You took most of his stuff."

"That's why I'm here," Mark said, breathing quickly. "To get the rest of it. How did you get in?"

"Spare set of keys. Kathy gave them to me. You don't mind, do you?"

"Why would I mind? You can come here whenever you like."

"It's just that I wanted to see the place for myself."

"Sure."

Mark looked toward the sitting room. He had not expected to feel this, but his brother's presence was an intrusion, an unnecessary complication he could do without. To make matters worse, Ben was clearly adrift in self-pity, one of the least attractive elements of his personality. For three weeks Mark had wanted to shake him free of gloom, to move him on.

"So what's left to take?"

There was an almost combative tone to Ben's question.

"Clothes, mostly," Mark told him. "Some suits. A couple of pictures . . ."

"Yeah, I saw those."

"And there's a box of papers underneath his desk. Bank statements. Insurance records mostly. Dad didn't keep a diary or anything, so none of it's any good to the police. I was going to take them home."

"Fine."

There was a prolonged silence. Mark scuffed his shoes against the kitchen's linoleum and thought about moving next door. When Ben spoke, his voice was removed, almost hypnotic.

"They say that when your father dies, it's actually quite liberating. The intercessionary figure has been taken out of the picture. There's supposed to be this feeling of transcendence."

"So is that what you feel? Liberated by what's happened? Transcendent?"

I don't have time for this, Mark thought. *Not now. Not tonight.*

"It's funny," Ben went on, ignoring the question. "I remember when we were children, when Dad first left, I had these feelings of guilt about it that went on for so long . . . It was as if everything was my fault, you know? We used to talk about this, you and me, don't you remember?"

Mark nodded. Ben was still looking out of the window, waiting for the moment to turn. It might almost have been a performance, a stage picture. From the fourth floor there was nothing to see but swaths of gray sky and a clutter of roofs.

Ben carried on: "It got to be ridiculous. I started to think that if I'd behaved better, eaten what was put in front of me, not cried so much as a child, that Dad wouldn't have left like he did. But what kind of shit is that to be thinking? It was his fault, not mine. It took me a long time to realize that."

"Me too," Mark said instinctively. "I had a kind of fantasy of reunion right up until my late teens. Like he would just suddenly reappear and beg our forgiveness. Turn up at school and say everything was going to be all right and then take us out for lunch at Garfunkel's. Did you ever have that?"

Mark shook his head.

"Maybe it would have been easier if Mum had had a boyfriend, someone who could have replaced him. I always felt that her life was structured to avoid pain after that, you know? I think that's why she never remarried."

Mark made a gesture of understanding, something with his face that he hoped would seem empathetic. In his experience, this kind of talk went nowhere. It was just the theorizing of the artist, the amateur psychologist enjoying his private confession. He thought for a moment that Ben might have been drinking.

"You getting much work done?" he asked, trying to steer him off the subject. "How's the picture of that girl going, the good-looking one? What's the deal on the exhibition?"

But Ben just ignored him.

"It never occurred to me until the other day that Mum might still have been in love with Dad." He lit a cigarette and exhaled very slowly. "Do you think that's possible? Do you think, even after everything that happened, that a woman could still love a man after being treated that way? It's not beyond the realms of possibility . . ."

But this was a step too far. The question actually embarrassed Mark. He hid his discomfort by opening up a nearby cupboard and pretending to rearrange the rusty tins and damp packets inside. "No," he replied eventually, "it's not beyond the realms of possibility. Listen, I'm in a hurry. Was there something that you wanted?"

And this gave Ben the opportunity that he had been seeking. Turning from the window, he said, "No, the will's straightforward. Everything to you. We've been through it."

So that's what this is about.

"Look, I've already told you. We can halve everything. The flat. The money. All his stuff. You just have to say the word."

"Forget it. I don't want to do that thing with Mum where we went through every room, dividing everything up . . ."

"He only left it to me because he didn't *know* you. He probably thought you would give it away or something."

"*Probably* thought?" Ben picked on the phrase as if it carried some sort of significance. It was now obvious to Mark that he was looking for a fight.

"Sorry, am I supposed to know what he was *thinking*? Tell me, brother, and let's be honest about this. If things hadn't worked out the way they had, if Dad had just been run over by a bus six months ago, what would you have done with forty-five grand in cash and a tiny fucking flat in Paddington?"

He waited for an answer. Ben remained silent.

"Well, there you go. You would have given it to me, or to Alice to pay her back for whatever you owe her."

He should not have said that. A mistake. Ben's face tightened into retaliation.

"I don't owe Alice anything, OK? I make money out of my work. Whatever her dad gives her is between them. It has nothing to do with me or with anybody else."

"Sure. Right. I'm sorry."

Ben moved past him, his shoulder brushing Mark's chest. They went into the sitting room.

"That's obviously what he was thinking, though."

Following him, Mark said, "What was that?"

"He knew that kind of money could really help me out. He knew all about Alice's family, the imbalance between us. It was just spite."

Now Mark raised his voice.

"Oh, get off it, will you? You and I both know that's a lot of shit. The will was altered for the last time over a year ago. He didn't know anything about Alice's family. He wasn't striking out at you from beyond the grave, or whatever kind of conspiracy theory you're trying to cook up."

Ben's eyes conceded the truth of this, but he said nothing.

"Listen," Mark tried to end the argument. "Dad was proud of

the fact that you were making a living doing the thing you loved. He told me that. Please just take his money. Buy yourself a couple of suits, take Alice on holiday, and sort out whatever it is you two are fighting about. Seb pays me eighty grand a year. I have my own flat. I've got equity, a company car, all the clothes and gadgets a bloke could need. You're a married man. You might have kids soon. Think about that."

"Always so organized," Ben muttered.

"Eh?"

"Always thinking about the future. Always an answer for everything."

"Well, at least one of us has his head out of the clouds."

"And that's you, is it, Mark? Tell me, has this thing got to you at all?"

They might have been teenagers again, bickering in the school holidays. The exchange was a graphic illustration of their relationship: Mark doing his best to push forward out of the past while justifying his more practical nature to an incessantly analytical brother who preferred blame and self-pity.

"What? Are we competing about Dad now? Who's more fucked up? Who's losing most sleep? You think I have to stand in a window looking moody and smoking a cigarette or I'm not *grieving* properly?"

It wasn't a bad comeback. Mark was quite pleased with it. For a moment Ben was silenced, although the respite did not last long.

"I'm just saying it's weird the way a guy like Jock McCreery, or that Yank Robert Bone, or any one of the stiff-backed suits from MI6 seemed more affected by what's happened than you do. You forgive and forget so easily. Nothing *gets* to you. Nothing makes you *feel*."

Now Mark squared up to him. He was taller than Ben, not stronger, but with an advantage of height and age.

"Jesus Christ. You know what the trouble with artists is, don't you? They have too much time to think. You invite misery on yourselves, fucking wallow in it. Then you marry a girl like Alice to justify your black moods. You're endorsing one another. It's pathetic. You wanna move on, brother. I thought you'd seen the light that night outside the pub, but I realize I was mistaken. Benjamin doesn't change his nature that quickly, never has. He feels too sorry for himself. Why don't you try growing up a bit? Just because I don't wear my heart on my sleeve doesn't mean I'm not *feeling* anything."

"What did you mean about Alice? What did you mean by that?"

But Mark had backed off to the door, empty-handed and set on leaving. Before long, Ben would be blaming him for arranging the failed reunion with Keen, for making him betray their mother, for any small resentment or prejudice that had been troubling him over the past three weeks. That was the thing he dreaded, Ben needling his conscience with hideous expertise. Best just to get away and not see him for a while.

"I'm gonna go," he said. "I'm not standing here taking this. You close up when you leave, do the lock. Next time we see each other maybe you'll be better company. In the meantime, try not to drag us all down with you."

22

"Why don't I put you in the picture, Yerm, clear a few things up?"

Macklin was walking east down Longacre with Vladimir Tamarov. He was at least six inches shorter than the Russian and they were moving quickly with a cold evening wind behind them.

"Nightclubbing as a business in Britain is worth two billion quid a year. You want me to say that again? Two billion quid a year, mate. Turnover year-on-year has gone up seven and a half percent. Wanna know why? It's not the clubs, Yerm, it's not your punters on the door. It's *diversification*. My favorite fucking word in the English language. Clothing, accessories, books, magazines, radio stations, CD compilations. Even T-shirts, for Christ's sake."

Tamarov nodded. He was thinking about going back to his hotel.

"Merchandising, that's what it's all about. We make seventy percent of our profits selling branded merchandise. The clubs are just a small part of it, and getting smaller in my humble opinion. I'll tell you another lovely English word if you like. *Sponsorship*. About half of all the eighteen- to twenty-five-year-olds in this country go clubbing on a Friday or a Saturday night. Millions of 'em, mate. They've got disposable incomes, they're fashion conscious, and they're out to get pissed . . ."

"I'm sorry," Tamarov said. "This word, please . . . ?"

"Pissed, mate. You know, drunk."

"OK," he replied, without bothering to smile.

"So you've got your big corporations, your mobile phone companies, your clothing brands, your breweries, and all they dream about is access to that market. They want to reach out and touch the kids. Now how do they do that?"

"Sponsorship," Tamarov said, like a student in a language class. If he was annoyed at being patronized by a supercilious English lawyer four years his junior then the Russian's level tone of voice gave nothing away. In time it might be necessary to remind Macklin who was boss, to apply an element of physical or psychological pressure, but for now he would let him continue. From the pocket of his overcoat he extracted a pair of brown leather gloves and put them on.

"Exactly." Macklin was leading him down Bow Street. "These companies pay for specific nights at the club. They put banners up on-site. Not so's it detracts from our brand, mind, but it gets what every boring blue-chip company craves. You got your latest digital WAP faxmodem espresso-making laptop associated with a brand like Libra, that buys you something priceless. It buys you *credibility.* Am I going too fast, mate?"

Tamarov's face was usefully inexpressive. He merely shook his head and said, "No, no," breath clouding out in the night air.

"Good," Macklin said. And then his phone rang.

Two hundred meters behind them, Michael Denby, a young MI5 pavement artist on the Kukushkin team, saw Macklin come to a halt beside the entrance to the Royal Opera House. He immediately stopped and turned toward the window of a nearby shop. Called up as a last-minute replacement for a colleague whose husband had "taken ill," Denby had forgotten to bring either a hat or gloves as protection against the cold. Mobile surveillance was the part of the job he least enjoyed. Taploe picked him, he knew, precisely because he was so ordinary—neither too tall nor too short, neither too fat nor too thin—and therefore less likely to be spotted by an alert target. He jangled coins in his pocket and thought of home as two teenage girls stopped beside him and peered into the window.

"There they are," one of them said, pointing at a pair of shoes. "Nice, aren't they?"

"Bit tarty," her friend replied.

Denby glanced down the street. Macklin and the Russian were moving again, heading south into Wellington Street in the direction of the Strand.

"So you've made up your mind then?" Macklin was saying into the phone, his voice a rumble of disappointment.

" 'Fraid so, mate." Mark felt guilty that he was letting his friend down. But the argument with Ben had forced his hand: he just wanted to go home and get a decent night's sleep. "There's a lot of things I've got to clear up at the flat," he lied. "Then the police want a final inventory. I just don't have time to come down."

"Fine. Whatever," Macklin said, and snapped the casing shut without adding goodbye. "Bad news, Yerm," he turned to Tamarov. "It's just gonna be you and me, mate. Keeno's had to cancel."

"This does not matter," Tamarov told him, after a moment of contemplation. "It does not matter at all. In fact it is better this way. I have important business that we need to discuss and then I would like to go home."

23

Stephen Taploe was at a dead end. For the best part of six months he had assumed that the investigation into Libra's activities would make his name within the Service. Secret dreams of promotion had raised him out of bed every morning; they had walked with him to the station and comforted him on the tube. He longed for the unfiltered approbation of his colleagues, their admiring smiles and whispered congratulations. But he could sense his entire career stalling on the fruitless search for conspiracy between Libra and Kukushkin. Six months of surveillance had produced—what? A thousand hours of phone taps and eavesdropped conversations revealing little more than Libra's predictable determination to make a success of the Moscow operation. GCHQ had fax and email intercepts—letters to real-estate agents, tax lawyers, employment agencies—that were consistently mundane, simply the logistical pileup of documents and contracts that would rain down on any company setting up a business in post-Soviet Russia. As well as occasional police reports from Moscow on the activities of known Kukushkin personnel, they had Watchers tracking Libra's meetings in London—the last of them between Macklin and Tamarov filed by Michael Denby two days before, complete with a ninety-five-pound attachment for "expenses" accrued at a lap-dancing club in Finchley—none of which had revealed anything that could be termed abnormal or suspicious. Taploe had always held with the basic, optimistic belief that massive surveillance would, in the end, bear fruit. But what had Paul Quinn uncovered? The odd attempt by Macklin to exploit a loophole in British tax law and three Russians working on the bar at the club's London site without adequate employment papers. Meager tricks played by companies the world over, little ways of wriggling around the rules. Taploe and Quinn needed something concrete, something with which to penetrate the cell structure of Russian organized crime in the United Kingdom. That was the purpose of pursuing the Libra connection, as a staging post into a much larger problem. And yet, increasingly, Taploe felt that he had missed his chance.

From his desk—tidy and well organized, it betrayed none of the accumulating chaos of the operation—he retrieved the initial police report into Christopher Keen's murder. No clues, no leads, no theories. Another dead end. Just blind panic at Thames House that an agent had been murdered and threats to shut the entire operation down. Taploe, in his defense, had pointed out that Keen had not been tortured for information; nor was it a signature mob killing, the motorcycle assassin favored by Viktor Kukushkin in Moscow. No, in a desperate bid to preserve control of the operation he had argued that Keen's death was a fluke, a random accident in a season of bad luck. There was no need to overreact, no need to take his team off the case. Just give it time and they would unravel the mystery. Just give it time and they would bring Kukushkin down.

His pleas had at least bought some time. Taploe, in effect, was now on final warning; without results in a matter of weeks, he would be back on Real IRA. He was convinced that a link existed between the shooting and Keen's work for Divisar, but it was impossible to prove. Investigations had shown that in the weeks before he died, Keen had been assisting a private bank in Lausanne with clients in the St. Petersburg underworld. Perhaps there was a link there. But how to establish that? Where to start?

There was a knock at the door of his office, three floors up at the northwestern corner of Thames House.

"Tea, boss," Ian Boyle said, setting a mug down on the desk. His tie hung at half-mast and the collar on his shirt was frayed.

"Just leave it there."

"You all right, sir? Look a bit knackered."

Taploe ignored the question and conveyed with a twitch of his moustache that he felt it impertinent.

"Get the file on Mark Keen, will you?"

"Sure," Ian replied, and retreated toward the door.

There was now a siege mentality about the operation, an imminent sense that a plug was about to be pulled. Something close to panic had begun to spread through the team, fanned by Taploe's failure to redirect the investigation. It was like Ireland all over again: the boss looking downtrodden and frustrated, his ambition coming up against a wall of compromise and bad luck. Ian returned with the file five minutes later, set it down, and left without speaking. Taploe exhaled heavily as the door clunked shut and immediately began flicking through the material: photographs, email printouts, credit-card receipts, phone logs, surveillance reports. In all probability, a file on an innocent man, just as Mark's father had insisted.

The idea, planted admittedly by Quinn, had been in his mind for three or four days. A last chance. The one person close to the center with access to unambiguous information who could reveal the truth about Macklin and Roth.

He picked up the phone and dialed Mark's office direct. A secretary answered at Libra Soho, first ring, with a voice like an advertising jingle. In a single breath she said: "Good morning Libra International how may I help you?"

"Mark Keen, please."

It felt like the final throw of the dice. To establish a source on the inside. Not the father, who could only ever have been peripheral, but the son.

"Who shall I say is calling?"

"My name is Bob Randall."

"Just putting you through now."

There was a two-second delay, then, "Hello. Mark Keen."

He recognized the voice like an old friend, the street consonants, the slackened vowels.

"Mr. Keen. Hello. My name is Bob Randall. I work for BT. Advanced telecommunications."

"Someone forget to pay our bill?"

Taploe felt that he should laugh, and did so.

"On the contrary, Mr. Keen, on the contrary. Not at all. Actually, I have a business proposition for you. A little venture that I think Libra might be interested in. I understand you're the company's executive director. How are you set for lunch next week?"

24

Sebastian Roth lived alone, in the palace of a self-made man. His Pimlico house, valued at £2.4 million, was actually two properties knocked together, with staircases at opposite ends of the building, like reflections of one another. He had bought both houses as ruined shells, and their conversion, including the construction of a forty-foot swimming pool in the basement, had taken eighteen months, a period in which Roth had lived in a suite at the Lanesborough Hotel whenever he was not traveling abroad.

He had no wish to share his life with a woman, and yet he longed for the diversionary pleasure of an affair, something to distract him from the relentless tide and pressure of work. Since adolescence, Roth had designed his life as a series of obstacles to be overcome: win that award; make that first million; buy that rival's company. The moral or social implications of his behavior rarely troubled him. He simply did not calculate into any decision the possible repercussions for those around him. His was an almost sociopathic indifference. He would do as he pleased, and deny himself nothing. A man in such a position, anointed with the twin blessings of private wealth and perpetual cunning, can begin to feel untouchable, as if no harm can befall him. If Roth was vain, he did not recognize it; if he was cruel or mendacious, he did not care. The arc of his life was aimed solely at the pursuit of his own pleasure.

As he was shaking her hand at the funeral, he had resolved to sleep with Alice Keen. It was as simple as that. This was just a challenge, something to lighten his days, the thrill of which would be derived as much from the planning as from the final seduction itself. The long, pale drawing room on the first floor of Roth's house was scattered with deep suede sofas and expensive works of art. In the corner nestled a Bang & Olufsen hi-fi, in the wall a widescreen digital TV. Yet he no longer derived pleasure from them. Studying a prospectus for investments in St. Petersburg, looking at spreadsheets for the Moscow operation, he cast his work to one side and busied himself with the first components of a plan. He would lure Alice with the promise of contacts and scoops, gradually allowing their relationship to assume a more personal character as her career thrived. At the funeral, he had witnessed the sheer opportunism in her eyes, a throttling ambition concealed by the trick of beauty. She was too good for Ben, Roth decided, and gave no further thought to their marriage. His only concern was that it would all prove too easy. His only dread was that his boredom might last.

25

Bob Randall arranged to meet Mark not at BT's head office in Newgate Street, but at the Whiteley's shopping center in Queensway, a vast Americanized mall heaving with coffee bars and marble.

"Will that be all right?" he had asked on the phone. "It's just that there are one or two individuals at my company—how can I put this?—that I'd prefer were left in the dark about our meeting. Sorry to be so mysterious. I can explain everything when we're introduced."

Taploe enjoyed the Randall alias: the role allowed him to loosen the tie of his self-restraint. When, for example, he shook Mark's hand at the top of the Whiteley's second-floor escalators, he felt almost hearty, and there was an uncharacteristic swagger in his walk as the pair made their way to a half-empty Mexican restaurant nearby. Taploe felt that he had made mistakes in his recruitment of Keen, mistakes that he was determined to avoid a second time round. Too often he had surrendered control, allowed his contempt for SIS to cloud his better judgment. This time things would be different: Mark would respect him from the word go, and differences of class or status would not become an issue. With an understanding of who was boss, Taploe was sure they could get things done. Indeed, he ordered two lagers from the waitress and felt very optimistic about it.

"So who at your company knows that we are meeting here this afternoon?" he asked.

Mark was still settling down in his seat and said, "Nobody. Just Sam, my office manager."

"It's in your desk diary?"

"Palmtop, probably. Why?"

They were facing each other across a tile-topped table, laughter echoing in the mall. Taploe preferred to make a target "conscious" of his identity at an early juncture in any conversation of this kind.

"Let me come clean right away," he said. "It was necessary to employ a little subterfuge to lure you here today. I don't work for British Telecom. I'm actually an officer with the Security Service."

Taploe waited for an appropriate reaction, but Mark's response unnerved him. He simply said, "OK," and removed his corduroy jacket.

"I work for MI5," Taploe explained, as if Mark had failed to understand.

"I'd gathered that," Mark said. "And you're investigating my father's murder?"

"Among other things, yes."

Their waitress, a tired-looking eastern European woman wearing thick black eyeliner, set two bottles of lager on the table and walked off. Mark's eyes followed her and then came back to the table.

"Other things?" he said.

Taploe poured the lager carefully into his glass and made an effort to compose himself. He felt that he had already lost ground.

"What do you know about my organization?" he asked.

"Back of a stamp," Mark replied, rubbing two days of stubble on his jaw. Taploe was worried that he looked bored.

"Right." He pushed up his sleeves. His arms were creamy and hairless and dotted with pale red freckles. "Our task is to root out criminal organizations working in the United Kingdom. Excise fraud, human trafficking, prostitution. We go after drugs smugglers, money launderers, football hooligans, any individual or group of individuals who may pose a threat to national security."

"You must be busy then," Mark joked and, like a ghost, Taploe caught a family resemblance in the grin that flashed across his eyes.

"Very," he replied.

"So how does my father fit in?"

"Well, why don't we order first?" By delaying his response, Taploe hoped to generate a little suspense. This, after all, was the part of the job he most enjoyed: the power afforded by privileged information. *Let him feel that he is about to become involved in something beyond the commonplace. Let him sense that he is at the edge of his father's secret trade.* Over time, Paul Quinn had been able to build up a comprehensive profile of Mark Keen, a psychology that suggested he would comply with today's pitch. Where Keen had been stubborn, Mark was biddable and kind; where the father had been haughty, the son was more modest and conscientious. Taploe also knew, from recent phone and email intercepts, of the ongoing argument with Ben. The two brothers had not spoken for days. Mark would be anxious to prove, if only to himself, that he had been affected by their father's murder. What better way to prove that than to work toward tracking down his killer? A song began playing out of a speaker above his head and Taploe felt rejuvenated, more able to control his adrenalin. Beckoning the waitress over, he ordered extensively from the menu, while Mark opted for the set lunch. When she was out of earshot, he continued.

"You want to know how your father fits in." Mark bobbed his head. "Well, before I answer that question directly, it would be useful if I could make some inquiries of my own."

"Go right ahead."

"First of all, at what point did your father tell you about his work for SIS?"

Mark again rubbed his jaw—it was becoming a reflex—and picked a fork up from the table. "After about two or three months."

"And he asked you to keep that information a secret?"

"Sure."

"And did you tell anybody?"

"I did, yeah."

"How many people?"

"Just one."

"Your brother?"

"My brother."

Taploe was about to say "Benjamin" but he thought better of it.

"Nobody else?"

"Nobody."

"Not even a friend, Mark?"

"Not even a friend." Mark looked annoyed. "What are you getting at?"

Steeling himself, Taploe bounced his moustache into a smile.

"Nothing unsavory, I assure you. But you must have found it difficult keeping that sort of information to yourself. A father who was a spy. A member of your own family involved in an organization—"

"Mr. Randall . . ."

"Call me Bob, please . . ."

"I don't know how much you know about my family, but that thought never crossed my mind. I didn't have anybody I would have *wanted* to tell. It wasn't difficult keeping Dad's past a secret. It was just between me and him and Ben."

"Now that's *exactly* what I wanted you to say."

Again Taploe smiled, and mistook the look of irritation on Mark's face for nerves.

"What you *wanted* me to say? I'm sorry, I'm confused. You're not from British Telecom, you're not here to do business with the club, and you're not from the police. You ask me a lot of questions about my father . . ."

Taploe leaned back and brought his hands together in a badly stage-managed gesture of conciliation. *Stick to the plan*, he told himself.

"I apologize," he said. "I was merely trying to conduct what I call a test."

"What you call a test," Mark echoed flatly.

"It's just that I would need you to be similarly circumspect with what I am about to tell you."

Circumspect. It was a word Taploe had not thought of in years. Appropriate to the requirements of secrecy. Exactly right for the purposes of their conversation. He must remember to use it again.

"The information I am about to share with you would have to remain confidential. In spite of the fact that it concerns your father, you would not even be able to discuss it with Ben."

Mark appeared to hesitate, as if reluctant to be drawn in, then nodded, saying, "I understand." Taploe proceeded to assess the immediate vicinity. There were six other customers in the restaurant, none of them within earshot: two teenage girls ten feet away having a giggly lunch; a young Middle Eastern man by the far wall dropping globs of mince and lettuce from a crunchy taco whenever he brought it to his mouth; three American students at the door making enough noise for a table of eight. No listening threat, in other words, from neighboring tables.

"We're looking into several possibilities," he said. "There may be a link between your father's murder and a post-Soviet crime group operating within the United Kingdom. Now I don't want to alarm you unnecessarily, but it's highly unlikely that your father was simply the victim of a random act of violence. The nature of the killing, the timing, the location, and so forth, all those factors point to another theory."

Mark took a sip of his lager and nodded stiffly. He was already looking less composed. Taploe hoped the beer would be tasteless, dry and catching in his throat.

"What about the Foreign Office?" he asked. "Do they have any ideas?"

"It's not really for me to speculate," Taploe replied, his voice a reedy whisper. "Not my area of expertise."

Mark held his elbow in his right hand, rubbing it, staring blankly around the restaurant. Body language. Had he turned the corner? His food had arrived but he had pushed his plate immediately to one side.

"We're working on two suppositions," Taploe told him, creating a small cone of salt at the edge of his plate. Something about this pleased him, the exactitude of it. "In his capacity as an employee of Divisar Corporate Intelligence, your father was assisting two organizations at the time of his death. Libra, of course, and, latterly, a small private bank in Lausanne. Running checks on large-scale financial deposits originating in St. Petersburg. Capital flight, for want of a better term. He may have mentioned it to you."

Mark shook his head.

"No, he didn't mention it. Didn't mention anything about it at all."

"But it's possible that your father made contact with these groups on their behalf?"

"It's more than possible," Mark replied. "It's a certainty. That's what Dad was employed to do."

"And thus the question must be asked: did he attempt to circumvent protocols imposed by an organized crime group either in Russia or here in London? *Did* he?"

For a moment Taploe thought that Mark was preparing to answer; he had intended the question to be rhetorical. Jumping in, he said, "Now I'm bound to say that I think this is highly unlikely. It would be unprofessional, naïve, and extremely dangerous." He counted out the adjectives on his fingers—one, two, three—and made a point of looking stern. "Furthermore, we've found nothing in his records to back up that theory. So—" Mark was shaking his head. "—if your father was doing his job—and we have no reason to believe that he was ever anything other than completely thorough in his affairs—he may have tried to encourage Libra or the Swiss to pull the plug on their operations because of an irregularity with the Russians. But, again, there's no record of any such concerns in the files at Divisar."

"So why the link with organized crime?" Mark asked. The table of Americans suddenly erupted in laughter and he looked across at them, eyeing with irritation a tanned, crew-cut jock with a pair of Discman headphones clamped around his neck. "What are you getting at?" he said.

Now Taploe paused for effect, like a bad comic looking for laughs. He was buoyed by the ease of the pitch, by how quickly Mark had turned. The center of their table was covered in small blue tiles and he tapped one of them in a clipped manner with the bitten nail of his index finger.

"Tell me," he said. "What do you actually know about Russian organized crime?"

"Just what I pick up when I'm over in Moscow."

"Well, let me begin by pointing out that the term 'Russian mafia' is something of a misnomer. More usually these groups originate from former Soviet republics such as Lithuania and Ukraine. Chechen gangs are particularly high profile in Russia, less so in the UK. But you may already be aware that the men your company have been dealing with in Moscow are of Russian origin. Libra has been negotiating with the Kukushkin syndicate. Am I right?"

"I don't have a clue," Mark said quietly. "I'm not given access to that kind of information."

"And who is? Mr. Roth? Mr. Macklin?"

If he was surprised that Taploe knew their names, Mark did not show it.

"That would be right, yeah."

"Let me fill you in. In August, Thomas Macklin banked two separate checks for around a hundred thousand U.S. dollars in an offshore company that he had registered in Cyprus a year before. Those checks were given to him by a known member of the Kukushkin crime syndicate and made out to Pentagon Investments. Do you know anything about that?"

"Pentagon Investments? Never heard of it."

"The payment may have been for any number of things. Services rendered, goodwill money, a piece of London real estate, something relating to business conducted between the two parties in Moscow or London. We don't yet know. What would seem most likely, based on our further investigations, is that Macklin and Roth have entered into a clandestine relationship with Viktor Kukushkin in connection with their burgeoning interests in the Russian capital. That is to say, a relationship over and above any protection money usually—"

To Taploe's delight, Mark swore under his breath—"*Christ!*"—halting him in midsentence. He waited several seconds before continuing.

"That is to say, the characteristic relationship usually established between organized crime groups in the FSU and overseas companies attempting to do business there. In other words, Mr. Keen, your boss is up to something."

Taploe watched Mark's face as it registered first astonishment and then a gradual, seeping disgust at what he was being told.

"*Up to something?*" he said finally. Taploe nodded and lowered his voice.

"We've had both of them under twenty-four-hour surveillance for the best part of six months." He failed to mention that Mark himself had been subject to the same level of scrutiny, yet felt no shame at the omission. "As a result, we remain convinced that Libra is being used by the Russians as a cover operation for money laundering, drugs smuggling, racketeering, and prostitution." These were as yet baseless accusations, a list compiled by Quinn simply to frighten Mark into cooperation. Nevertheless, Taploe reeled them off with a straight face. "What we need is proof. Proof that Roth and Macklin have entered into a mutually beneficial relationship with the Russians which your father accidentally uncovered and for which he was killed."

Mark appeared to be staring at the paintwork of the restaurant, as if the sweeping waves of orange were making him feel nauseous and confused.

"You really think that's true?" he said. "You really think that's what happened?"

Taploe knew that he could play on his rage, on his adulation for Keen. He wanted Mark to feel disgust, then the tremor of excitement at his first glimpse into a clandestine world, the thrill of the son initiated into his father's secret trade. Above all, Taploe had to lead him to a point where refusal would cease to be an option.

"Mr. Keen," he said and, for a moment, thought about reaching across and touching Mark's shoulder, just for added effect. "I can understand that it must be very hard for you to hear these things about people you have worked alongside for so long, about people you undoubtedly trust. These men are friends of yours, after all. But the reality is that you are most probably working for a company which is laundering money for the Russian mafia."

Mark again shook his head. "How does that work?" he said. "I hardly know anything about the Kukushkins. What the fuck are they doing in London anyway?"

Taploe sniffed.

"Well, you see, that's what I need your help in finding out."

"*My* help?"

"Yes." Taploe looked over Mark's shoulder as the two teenage girls stood up and walked out of the restaurant. One of them dropped a five-pound note onto the table as a tip. "We need somebody on the inside, somebody close to Roth and Macklin who can find out what's going on. You have access to confidential papers, to computer software, travel arrangements, tax returns, everything we require to build a watertight legal case. I need as much of that as I can get my hands on and I need it quickly. Now, can you help me?"

Taploe made it sound like a personal crusade. When he had pitched Mark's father, the circumstances had been very different. The guilt, his loyalty to the old firm. But Mark would be lured by a sense of right and wrong. Taploe was convinced now that the target could not reasonably refuse.

"I know it's a lot to ask," he said, risking understatement, "but I'm sure you're just as anxious as I am to bring these men to . . ."

Mark was holding up his hand. "No, it's not that," he said.

"What then? We can pay you, of course. If that's a problem."

This was a mistake. Mark looked disgusted.

"*Pay* me?" he said, and Taploe saw that he had moved too quickly. Panic engulfed him and he felt his thighs tighten under the table. "I don't want your money. If I help you, I'll do it because of my father. I don't want to be paid for trying to find out who killed him."

"Fine," he said. "Fine." He tried to smile. "But nevertheless the idea interests you . . . ?"

Mark looked down at his food, now lukewarm and congealed. A hard seal of oil had formed on the mince, on the shreds of tired, moisture-seeping lettuce gradually collapsing into rice. It was a dreadful silence.

"Yes, it interests me," Mark said finally, and Taploe felt a surge of relief. "But we'll need to talk more. To clear up how I go about it. I can't just start snooping around the offices without knowing what I'm looking for, without knowing what to do."

It was music to his ears. Mark was complying on instinct, allowing his anger to make a judgment for him, conscious only of his rage at Macklin and Roth, and ashamed at how easily they had duped him.

"Who else knows about this?" he asked.

"Nobody," Taploe replied, hardly aware of the question. "You're the only person, Mark, the only person. And it has to stay that way. You understand that you can talk to nobody about this? Not even to Ben?"

"Yes," Mark replied impatiently. "Yes, I understand that."

"Then good. So perhaps before we go any further I can lay down some ground rules."

26

One of the happier corollaries of a stubborn nature is that it makes tough decisions easier to stick to. Ben woke after his first decent night's sleep in weeks and concluded that enough was enough. For too long he had been adrift in the consternation of grief: it was time to get his life back on track. He would call Mark, fix to meet him for a drink, apologize for what had been said at the flat in Paddington—and accept his offer of a share in Keen's will. The money would do him good. Twenty grand to spend on organizing the exhibition, on taking Alice away on holiday, buying himself a new suit, and maybe fixing up the car. What was the point in taking a stand against a dead man? Nobody respected him for it. Better to embrace the future, as Mark had suggested. Better to concentrate on his work, on his marriage, and to put the past behind him.

To that end, Ben left the house at eight thirty and drove through rush-hour traffic to Cork Street, where there were three or four galleries that had expressed an interest in showing his paintings. He was not used to making such an early start. While his friends would wake up at six or seven and make their way on slow, packed trains to offices spread out across London, the rhythm of Ben's mornings was quite different. He would set the alarm for eight—later, if he had been out the night before—and then snooze until nine or sometimes ten. Alice would be long gone by then, to the gym and on to the *Standard* or a meeting in town. He would make coffee, run a bath, amble out to buy a paper or croissant, and only think about going up to his studio as the morning was drawing to a close. That still left time, after all, to put in a seven- or eight-hour day, and anyway, he felt at his most creative in the afternoons and early evenings. This was the routine that best suited his temperament and it had served him well for years. Today, however, was different. Today felt like a new dawn. It was as if a bubble had burst inside his life, the liberation he had spoken of to Mark. Heading east, Ben stared at the drivers of other cars as if for the first time: cabbies pontificating into their rearview mirrors; electricians in rusty vans with tabloids furled on the dashboard; salesmen pale as clouds turning tuning dials on radios. Ben had the odd sensation that he was seeing the world with fresh eyes, and weighing up his place in it. The feeling of being completely alone, orphaned in a literal sense, was at once very acute and yet not in itself alarming. Making a left turn into Mayfair, he spotted Roth. Ben's eyes just settled on him, coming to a halt at the lights. He was eating breakfast in the window of a branch of Starbucks, a cup of coffee in his hand. Even at a distance of fifty feet, success emanated from him like a suntan. He was wearing a pale blue shirt and eating what looked like a pain au chocolat. A silk tie was slung up over his shoulder, doubtless to protect it from stains, and he was not alone. At the stool beside him sat a woman whom Ben thought he recognized. A slim, late-thirties blonde, not quite attractive, yet professional and striking. Where had he seen her before? The lights were changing and he thought about pulling the car to the side of the road to get a better look, but a bus was tight on his tail and Ben was forced away in the traffic. It was starting to annoy him. They had not looked like lovers: on reputation she was too old for Roth, who preferred younger women, models and dancers from the clubs. She had a briefcase at her feet and appeared to be writing things down. Where had he met her? Where had he seen her before?

He was already on Cork Street by the time he remembered. McCreery's house. The wake. Coming inside from the rain, and a woman passing them in the hall.

"Well, that was nice," Alice had said. "What a fucking cow."

"Keep your voice down."

"I don't believe it. I just met that woman five minutes ago and she blanks me, the death stare from hell."

"Who, the blonde?"

"The blonde. Some cow from the Ministry of Defence. Dulong, I think her name was, Elizabeth or Lisa. Friend of Roth's."

Alice had been quite upset about it, needled and annoyed. On the way home she had mentioned Dulong two or three times, calling her a bitch and making jokes about her clothes. Only then, by comparison, did it occur to Ben how little Alice had talked about her conversation with Roth. He would ask her about it when she returned home.

27

Act as though nothing has changed. Do your job as if it were just another ordinary day. Make telephone calls to DJs, suppliers, bar staff, journalists, whoever you would normally talk to just to keep Libra up and running. Long-standing appointments? Keep them. A lunch with Macklin or Roth? Do not back out of it. You need to pick their brains and still make out that you're their best friend in the world. Don't overplay anything, Mark. Try to remain relaxed at all times. If you start to act suspiciously they will soon become suspicious of you. You have to make sure that when they go home at night the last thing they're worrying about is Mark's loyalty to the firm. If you need to contact me, use the code word "Blindside." Do not send emails from the office or make calls from your desk. Go to a public telephone or Internet café and I can be with you in twenty minutes. My experience tells me that you will get opportunities when their backs are turned. Act on what we've taught you in the last two weeks and it will all be wrapped up in no time.

Randall's advice rang in Mark's ears, and yet he took to the task with an ease that could only have been bequeathed by his father.

A genetic facility for the double life; an ordinary man in extraordinary circumstances concealing his true purpose from the world.

A week after the first meeting in Queensway, Mark had set to work. His first destination was the club's main site in Kennington, where Roth kept unlocked offices containing papers, financial records, and computer data that MI5 had never seen.

It was midmorning, the time of day Mark most enjoyed visiting the club, when he could be alone in the vast, cavernous rooms with only a few cleaners for company. The floors were still sticky with drink and sweat from the weekend and Mark's shoes squelched as he made his way across the lower level to a private staircase at the western end of the building. Through a security door, then up to level two, past the main bar and into a suite of dingy offices that reeked of stale air and sweat. He looked into all three rooms to check that he was alone, then fired up the closed-circuit televisions at the end of the corridor to warn him of any approaching employees. Having made photocopies of up to fifty documents in Roth's filing cabinet, Mark turned his attention to his desk. The central drawer was locked, but he knew that he kept a key in a CD case behind the door. Sure enough, there it was, and he began searching through the debris of flyers, demo tapes, and foreign currencies littering the interior. The contents were like historical artifacts, decade-old junk and trash from Libra's earliest days. This was pure nostalgia, a glimpse into their vanished past, a time before the suit and tie and the Ibiza spin-off, when all that mattered was *Time Out*'s good opinion and three hundred punters on the door.

Then, right at the back, beneath a rave flyer from 1992, Mark found two floppy disks. They were unmarked and covered in fluff and dust, but he copied them onto his laptop with the certain conviction that he had uncovered something valuable. Weren't disks, after all, the holy grails of espionage? Then, having replaced the key behind the door, he left the office. The entire visit had lasted just over two hours. He had moved through the building as if it were just another ordinary day, his role changed without visible effect from servant to spy.

Two days later, with Macklin in the Czech Republic and Roth skiing in Courcheval, Mark worked late at Soho headquarters and spent five hours going through the contents of their offices. He had doubts about this which he had kept to himself: namely, that any incriminating evidence would almost certainly have been secured in the basement safe, access to which was restricted solely to Macklin and Roth. Nevertheless, he followed the procedure mapped out by Randall: filing cabinets and desk drawers, and a thorough search of both rooms for compartments or concealed spaces.

Look behind pictures, Randall had told him, *below carpets and underneath chairs. There may be documents hidden there, sequences of numbers or letters which we can make sense of in the context of other intelligence. Search for evidence of private financial accounts, correspondence from unusual sources, particularly the Cayman Islands, Jersey and Isle of Man, Turks and Caicos, and other offshore territories. Make copies of bank statements, insurance records, anything and everything not immediately recognizable as Libra's characteristic business. It's possible Kukushkin are using Libra as a front for buying assets vital in regard to the facilitation of money laundering. Check Macklin's records in particular. In the first instance, the legal end of transactions of this kind would almost certainly originate with him.*

Finally, at 1 a.m., Mark switched on the computers in both offices and trawled them for information. It quickly became apparent that this was a hopeless task, too vast for one man alone at night with no idea of what he was looking for. Thousands of emails and documents relating to every aspect of Libra's business: it would take a team of a dozen experts hundreds of hours to analyze them. Instead, acting on a separate request from Randall, Mark made hard copies of Roth's and Macklin's appointments diaries and placed them in a sports holdall now three-quarters full with documents. It was almost 2:30 by the time he left the building, punching in a four-digit code to activate the security alarm. Shouldering the holdall, he walked north and flagged down a taxi in Soho Square. Giving the address of his flat in Kentish Town, Mark zipped open the bag and glanced through Roth's appointments: dinner with EMI in ten days' time; two meetings scheduled for the end of the week with American representatives of a major Los Angeles record label; a haircut the day before that. Nothing unusual, in other words. Nothing encoded or obscure. Just another fortnight in the life of Sebastian Roth.

But then he saw it, two days back, an appointment that had been scheduled just hours before Roth was due to leave for the Alps. In his neat, looping script was written:

LUNCH 1 P.M.—ALICE K.

28

"I'll tell you one thing. Seb wants to fuck my sister-in-law."

"Come again?" said Taploe.

"They had lunch a week ago. I saw the appointment in his diary."

"Yes, we noticed that. Did you say anything?"

"Of course not."

"Not to him. To *her.*"

"No. She'd only lie about it, say it was for a story or something."

Taploe took a Kleenex out of a small cellophane packet, blew his nose into it, and said, "Has she been unfaithful to Ben before?"

Mark paused, wondering if the question was relevant to their investigation or simply an invasion of his family's privacy.

"Why don't you ask her?" he said eventually. "I imagine so, yes. It's not something I like to think about. Besides, they may only have had lunch. There is that possibility."

Taploe scrunched the Kleenex into a tight ball and dropped it on the floor beside the accelerator. They were sitting in a Security Service Astra in the basement car park of a Hammersmith hotel.

It was an excessive precaution: Taploe might just as well have met Mark in the broad daylight of a London park, but he felt it useful to create an atmosphere of intrigue.

"Is Ben faithful to her?" he asked.

"What, *brother*? Screw around behind Alice's back? Christ, no. She'd cut his dick off. Ben hasn't looked at another woman since 1993. He once copped off with a girl on a stag weekend—long time before they were married—and Alice didn't let him forget it for years. Constant nagging, guilt trips, endless fucking about. You would have thought he'd got the girl pregnant, the way she carried on."

Taploe sniffed.

"Sorry," Mark said, sensing that he wanted to get back to business. "You were saying about the stuff I got from Kennington."

"Yes, we're still examining it." Taploe was hoping to conceal the fact that it had proved largely useless.

"And the disks?"

"Nothing, I'm afraid."

"Just old crap?"

"Just exactly that."

A bottle-green Audi swung out in front of the Astra, blinding them briefly with the sweep of its headlights. Mark was concerned that the driver might see his face and he shielded it as Taploe opened the window and tapped his thumb on the steering wheel.

"Let's talk for a moment about the computers."

Mark seized on this.

"That's what I don't understand," he said. "Surely you have a way of hacking into our network from the outside? You can read anything that comes out of there."

"Used to," Taploe replied. It was a moment of uncharacteristic candor. "We lost that level of surveillance three weeks ago. A manpower issue."

"Terrific."

He omitted to add that the entire Kukushkin operation was gradually, inevitably being pushed to one side. Lack of concrete evidence. Death of a joe. The Wise Men had lost their faith in Taploe and were moving on to pastures new.

"But it shouldn't make any difference," he said. "That's why you're so important to us. With you on the inside we can get at everything we need."

"How?" Mark asked. "Everything sensitive is password protected. I was trying to get into Mack's email system . . ."

". . . There is an alternative," Taploe interrupted.

"An alternative?"

"Does Libra have technical backup? A team of troubleshooters who come in if your network goes down?"

"Sure they do. The people we bought the computers from."

"And where do you keep the file server?"

"In the basement," Mark said.

It was as if the idea had only in that instant fused in Taploe's mind, regardless of the fact that Quinn had conceived the plan two days earlier. He said, "Then let's kill two birds with one stone."

"I'm not following."

"Next week—we'll set a date—at a specified time, ideally when Macklin and Roth are out of the building, my people will stage-manage a computer attack at your offices in Soho. In other words, put a virus into the network from the outside. All the computers go down. Secretaries start to panic, people lose their work. Now, in the absence of Roth and Macklin, you're the man in charge, is that correct?"

"Correct."

"So it would be you who would call in the technicians?"

"Not necessarily. Sam would do it, the office manager. But she's just gone on maternity leave."

It felt like Taploe's first stroke of luck in weeks. "Good. Then you're the one who makes the call. As soon as the network goes down, inform the staff that help is on its way. Only you've telephoned *us*. Your normal technicians never need to know. Instead, we send A-Branch plumbers who fix the system, copy every hard drive in the building, and get access to the basement safe, all inside three or four hours."

"You can do that?"

"We can do that," Taploe said. "Closer to the time, we'll go through it all in more detail. For now, you should be getting back to work."

29

Jenny telephoned to say that she would be half an hour late for her appointment with Ben. It was 9:45 in the morning. Having finished his third cup of coffee of the day, he walked downstairs and retrieved the post from the metal box bolted to his front door. The number of messages of condolence he now received in relation to his father's death had dwindled to perhaps one or two a week. And none today, it seemed. Just an electricity bill, addressed to Alice, and something from a French mail-order clothing store she liked to use from time to time. The obligatory bank statement, a takeaway flyer, and a postcard addressed to the house next door in Elgin Crescent that had obviously been delivered by mistake. Then, second from the bottom, Ben discovered an airmail envelope made out in his name containing what felt like a substantial letter. A return address had been written on the reverse side.

Robert Bone
US Post Office/Box 650
Rt 120

Cornish, New Hampshire 03745
United States of America

Inside the envelope he found a typed, six-page letter written on fine, watermarked paper and folded twice with care. Only Ben's name was handwritten, the barely legible scrawl of a hyperactive mind. He began to read:

Dear Benjamin

We met all too briefly at the service to commemorate the death of your father who was, as I hope I communicated to you at the time, a close and dear friend of mine. I promised as my wife and I departed that afternoon that I would write you and Mark with some of my recollections of Christopher, both the good times and the bad. However, I also believe that what I have to say may help to cast some light on the reason why your father was killed.

Ben read that last sentence twice and found himself speeding through what followed:

Your father was loyal to his friends, an erudite and sophisticated man, troublesome on occasion, at times maybe even a little impossible. The Keen temper was famous on both sides of the Atlantic! He loved Russia as his second home: its beauty, its fine tradition of literature, of poetry and music. Most of all, and this may sound odd of an Intelligence man, he loved the honesty of the people, what he described to me as "the lack of evasiveness in the Russian soul."

When Jock spoke at the funeral he touched on all of these

things but I could sense from talking to Mark and to you even briefly on the driveway that there was a good deal missing, too many gaps left unfilled.

As you will no doubt be aware by now, Christopher worked for British Intelligence for almost twenty years. In 1977—his first year with the SIS—he was posted to Berlin, where he remained for the next four years. (Most of what I'm about to tell you is classified information, so I would ask that you bear that in mind when you consider who to speak to about it.) I first met Christopher in the winter of '79, as one of the agency's Station Chiefs. Liked him immediately, almost as a brother. Your Foreign Office can specialize in disdain, but Christopher wasn't arrogant in that sense. I gained the impression that he was unlike his other colleagues, just eager to do the best job he could. Anyway, that Christmas Brezhnev drank one too many eggnogs and decided to send troops into Afghanistan, and for a while we all thought we might be on the brink of another global war. But the powers in Washington—I'm talking predominantly about hawks in the Reagan administration like Casey at the CIA—saw the invasion as an opportunity. Even if the Afghan resistance wasn't ever going to be able to defeat the Soviets, they decided that at least the United States could prolong the agony and visit upon the Russians the equivalent of their own Vietnam.

To that end, and on a very clandestine basis, America began arming and supporting the mujahideen and soon Central Asia was crawling with every intelligence outfit in the civilized world: the Chinese, the Iranians, the French, the Italians, Pakistan's ISI, of course—and MI6. Jock, for example, because of his background in the military, was instrumental in training senior members of the resistance in combat techniques, even flying some senior mujahideen figures to the Highlands of Scotland for exercises with the SAS. If there was a difference in the American and British approaches to the war, it lay in operations like these. While we tended to view the conflict as essentially ideological—a stepping-stone, if you like, on the way to winning the Cold War—MI6 took a more traditional approach, seeing Afghanistan as an opportunity to recruit Soviet military and government personnel as agents who would return to Moscow and bring them valuable intelligence in five or ten years' time.

Meanwhile, Reagan, Casey, and later Bob Gates were still playing the Great Game, trying to manipulate the future of an entire continent by playing factions off against one another.

Ben stopped reading and took the letter upstairs. He wondered when Bone was going to get to the point. Most of what he was saying had been reported, ad nauseam, in the papers after 9/11, articles that Ben had tended to skip through laziness. Was this just another stranger promising to throw light on the mystery of Christopher Keen? At least Bone had managed to get over the page. The sheer bulk of his letter was impressive, if only because many of the others had been so inconsequential. He poured himself a glass of water and continued reading in the studio:

Your father and I were posted to Kabul in the late winter of 1984, about a year before the introduction of the American Stinger missile drastically turned the tide of the war in favor of the mujahideen. Christopher was an undeclared SIS officer working out of the British Embassy while I operated under cover of a Dutch aid organization which was predominantly a front for American espionage activity. It was a coincidence that we were there at the same time and while I spent a lot of hours on the road, shuttling between Peshawar and Kabul, we still managed to see quite a bit of each other and I was grateful to have a friend out there. What fascinated both of us about the invasion was the opportunity it provided to see the Soviet forces at first hand—how they operated in a military situation and so forth. (Don't forget that this is the height of the Cold War, when the Soviets were still thought of as the Great Satan by Reagan and Thatcher.) A lot of people would be embarrassed to admit this in light of what happened within five or six years, but there were still a lot of high-profile individuals who gave credence to the idea that the Soviet Empire was aggressively expansionist and posed a serious threat to Western democracy.

What we discovered was that the Soviet machine was anything but effective. The army was riddled with corruption and petty crime. Drug and alcohol abuse were endemic and the conditions under which most soldiers were forced to live wouldn't have been unfamiliar to a hostage in downtown Beirut. Added to that you had non-Slavic elements in the Soviet army who were Muslims not only hostile to the Communist system as a whole but also being asked to fight their own people—ethnic Tajik, Uzbek, and Turkmen Afghans who were their Muslim brethren. It was a crazy situation.

Now as an intelligence officer, a situation like that looks like a big opportunity—and that's how your father saw it. Pretty soon his whole raison d'être for being out in Central Asia was to recruit members of the Soviet armed forces and medical staff as agents for British Intelligence. The Russians had made Afghanistan into a big black market, and soldiers with nothing better to do would just wander around bartering gasoline, food rations, military clothing and footwear, even selling their own weapons and ammunition to get hold of drugs or alcohol. So it was possible for an experienced intelligence operative, fluent in Russian as your dad was, to engineer situations in which he encountered the enemy at first hand.

One individual like this was a young soldier who began there and then to spill his guts about everything that had been happening, not aware who your father really was, and probably not caring too much either. His name was Mischa Kostov and Christopher couldn't have known it at the time but he was just about the best potential Soviet agent he was ever going to get his hands on. Mischa—I never met him, of course, but I know he was a sweet kid—was recruited to the army at the age of twenty, and drafted, I think, in April of '85. As he told it to your father, he'd done about ten weeks of basic training in desert and mountain warfare at a camp in Termez before being sent by train to a Soviet assembly point in Ashkhabad and then on to Kabul by air. This was standard procedure and at this point in his military career the kid's excited—not only does he get to serve Mother Russia, but the future looks rosy once he gets home. Afghan veterans were given preferential treatment when it came to getting jobs or a place at a good university, a decent apartment in Moscow. Added to that, a guy from the Russian army serves two years in Afghanistan, it's counted as the equivalent of six back home, so if everything goes OK, Mischa is on to a fast-track promotion and treble his salary.

Only he finds there were guys in his unit who are only fighting for personal gain. There's nothing ideological going on. Mischa's a young man and he's starting to realize that this is a selfish world we live in, that everybody's out for themselves. Patriotism? Forget it. Most of his comrades have been told they're going to Afghanistan to fight Iranian and Chinese mercenaries, to build kindergartens and schools for Afghan kids. And then they get there and see that this is bullshit. The soldiers are bored, too, restless and—in '85/86—increasingly conscious that they're never going to win the war. These are men quite a bit younger than yourself, Ben, with no women around and nothing to do but smoke hashish or opium, maybe shoot up some koknar. We smoked some weed in Vietnam, but Afghanistan was like Woodstock. The Agency later estimated that at least half a million young Soviet men were exposed to narcotics of one kind or another while serving tours of duty in Afghanistan. And when they went back home, they took that problem with them.

Then, of course, there was alcohol. These are Russians, after all. At one point—independent of Christopher and Mischa—I interrogated a Soviet soldier who told me the guys on his unit used to drink eau de cologne, antifreeze, glue, even brake fluid just to get themselves drunk. But far as your dad could tell, Mischa was more clearheaded. The army was rife with smuggling, pillaging, reprisals, torture, but he stayed out of it, keeping his head down. Only the gradual effect of the corruption on his morale was taking its toll and that's what your father relied on, that's the cynical line we had to take. There were men coming into Mischa's unit from the front lines every day and the stories they had to tell were just horrifying. Hygiene, for one, nonexistent. Here they are trying to fight one of the most sophisticated, battle-hardened resistance armies in history and the Russian soldiers are having to contend with dysentery, hepatitis, yellow jaundice, malaria, typhus, skin infections brought about simply by not having access to a shower or even hot water—sometimes for a month at a time. Clean sheets, clean underwear, are unheard of for these men. When they eat, it's off aluminum plates that haven't been cleaned in weeks. In the desert areas there's sand and lice everywhere, heatstroke and dehydration, then frostbite in winter. Mischa was tough, and he could cope with this, but what he couldn't stand was listening night after night to guys who were being destroyed by war.

After a while he was posted west toward the border with Iran and became involved in some of the heaviest fighting any unit had known out there. Your father began to worry that he wasn't going to make it back. Forgive me for saying this, Ben, but I think in a sense Mischa had become almost like a son to him. Of course he did return to Kabul and it was then that he told Christopher that several of his comrades had come into conflict with older soldiers in their unit. The Soviet army has what they call "stariki," veterans who, regardless of rank or ability, have an unwritten right to make life as tough as they can for younger conscripts. If you'd served less than six months in the army, it could get rough, and young recruits, some of whom were just sixteen or seventeen years old, were forced to scrub toilets with toothbrushes, run around camp wearing gas masks until they fainted, or just woken up in the dead of night for no better reason than that's what the stariki wanted. The culture was so ingrained you could even get higher-ranking officers at the mercy of their subordinates simply because they were younger or had served less time. And of course if they tried to complain to their commanding officers the treatment was only going to get worse. The irony was that these soldiers were out there to fight the mujahideen, but their real enemy turned out to be themselves.

There was one Muslim guy on Mischa's unit who, as far as we could tell, was straight out of high school in Uzbekistan. Like I said before, there was a lot of bad feeling between the Slav majority and the "churkas," Soviet Muslims from the southern republics. The bullying in this case got so bad he went missing for two days. The regiment drove themselves crazy looking for him, wondering if he'd deserted to the rebels, but eventually he got tracked back to his village in Uzbekistan. Somehow he'd managed to get a pass back home and just run away. So the Soviets put him in solitary for three weeks and then he gets called back to the front and life in the barracks deteriorates further. Bullying and punishment on a level Mischa didn't even want to talk about. He was ashamed, I think. This is a proud son of Soviet Russia with scales falling from his eyes. Christopher later found out that the stariki beat this Muslim kid every night with an iron bar and that he was raped by another soldier on at least two separate occasions. He wrote a letter home to Uzbekistan, begging his father to get him out of there, but what could his dad do? The kid's already gone AWOL once, he's a stain on the family. So no help comes and the inevitable happens. One night he crept out of bed at 2 a.m., took a knife into the bathroom, and slit his wrists. He was eighteen years old.

That spring, Mischa was posted back to the front, this time south toward Kandahar, but a new company commander, name of Rudovski, had been assigned to his unit because the previous guy got killed. Rudovski came with a sidekick, Domenko, a sergeant smacked out on liquor and char twenty-four hours every day. This was when the atrocities started, a summer of mindless slaughter to which Mischa bore terrible witness. The worst of it came in August when the unit captures a dozen Afghan kids armed only with a few bird guns, just trying to do their bit for the resistance. The Russians are only about ten clicks from their base and Mischa suggests handing them over to the Afghan Security Service. But Rudovski has other ideas. He orders the Afghan kids to strip naked and starts tying them up, hands and feet. Then he lays them on the road and Rudovski tells one of the drivers to run them over with an armored personnel carrier. The BMP driver said he wouldn't do it and neither would several of the other soldiers. Rudovski knew enough not to ask Mischa. So eventually he turned to Domenko and says something like "Show these cowards how to love the motherland," and then Domenko climbs into the BMP and just drives over the kids and crushes them.

When Mischa got back to Kabul he told your father about all of this and the information went into a CX that was read at the highest levels of government in both the UK and the United States. But by then he was a changed man, addicted to opium, couldn't function without it, and he'd become sloppy. Christopher, who was maybe more involved than he should have been, and too upset about what was going on, was intent on somehow getting Mischa out of Afghanistan, even if it was only as far as Islamabad. He was afraid, as I was, that Mischa would blow his cover. But he couldn't get authorization from SIS. Nothing could be allowed to disturb the illusion that Western intelligence agencies were adopting a passive role in the Afghan conflict, offering humanitarian assistance and nothing more. No matter that the Soviets knew all about CIA and SIS activity by that stage. What happened is that Mischa was blown. The army had gotten suspicious and he was observed en route to a clandestine meeting with your father and then later executed by court martial.

This is highly classified information, Ben, but it's central to my theory about what happened in London and I don't think it's right that you and Mark should be prevented from knowing the truth. When the Soviet archives were opened up and Western intelligence analysts were able to unravel many of the most closely guarded secrets of the Cold War, I discovered that Mischa's father had worked for the KGB. SIS and Christopher had always believed that he was simply a middle-ranking civil servant in Moscow, but through my old contacts at the Agency—I quit in '92—I was able to find out that Dimitri Kostov had operated within a First Chief Directorate section known as Department V. Department V was a relatively new section of the KGB created in the late '60s to replace the Thirteenth Department of the FCD, which organized what we used to call "wet jobs." Assassinations, for want of a better word. Nominally, Department V was tasked only with carrying out acts of sabotage, but under the control of Andropov there's strong evidence to suggest that assassinations continued.

My fear is this. When Mischa was blown, SIS was concerned that he may have divulged your father's identity to the Soviet military prior to his execution. Christopher was taken out of Afghanistan as a precaution and reassigned to China. His career never recovered and when SIS was overhauled under McColl in the early '90s, he was pushed out. Something very similar happened to Mischa's father, almost like a mirror. When it was discovered that his son had been betraying secrets to the British, Kostov was discharged from the KGB and sent to Minsk to process employment records. He turned to drink, lost his wife, and only came back to Moscow after the putsch when his old KGB friends, most of whom were running the country in one guise or another, were able to find him work.

That's what I know. Kostov had numerous aliases—Kalugin, Sudoplatov, Solovyov—and I've never been able to track him down. Time and again I would talk to your father about the possibility of Kostov coming after him but he just wouldn't talk about Mischa. He felt like he'd killed a man, sent him to his death. And coupled with the guilt he felt about you and Mark, the pain was often hard to bear. Your father was a proud man and would just laugh off my concerns. "How would Kostov ever find me?" he used to say. "He doesn't even know my name." I was just a conspiracy theorist, another paranoid Yank who couldn't let go of the job. But nobody's identity was secure—a list of SIS officers worldwide was posted on the Internet about five years ago. Your father's name was on that list.

I would urge you to take this information to the police if I thought they would be permitted to act on it. I tried to alert SIS to the problem a long time ago, but my bridges are burned there now. Everything falls on deaf ears.

It frustrates me to end on such a downbeat note, but I loved Christopher and his loss has affected me. Please contact me at the address stated if you want to talk through any of what I've written here today. Together I believe we can solve this situation and maybe help to put the past behind us.

Yours sincerely,

Robert M. Bone

When he had finished reading the letter, Ben continued to stare at the base of the final page, as if expecting further words to appear. For some time he remained like this, a cross-legged figure in the center of the room, unsure of how to proceed. Oddly, there was still an instinctive part of him that wished to remain ignorant of his father's past, a stubborn refusal to grapple with the truth. Under different circumstances, he might even have scrunched up Bone's letter and thrown it petulantly into the nearest bin. That, after all, was how he had survived for the best part of twenty-five years.

But almost every sentence Bone had written, every one of his recollections and theories, had been revelatory, clues not simply toward the solving of a murder, but vital pieces in the jigsaw of his father's life. Ben immediately wanted to share the letter with Mark, and yet a part of him enjoyed the buzz of privileged information. This was the breakthrough the police had been searching for, but it was also a secret glimpse into a world that his brother could only have guessed at.

30

Mark called Bob Randall from a phone booth in the ticket hall of Leicester Square underground station. He lost his first twenty-pence piece in the teeth of a broken callbox, but reached the contact number at his next attempt. A man answered, sneezing as he picked up.

"Can I help you?"

"This is Blindside."

"Hold the line."

Taploe was put through in under ten seconds.

"Randall," he said.

"We may have a problem."

"Elaborate."

"I just got to the office. Macklin's breakfast was cancelled. Lunch as well. It looks like he's going to be there all day. I told him I was going out for a coffee so I could get to a phone and tell you."

"I see. So do you still want to go ahead?"

"Do you?"

"There's no problem at our end. The network will go down at

11 a.m. as arranged. We have the team standing by waiting for your call. But you sound unsettled."

Mark had not wanted to betray any of his anxiety. *Think of Dad*, he had said to himself. *What would my father do?* He braced his foot against the wall of the callbox and said, "I'm fine. Don't worry about me. I just thought you should know."

"Well, I'm pleased to hear that. So let's press ahead. This is information that we need. Now, where are you?"

"Leicester Square tube."

"Well, it's almost half-past. Get back to the office. We'll expect to hear from you within the next forty minutes."

"Sure."

"And Mark?" Taploe said.

"Yes?"

"Don't forget the coffee."

"What?"

"You told Macklin you were going out for a coffee. Make sure to bring one back."

Half an hour later, Mark was sitting in an armchair in his office when he heard the distinct rumble of a Macklin "Fuck" coming through the walls. Another voice—Kathy's—cried out, "What the hell happened?" and then a door opened in the corridor.

"Why's the fucking email not working?" Macklin shouted. "Where's Sam?"

"Maternity leave," somebody said.

"Fucking great."

He swerved into Mark's office, a shirt button popped open on his belly. Mark lowered the magazine he was pretending to read and tried to look distracted.

"Your computer working, mate?" Macklin asked him.

"Mine just crashed as well," Kathy said, coming in behind him.

Mark stood up with perhaps an exaggerated nonchalance and walked across to his desk. Hitting a key at random, his stomach a swell of nerves, he prayed for total system failure.

Granted.

The small, frowning face of an Apple icon appeared on-screen and nothing Mark could do would remove it. Turning to face Macklin and Kathy he said simply, "Shit." At the reception desk, thirty feet away, Rebecca, a temp who had replaced Sam as office manager, answered a telephone call just as her own computer froze irreparably. She had been in the middle of writing a frank and erotic email to a one-night stand and was worried that it would now be discovered on the system.

"Well, that's fucking great, isn't it?" Macklin was saying. "I had twenty fucking messages downloading and now they're all shot to fuck. Some cunt in the Philippines, probably, a prepubescent anorak who thinks it's a fucking laugh infecting every computer in the civilized world with Macintosh Clap. Doesn't he have something better to do? You know, watch football, play Virtual Cop or something?"

Mark caught Kathy's eye and grinned. "It may not be that bad," he said. Momentarily forgetting the temp's name, he called out to her, "Is yours down too?"

"Yes," Rebecca replied from across the room, covering the telephone with her hand. The conspiratorial way she then soundlessly mouthed the word "Frozen" made Mark wonder if she fancied him. "Well then, I'll get someone to fix it," he said.

"Who does Sam normally call?" Macklin asked. "Of all the fucking days to be on holiday . . ."

"The number's in her magic book," Kathy told him.

At this, Mark stepped in.

"Don't worry, I'll call them," he announced, and then panicked that he might have sounded too enthusiastic. Why would *he* do it, after all, when Kathy was around and knew where to find the book? *Rescue this. Say something.* "Mack, you go next door. Kathy, make him a cup of tea. Virus or no virus, it'll be fixed by lunch."

"What makes you so sure?" Macklin asked.

"Vibes, man," Mark replied.

He was impressed by how precisely the men from A Branch looked exactly like computer technicians. For some reason he had been expecting lab engineers wearing white coats and protective helmets, but the three men who came to the Libra offices within half an hour of Mark's call were spotty, unwashed, socially inept youths. None of them looked at Mark. They had already performed a complete dry run of the operation the preceding weekend and knew exactly which rooms to target and where to locate the safe.

"Is there a unit in there?" one of them had asked Kathy, nodding toward Roth's locked office.

"Yeah," she had said.

"Any chance of getting a look at it?"

"Sure."

And total access was thus provided. Over the course of the next four hours, every computer in the building was disassembled and a copy made of its hard drive. Meanwhile, having been shown to the basement by Mark, a security specialist plugged phony wires into the mainframe—purely for the purposes of cover—and then calmly broke into the Libra safe, making a thorough photographic record of its contents. Mark, who had told an increasingly agitated

Macklin that he would "keep an eye on things downstairs," watched all this unfold from the basement doorway and felt the thrill of his participation in it. *This'll make our case*, Randall had told him, and he was surely right.

Yet there was a single flaw, a problem that nobody could have foreseen. Just after two o'clock, as Macklin was leaving the office to buy himself a sandwich for lunch, he turned to Rebecca in reception and, laying the groundwork for a future date, said, "Sorry about all the computer geeks, sweetheart. Can't be helped, I'm afraid."

"That's all right," she replied. "But it's a bit weird, Mr. Macklin. They got here so quickly."

Macklin, who was wondering what chance he had of getting her into bed before the end of the week, only half-absorbed this observation and said simply, "Oh yeah?"

"Yeah. Sam left me a note before she went away, basic stuff saying where everything was. I had the number for the computer technicians and called them after what happened. Only, thing is, they said they were busy, couldn't get here till three or something. Then they go and show up twenty minutes later."

"Is that right?" Macklin said. "Is that right?" She now had his full attention. "After twenty minutes?"

"Yeah."

He frowned.

"Maybe they had a cancellation. Did you ask?"

Rebecca shook her head.

Macklin eyeballed the only visible technician in the room, a twenty-four-year-old A-Branch recruit named Frank who was pretending to rewire a circuit board outside Mark's office.

"Hey, mate," he called out.

"Yeah?"

"How come you got here so quickly?"

Trained never to open his mouth until he knew the score, Frank continued facing the wall and replied, "What's that?"

"I said, how come you got here so quickly?"

Half-turning now, Frank frowned at Macklin and muttered, "Not following you, mate."

"Well, it's just that the lovely Rebecca here phoned your offices this morning and you said you was busy till three."

"Beats me. I just go where I'm told," Frank said. Thinking on his feet, he added, "I know there was talk of a big job last night. Maybe it got called off."

"Right."

Macklin seemed satisfied and looked back at Rebecca, raising a fat eyebrow in a manner he intended as flirtatious.

"Well, there you are, sweetheart," he said. "Mystery solved. So what are you doing for dinner tonight? Fancy some sushi or something?"

Afterward they had Frank to thank for reacting as quickly as he did.

No sooner had Macklin left the building than he put his tools to one side, smiled at Rebecca, and walked calmly down to the basement. Mark, who was startled when the door opened at the top of the staircase, signaled frantically to the locksmith and leaped to his feet.

"Problem," Frank said, matter-of-factly.

"How so?" the locksmith replied.

"Girl upstairs, temp. She's not as lazy as she looks. Turns out that as soon as the system went down she called the regular technical support team. As luck would have it, they were too busy to get here till three. But it's already gone two. Unless someone gets on the phone smartish and cancels the appointment, this place is gonna be crawling with Mac technicians wondering who the fuck we are."

"Jesus," Mark said.

Frank's voice was a low, logical statement of the facts. "You got the number?" he asked.

"I can find it."

"Then do it now. Our friend just popped out for a sandwich. He's due back in less than five minutes."

"Rebecca. Give me Sam's magic book, will you? I need to find something out."

Mark prayed that she would retrieve it without asking any awkward questions. Without stopping to make conversation. Without wondering why he had a film of sweat on his forehead in the middle of winter.

"Of course, Mr. Keen, of course."

"Call me Mark," he said. "I think she keeps it in the drawer . . ."

"Yeah, here it is. Everything all right?"

Frank passed them at the reception desk, sucking on a carton of Ribena.

"Everything's fine, yeah. It's just so hot down there." Lowering his voice, Mark whispered, "These guys are taking forever."

And Rebecca smiled, enjoying the shared confidence.

She handed him the book and followed Mark with her eyes as he walked away.

"Mr. Keen?"

"Yes?"

Mark turned round. Rebecca was touching her neck, swinging this way and that in her revolving chair.

"It's just that I was wondering if you could show me how the fax machine works. I'm having trouble receiving."

Wondering if this was a pass, Mark said, "Sure. Just let me do this one thing and I'll be right back with you."

"Great."

He closed the door of his office, heat spread across his body. Flicking through the book—*where?*—Mark searched for the number. *What's the name of the company? What the fuck are the computer men called?*

But Sam was efficient. Sam laid things out. In the section marked "Computers" he found a list of companies, topped by a firm of Apple specialists whose name he instantly recognized. Dialing the number with dervish speed, Mark found himself in an automated queue.

For general inquiries, press 1.

For information about our range of software products, press 2.

For customers experiencing problems with the latest version of Windows, press 3.

For corporate accounts, press 4.

Mark hit "4" hard with a rigid index finger and swore as music drifted through on the line. A boy band. Guitars and harmonies. He could feel his back becoming soaked in sweat. And then, through the window of his office, Mark saw Macklin coming back with a sandwich, his thin hair pushed to one side by the wind. *Stop and talk to the girl*, he prayed. *Try and get your fat arse laid.*

"Hello, can I help you?"

A woman, young, with a voice not unlike Rebecca's, was on the line.

"Yes. Hello. Listen, hi, I'm calling from Libra."

"Yes?"

"We've solved our problem."

Nothing.

"Remember we called you?"

Silence.

"About a virus."

"A virus?"

The woman sounded bored. Not taking things in. So many calls to field in a day and nothing interesting about this one.

"Yes. A virus at the Libra offices." Macklin was eating his sandwich and seemed to be laughing at something Rebecca had said. *Stay there, you prick. Keep talking.* "One of our office managers called you. You said you had a team coming out here at three."

"At three?"

More silence, deep as a cave.

"I'm just going through the book now, sir."

"Is it there?"

Impatiently the woman said, "Just a minute, I'm still looking." Then, "Here it is. Yes, three o'clock."

"And?"

"And what, sir?"

"Well, I'd like to cancel it. If it's not too late."

"I see."

Mark experienced a weakening sensation in his arms. "Are they already on their way?"

"Just a minute, please."

And he was forced to wait as the woman abandoned the line to "Careless Whisper." One minute went by. Two. He looked out into the office and could not see Macklin. Then there was a knock on his door.

"Just a minute."

Macklin came in anyway. "Keeno, can I just . . ."

Mark looked up and signaled sternly with his hand. Eyes set like stone and the words "gimme five minutes" mouthed with absolute intent. Macklin said, "Sorry, mate, I'll wait then," and closed the door.

"Hello?"

"Yes." Mark pressed the phone tighter to his ear.

"That's fine, sir."

"It's canceled?"

"Yes, sir."

"They're not already on their way?"

"What?"

"I said the team, they're not already on their way?"

"No."

"Well, that's great news."

Anxiety fell from his body, a storm cloud shedding rain.

"Was there anything else?" the woman asked.

"No, nothing else," Mark said, sitting back in his chair.

"Well, that's fine, then," she said, and hung up the phone.

31

Tracy Frakes had been waiting for the letter for three days.

On Tuesday morning, Mark had left the house at 8:45, forty minutes before the fat postman ambled up Torriano Avenue and dropped a single postcard into his letterbox. There was no second post that day, so Tracy had gone home and spent the rest of the afternoon with her kids, taking them to the movies and then on for a meal at McDonald's.

The following morning, she had woken at five, driven west to Kentish Town, and had difficulty finding a parking space with a decent view of Mark's property. He had left earlier than the day before—at 7:25 a.m.—and Tracy had thought he looked attractively disheveled, his hair still wet from the bath, lost sleep staining his eyes. Then she had to wait another two hours for the postman, the same overweight blob as the day before, passing the time reading *Glamour* magazine and a brand-new book by John Grisham. Once the postman was safely out of sight, Tracy had entered the property, only to find that Mark had been sent two bills (gas and water), an invitation franked by *Q* magazine, another postcard (this time from Argentina), and a piece of junk mail from a home-tailoring service in Epping. Nothing, in other words, from America. She would have to wait for second post and most probably come back tomorrow.

By Thursday, Tracy was bored of the assignment. Another 5 a.m. rise, another headlight drive to Kentish Town. She didn't get called by Taylor all that often, and had been hoping for a decent black bag, a job that entailed something more than just fiddling about with someone's post. Taylor had recruited her straight out of prison six years earlier, hoping, he said, to take advantage of her "unique gifts for theft and petty larceny." He was a right twat, Taylor. Ten stone of Yorkshire ponce who treated her like a street urchin. Still, the money was good, and it was nice to get out of the house. Tracy wondered what she'd buy for her boys when the check came through. Come to think of it, she wondered what she'd buy for herself.

At eight on the dot, Mark came out. A bit nervous this morning, looking a bit stressed and concerned. He was wearing a classy suit cut in navy blue corduroy with trousers that flared just above the shoe. Tracy thought he looked handsome; she wondered what he did for a living, whether he had a girlfriend or family. That was an element of the work she really enjoyed, the mystery of a target's identity. Once, she had broken into an office block in Bracknell and seen the company chairman that very same night on the news. To get so close to someone, to see their furniture, their clothes, to rifle through drawers and cupboards and leave no trace of her passing. There was real skill to it, a gift for ghosting through. It annoyed Tracy when intelligence people made a mess of things, when there were stories in the papers about break-ins going wrong. She couldn't see any excuse for it, for leaving a room disturbed. They'd all been trained properly; people just got sloppy, stopped taking pride in their work.

Mark came toward her now and, for the first time in three days, walked right past Tracy's vehicle. She had to pretend to apply makeup in the rear-view mirror as he headed south for the tube. Then it was another two-hour wait for the postman, finishing the Grisham as the minutes crawled by. At 10:05, a woman wearing a dark blue Post Office uniform with a red canvas bag turned into the avenue and began distributing letters, working more quickly than the overweight blob, who must have been off sick. Four minutes later she left her trolley at the gate of Mark's house and took three letters up to the door, pushing them through the letterbox and then turning back to the road. When she was out of sight, Tracy moved quickly. Reaching into the back seat for her clipboard and charity ID, she stepped out of the car, made a brief check of the surrounding doors and windows, and walked across the street. She was inside Mark's house within four seconds—her quickest time so far—and closed the door behind her with a soft bump. An airmail envelope had floated out about four feet into the room. Flipping it over, she read the return address on the reverse side:

Robert Bone
US Post Office/Box 650
Rt 120
Cornish, New Hampshire 03745
United States of America

Bingo. She would get it to Taylor by noon. A quick glance through the front door's fish-eye lens and Tracy was out on the street. Job done. With any luck, she'd be home by three.

32

It wasn't there.

Ben rummaged through the contents of the shoebox where he had hidden the original copy of Bone's letter, but there was no sign of it. Tapes, random playing cards, paper clips, packets of gum, but no trace of an airmail envelope bearing Bone's handwriting. Just two days before, Ben had come home, made a photocopy of the letter at a local newsagent, and placed the original for safekeeping in his studio. Alice could not have taken it because she would not have known where to look. And yet somebody had been through the box.

He shouted downstairs: "Have you seen the letter?"

Alice took a long time to reply. It was Saturday morning and she was reading the papers in bed.

"What's that?"

"The original copy. The letter from Robert Bone. Not the one in the car."

Again, a long delay. Then, tiredly, "No."

He walked downstairs and went into their bedroom.

"You sure? You didn't send it to your friend in Customs and Excise, the one who was going to check on Kostov?"

"I'm sure."

Alice looked puffy and tired, trying to lock herself into the privacy of a weekend and not wanting to be disturbed. Ben had brought her a cup of coffee at ten and barely received a word of thanks. He was trying to make an effort with her but she seemed distant and cold. In the past, Saturday mornings had been almost consciously set aside for sex, but even that was a chore now.

"I'm going out," he said.

"Where?"

"Thought I might go for a walk round Regent's Park, maybe take a look at the roof on the British Museum, go to an exhibition or something."

"All day?" Alice asked.

"Probably, yeah."

She had told him that she was having lunch with a friend and afterward going in to the *Standard*. Another Saturday apart. Another weekend when they did separate things.

"Did Mark ever call you back?" she asked.

"No. I've left twenty messages, sent a dozen emails. He must be ignoring me."

Peeling a satsuma in bed, Alice said, "Now why would he do that?"

The tone of the question suggested that she could well imagine why.

"I have no idea," Ben replied. "I'm trying to make it up to him."

Didn't she realize that? Hadn't she seen that he was trying to move on? Or was it simply that she didn't care?

"I mean, maybe he's busy," Alice suggested. "Maybe his phone's not working. Maybe he just wants to be left alone."

"Well that's great, isn't it? I have a lot of stuff I need to talk to him about and he won't fucking get in touch."

"Relax," she said, an instruction that had the effect of making Ben feel even more on edge. "Where do they say he is when you call Libra?"

"They say he's *around*. That's all they seem to know. That he's *around* or *in a meeting* and *can they take a message?* And his mobile just rings and rings. I don't even get to say anything."

Alice smiled as juice from the satsuma dropped onto the sheets.

"So, as I was saying, I'm going out," Ben told her. "Thought I might take the car."

He picked up a bottle of mineral water from the floor, took a slug, and scratched at his neck. Alice said, "OK," then, out of nowhere: "By the way, I had lunch with Sebastian yesterday."

The water caught in Ben's throat. He had been walking out of the room.

"Sebastian?"

He knew exactly who she was talking about.

"That's right. Sebastian Roth."

Why was she telling him this now? To start a fight? To assuage her guilt? To bury the news in everyday chitchat in the hope that it would just go away? Alice never did anything without first exactly calculating its impact.

"How did that happen?"

"He invited me."

"He invited you?"

"That's right."

"Just you? Nobody else?"

"Just me." She was pretending to read the paper.

"And how was he?"

"Great."

Ben moved across to the window and stared out at Elgin Crescent. He was aware of Alice chewing elaborately.

"So did you get a story out of him? I mean, that was the point of the meeting, right? For the paper?"

"Sure."

"Well, go on then."

"Go on what?"

"Well, what was the scoop? Why else would you bring it up? There must be a point to this announcement."

It depressed him that they had so quickly descended into yet another argument.

"There's no point to it," she said. "You're making too much of a harmless piece of information. I just thought that you'd be interested."

"Well, I am."

"Well, *good*." Alice sighed theatrically and let the newspaper flap onto the bed. "We talked about your father, actually. Then we talked about Seb's new restaurant . . ."

"*Seb*?" Ben said sarcastically. "You call him '*Seb*'?"

Alice ignored this.

"He wants me to do a feature," she said. "A big interview for the paper."

"I didn't know Libra were opening a restaurant."

"Well, there you go. That's why we need journalists in the world, Ben, to keep people like you informed. Anyway, it's not Libra officially. It's just him and his lawyer."

"Tom Macklin?"

"Right."

"How come Mark never said anything?"

"Well, maybe because he doesn't know anything about it." Alice threw back the duvet. Her legs looked supple and warm and Ben suddenly wanted to touch them. Her pale naked body breezed past him as she said, "Maybe he would have said something if you two ever spoke," and went into the bathroom.

"Did you mention anything to Roth about Bone's letter?"

"Christ, no." She was coming back into the room. "You told me to keep quiet about that. I haven't told a soul." He scanned her face for the lie as he said, "Good." For all Ben knew, Alice and Roth could have skipped lunch, booked themselves into the Charlotte Street Hotel, and fucked from noon till six. That was the extent of the trust he held for his wife. He heard the lock click on the bathroom door and sat down on the bed. There were shards of satsuma skin hidden in the white folds of the duvet.

"Well, I'll be off then," he said, shouting through the door.

"Fine," Alice called back.

And then he heard the hot blast of water pouring into the bath and assumed that the conversation was over.

33

For Mark, this was the spy's life. Secret codes, surreptitious phone calls, meetings in underground car parks, the total concealment of everyday life. Joking with Macklin, smiling at Seb, and nobody at work with the slightest idea that genial, approachable Keeno was a source feeding privileged information to an officer in MI5. It was just as he had imagined it. Just as his father had described. Mark had an aptitude for spying, a talent for secrecy and sleight of hand. It ran in the family. The Keen inheritance.

And now safe houses. Randall had made contact via email insisting on a meeting on Saturday morning. Something important had come up, something vital to the operation. Mark was given exact directions from Kentish Town to an MI5 property west of the Kilburn High Road and set out shortly after breakfast. For security, Watchers posted along the route tracked him all the way to the front door. He arrived at 10 a.m.

The flat was located on the first floor of a converted, semi-detached house in Priory Park Road. When Mark rang the bell, Ian Boyle opened the door and smiled warmly. Only twice before in his career had Ian had the opportunity to meet the target of his own surveillance at first hand, and he was intrigued to witness Mark close-up, the full weight and presence of the man unseparated by lens or windscreen.

"All right there?" he said, waving him inside. "You find us OK?"

"No problem," Mark replied.

There were flyers littering the narrow hall and a citrus smell of carpet cleaner and detergents. Directly ahead, a steep staircase led up to the flat with a bicycle partly blocking the way. Ian had to push it to one side and said "Sorry" as oil from the chain rubbed up against the wall.

"Bloody thing's always getting in the way," he said. "Good for exercise, though. Keeps me in trim."

To illustrate his point more vividly, he patted his stomach, leading Mark upstairs past bedrooms with closed doors and a bathroom in the process of being redecorated. Taploe was waiting for them in a bright, yellow-painted sitting room off the top landing, standing by a window that overlooked the street. Dark blue velvet curtains were drawn against the light and he appeared to be chewing gum.

"Mark." Taploe turned quickly, moving forward with his hand outstretched, like an edgy host at a cocktail party. "How have you been?"

"Fine," Mark told him. "Fine."

"Good. Great. Thanks, Ian." Taploe's thin, nasal voice was unusually rushed. "We'll be fine if you just leave us in here."

"Right, guv."

The source of his nervousness, perhaps, was a bulky, shaven-headed man hunched forward uncomfortably in an armchair on the opposite side of the room. Younger than Mark by perhaps five years, he had the look of an electrician or plumber, wearing a green Fred Perry T-shirt, scuffed cream trainers—the laces slackly tied—and dark denim trousers swollen with fat at the thigh. Mark did not recognize him, but assumed he was one of the plumbers who had helped strip the hard drives at Libra.

"This is a colleague of mine. Paul Quinn. A legal financial expert," Taploe explained, speaking in short, abrupt sentences. "He's going to be helping us today. Paul, this is Mark Keen."

Fifteen stone of concentrated indifference half rose from the armchair to shake Mark's hand.

"All right, mate?" A London accent, low and nebulous. Mark wondered how such a person could know anything at all about the complexities of the financial markets.

"The journey was no problem?" Taploe's head bobbed up and down as if to encourage a positive response from the question. "You found us OK?"

"No problem," Mark said. The room was very small and a wide coffee table threatened to strike his shins at any moment. He sat down on a low, two-seater sofa with coat-hanger springs and said: "The journey was fine. No trouble."

Above Quinn's head, not incongruously given his youth and appearance, hung a worn, faded poster of *Enter the Dragon*: Bruce Lee stripped to the waist, three fresh scars torn like cat's claws across his chest. The bright yellow room was otherwise bare. A row of bookshelves on the facing wall contained nothing but outdated telephone directories and a small vase of dried heather. A hundred-watt bulb burning in a lampshade overhead left a blob of blinding color on the backs of Mark's eyes whenever he closed them.

"First things first," Taploe said, sitting down and jerking his knee away when it accidentally brushed against Mark's thigh. "The

Soho operation was a big success. Really first-rate. Enough information to convict Macklin and put him away for a very long time." There was a slight shaving cut on the underside of his chin and he touched it. "I wanted to thank you in person for all your help so far. You've been invaluable to the operation as a whole. Really turned it around."

"Don't mention it."

"Which brings me to explain why Paul is here. I thought it would be better if what has become a somewhat complicated situation was explained to you by somebody with an expert's grasp of finance. A specialist, so to speak."

Across the room, Quinn inhaled briskly through his nose, a sound like a rhino bathing. Mark smiled at him, trying to establish a connection, and was met by a look of intense, intelligent concentration that did not preclude the later possibility of empathy or rapport.

"Paul is a lawyer by trade." He was also Taploe's closest colleague on Kukushkin, the engine of the case. "He helps us out from time to time with complex financial cases. When we can't see the wood for the trees."

"I see." Mark suspected that this last remark had cost Randall something in terms of his own pride and smiled at Quinn to flatter him.

"What we've been able to establish from the hard drives and safe is a highly sophisticated money-laundering operation with Thomas Macklin at its core."

"Seb's not involved?" Mark asked immediately, a question that caused Taploe to grimace nervously.

"Not in the first instance, no," he replied, and then passed the buck. "I'm going to let Paul take it from here. Otherwise there's a danger we could repeat ourselves."

"Sure," Mark said.

They were down to business now. Quinn, who was focused and alert right from the start, moved forward to retrieve a thick red folder from the floor beside his chair. Loose papers bulged from within, secured uncertainly by strained elastic bands. The history of the case, all the raked-up dirt and bad news. Laying the file on the coffee table in front of him, he coughed damply and said, "Right. Let's kick this thing off." There were no preliminaries, no small talk. "Tell me what you know about the way Libra is set up, your actual holding companies and so on."

Mark put his elbows on his knees.

"London Libra is owned by an offshore company registered in Cyprus, to limit tax liability. Same thing goes for New York and Paris, two separate holding companies in Jersey controlling all the money from both clubs."

"And what else?" Quinn was confident and eager for information in a way that encouraged Mark. There was an idealistic quality to him, a young man's zeal. "What do you know about private investors, Macklin's role in all of this, the structure of the new Russian operation? How much do you know about that side of things?"

"The Russian club is going through Cyprus and our regular bank in Geneva. Same with the money from Ibiza in the summer and the cash from merchandising. France and Manhattan are two separate entities. Otherwise everything gets paid out of Switzerland. Staff, ground rent, booze, DJs, hardware. Everything." He felt like a corporate whistle-blower, spilling all the secrets. The feeling of this was intoxicating. "As for private investors, Seb still owns about sixty-five percent of the stock. Tom just looks after him, signs the checks and all that. Probably has a bit of equity, too. I don't know. Those two are like brothers."

Taploe stood up from the sofa and moved toward the window.

"Brothers," Quinn muttered. "But Macklin has power of attorney over Roth's affairs, is that right?"

"That's right."

"So in theory he can do whatever he likes?"

"In theory," Mark said. "But I'm not a lawyer, so I wouldn't know."

"Well, I am a lawyer and I'm telling you that's the situation." For the first time Quinn grinned, a crease at the edge of fat lips. Mark liked him. "When it comes to his relationship with Roth, Macklin is the main man, the *consigliere*, if you like. We reckon he's been buying up chunks of London real estate on behalf of the Russian mob, small businesses, too. As of this moment I have him as the main signatory on two hotels in Paddington, an entire residential block north of Marble Arch, a couple of bureaux de change out at City Airport, a minicab operation based not too far from here, even a chain of laundrettes in fucking Manchester. He's also looking into buying out a majority share in a Bayswater casino. Might have even done so by now. In other words, operations with a high-volume cash element which can be used to facilitate money laundering on a massive scale."

Suddenly Mark felt heavy in the stomach. He leaned back on the sofa so that his head was resting against the wall.

"Where's he getting the cash from?" he asked. "The Russians?"

"Exactly." Taploe had interrupted, frustrated at having remained silent for so long. In Quinn's company he often felt second-rate, shamed by the younger man's greater self-confidence and expertise. "We think Macklin is operating as one of several frontmen for the Kukushkin syndicate, buying up properties on their behalf and helping to clean illegal money."

"Which is what you suspected he was up to all along."

"Yes, it is." Taploe's eyes softened, as if he had been paid an unexpected compliment. "But now I have proof."

"Still," Quinn said, rubbing his scalp, "that's just one side of a more complicated situation." He began removing rubber bands from the red folder and placing them at the edge of the coffee table. "Do you know what I mean by the term 'double dip'?"

"No idea," Mark said.

"Well . . ."

Taploe cut him off in midsentence.

"In the model double-dip operation, an individual—or group of individuals—pretends to be depositing cash sums in a legitimate bank account while in reality he—or, of course, it could be she—is making payments into a separately located dummy account of exactly the same name."

Mark, confused, instinctively looked to Quinn for confirmation of this.

"That's actually right," he said, deferring uneasily to the boss. "Now, London Libra is owned by a single asset offshore based in Cyprus?"

"Right."

"Only when it came to your new venture in Moscow, Macklin devised what you might call a new strategy." Quinn moved forward heavily in his chair, to the point where Mark began to worry that it might actually topple over. "He seems to have convinced Roth not to own the club in his own name and not to be a signatory on any of the accounts."

"Why?" Mark asked.

"Simple. Same as what you were saying before. Because it would limit Roth's liability for creditors if Moscow went tits up. At the same time he reduces his capital gains bill in Russia. Roth apparently agreed—makes sense, after all—so Macklin went ahead and set up a second separate holding company in Cyprus. Called it Pentagon Investments, just so no one would pay much attention. He then appointed a small number of nominee directors—under his own control—and got his hands on a couple of bent accountants to cook the books."

Mark was struggling to keep up. His brain was a mulch of facts and theories, a puzzle he could not solve. He thought back to all the days and nights he had spent with Macklin, the restaurants and nightclubs in Moscow and St. Petersburg, all those endless plane journeys out of Heathrow with nothing to do but listen to Tom's stories. When had it all started? Macklin had led a double life wildly more dangerous and clandestine than his own, right under the noses of men who trusted him like a brother. *All of us are spies*, his father had once told him: *all of us inhabit a private world, a place of secrecies and evasion.*

"I'm not getting this," he said, shaking his head. "Where does the double dip come in?"

Quinn scraped his trainers against the carpet and coughed, folding bulky arms across his chest.

"Basically," he said, "like this. The main Libra holding company in Cyprus—the one you've all been told about—is still operational for London, Ibiza, T-shirts, compact discs." He pronounced "Ibiza" as "Eye-Beetha," an affectation for which Mark had always lacked the courage. "Then there's Pentagon Investments, which is used for Moscow. But Macklin has been playing both ends. Unknown to the Russians he's also set up an identically named dummy Pentagon account in the Cayman Islands. Every now and again, when he thinks no one's looking, Macklin has been redirecting some of the Russian cash into that account for his own personal enrichment."

"That's the double dip," Taploe said, stating the obvious. Quinn ignored him.

"At a guess," he said, "there's now something in the region of one point eight million buried away out there. Give or take."

"Holy fuck," Mark said, language Quinn seemed to enjoy. "And the Russians have got enough money they don't notice that's gone missing? How's this all getting generated?"

"Lot of ways." The room was now very warm, and Quinn's face looked cooked beside the bright yellow walls. He was flying. "Narcotics, prostitution, arms deals, precious metals, oil, timber, stolen cars, icon smuggling, you name it. He's entrepreneurial, your average Russian mafioso, and he robs people for a living. About thirty percent of the capital flight out of Russia these days is illegally earned. *Thirty percent.* And it has to get washed. Now and again a man like Viktor Kukushkin will try and improve his public image by donating a couple of million dollars to local charity. Generally speaking, though, he wants to hold on to his cash. And that's where blokes like Macklin come in. He's been cleaning Kukushkin's money through the hotels, through the cab company, through the bureaux de change. There's lots of it and it's moving all the time. You'd need a hundred officers working round the clock just to keep track of half of it."

"And Libra is a part of this?" There was resignation in Mark's voice, still a sickening loom in the stomach. "Tom's been laundering through the club."

" 'Fraid so." Quinn lifted several pages from the file and scratched at his left ear. "Nightclubs make ideal cover. Again the high cash element, again the rapid turnover. You charge punters sixteen quid for a couple of gin and tonics with ice and lemon, you're gonna make a lot of money very fast. Those invoices you've been signing off—most probably faked. Macklin has been doubling your weekly turnover for more than eighteen months, drawing up fake balance sheets, inventing staff and security personnel, saying he sold a hundred crates of Bacardi when he only sold fifty. That kind of thing."

"But I *saw* all of those," Mark insisted. "I see it all the time. Everything goes across my desk."

"You've been away a lot," Taploe said quickly, as if there were a way of letting Mark down gently. "Traveling overseas, delegating responsibility, seeing to your father's probate . . ."

"We also suspect that Macklin has other people working for him on the inside," Quinn continued. "But it's too early to tell."

"Inside *Libra*?" Mark stood up out of the sofa. The room was so small he barely had space to move. So much of his anger at Macklin and Roth had grown out of a conviction that they were in some way responsible for his father's death. And yet the scale of the deception purely within Libra, the liberties Macklin had taken with Mark's friendship and trust, momentarily seemed worse even than any involvement he or Roth might have had in the murder.

"One of these is a former employee of yours," Taploe said. "Left the company some time ago. A Mr. Philippe d'Erlanger."

Mark looked up. "*Philippe?*"

"He's been running an Italian restaurant in Covent Garden

and—how can I put this?—*assisting* Mr. Macklin with his business affairs."

"Assisting in what way?"

Taploe moved toward the window and pinched a clump of curtain fabric.

"He's one of the nominee directors of Pentagon, for a start. For the moment, however, what we're most interested in is his rapid turnover of female staff."

"Rapid turnover of female staff," Mark repeated.

"That's right." Quinn now took over. "Waitresses, bar staff, cloakroom attendants, the pretty girls on reception who smile at you when you walk in then don't speak any English. Birds from Poland, Romania, Bulgaria, Russia, the Balkans. They find jobs at the restaurant, then disappear when they're offered more lucrative ways of making a living."

"You mean prostitution."

"I do mean prostitution, yes. We know that Kukushkin has control of a network of apartments all over London that are being used by call girls with connections to organized crime. We've had d'Erlanger under surveillance for some time, although at present his role seems to be limited."

"Limited to what?"

"He simply acts as a middleman. The gangs organize to bring girls to the UK from locations right across central and eastern Europe, promising them jobs as au pairs, waitresses, dancers. D'Erlanger is one of several businessmen in London who offer them work so that they can remain in the country, then they run up debts, get their passports taken away by the gangs, and discover that the only way to break even is spending fourteen hours a day sucking cocks in South Kensington. Maybe you've noticed this with staff at Libra—barmaids or girls in admin who were given work by Macklin and then farmed out to Vladimir Tamarov."

"Tamarov?" Mark said. "The lawyer?"

"For lawyer, read gangster." Quinn spoke the word with relish. "Tamarov is number two in the Kukushkin organization and certainly their main player on the UK mainland. We think he's the one who controls the girls. There are three known Tamarov-controlled escort agencies on the Internet, all of them based in London."

"And you've been following him?"

"Him and others, yes." Taploe came forward, encouraged Mark to sit down, and then looked across at Quinn. "This is part of the reason why I've brought you here today. Tamarov has a bodyguard, a middle-aged Latvian thug by the name of Juris Duchev. In the past Macklin tended to meet him as a first point of contact in London or Moscow. Increasingly, however, he's been seeing Tamarov in person. Both Tamarov and Duchev are in London for the next three weeks. How would you feel about getting close to them, forging some kind of relationship?"

Mark laughed.

"You want me to make friends with the Russian mob?"

Taploe opted for flattery.

"Look," he said. "So far you've shown a real facility for winning people over. It's one of the reasons Paul and I are so grateful to have you on board." Tellingly, Quinn looked at the floor. "You obviously have your father's gift for intelligence work. The personal connections you could make would be worth months of surveillance."

Mark frowned. "What makes you think they'd trust me?"

"Just that," Taploe said, as if the simple fact of Mark's good nature provided him with the answer. "And we have fresh SIGINT which suggests that Macklin is now looking to bring someone in."

"You've heard him say that? That he wants me?"

"Not in so many words. But it's clear that the relationship between Libra and Kukushkin has become so complex, so far-reaching, that Macklin needs a partner. Someone other than d'Erlanger. Someone like yourself, in fact."

And so Mark found himself lured, flattered, finessed into a new area of intelligence work in which he had not anticipated being involved. From informer to plant, the ghost in the machine. It felt at first like a promotion, and appealed as much to his vanity as to any sense of duty toward his family. Yet Mark must have looked unsettled at the prospect because Taploe said, "There'd be no danger. You'd be under our watchful eye all the way."

"But why do you even need me to do it?" He was beginning to wonder if he had the nerve, the wherewithal to pull it off. "Why don't you just arrest all three of them? It sounds like you've got more than enough evidence."

"For legal reasons, mostly." Quinn stretched and a hair-scattered bulge of pale stomach appeared briefly beneath his shirt. "What the Yanks like to call attorney–client privilege. We had no right to do what we did at the Libra offices. Any information gathered from the premises under those conditions couldn't be presented in a court of law." He scratched a patch of fatty, dry skin on his arm. "We'd have to go through due process, obtain a writ, even get formal permission from the Law Society to go through Macklin's files again."

Mark frowned.

"So what was the point of it?"

"Evidence gathering. Building a picture." Taploe arranged his hair. "We need hard evidence against Kukushkin and Tamarov, not just against Macklin and the Belgian. And we're still trying to find out whether Roth had prior knowledge. Perhaps Paul didn't make it clear, but Roth's name is all over the documents. It's not unreasonable to suggest that he's been using Macklin to cover his own tracks. Roth could be double dipping Kukushkin, he could be a secret cosignatory on the Pentagon account, a director with the power to change the banking mandate. It's just too early to tell. The one thing we're trying to avoid is scaring off the Russians. I don't want simply to arrest a Thomas Macklin when six others just like him could grow overnight in his place. That's part of the reason I've never tried to recruit him. He might agree, but then tip off Tamarov or Duchev, even Kukushkin or Roth. And then what do we have? Probably Macklin in a body bag within forty-eight hours and an entire network of organized crime evaporated overnight. You *know* Sebastian, Mark. An operator as clever and capable as that would surely know what was going on in his own backyard."

"I suppose." Mark shrugged his shoulders. He felt like a child being sent out to play in the road.

"The trick is to let them do the talking," Taploe said, priming him for the task ahead. "Nurture any awkward silences. That forces people to open up. Agree with what Tamarov says, match his opinions with your own. If he feels that he can trust you then anything is possible."

"I'd also need you to find out whatever you can about a bloke called Timothy Lander," Quinn said.

"Go on."

"He's a banker, we think, based in the Caymans. Not, as far as we can tell, associated directly with Pentagon, but it's a tight community out there and there's a possibility a connection will be made. Your father made a series of telephone calls to his office in Grand Cayman in the weeks leading up to his death. There's no record that they've met, but the coincidence seems strange."

"I've never heard of him," Mark admitted.

"Well, I've asked our SIS station out there to look into it." Taploe suddenly looked pleased with himself. "The UK police are also interested in some work your father was doing for Divisar on behalf of a Swiss bank. Not Geneva based, but an investment house in Lausanne. Macklin or the Russians may have interests registered there which your father stumbled upon."

"Yes."

"So it's a big task we're facing," he said. "Much as we appreciate what you've achieved so far, there's still a great deal of work to be done."

34

A brilliant midwinter afternoon, clean white light pouring into the great Court of the British Museum. Ben felt bathed in limestone. He walked a circuit of the reading room and was revived. *Let Alice have lunch with whoever she likes. At least she has nothing to hide. At least there are no secrets between us.*

Long, chrome-legged tables with plastic tops were set out in rows perpendicular to the northwestern edge of the great Court. After half an hour Ben bought himself a cup of tea and sat down beside a young American student with bug eyes and a sprout of goatee beard. He was talking to a Japanese girl.

"You wanna know what really *amazes* me about the Kennedy assassination?" he was saying. "It's that the guy who shot him is most probably still out there."

"Unless the CIA already killed him," the girl replied. She had a faultless English accent and wore blue-rimmed glasses that were too big for her face.

"Sure," said goatee. "But if they didn't, I mean, if he's still at large, just imagine what goes through that guy's mind, like last thing at night. He'd be—what?—like *seventy* now?"

"I guess."

"Ben?"

A man was standing beside the table holding a guide to the museum in one hand and a walking stick in the other. McCreery.

"Jock." Ben stood up so quickly that his thighs knocked on the underside of the table, spilling a splash of tea onto the white surface. "Fancy seeing you here."

"Ditto. Are you on your own? Not with Alice?"

"Not with Alice," Ben said, and left it at that. "I thought you lived in Guildford."

It was a pointless remark, but he had been stuck for something to say. McCreery was Mark's friend, a stranger to Ben, a background figure in the chaos of death. Shorter and more overweight in the lower part of his body than Ben remembered, McCreery was wearing a bright green windcheater, hiking boots, and denim trousers with that pale fade particular to jeans worn by men in late middle age. He looked suitably dressed for a long walk on the Downs.

"I do live in Guildford, yes," he explained, leaning on the stick. "But I'm in town for the weekend. Haven't been here since Foster stuck the roof on. Appalling, isn't it?"

"I think it's incredible," Ben told him, and wondered if McCreery would respect his honesty.

"Do you really? For me it's highly derivative of Pei, you know, the Oriental chap who messed up the Louvre."

The Japanese girl appeared to swallow hard as Ben said, "Right. Look, do you want to sit down?"

"If that would be all right. Are you sure? Thank you."

Goatee shuffled along and McCreery squeezed in, laying his walking stick at an angle across the table.

"What did you do to your leg?"

"Rheumatism." McCreery gave a self-deprecatory shrug. "Runs in the family, I'm afraid. My late father suffered from it, his father before him. There's been a long line of McCreerys hobbling about in their fifties."

Ben made a small noise in the back of his throat and wondered how long McCreery would stick around. Already he could feel the afternoon slipping from his grasp. They had only one subject in common and he was not in the mood to discuss his father. Sure enough, McCreery soon embarked on a conversation about the funeral.

"So who did you talk to at the wake?" he asked.

"Oh, everybody and nobody. A lot of my father's colleagues. People from Divisar and . . ." Ben searched for the appropriate euphemism ". . . your company." McCreery smiled in an effort to acknowledge his tact. "To be honest, I found it hard going. Alice was great. You and your wife were both very kind. But I just couldn't get my head round the whole thing, you know? Sort of took the wind out of me."

"Of course," McCreery said. "Of course. I must say that both Gillian and I were rather concerned about you."

"About *me*?"

"Yes. Conscious that you didn't want to be there, that you'd rather have been somewhere else. I went upstairs to my bedroom at one point and saw you standing alone on the drive. Felt for you, old chap. Bloody awful thing. I'm so sorry."

Ben didn't know whether to be embarrassed or grateful.

"Well, I just went out for a smoke," he said. "Just to grab some air, that was all."

"Of course."

McCreery bobbed his head gently and looked up at the roof. He appeared to be giving it a second chance, but then frowned and finally settled his gaze on a nearby Egyptian sculpture. Changing the subject, he asked after Alice and then briefly discussed an article she had written in the *Standard* a few days earlier. Ben began to warm to him, if only because McCreery appeared to be showing a genuine interest in his family's welfare. He asked thoughtful, intelligent questions about the police inquiry, and seemed acutely sensitive to the unique psychological predicament in which Ben and Mark had found themselves. McCreery's concern was all the more touching when Ben considered that he too had lost a friend, a man he had worked alongside at MI6 for almost twenty years. The idea of losing one of his own close friends was one of Ben's deepest fears.

"I guess it's been difficult for you, too," he said. "Dad was your best mate. It can't have been easy."

McCreery sighed.

"Well, it's funny," he said. "One gets older, one has to adjust to sudden loss. The booze, accidents of one kind or another, bloody cancer. But there was something very special about Christopher. I think it's a great tragedy that you never had the opportunity to know him as well as we all did. A very great tragedy indeed."

Ben remembered the conversation on the drive at McCreery's house, Robert Bone saying something very similar about Keen. He thought of Bone's letter and wondered if McCreery could be trusted with its contents. "You know, when people die, everybody writes, don't they?" he said. McCreery looked slightly confused. "I mean, the husband, the wife, they always get a letter. Then you write to the children, to the parents if they had any, to all the close relatives of the person who's died. But the friends just get left behind. Nobody thinks of them. They've maybe just lost the one person in the world that they could confide in, someone where the roots might have gone even deeper than a marriage. A friend from school. A friend from childhood. But nobody thinks of them. They just get forgotten."

McCreery produced a wonderful smile that broke up the general blandness of his features, the pale, puffy cheeks, the thinning gray hair. His eyes seemed to congratulate Ben for the observation.

"Yes," he said. "I must say I didn't receive a single letter of condolence about your father. Not a single one." Making a joke of it, he added, "And you?"

"Fifty-three at the last count," Ben said, and they both started to laugh.

"Including mine?" McCreery asked.

"Including yours."

It was a lovely moment, rueful and sustained. Goatee and the Japanese girl were long gone, and they were now alone at the table.

"Makes me think of my own son," McCreery said. "My eldest, Dan."

"You have children?"

"Two, yes. We've just had the most almighty bloody row, as a matter of fact."

"What about?"

"Well, I can't really stand Dan's wife," McCreery replied, matter-of-factly. "And I'm absolutely certain that she can't stand me."

"That's not easy."

"No, no, it's not. How do you get on with Alice's parents?"

"So-so," Ben said. "Her mother drinks too much, does a lot of charity work and Chardonnay. Dad's a self-made millionaire. Wants to play golf with me the whole time and calls Alice his 'princess.' Still, they're decent people." McCreery smiled as Ben repeated his earlier question. "What did you argue about?"

And it took him several seconds to compose his thoughts. The great Court was now very crowded and there was a long queue at the café.

"Well, I think Bella—that's my daughter-in-law—is of the opinion that Gillian and I rather ruined Dan's life," he said.

"How's that?"

"Oh, the usual Foreign Office whinge. Winging him around the world as a small boy. Germany, London, Moscow. She thinks he never settled, never put down any roots."

"Is that important?"

"Well, apparently." McCreery squeezed his eyes shut and blinked rapidly. "She's done a bit of a job on him, actually, convinced Dan that we were somehow unsuitable as parents. Let's see, at the last count I was an imperialist snob, a racist, and—let me get this right—a typical Tory homophobe."

"Jesus." Ben looked taken aback but tried to keep the mood light. "She really doesn't like you."

"Yes, I'd made the mistake of voicing my disapproval of the FCO's current willingness to allow gay ambassadors to cohabit with their—dreadful word—'partners' overseas. Bella, quite rightly I suppose, thought this was an appallingly reactionary stance and encouraged Dan to leave the restaurant."

"You were in a restaurant?"

"We were in a restaurant."

Four German tourists bearing trays of tea and sandwiches approached the table and sat down. McCreery acknowledged them with a nod.

"There's actually a rather sobering thought behind all this," he said. "We are terribly possessive as a species, Ben, particularly women, I think. It has something to do with insecurity, with the human need to establish territory. Bella perceives Gillian and me as a threat and has very systematically gone about the process of pushing us away."

"It sounds like it."

"Yes, she's a bloody fool. I have no designs on my son, no wish to prevent him from living the kind of life he wants to lead. But she wants him for herself, you see. She feels threatened. One or two of his friends have told me that it's much the same thing for them. She's turned him against them and they never see Dan anymore. She simply won't allow it."

Ben secretly felt that Dan sounded ineffectual, but he was nevertheless sympathetic to McCreery's dilemma. His father had been lucky to have him as a friend. McCreery did not appear to take himself too seriously, yet he possessed a serious, analytical mind and an appealing honesty. He wondered if he had been unfairly critical of intelligence men, and felt guilty for having prejudged McCreery, even if some of his opinions were wildly out of date. He was on the point of going to the car and fetching the copy of Bone's letter when McCreery announced that he wanted to move.

"Do you mind if we walk around a bit?" he said, picking up his stick. "It's just that my leg's a bit sore."

"Of course," Ben replied. "Of course."

"You don't have to be off anywhere?"

"No, nowhere at all."

"Well, good then. I must say, I'm enjoying our little conversation."

McCreery stood up and moved back from the table. He sought his balance on the stick and put a hand on Ben's back.

"It's bloody good to have run into you, actually," he said. "Really made my afternoon. Now let's go and feel smug about the Elgin Marbles or something, shall we? That always gives me a kick."

35

You see things as a Watcher. You see the private lives of public men, the lies and the cop-outs of power. You witness acts of violence, acts of greed. Above all, there is the interminable tedium of nothing going on. Ian Boyle had seen it all. This was not his first adultery.

He was assigned to Roth from 9 a.m. on Saturday morning, taking over from Graham, who had done the overnight shift in the Southern Electric van. He had to wait a couple of hours while Roth preened himself inside and then left the house at 11:16, looking tanned and spruce, the innocent ease of the guilty man. His 6-series BMW was parked on the corner and Ian followed it at a three- or four-car distance as Roth drove north via Chelsea toward the bustle of Notting Hill. He had a pretty good idea where he was going: the rumors had been rife all week. Sure enough, Roth pulled up outside the house on Elgin Crescent, then checked his hair for a long time in the rear-view mirror before making a call on his mobile phone. To her. Inside. Ian saw it all. When he had finished speaking, Roth put the hazard lights on and started the engine. He wasn't staying.

She came out pretty quickly. Looking beautiful, the way she always did, a terrible temptation for a man and aware of that power and using it all the time. They didn't kiss as she stepped into the car, but that was probably just a precaution for the neighbors. Instead, there was a movement, a kind of visible friction in the front seat, and Roth appeared to hand Alice what must have been a present. And then they were off, his hand stroking the back of her neck, then changing gear, then touching her again. Ian felt terrible for Benjamin.

He followed them to the Lanesborough Hotel. They went in separately and stayed for more than four hours. While he was waiting, Ian discovered that the room had been booked under a false name. A Mr. Dulong, of Edinburgh. It was a week before he discovered just how sick that was, just how conceited Roth had been. At one point Ian phoned Taploe and told him what was going on, but the boss had just sounded vindicated, as if Roth's behavior justified the increased surveillance, proving a larger crime.

The only thing that surprised Ian about the whole sorry, shabby affair was how angry Alice looked when she emerged from the hotel at 4:46 p.m. As if they'd had a row. It wasn't the look, at least, of a woman who'd had herself a good time. But then Ian had never been very good at reading the female face; perhaps that was why he had never risen any higher within the Service. His own wife, after all, had tricked him for months: all that time saying she was going to be late back from work and all that time fucking another man. Ian thought about Ben again and wondered if it would be unethical to get a message to him through Blindside.

Coming down the steps of the hotel, Alice pulled a phone from her bag. Ian noticed that her hair was still slightly wet at the back of her neck, a flush in her cheeks from the shower. She dialed a number and began looking round for a cab. And then she was talking, arguing, jabbing the air with her hand. Ian had a good idea who she was speaking to, a hunch of intuition. Ten quid, he said, laying a little wager with himself as Alice stepped into a cab. Ten quid that the spoilt little bitch is feeling guilty about what she's just done and is taking it out on *him*.

36

"Alice, what I'm trying to tell you is that I just don't have time to talk about this now . . ."

Ian was right. Ben was standing outside a smoky pub in Russell Square, Bone's letter in his hand, fending off an Alice moan.

"All I'm asking," she said, "is that you show me a little sympathy. I've been at work all day and nobody was around to help me out and I just wanted someone to understand that. All you've done is spent the last five minutes saying it's not that big a problem. It's just typical male behavior."

Ben momentarily moved the phone away from his ear, staring at it in disbelief.

"That's all I *was* doing," he said. He could see McCreery staring at him from inside the pub. "I was *trying* to understand, Alice, trying to show you a little sympathy. But you aren't interested in seeing that, in listening to what I'm saying. You just want to use your situation at work as an excuse to get angry with me, as a way of making me feel bad instead of you. And now you're saying that it's 'typical male behavior.' I can't fucking believe that we're even having this conversation . . ."

He heard the squeal of the taxi's brakes. "Are you in a cab?" he asked.

"Yes," she said.

"Look, try to understand this." Ben hoped that he could end the conversation with one swift speech. "I am your husband. I automatically understand and share anything that affects you. That's what it means to love somebody. You hurt when they hurt. So take it as read that I am *sympathetic*. Take it as read that if my wife calls me up in the pub while she's having a shitty day at work, I am *understanding*. But if all you want is sympathy and a kind of mute approbation, get a dog." McCreery was now standing at the bar, buying them a third pint. "The difference between me and a cocker spaniel is that I am able to offer you something more than a dog can; that is, a *solution* to your problem. And I don't know why it's suddenly fashionable for women to consider that as some sort of male flaw. If I were you, I'd be grateful for the second opinion."

"So what *is* your solution?" she said.

"I've just told you. I told you ten minutes ago, at the start of this fucking conversation. Go home, take a bath, watch a DVD, and relax. You can go back in tomorrow, get one of the work experience people to help with your research, and finish the piece. Now I'm here with Jock, we're talking about the letter. I can't do anything about this at the moment. I have to go."

If he hadn't hung up, she would have kept him on the line for another half an hour. Ben ended the call, switched off the phone, and put it in his jacket pocket.

McCreery was still at the bar, a pint of Guinness settling on the counter next to a tumbler of whisky.

"Everything all right, old chap?"

"Sure. That was Alice on the phone."

"Woman trouble?"

"Woman trouble."

He handed the letter to McCreery.

"Like I was saying before, I'm only showing you this because I think you have a right to see it. I can't go to the police because I don't know how the Secrets Act works. But it seems important that you should get a look at it."

Very calmly, McCreery extracted Bone's letter from the envelope.

"This is the photocopy?" he said.

"That's the photocopy."

At a nearby table, a group of men erupted into laughter and one of them knocked over a glass. Ironic applause amid mutterings of, "Nice one, Dave." McCreery frowned as he held the letter in his hand, six pages of crumpled A4.

"How long did you say you've had this?" he said.

"Just a few days. I made the copy when I received it. For Mark," Ben lied. He did not yet want to tell McCreery that he had been planning to give the copy to a contact in Customs and Excise.

"Mark didn't get one himself?"

"I have no idea. I haven't spoken to him in days."

"Why don't we sit down? I'd like to read it."

They returned to their table in a quieter corner of the pub. Ben felt that he had drunk too much on an empty stomach, two pints of Guinness as McCreery regaled him with stories about his father. His head felt light and dizzy. It took Jock ten minutes to read the letter, his face occasionally jolting into a look of disbelief. When he had finished, he said, "Do you mind if I read it again?" Ben took the opportunity to visit the gents. Before he returned, he bought himself a packet of cigarettes from a vending machine and some crisps and peanuts at the bar. McCreery was on the final page as he sat down.

"Bob has always had some fairly potty theories about what went on in Afghanistan."

"So you knew him?"

"Oh, absolutely."

"What kind of theories?" Ben asked.

McCreery waved his hand dismissively over the table, as if to swat them away.

"Oh, I won't bore you with that now. Suffice to say, the Yanks have had it up to here with his conspiracies." He chopped a hand against his forehead and took a swig of his double Scotch. "I had a nasty feeling he'd do something like this."

"So it's true."

Ben laughed nervously as he asked the question.

"Oh, god, no. Well, not all of it, in any event. All this stuff about Bob being Station Chief in Berlin is complete balls, for a start. I don't know what he's talking about. Bone was a Cousin, certainly, but very low on the food chain."

"A Cousin?" Ben asked.

"CIA." McCreery assumed a quieter voice. "He did end up in Afghanistan, but Christopher would hardly have regarded him as a friend. Far as I'm aware, they only met half a dozen times. Bob was a bit fuckstruck by the Brits, to be honest, a complete Anglophile. Boodles and the Queen, all that empire jazz, made him drool like a puppy. So an old-school operator like your father would have been right up his street. Old Bobby Bone loved a bit of posh."

McCreery appeared to look back at the letter and emitted a gusty laugh on page four.

"And this bit's absolute cock," he said, waving the paper noisily in his hand. Ben couldn't tell whether McCreery was genuinely irritated or just being loyal to the firm. "Neither was your father continually based in Kabul, nor was he undeclared. He simply made visits to the Afghan capital from time to time. Until later on. Bone was mostly working for an aid organization, and then only as a conduit for American funding. The Yanks were chucking so much money at the Soviet problem they didn't know if it was arseholes or breakfast time."

"So why would Bone just make all this stuff up?"

With a theatrical lurch of his eyebrows, McCreery intimated that the American was simply demented.

"God knows," he said. "Perhaps some of it's true. I ran agents for years that Christopher knew nothing about. That's the business we were in. And Bob's analysis of the Soviet army is pretty accurate. The drugs, the bullying, the corruption. But the idea that a foreign diplomat—particularly a tall, white, elegantly attired Brit like Christopher Keen—could just walk around the bazaars of Kabul calmly recruiting disgruntled Russian soldiers is frankly lunatic. One might as well try hitchhiking in Piccadilly. Your father was a pedigree intelligence officer, my god, but even that would have been beyond his considerable talents. Besides, one didn't have authorization to go after members of the occupying forces. That wasn't our brief. We were anxious to get our hands on Soviet military technology, certainly, but their officers were exceptionally well disciplined and very unlikely to turn. As for their subordinates, the Office already had highly placed sources in Moscow who completely negated the need to pitch lower echelons."

"Echelons," like "Cousins," was another euphemism with which Ben was unfamiliar. Instead, he said, "What about what Bone says about the SAS?" he asked. "About you training the mujahideen?"

McCreery hesitated.

"Quasi-accurate, at best. We certainly sponsored de-badged British soldiers to report on the muj, and SAS did take a contingent to Scotland for training. But not to the Highlands, as our friend attests. The exercises took place in the Hebrides."

"And you were there?"

McCreery rolled his neck and implied with a glance that Ben should ask a different question.

"Sorry," he said. "I didn't mean to pry."

"Oh, heavens, don't worry. I'm just not at liberty to discuss specific operations in which I may or may not have been involved. Bit old-fashioned like that. Take my responsibilities rather seriously."

"Of course."

"Unlike dear Mr. Bone, it seems, who has committed a flagrant breach of security. Still, that's the American way. Shoot first, ask questions later."

"Friendly fire," Ben said, without really meaning to, and Jock smiled. "So what *was* my father doing in Afghanistan? Can you at least tell me that? Can you tell me if there's any link between him and this guy Kostov?"

McCreery coughed.

"Let me give you a little history lesson," he said. Whisky in hand, hair faintly disheveled, McCreery might have been a professor of poetry discussing Yeats down the pub. "Throughout the 1980s, the Afghan resistance received arms and ammunition from a number of different sources: China, Egypt, the Pakistani intelligence service. Even bloody Gaddafi got in on the act. Additional bulk funding was provided by the Saudis, the Reagan administration, and, to a lesser extent, the Frogs, the Japs, and our own Conservative government. Mrs. Thatcher was a huge fan of Abdul Haq, for example, a key mujahideen figure who was eventually murdered by the Taliban. Quite an alliance, I'm sure you'd agree, but we were all aware that the Soviets were trying to surround the oil fields of the Gulf, which would have been catastrophic for the international community. At that time the CIA station in Islamabad was America's largest international intelligence operation, far bigger than Nicaragua, Angola, and El Salvador combined. Bone is right about a lot of this. Now, there was a hawk in Texas, man by the name of Charles Wilson, a boneheaded Congressman of the McCarthy mold, who was paranoid up to his eyeballs about Reds under the bed. Yes, for him—and for others with Reagan's ear—Afghanistan *was* to be the Soviet Vietnam, no question. Wilson was a big fish in the House Armed Services and Intelligence Committee and he pushed a lot of money the way of the mujahideen."

Ben was beginning to glaze over with facts. He felt suddenly cold from the open pub door and put on his coat.

"Alas, Wilson and others in Congress backed the wrong horse, and America has been paying for it ever since. Bone, as a CIA man, has a vested interest in playing down those failings at the expense of my own—and your father's—organization. Allow me, for example, to illustrate the mess that many of us are still to this day cleaning up. Bill Casey, the head of the CIA whom Bone refers to in his letter, took a liking to an individual by the name of Gulbaddin Hekmatyar, who was the leader of the most fanatical group of mujahideen, Hezb-i-Islami. By fanatical, I mean pan-Islam, that is to say an organization virulently opposed to all things Western, from *Dallas* to Warren Buffett. This was an irony apparently lost on the Pentagon, who clearly thought he was Mahatma Gandhi. Both the Pakistani government and its intelligence service—without either of whom the Cousins simply couldn't operate—were also card-carrying members of the Hekmatyar fan club, which rather explains the relationship. No matter that he'd organized the killing of other mujahideen leaders in order to cement his power base, and had never been directly involved in any confrontation with the Soviet invasionary forces. That didn't seem to bother the Yanks. Perhaps eventually, they wanted a fundamentalist regime in Kabul to destabilize the communists in the north. Who knows? Always playing god, the Americans, never keep things simple. And, of course, these U.S.-backed fundamentalists have had a field day ever since, knocking off Sadat in '81, blowing up U.S. Marines in Lebanon. When it came to the Gulf War, in fact, Hekmatyar was one of the first public figures to denounce American involvement in Kuwait. Lovely way of repaying the favor, don't you think?"

"I'm sorry," Ben said, licking peanut salt off his fingers. "What does any of this have to do with Kostov?"

"I'm coming to that." McCreery reacted as if Ben were being impatient. "I'm trying to paint a picture of blatant American incompetence which feeds into the Mischa situation."

"So Mischa *did* exist?"

"Oh, absolutely. He must have existed. Yes." McCreery scratched the back of his neck. "Now, at one stage your father helped to set up an organization called Afghan Aid, which nominally worked on medical and agricultural projects for refugees. However, it also provided support for Ahmed Shah Masood, a far more sensible and moderate muj leader who was later to command the Northern

Alliance. You may recall that he was assassinated immediately prior to September eleventh."

"Yeah, I remember reading about that."

"Well, he was another favorite of Thatcher's."

"I see."

But then silence. Ben had been expecting McCreery to elaborate further, to steer his little history lesson toward Mischa, but the monologue appeared to have ended. Perhaps the guarded spook who had spoken with so little candor at his father's funeral was simply preprogrammed never to divulge useful information.

"Is that it?"

"Is what it?"

"Well, what about Mischa? Did my father recruit him or not?"

McCreery actually laughed at this to the point where Ben might have lost his temper.

"What's funny, Jock?" he said. The use of his first name felt oddly impertinent, regardless of the fact that they had spent most of the afternoon together.

"Well, I'm simply not in a position to talk about that in much detail. It's very much still under wraps. You can understand—"

"No, I *don't* really understand. Forgive me for saying so, but this is exactly what happened at the crematorium. A few carrots dangled in front of the congregation, and then you withdraw. MI6 have access to a well of memories that for some reason must remain secret, because that is what the State has decreed. Now I respect that, Jock, I really do, but I need to know about Kostov. I need to know whether Bone is telling the truth. So far all you've given me is a potted history of Mrs. Thatcher's affection for a couple of guys whose names I can't pronounce."

McCreery gave an affectionate shrug that appeared to suggest compliance.

"Forgive me," he said. "You're absolutely right. Old habits die hard. And if I appeared evasive at the funeral service, it was only because I was in the presence of one or two people who would not have taken kindly to *Spycatcher* from the pulpit." McCreery laughed at his own joke. "If you want to know about Mischa and Dimitri Kostov, I can tell you, but only with the cast-iron guarantee that any information divulged will go no further than this table."

"Of course, Jock . . ."

"That means even Mark." McCreery looked very insistent about this. "And Alice, of course. *Particularly* Alice, as a matter of fact, in view of her chosen profession."

"I can guarantee that."

McCreery looked around, as if to be sure that any further conversation would be muffled by the swirl of noise in the pub.

"Are we OK to talk about this here?" Ben asked.

"I think so." He leaned forward. "Mischa Kostov was a source for the Americans. An agent of the CIA." McCreery's voice was a ham actor's whisper. "The story Robert Bone relates is accurate in as much as it refers to an actual relationship between a Western intelligence service and a member of the Soviet armed forces. But I would recommend that for every mention of your father's name you substitute that of a Cousin whose identity I am afraid I am not at liberty to divulge. Suffice to say that he was a close friend of Mr. Bone. His mentor, in a manner of speaking."

McCreery shuffled forward and frowned. He seemed troubled by his leg.

"Mischa's father, Dimitri, was indeed a KGB officer whose aliases included Vladimir Kalugin and—I think I'm right about this—Leonid Sudoplatov. He was not, however, a member of Department V, and certainly never carried out Kremlin-sponsored executive actions. That's absolute nonsense. The other rather important thing to bear in mind about Dimitri Kostov is that he died in 1997."

Ben was halfway through what must have been his fifteenth cigarette of the afternoon when the lower part of his mouth fell away, issuing a broad cloud of uninhaled smoke out in front of his face.

"Kostov is dead?"

"Yes. As is Mischa, though in rather more violent circumstances. Exactly as Bone attests, he was shot in Samarkand by order of court martial sometime in the late 1980s."

"So my father never had anything to do with him?"

"Nothing at all. The Yanks lost him. He was their joe." McCreery picked the letter up from the table. "Which makes Bone's suggestion that Mischa was like a son to Christopher particularly unpleasant in the circumstances."

"Yeah, I could have done without that," Ben admitted, eating a crisp.

"I'm sure you could."

"So who *did* kill my father?"

It was the only question left to ask.

McCreery paused. "Between you and me—and again I would ask that this is something we keep strictly *entre nous*—the Office has been working very closely alongside Scotland Yard to unravel that very question. Right now, we're looking at one or two irregularities with regard to your father's relationship with a Swiss bank."

Ben shook his head. "What does that mean?"

McCreery shuffled forward and seemed troubled by his leg.

"Shortly before he died, Christopher was doing some work for Divisar on behalf of a private bank in Lausanne. There may be a connection there. We're also looking into a series of telephone calls that he made to a Timothy Lander in the Cayman Islands."

"That's not a name I've heard before. How come the police haven't told us about it?"

"As I was saying, that part of the investigation is still very much under wraps."

"So you're claiming that almost everything in Bone's letter is faked-up to deflect attention away from the fact the CIA lost an agent in Afghanistan nearly twenty years ago?"

McCreery wiped away an imaginary speck of dust from the surface of the table and said, "To all intents and purposes, yes."

For the last time, Ben took hold of the letter and began going through it, picking out the facts.

"So it's bullshit that Dad worked for British Intelligence for twenty years?"

"Seventeen."

"And he never went to Berlin?"

"No, he was in Berlin, but declared, and only for eighteen months. That was immediately after he left your mother in the mid-1970s."

Ben flicked through three more pages until he found what he was looking for.

"And what about this?" He stabbed the letter with the end of his thumb. "Was he ever assigned to China?"

"Never went there in his life." McCreery finished his whisky. "And Bone didn't quit the Cousins in '92, either. He was thrown out after the Kostov cock-up, turned to the drink and became a teacher. Humanities, if I'm not mistaken. Now there's an irony."

Taking the letter back from Ben, he added, "Just look at the way he phrases certain things as a means of disguising his guilt. It's bloody amateur hour. Here, on the third page." McCreery quoted, from the text. "*I never met Mischa, of course, but I know he was a sweet kid.* Don't you see, Ben? That's a blatant lie. The sheer *nerve* of the man. And what does he say later on? That he interrogated a Soviet soldier *independently* of Christopher and Mischa? Total cock-and-bull. The Soviet soldier *was* Mischa. How else do you think Bone knows so much about the Russian military?"

"All right, all right," Ben said quickly. He felt compelled to add: "It's not that I don't believe you. I just want to get to the bottom of who killed Dad. That's it. Everything else is irrelevant . . ."

". . . and I can understand that."

"But Bone's not a sadist. He bears no grudge against me. Why pull me aside at the funeral and then write six pages of bullshit about Kostov and M16? Why involve me at all?"

"Alice," McCreery replied instantly.

"Alice?"

"Think about it. She works for a major newspaper. Bone's hoping she'll leak the story to the news desk and embarrass the Brits."

"But she would never do that." It was a statement that lacked conviction.

"Bob's not to know that, is he? This is not a benevolent individual we're talking about. Bone and Masterson were two of the most unsavory characters I've ever had the misfortune of coming into contact with in over thirty years of intelligence work."

Ben seized on the mistake.

"Masterson is the mentor?" he said. "The one who actually recruited Mischa?"

"Oh, dear." A pantomime of embarrassment played across

McCreery's face. He touched his mouth with his hand. "I shouldn't have revealed his name. That was an error. I apologize."

"Don't worry about it, Jock. I'm not going to tell anyone."

"Good. Good. Well, look, I must catch that train back to Guildford." McCreery was standing, fetching his stick. "In the meantime, if I could just hang on to the letter and take a longer look at it, that would be most helpful. We've already lost one and you can imagine that we don't want this sort of thing lying around . . ."

Ben hesitated. To refuse would seem odd. He made a mental note of Kostov's aliases for the benefit of Alice's contact in Customs and Excise and said, "Of course. Be my guest."

McCreery looked pleased. He pocketed the letter, saying, "Your other one's bound to turn up."

"Sure it is."

"And look, I don't need to tell you again that the fewer people that know about this, the better."

"I understand that."

Ben was also on his feet, watching McCreery pull a windcheater over his head. He had the sudden but irrefutable feeling that he was being palmed off. The mood of their conversation had changed markedly.

"Have you spoken to Bone since you received it?" McCreery asked.

"No," Ben said, falling in behind him as they walked to the door. "He didn't leave a number. Just a P.O. Box address in New Hampshire."

"I see."

It was as if McCreery was more than just late for a train. He seemed hurried, his job done. Out on the street they turned to one another.

"Well it was super to see you, it really was." The charm in his eyes, all the warmth and friendliness engendered in the course of the afternoon, had evaporated. Now McCreery looked distant and removed.

"Yeah, it was good to see you too, Jock."

"And good luck with your art," he said, employing a term that Ben detested. "Don't worry, old boy, don't worry," he called out, hobbling around the corner. "We'll get to the bottom of this thing, you'll see. It's all just a question of *time.*"

37

"Something's not right, brother. Something is not *right*." Ben was pacing in the kitchen at Elgin Crescent, sections of Wednesday's *Guardian* scattered across the floor.

"The letter goes missing from my studio, your version never even shows up. Jock says it's crap from start to finish, then insists I keep the contents to myself. Somebody, somewhere, knows something that we don't. Somebody, somewhere, is covering something up."

Seated calmly at the kitchen table, Mark smiled to himself and invited Ben to sit down.

"I'd prefer standing," he said.

"Fine. Then why don't you begin at the beginning? Why don't you just tell me what this Yank actually *said*." It took Ben fifteen minutes to describe the contents of Bone's letter in detail. He was flustered but remained concise. He told Mark about Mischa, he told him about Kostov. His brother listened carefully, but in the manner of a card player who knows he holds the ace.

When he had finished, Ben said, "You don't look like this is making any impact on you at all."

"I don't?"

"No. You don't."

"Well, where did the letter come from?" Mark asked.

Ben looked at him.

"That's all you have to ask? That's the one thing you want to know? Where it *came* from?"

"Well it's a start." Mark was aware that he sounded smug, that he was playing the old hand and professional spook, but it was fun watching Ben flounder around in a misconception.

"You're not interested in Sudoplatov?" his brother asked. "You don't want to know about Kalugin?"

Mark tilted back in his chair. He put his hands behind his head and grinned again.

"What the fuck is so funny?"

Not for the first time, Mark weighed up the possibility of telling Ben about Blindside. Just to see the look on his face; just to put him in the picture.

"Nothing's funny," he said. "I promise you, nothing's funny at all."

"Then why are you looking at me like I'm a fucking idiot?"

"Because if Jock says the letter's a crock of shit written by a drunk who got thrown out of the CIA then I'm inclined to believe him. If Mischa was an American failure, if Kostov actually *died* in 1997, then what the fuck are you getting so upset about?"

"I'm not upset," Ben said.

"Yes, you are."

"I'm just annoyed."

"About what?"

Mark wondered if some of the tension between them had been precipitated by the will. Ben had asked for his share of the money, but had done it grudgingly, as if the request put him in Mark's debt. He noticed that he didn't answer his question.

"Look," Mark said, trying to make him feel better. "Did this Bone guy leave an address?"

Ben's reply was sarcastic.

"No. This Bone guy did *not* leave an address. Just a P.O. Box number in New Hampshire."

"Exactly."

Ben looked at him as if he had lost control of his senses.

"*Exactly?*"

Mark stood up. He had weighed up the odds. So what if Ben found out about Kukushkin and Randall, about Tamarov and Tom? Where was the harm? An electric combination of vanity and common sense persuaded him to break cover. He drained the coffee he had been drinking, half a cup in a single gulp, and said, "Is that locked?"

Ben looked at the kitchen door leading out into the garden.

"What, that? No. I go out there all the time."

"Then let's get some air. Let's go outside for a chat."

The garden was colder than it looked, furniture damp to the touch, a settling of dew on the grass. Mark peered over neighboring fences—both sides to check if they could be overheard—then returned to the terrace, where he sat in a narrow wicker chair buckled by English weather. Ben remained on his feet and said, with undisguised derision, "Well, this makes a nice change."

Mark was wondering where to begin. Somehow he had always

known that he was going to tell Ben. It was just a question of the timing.

"What are we doing out here, brother? It's fucking freezing."

Mark leaned forward in the chair, little creaks and snaps. Then he looked away from the house, toward the south end of the garden, and said, "We're out here because I know the real reason why Dad was killed."

Ben took the news evenly, with no discernible movement beyond a slight creasing around the eyes.

"Say that again?"

"Sit down, Benjamin."

Mark only called him "Benjamin" when things were serious. He had called him "Benjamin" when the cancer was quickening and their mother had six weeks to live. Ben buttoned up his coat, settled on the edge of the garden table, and waited.

"I'm not supposed to tell you this." Mark looked very serious, all the playfulness and swagger gone from his face. He seemed burdened by some terrible responsibility, an expression that managed to irritate his brother still further. "For the last couple of months I've been working for a man called Bob Randall. He's an officer with MI5."

Ben found that he could not laugh.

"*MI5?*"

"Yes."

"Well, that explains a lot." The lightness of this reply belied Ben's total surprise; he experienced a jealous kick of sudden and unexpected resentment.

"Seb and Tom Macklin have been under surveillance for almost a year. Tom has been laundering money for a Moscow crime syndicate run by a man called Viktor Kukushkin. He's tricked everybody, maybe even Seb; nobody knows to what extent the boss is involved. For months, Tom's been buying up real estate, fixing invoices, moving money around the clubs, dealing with a character called Vladimir Tamarov who's Kukushkin's number one over here. They're running hookers in from eastern Europe, pushing class As, the whole lot."

Ben was shaking his head.

"And Dad found out about this while he was working for Divisar?"

"It looks that way." Mark glanced up at the house. It was as if the entire edifice of Elgin Crescent might be eavesdropping on their conversation. "That's why we have to talk out here. I don't want to come over all Harry Palmer, but there's a very small chance your place is wired."

Now Ben laughed.

"Don't be ridiculous," he said, dismissing the notion because it gave him a moment of power. "What do I have to do with it? Nobody bugs the home of a *painter*."

"Fine," Mark replied, and was forced to concede that he had perhaps overreacted. "Still, it's better not to talk about anything sensitive when you're inside the house."

"OK, James," Ben whispered, mocking Mark's tone. He pursed out his lips and looked camp. "Are you licensed to kill, brother? Have you got gadgets and herpes?"

Mark didn't laugh.

"Macklin has been redirecting some of the Kukushkin money into a secret offshore bank account in the Cayman Islands. Before Dad died he had several conversations with a banker out there called Timothy Lander."

"I've heard that name." Ben stood up. The backs of his legs felt damp beneath his clothes. "McCreery used it. Told me exactly the same thing."

"About Lander?"

"About Lander."

"Well, there you go." Mark was glad that Ben at last looked appropriately respectful. "Five and Six are both trying to find the same guy. I reckon Lander queried what was going on, told Dad about it, and Macklin had him shot before he whiffed the gig to the Russians. Either that or he simply found out that Viktor and Tom were in bed together and threatened to go to the police."

"So the whole Kostov thing really is bullshit?"

"Total bullshit. A red herring. Probably dreamed up by Kukushkin to throw us off the scent. That's why I asked you where the letter came from. Kukushkin's people in New York probably rented out the P.O. Box, got hold of Bone's stationery, then faked the letter. That's why there was no fixed address. The Russian mob's full of former KGB and soldiers who did time in central Asia. They'd know all about what Western intelligence got up to out there during the Soviet invasion. It would have been easy to make something up, to take the names of dead men like Mischa and Kostov and reinvent their lives for a smoke screen. I bet Jock is running a trace on the P.O. Box right this minute, finding out who's been renting it."

"So Jock knows about all this?" Beneath his relaxed demeanor, Ben felt humbled by the realization that for weeks he had been a small, nearly irrelevant player in a drama of bewildering scale and complexity.

"Not my end of it," Mark replied. "I have to keep that hush-hush. Far as I know, Five have just used the local cops in Moscow. The other day my controller said they were finally bringing in SIS to help trace Lander, but otherwise the Friends have been kept right out of it."

"Listen to you," Ben said. "Got all the lingo. The old man would be proud of you. Like looking in a mirror."

Ben had meant this only lightly, but Mark's face hummed with pride. He said, "Thank you," and reached out to hold Ben's wrist. His touch was very warm and certain. "I'm doing this for him, brother," he said. "And for us. Got to try and help. Got to dismantle the whole Kukushkin thing. Want to make sure nothing like this can ever happen to anybody else."

"Well, I think that's great." And Ben felt that he was twelve or thirteen years old again, looking on his older brother with a rapt and fascinated attention. He possessed little of Mark's instinctive decency, his natural sense of right and wrong. A part of him dismissed this element of his brother's personality as wrongheaded and idealistic; yet there was something to be envied in Mark's secret life, a sense that he was honoring their father's memory.

"What are you thinking?" Mark asked.

"Just that I hope you're being careful. And that if you need any help I'll do what I can."

"I appreciate it. Thank you."

"And you trust this guy Randall? You really think he knows what he's doing?"

"A hundred percent."

A cold wind cut across the garden. Mark stood up out of the wicker chair, rolling his neck like a doll. Ben experienced another stab of frustrated envy, a craving to be involved.

"Are you sure there's nothing I can do to help?" he said.

Mark looked at him and stepped down onto the grass. He was

touched by Ben's concern and already feeling the relief of having confessed his secret to the one person he could trust. Perhaps Ben's presence would take the sting out of the job; perhaps Ben could act as a buffer for all the stress and concern.

"No," he said. "There's nothing you could really do, mate."

"It's just that I get so fucking bored all day up there in the studio. Maybe if I could just do something, even if it was only for Dad . . ."

"Well, look," Mark began, recognizing the sentiment, "why don't you come and meet the Russians sometime, make it look like there's nothing going on? I'm going to a place with Tom on Friday, supposed to befriend one of them and get him on my side."

Ben leaped on this.

"Christ, yeah," he said. He had not expected such a big role. "Sure I'd do that if you thought it would help."

"It'll make good cover." Mark was discovering a certain logic to the idea. "They'd never suspect anything if the two of us were out together."

But how would he square it with Randall and Quinn? Why, when he had been so at ease with the masquerade, had Mark suddenly called on Ben for support? He made light of his decision with a joke.

"It's actually a lap-dancing place in Finchley Road. You might enjoy yourself."

"Or find something out," Ben added quickly. "Maybe stumble on some useful information . . ."

"Well, that's right. The important thing is not to say anything to anyone, not to let on that you know. And don't mention what we've talked about to Alice, and certainly not to Jock."

"Fuck Jock," Ben said, with authority.

"Forget everything until we talk. I'll give you the address of the place when I've got it. Until then keep your mouth shut. We'll sort everything out tomorrow."

38

It was a cold night and Ben walked at pace along Finchley Road, searching for the entrance to the club. He hoped to discover Macklin and Mark waiting for him in the foyer, or just pulling up in a cab, because what if somebody he knew—a friend, perhaps, maybe even a gallery owner—spotted him as he walked inside alone? How would *that* look? A married man of thirty-two using lap-dancers for kicks?

Moving north into residential Hampstead, he noticed red rope cutting off a section of pavement and a chunky, stubbled bouncer breathing clouds of air into thick leather gloves. A blue neon sign hung over the door. Two skinny office boys wearing chinos and polo necks were mustering the courage to go inside.

"Evening, sir."

The bouncer was built like a bag of cement. With a single, murderous flick of his eyes he analyzed Ben's shoes, trousers, jacket, and tie, then waved him past the rope. Ben moved toward a small booth inside the door and paid an entrance fee of fifteen pounds.

The girl who took the money had a copy of *OK!* magazine hidden beneath the counter.

"Just head down the stairs, love," she said, music thumping from below. "Somebody'll take care of you in the lounge."

Ben was struck by how smart the club appeared; somehow he had been expecting condoms on the floor, lurid pink lights and posters of models wearing plastic swimwear. At the foot of the staircase he was greeted by a middle-aged waiter wearing black tie and ferocious aftershave. Beyond him, through double doors, he could see girls in next to nothing drifting past the glass.

"Good evening, sir." The waiter had a southern European accent, possibly Greek. "I show you to a table?"

"Actually I'm meeting some people," Ben told him. "My brother, Mark Keen. One of his colleagues, Thomas Macklin. I don't know if you've heard of them. They're with some Russians . . ."

"Oh, yes." The waiter seemed to know all about them. "The party from Libra," he said, leading Ben through the double doors. "They haven't arrived yet. But I can show you to their table. Mr. Macklin has made a reservation with us."

It was like the Savoy all over again, deference and respect if you could pay for it. Two girls, both blond and staggeringly tall, looked up and caught Ben's eye as he walked the floor. He smiled back, aware of bikinis and high heels, of other women scoping him from nearby. The club was comparatively small, a low-ceilinged room no bigger than a decent-sized swimming pool, decked out with expensive mirrors and dimmed lights. Ben had been expecting something on the scale of Libra, perhaps three or four floors with room to move, but this was an intimate space, with a seating area of just ten or fifteen tables and a tiny spotlit stage skewered by a chrome pole.

He passed the office boys—already sitting down and drinking beers—and was shown to a long table flush against the far wall. Ben sat at the top end, facing the stage, his back tucked into a corner.

The waiter asked if he wanted a drink.

"That would be great." He was making himself feel more comfortable, shuffling into his seat. "I'll have a vodka and tonic, please. Ice and lemon."

There were five other men in the club. Aside from the office boys, two thick-set Arabs with heavy moustaches were being entertained by a gaggle of girls at a table near the stage. One of them had his right hand on the neck of a bottle of champagne and his left curled around the narrow waist of a woman whose face Ben could not see. Above them, a black girl was dancing in sinuous loops on the stage, one of twenty or thirty lap-dancers dotted throughout the bar. Ben felt exposed, as if he did not belong in such a place. Yet the atmosphere was enticing; it fed into his excitement about the Russians, the sense of being involved in something clandestine and underground. He began looking around for Mark, checking his watch theatrically, and lit a cigarette to give an impression of cool. *Maybe they've stood me up*, he thought, though it was still only ten past ten. Then a song he had hoped never to hear again—Michael Bolton singing "How Am I Supposed to Live Without You?"—began playing on the sound system and a lap-dancer was walking toward him.

She was six foot and blond, wearing a tight leather dress. Not Ben's type: plastic and exercised. When she sat down she deliberately let her leg touch his.

"Hi there, honey." An American accent, with breath that smelled of mints. "My name's Raquel. Mind if I join you?"

Ben found himself nodding, but he was looking around the

room. He didn't want to appear rude, but needed to find a way of making the girl go away.

"This your first time here, honey?" she asked. Her skin looked tanned under the lights.

"First time, yes."

The legs of Ben's chair caught on a piece of loose carpeting and he was forced to sit at an awkward angle.

"You're American," he stated obviously.

"That's right."

Everything he could now invent to excuse himself from the conversation sounded like a lie. That he was waiting for friends. That he was happy just sitting alone. That he thought America was a terrific place and really misunderstood by most Europeans. It was like being drunk and trying to persuade someone that you were sober. Finally Ben said, "I'm waiting for Macklin. For Thomas Macklin."

And Raquel's face lit up. "Oh, you're waiting for *Tom*?"

"You *know* him?"

"Sure. Everyone knows Tom. Comes in here all the time."

And again, Ben felt her leg against his, a lighter touch this time, the soft enticement. Raquel was sliding her hand across his knee, saying, "So, you wanna little dance?"

"No, no, thanks. I'd prefer just to sit here. On my own. They'll be here any minute . . ."

To Ben's right, the black girl was now gorgeously topless, gripping the pole like a microphone, and nowhere for his eyes to fall. Suddenly Raquel was swaying into his lap, her breasts a silicone mold. He said, "Look, this isn't such a good idea," but his voice lacked clarity and resonance. Her face was suddenly so close to his cheek that he could feel the heat of her skin against his own.

"Naughty boy, Benjamin. Naughty boy."

Macklin. *Fuck.*

Ben practically threw Raquel off his lap and was greeted by a startling spectacle: Thomas Macklin wearing an electric-blue suit, flanked by two unidentified men in jacket and tie, his brother beside them, grinning like the Cheshire Cat.

"Hello, there, Benny boy. Having yourself a good time?" Macklin leaned over to shake his hand. "I see you've made Raquel's acquaintance. How are you, sweetheart? Looking gorgeous as ever."

Raquel kissed Macklin full on the lips and said, "Hi, Tom" with a white smile. Ben was hot with embarrassment as he rose awkwardly from his chair.

"Brother, these are some of my colleagues from work." The grin on Mark's face was still evident. "You know Tom, of course. And this is Vladimir Tamarov, a lawyer from Russia, and his associate, Juris Duchev, from Latvia. They're helping us out with the Moscow thing, tying up some loose ends."

Ben got a good look at them. Duchev was past forty, balding and squat, with tired, bloodshot eyes and skin the color of pancake mix. He was wearing black flannel trousers and a Soviet-era woolen jacket that looked utterly out of place in the club. His expression was so hard and unkind he might never have smiled. Vladimir Tamarov also wore a look of absolute indifference to his surroundings. Tall and athletically built, he was dressed in what might have passed for Armani, with an expensive-looking watch visible on a thick, tanned wrist. His hair gleamed with oil, combed in swept-back strands that ended in dry curls at the back of his neck.

"Good to meet you," Ben told him, standing uncomfortably with his weight on one leg. It occurred to him that he was shaking hands with the men possibly responsible for his father's death. Did Mark realize that? Had he thought this through?

"Good to meet you also," Tamarov replied, ignoring a peroxide blonde who drifted past him wearing a black lace corset and thigh-high leather boots.

There were quick remarks now and drink orders, the group settling down at the table. Ben was conscious that he owed money to Raquel, but she seemed happy to remain at his side, her hand now confidently parked in Macklin's lap. Tamarov sat on Ben's right, his back to the wall, with Mark and Duchev beside one another at the other end of the table.

"Where's Philippe got to?" Macklin asked, turning and looking back toward the entrance. His voice was loud and controlling, any civility erased by drink.

"Went to the gents, I think," Mark said.

"Taking his fucking time about it. So, how you been, Benny boy?"

"Not too bad, *Tommy boy*," Ben replied, and was surprised to see Tamarov smiling as he removed his jacket.

"You not like me calling you that?" Macklin grabbed Ben's shoulder and squeezed it hard. "Hey, Keeno!" Again he was shouting down the table. "Little brother here doesn't like me calling him 'Benny boy.' Now, what do you think about that?"

Tamarov glanced at Ben, the unspoken solidarity of sober men, and raised his eyebrows in a way that suggested he was tired of Macklin's behavior, that he thought of him as foolish and embarrassing. Ben nodded back, and wondered if he had gained his trust.

"I told ya," Mark replied, wearing the mask of work, the banter and the easy charm. "Ben don't like to be messed around, Thomas. He's the artist in the family, the thinker."

"Ah, you are the artist?" Tamarov said, drawing Ben out of the exchange. His voice was low and matter-of-fact, a heavy accent.

"That's right."

"Mark tells me earlier you are painter, this is correct?"

"That's correct."

"I buy paintings, collect for my pleasure."

"You do?"

It was an early skirmish. Was Tamarov telling the truth? Drinks were being set down—champagne and vodka all round—and Ben concentrated on the swarm of bikinis and miniskirts now descending on the table. Mark shifted along so that a Thai girl with flowers in her hair could sit between him and Duchev. Duchev, looking like a coal miner who had wandered into the wrong party, grimaced as a thick-boned brunette tapped him on the shoulder and invited herself to sit down. They began speaking and Ben assumed that she was Latvian. Raquel then began massaging Macklin's shoulders, saying how much she liked his suit and helping herself to champagne. He would have to speak to Tamarov.

"So why do you do it, please?" the Russian asked. He had a very direct and concentrated manner, cold, striking eyes that could detect the flaw in a man.

"Why do I do what?"

"Painting. Why did you become artist?"

For the sake of the job, it seemed important to Ben to take care with his answer.

"I do it because it's the only thing I know how to do," he replied. "I can't bank. I can't farm. I can't teach. But I *can* draw. And I have a need to do it, to get this stuff out of me."

It was an answer he had employed many times before, but Ben now added to it by drumming his chest in a manner that he thought might appeal to a Russian. The music in the club was now very loud, the throb of a Latin salsa.

"I see." Tamarov seemed unaffected by events around him: the laughter, the wisecracks, the two bored black girls nearby, yawning into their mobile phones. "And how do you feel about the way art is going in this country?" he said. "In England?"

"You ask a lot of questions," Ben said, and regretted it. That wasn't the way to win him round. Tamarov let him fall through an embarrassed silence, twisting ice in his glass. Forced into a quick reply, Ben said, "I think a lot of so-called modern art is bullshit. I'm trying to do something more lasting. More authentic."

"I see. Yes, the way that painting is presented here concerns me. You have this so-called artist, a man who leaves his clothes in a Tate gallery, and he is made famous for this. But then England has chemists, engineers, you have architects, and nobody knows their names. Why is this, please?"

Tamarov looked very much as though he wanted an answer.

"Well, it's just laziness on the part of the media, laziness on the part of the public," Ben told him. Raquel was laughing at something Macklin had said and he could feel her leg moving under the table. "People respond to modern art in the same way that they respond to sex."

Tamarov frowned. "To sex?"

"That's right. To sex. They respond purely on the basis of appearance. There's nothing deeper going on. 'Does this installation turn me on?' 'How does this video make me *feel*?' Those are the kind of questions they're asking themselves."

Tamarov asked for a translation of the word "installation" and Ben did his best to provide one. Then the Russian began nodding slowly, as if deep in thought.

"Well, this is true," he said finally. "An appreciation of older paintings, the work of Matisse or Renoir, this is much closer to love. My feelings for them will become deeper, as they would for perhaps a friend."

Ben could only smile awkwardly. It occurred to him that he was in the middle of a lap-dancing club holding a conversation about art and friendship with a money-laundering Russian gangster who could have murdered his father.

"Your British culture is only about shocking people," Tamarov continued. "This is what happens when the morons take over. They play to the—what is the expression Sebastian is always using—the *lowest common deconimator.* Is this correct?"

"Lowest common denominator, yes," Ben said, noting the clear reference to Roth. "And they *are* the lowest common denominator. I mean, what are their obsessions? Celebrities, gossip, and fucking."

When Tamarov smiled, it was strange to see a face so controlled, so basically intimidating, giving way to an amusing idea. It was the reaction, Ben realized, of a man who liked what he saw, a thought that appalled and gratified him in equal measure. He was doing a good job. Then there was a sudden commotion at the table, Macklin breaking off from Raquel and swinging round in his chair. Twice he shouted, "Hercule!" in a voice loud enough to be heard above the music, and Ben looked up to see a skinny, well-dressed man approaching the table, drunk and disoriented, with a stunning Indian girl in tow.

"Sorry, Tom." Philippe d'Erlanger had only a faint Belgian accent and he was speaking quickly. "I am coming back from the toilet and I meet Ayesha and we do a little dance together and I was delayed. Hello, I'm Phil."

"Good to meet you." And now Ben was shaking the hand of a drunk Belgian who ran eastern European prostitutes out of a restaurant in Covent Garden. It worried him that a part of him found this exciting.

"You are Mark's brother, yes? Benjamin?"

"Benny boy!" Macklin corrected, a clammy hand going back onto Ben's shoulder. He could feel the weight of it, the sweat, and wanted to throw vodka in Macklin's face.

Raquel was laughing as he said, "That's right, I'm Ben, Mark's younger brother." D'Erlanger sat down. "So you work at Libra?" he asked, noting a tiny particle of cocaine at the base of the Belgian's nose.

"Used to, in the past," he replied. "Now I own a restaurant. This is Ayesha, by the way."

The Indian girl was perched delicately on d'Erlanger's lap, her fingers playing gently in his hair. She looked at Ben and flirted shamelessly, eye contact that he felt as an energy moving right through his body. Her thighs were slim and dark, the left leg crossed over the right so that the light cotton of her dress rode up almost to the waist. Ben nodded at her and took a sip of his drink.

"So you two were dancing back there?" he asked.

"Yes, it was very agreeable." D'Erlanger was grinning inanely. "They have a separate area where you can be more private. VIP, I think they call it. Very Important Persons."

He laughed uproariously at his own joke, but Ben noticed the exhaustion in his face, tired, jaundiced skin and bruises beneath the eyes. A nocturnal creature. Stress-driven. Greedy.

"So this is better than Moscow, no?" he was saying, this time to Tamarov. "More relaxed, I think."

"What do you mean?" Tamarov asked.

D'Erlanger turned back to Ben. His attention was everywhere.

"We've just been in Moscow," he said. "Have you ever been, Benjamin?"

Ben said that he hadn't.

"Well, I will tell you . . ." He rubbed his nose, wiping sweat off his cheek. ". . . everywhere you go there are security persons, men maybe only twenty or twenty-five years old carrying guns and leather jackets, like they think they are Bruce Willis or something. And not just in nightclubs, but in supermarkets, in cinemas, in shops. What are they called, Vladimir?"

"*Okhrana,*" Tamarov told him.

"That's right. *Okhrana*. The Muscovites are obsessed with staying alive, with security. We go to one restaurant with Thomas and Juris—it's called the Prado or Prago or something . . ."

"Praga," Tamarov said.

"Thank you, yes, Praga, and this is a typical Stalin wedding cake near the Kremlin where you have maybe eight or nine different restaurants, themed and so on, and we cannot move because of all these clowns, these *clowns* with their Range Rovers and their bulletproof vests and Walther PPKs . . ."

Again, d'Erlanger laughed at his own joke. Ayesha smiled back adoringly, his oldest friend in the world. Then, when she thought that no one would notice, she stared intently back at Ben, a second moment of flirtation that took him by surprise. There was a promise of paradise in her eyes.

"So Vladimir, he books a table for us and we have to pass through metal detectors, body searchings, as if we are terrorists or something." Ben could hardly concentrate. "Can you imagine this at my restaurant, Benjamin? You come to eat at my place in Covent Garden and I have one of my waitresses take you into a back room and maybe do a strip search before you can order a soup . . ."

Again, d'Erlanger laughed hugely. Ayesha was still trying her best to look amused but Tamarov had a face like stone. Movement at the opposite end of the table ended the conversation. Mark had stood up and was excusing himself from the Thai girl. Seeing this, Ben said, "I'm just going to the bathroom." Nobody paid him much attention. "You going too, Mark?"

"Yeah, for a piss," his brother replied, passing behind Macklin's chair. Ben nodded conspicuously at Tamarov as he squeezed himself out and walked with Mark to the gents.

Inside it was quiet, two doors separating them from the rest of the club. Ben checked that they were alone as Mark washed his hands at the sink.

"I have to talk to you," he said. There was a note of urgency in his voice. "Something's come up."

"Not now, brother," Mark whispered. "This is hard enough as it is."

The door swung open and a stooped, elderly man walked into the bathroom. Mark moved away from the sink and locked himself in one of two cubicles. Ben pretended to look at himself in the mirror and adjusted his tie. The man left without washing his hands.

"D'Erlanger has been to Moscow with Macklin and Tamarov. He must be involved in something out there . . ."

"Ben . . ."

"What were you talking to Duchev about?"

Mark came out of the booth. He was frowning. "What?"

"You guys were talking about something while I was with Vladimir."

"He's retiring. He's bought some property in Spain. He doesn't like the weather in Latvia and wants to build his own house south of Granada. Why?"

Instantly, Ben said, "Well, you could use that."

"Sorry?"

"You could rob him of his dream." In the tight confines of the bathroom Ben was rushing on sheer adrenalin, eager to help out. "If Randall needs evidence on Kukushkin from within, Duchev would be the man to give it to him. They could recruit him as an agent, threatening to take away the land . . ."

"What?" Mark looked appalled. "What the fuck are you talking about?"

"Just that. Just what I was saying."

"Have you done a line, brother?"

"Of course I haven't done a line. You think I'd do coke before something like this . . . ?"

Mark was shaking his head, an exhausted, disappointed smile. "This was a big mistake, bringing you in on this. I didn't realize how fucked you'd get. I don't know what I was thinking . . ."

"What?"

"I should never have got you involved." Ben came toward him.

"You got me involved because you can't do this thing on your own. You need me to help you out, to do it for Dad . . ."

"No." Mark was intractable. "I don't need you to help me out. It's not safe. I asked you along tonight so you could see the Russians for yourself, to prove to you that Bone's letter was a fake. I didn't get you along so that you could start playing I Spy like it's a game or something. The two of us just being in here is bad enough. You shouldn't have followed me from the table."

Ben turned away, looking at his reflection in the mirror. "You're drunk, brother," he said. "You're paranoid."

"I am not drunk, Benjamin. I am not paranoid. You just need to calm down." Mark was very careful not to raise his voice. "Do you know anything *about* Duchev? Do you realize how dumb it would be to try to recruit someone like that? This is one of Kukushkin's most trusted employees. This is a guy who, four years ago, took a leading Moscow mafioso into the countryside in the boot of a car, found a nice isolated spot, chopped off his fingers, hammered out his teeth, and then set fire to his vehicle. The bloke was *still alive*. That was just a job for Kukushkin, a favor. All in a day's work. That's what I'm dealing with, brother. This is the kind of person I'm up against."

"What about Tamarov?"

"What *about* Tamarov? Go back to your paints and charcoals. He's just sussing you out. Can't you see that? He's sussing *both* of us out. These guys, they value loyalty and honor above everything else. You make friends with him and he'll become fucking *depraved* if he realizes what we're up to. A man like Tamarov is either your best fucking friend in the world or the worst mistake you ever made. That's what I need you to bear in mind so that you don't fuck this thing up."

"You should get out of this," Ben said calmly. "I can see you're not . . ."

Mark flashed him a look of contempt. "Drop it," he hissed.

"All I said was that d'Erlanger went to Moscow. That's all I came in here to tell you."

"And?" Mark's hand was coiled into a fist, leaning on the bathroom sink. "You think that's big news? What do you think MI5 do all day if they're not tracking—"

He did well to stop talking as quickly as he did. The internal door of the bathroom had shifted fractionally in a movement of air created by someone entering on the other side. When Tamarov came into the room his eyes narrowed in the brighter light and he stopped in his tracks. He looked first at Mark, then at Ben, and said, "Everything OK?"

Ben let his brother do the talking.

"Oh, fine," Mark replied. "Fine. We're just having a chat about one of the girls. You all right, Vladimir?"

"Not too bad," Tamarov said, standing with his back to them at the urinal.

"Good."

"So you like one of the girls?"

He had twisted his neck round and directed the question at Ben.

"That's right," Ben replied, falling gratefully into the lie. His pulse was sprinting like rain and he hardly dared look at Mark. "Her name's Ayesha. The one with Philippe. She's nice, eh?"

"Very beautiful, yes. I could tell you liked her. We are talking, Mark, and your brother is very interesting on the subject of modern art. But his eyes they keep moving to this girl. He cannot take them off her." Tamarov laughed, zipping up his fly. "But you have a problem, I think. Philippe is very drunk and he is carrying a lot of cash. You will have trouble persuading her to leave him."

Ben smiled—though it looked to Mark more like a grimace—and did his best to keep up the charade.

"Oh, that's OK," he said. "One dance is enough for me. Besides, I'm married, Vladimir, and that American girl took me a bit by surprise."

"Yes," Tamarov said, washing his hands at the sink. "By surprise. Perhaps this is what you were talking about when I came in."

There was a dreadful silence, the sound of taps and muffled music, and they left the bathroom together. Mark allowed Ben to walk ahead of them and tried to gather his composure. They were at a set of double doors leading back into the club when Tamarov took hold of his arm.

"Come with me to the bar," he said. "I want to speak to you in private."

"Sure," Mark replied coolly. He desperately wanted water, ice, something to take the dryness from the roof of his mouth. They were moving through the darkened VIP area, Ben up ahead and girls on all sides dancing in the laps of half-hidden men.

"What will you have?" Tamarov asked him.

"Just something soft," Mark replied. He was still irritated by Ben. "I have to be up early in the morning."

Tamarov ordered two Cokes and jerked his head contemptuously in Macklin's direction.

"Thomas must also be awake early tomorrow," he said, looking across at the table. "We have important series of meetings on Saturday, no? But I think he does not care."

"Oh, Tom's all right," Mark said, thinking that a display of loyalty would play in his favor. "He just likes a drink from time to time. Likes to let his hair down."

The barman set down two Cokes on the bar and Tamarov paid him with a stiff fifty-pound note. Then he trained his eyes on Mark, saying, "What has he told you about me? About who I am?"

Mark didn't flinch. "That you're a lawyer."

"But by now you understand how business works in my country? You understand that in order for your operation to succeed it has been necessary for Thomas and Sebastian to make certain arrangements?"

"Sure," Mark said casually. "I understand that."

Tamarov moved his mouth slowly from side to side, like a man tasting expensive wine.

"So I want to speak to you privately today because we have not met before tonight and there are matters on my conscience that I need to discuss with you."

"On your conscience," Mark repeated.

"Let me be clear." Tamarov straightened his back and swallowed a mouthful of Coke. "Your father was working for Sebastian at the time of his death. I am aware of this. We were all aware of it. This is how business is done."

"I'm not sure I'm following you."

"What I want to say is this." Now he reached out and put his hand on the shoulder of Mark's jacket. It was like being touched by a priest. "When I heard about your father's murder, I was shocked. It came to me as a surprise. It came to all of us as a surprise. Do you understand what I am telling you?"

For a time there was nothing between them but pop music and distant, idle chatter. Girls in peripheral vision and Mark calculating all the time. Under pressure, he made a decision.

"Vladimir, if you're trying to tell me that you work for Viktor Kukushkin, that you're one of his lawyers, then that doesn't surprise me. I'm a big boy. My father told me about Kukushkin's organization and, to be honest with you, on my trips to Moscow with Tom, I put two and two together."

Tamarov flattened down the dried curls at the back of his neck and seemed relieved to have cleared the air. "I appreciate your frankness," he said. "But I am trying to tell you something more than this."

Now Mark did not respond. It was something Quinn had talked about at the safe house. *Page One, Rule One: If you don't know what's going on, keep your fucking mouth shut.*

Tamarov leaned forward.

"I must ask you a personal question," he said. "I hope that you will not be offended by it."

"Go on."

"It is only that I hope you do not feel that my client was in any way involved in what happened . . ."

"Jesus, no." Mark could not tell if the lie rang hollow. "Christ, that thought never occurred to me. You think I'd still be working for Libra if I thought they had anything to do with what happened? You think I'd drink with you at this bar?"

"Then I am very relieved." Tamarov swayed back and removed his hand from Mark's shoulder. "This has been a burden for me tonight, and for Juris also. As I was saying to you, your father's tragedy came as a surprise to all of us in the organization."

"Juris also works for Mr. Kukushkin?" Mark asked, because he had to.

"He is an associate," Tamarov replied after a pause.

Both men glanced back at the table. Ben, Mark was pleased to see, was now talking to Ayesha in the corner. That would keep him out of trouble. Macklin, Raquel, Duchev, and Philippe were laughing among themselves in a separate conversation.

"And your brother?" Tamarov asked. "What does he think?"

"Ben?"

"Yes. Ben."

"Oh, all brother cares about is paintings."

Tamarov's mouth dipped.

"I like him very much," he said. "Benjamin is good person. It is not easy for him to live with everything that has happened. I also lose my father, when I was seventeen year old."

"I'm sorry to hear that."

"A car crash outside Moscow. He was killed with a friend, coming back from a day of fishing in the country. My mother was very sick and I had to inform my younger sister and brother of this news. They are twins, only ten years old at the time. When I tell them what has happened they are screaming, like animals on the floor."

"That's terrible. I'm really sorry."

Two girls approached them at a gentle sway but Tamarov waved them off.

"I remember afterward, going through his . . ." He searched for the word. ". . . his possessions. My mother was ill for some time and it was left to me, only a young man in Soviet Russia, to arrange the funeral. This was an intimate thing, you understand, for a boy to go through his own father's books, his clothes. Later I read an American author. He says: 'There is nothing more terrible than to face the objects of a dead man.' I always remember this."

"I had to do the same thing," Mark said, and for a moment he was out of the role, alone in Keen's flat that first time: finding a razor lying beside the bath, clogged with his father's hair; suits and ties in cupboards, never to be worn again; a Bible in a drawer just a stretch away from his pillow; even an unopened packet of condoms gathering dust under the bed.

"So we have something in common," Tamarov announced.

"Yes, we do." And for no better reason than that he was unsettled and short of ideas, Mark picked up his drink and proposed a toast. "To the future," he said.

Tamarov looked pleasantly surprised.

"Yes, to the future," he responded, and smiled. He appeared to be on the point of adding more when Duchev approached. Acknowledging Mark with a granite nod, he said something quickly to Tamarov in a language that was not Russian.

"Es atnācu uzzinat kā klājās. Nu, kā iet?"

"Vies iet labi," Tamarov replied. "Esmu pārliecināts ka brāļi nekā nezina."

Latvian, Mark assumed, and attempted to commit certain phrases to memory. Tamarov had used the word "labi," which he knew meant "fine" or "good," but he would struggle to remember anything useful for Randall.

"Juris is wondering where we get to," Tamarov said. "I was just telling him that we come back and sit down." Again the pair spoke briefly in Latvian, this time with distinct names emerging from the flow of language. *Philip. Toms.* Something about *piedzá rušies.* Mark noticed that Tamarov dealt with Duchev as a young, successful executive might speak to his foreman or chauffeur: with an authority checked by respect for the older man's experience and loyalty.

"What's happening over at the table?" he asked.

Duchev seemed to wait for permission to speak. Air conditioning had rendered the club almost odorless, but Mark could pick out the strong smell of his sweat.

"We find out," he said.

Together they returned to the group and found Macklin holding court at the table, spittles of champagne now staining his electric-blue suit. Raquel, Ayesha, Philippe, and Ben were listening with rapt attention to a high-volume monologue about prostitution.

"Thing about hookers," Macklin was saying, "is you have to watch out for the fibs. I learned this early on, Benny boy, right from the word go. Brass says she's seventeen, more than likely she's five years older, ten from time to time. You go for someone who's thirty, take it from me she's getting on for the menopause and it's like fucking your mum. 'Mature' is the same deal. You know what they mean by that, don't you, Ben? Ropey as fuck. Ditto 'sophisticated.' Don't make me laugh. About as classy as these birds get is watching *Countdown* on their coffee break."

Tamarov did not bother sitting down. A tall black girl with muscular, gym-stiffened arms had caught his eye. He returned with her to the bar. Noticing this, Macklin raised his voice and directed it at Duchev.

"Good for old Vladimir," he shouted. "Look at your boss having fun. You wanna get some yourself, Juris, before it gets cold. Bit like the Hungry Duck in Moscow, eh?"

Duchev said nothing. Macklin turned his attention back to Mark and Ben.

"So, Keeno, I was just telling your brother here about my life of iniquity and vice."

"Yeah?"

"Yeah." There was a layer of gleaming sweat like fat melting on Macklin's face. "Shall I tell you my golden rule, Benny boy, my golden little rule?"

"Why not?" Ben said tiredly.

"If it flies, fucks, or floats, rent it, don't buy it."

When Ben failed to laugh, Macklin launched a further tirade.

"Well, look at that," he said. "He's like Sebastian fucking Roth, your little brother. Clean as a whistle and tied to the sink."

"What do you mean by that?" Ben said, and might have lost his temper.

"I mean our Seb is too busy kissing government arse to have himself a good time. Spends his nights at the opera with the cream of New Labour, having intimate little dinners with the movers and shakers of Whitehall. God knows why he bothers. Fancies himself for a place in the House of Lords, I reckon. Very ambitious, our Seb."

"Easy, Tom," Mark said, but Macklin was on a roll. "Come on, you know what I'm saying, Keeno. Those trips abroad, we hardly ever see him." He started talking directly at Raquel, at Ayesha, at anyone who would listen. "Me and Mark, we go off to Moscow nowadays and we have ourselves a right good time. But Seb, no, he keeps his distance, hobnobbing with his cronies in the Kremlin. Who does he think he is?"

"Tom, leave it," Mark said again, and this time his tone was more forthright. Duchev had turned away, but was surely processing every word.

"Fine," Macklin replied. "Fine. I'm only telling you the truth. Way I see it, Benny boy, man like you wants to give himself a treat from time to time. I saw you when I came in here, Raquel giving you the once over. You were loving it, mate, *loving* it. Wasn't he, sweetheart?" Raquel smiled obligingly. "I'll tell you this for nothing. I had a Thai bird last night, fucking unbelievable. Nipples like indoor fireworks. You don't know what you're missing."

Ben lit a cigarette. At that moment he would rather have been anywhere else in the world but listening to Macklin talking about his sex life.

"Philippe's been there, haven't you, mate?" D'Erlanger, who had been quiet for some time, looked awkwardly at the table. "Don't be shy, Hercule, don't be shy. Down the Caymans, wasn't it? You and Timmy Lander went retail. He told me all about it."

Neither Ben nor his brother could prevent the looks of shock that sprang onto their faces.

"Timothy Lander?" Mark said quickly.

"That's right." Macklin's hand was scraping up Raquel's back. "Night on the tiles, wasn't it, Poirot?"

"Do I *know* him?" Mark asked. "From Libra?"

"Tim?" Macklin frowned. "Don't think so, mate. Top bloke, though. Old friend of mine from college; runs a diving school out there."

"You sure?"

"Sure I'm sure. Philippe was going out a while back and I asked Tim to—how shall I put this delicately?—show him a good time." Macklin appeared to be affected by a memory, pleasure briefly leaving his face. "Matter of fact, I tried to hook your old man up with him, Keeno, when he was planning a holiday out there. Told me he wanted to do some diving out in the Caymans, so I gave him Tim's number. That was just before the, er, accident, you know. Sorry about that. Here, have another drink."

39

"Timothy Lander is a fucking *diving* instructor."

"I knew that."

"You *knew* that?"

Taploe secured his seatbelt and managed to look suitably contrite. He said, "We found out shortly after our last meeting. Paul had a call from the Cayman Islands which confirmed it."

"From the Cayman Islands? Not from SIS?"

"Why would SIS be involved?"

Mark was sitting opposite Taploe on the leather back seat of an MI5 cab. He frowned and said, "Because you said their Station out there was looking into it." For the first time, he had begun to doubt Randall's integrity. He wished Quinn were in the car, somebody whose word he could count on. With Paul Quinn, he knew where he stood. "Or was that just a lie designed to make me feel better? Maybe you knew all along that Lander was a red herring. I mean, how hard is it to trace somebody when you have their fucking phone number on my dad's records?"

"I never lied to you about Timothy Lander." Taploe's nose seemed to twitch, as if he had suffered a grave insult. "Paul found a Stewart Lander working for Citibank, but nothing under Timothy. It was only by chance that his name came up."

Mark shook his head and looked out of the window.

"Now I need to know more about last night," Taploe said. "The club. Everything you can recall."

Ian, who was driving, switched lanes abruptly on Marylebone Road and shot the cab up on to the Westway.

"I told you most of it on the phone."

"Well, then, let's start with Tamarov. Why do you think he brought up the subject of your father?"

"How the fuck should I know?" Mark was tired and fractious. He had left the club at three in the morning and been debriefed by Taploe for thirty minutes on the telephone before grabbing just two or three hours of sleep.

"Well, can you hazard a guess?"

"To clear his conscience?" Mark suggested. "To take me off the scent?" Taploe appeared to agree with this assessment and nodded discreetly. "Or," Mark added, "because he was actually telling the truth. Because Duchev and Kukushkin really *did* have nothing to do with what happened to my father. Because the shooting was just a run-of-the-mill murder that is never going to be solved." He wondered whether to tell Randall about Bone's letter. The more he thought about it, the crazier it seemed just to dismiss the theory about Kostov. What if Jock *was* lying, as Ben suspected? But then maybe Randall already knew about Mischa. He had recruited Mark using Kukushkin as a lever, the treachery of Macklin and Roth, yet there was no specific evidence linking any of those figures to the murder. Maybe Five and Six were in it together. Mark stared at the floor of the cab and did not know who to trust.

"We will solve it," Taploe was saying. "It's just a matter of time."

"Time," Mark muttered.

"Now, you said that Tamarov was upset with Macklin for being drunk?"

"That's right." Mark was still staring at the floor.

"How drunk was he, as a matter of fact?"

"Very."

"Can you be more specific?"

Mark lifted his head with bored indifference. "You want a urine sample?"

Ian grinned in the rearview mirror.

"Well, what about d'Erlanger?" Taploe asked, ignoring the sarcasm.

"Not booze. Cocaine."

"I see. And at the bar you said Tamarov openly admitted to you that he was Viktor Kukushkin's lawyer. Is that correct?"

"That is correct."

"Now why did he do that, do you think?" But Mark had had enough.

"Fucking hell. How many times do I have to tell you? I don't have answers to these questions. If you don't know what's going on, then pull me out. If you think Kukushkin is already on to me, I'm not exactly keen to stick around."

"Nobody is suggesting for a moment that Kukushkin is on to you. Do you have reason to suggest that that might be the case?"

Shaking his head, Mark stared at passing cars.

"Look, I am trying to piece things together," Taploe told him. "I am trying to help you, trying to run this operation. All I want to know is what your instincts tell you. I wasn't there last night. I need to see things through your eyes."

Ian pulled away sharply at a green light and, for the third or fourth time in the journey, Mark was jolted back in his seat. A motorcycle courier buzzed past his window, weaving down the blind side of a single-decker bus.

"My instinct tells me everything is fine," he said. "Like I told you, the best thing you can do is get to Duchev. He's on the way out. Retiring. You threaten to confiscate this land he's bought in Spain, that's a big lever. Juris has dreams of growing oranges and lemons on the plains of Andalusia. He talked about it for a quarter of an hour. You tell him he's got more chance of growing cress at Wormwood Scrubs, that's going to make an impact, believe me."

Taploe seemed impressed by the idea. He pinched a tuft of his moustache, as if removing an imaginary speck of food, and steadied his balance on a loop of plastic tacked above the door.

"That is something I've been thinking over since we talked this morning," he said. "But it needn't concern you. If I pitch Duchev, that won't affect your ongoing relationship with Tamarov. That is the vital element here. Now, your brother. Why do you think Tamarov was so friendly toward him?"

Wary of questions about Ben, Mark again answered aggressively.

"I don't know," he said. "I don't know why he was friendly to Ben. To get him onside? To test him? Isn't it possible they just *liked* one another?" He was conscious that Ben had conceived the plan for Duchev and wanted to protect him. "I mean, maybe you guys are looking for conspiracy where no fucking conspiracy exists. You think Timothy Lander is a corrupt investment banker in the Cayman Islands and he turns out to be Jacques Cousteau." Expecting Ian to laugh at this, Mark looked into the front seat, but he saw that Boyle's eyes were concentrated on the road.

"What about what happened in the toilets?" Taploe asked. "You were talking in there with your brother when Tamarov came in. How did he react at that point?"

Mark stayed back in his seat and bluffed it out. "Like he'd just bumped into a couple of guys who were talking in the gents. Like any normal bloke in a club who needs to go for a piss. Ben and I are brothers. Can't brothers talk in public without somebody getting suspicious?"

"You tell me."

Ian overtook an articulated lorry at speed and Mark slammed down his passenger window. The air in the cab had been fuggy and stale and his throat felt swollen with lack of sleep. When the wind funneled across the seats it dampened Taploe's eyes.

"That too much for you?" he asked.

"Leave it," Taploe replied.

The cab slowed.

"You asked about Ben and Vladimir," Mark said. "OK, I'll tell you. Vlad told me his father died when he was seventeen. So maybe he feels sorry for Ben. Maybe he feels sorry for me. Maybe there's some empathy there."

"Excuse me, boss, but that tallies with our diligence." Ian was shouting above the noise of the road. "Tamarov's old man was killed in a car accident outside Moscow. March 1982, if I recall correctly."

Taploe fidgeted in his seat, barely acknowledging the intrusion.

"Well, if that's the case, that's certainly something you could use to your advantage in forging a relationship with him." Ian appeared to nod in agreement. "But you are not, I repeat *not* to involve your brother in any Security Service operation ever again. That was foolish and unnecessary."

Mark should have backed down, but the combination of his already dark mood and a sense of loyalty to Ben got the better of him.

"My brother did all right," he said.

"That's not what I was told."

Ian brought the taxi off the Westway and turned toward Shepherd's Bush. A man wearing a tan overcoat tried to hail the cab by waving a furled-up newspaper frantically above his head. Mark saw him swear loudly as they sped past.

"What were you told?" he asked.

"We had Watchers in the club. Two young men. They went in immediately before Ben and sat down at the next-door table."

"The guys in chinos? The two blokes in polo necks?"

"The very same." It was a small moment of triumph and Taploe enjoyed Mark's discomfort. "They said your brother looked nervous all evening. Now how would you explain that?"

Mark was caught in a lie.

"Well, that's just their assessment," he said. "They have to write something, don't they, to justify their jobs."

Taploe cast him a withering look and glanced at his watch.

"Is he conscious?" he asked, still staring at his wrist.

"What does that mean?"

Ian answered from the front seat.

"It means does your brother know about Blindside? Have you told him that you're helping us?"

Taploe scrutinized Mark's face intensely for his reaction.

"Fuck, no," he said. "I'm not stupid."

The interrogation might have continued had Mark's mobile phone not rung. He withdrew it from the pocket of his suit, glanced at the readout, and could hardly believe his eyes.

"It's him," he said.

"Who?"

"Tamarov."

The phone was already on its third ring.

"Well, answer it." Taploe sounded petulant, fearing the loss of the call, and for an instant Mark saw the depth of his ambition.

"Hello?" he said, picking up.

Taploe could only hear Mark's end of the conversation.

How you doin', mate? It was a good night, wasn't it? Yeah, I'm suffering a bit with no sleep, but I'll be all right.

He was forced to concede how naturally Blindside dropped into the role: Mark was improvising with ease, no sign of edginess or nerves.

Well, he said he enjoyed meeting you too, Vlad. Yeah, sure, absolutely. You wanna meet up, that's fine, sounds very interesting. OK. Well, I'll see you there in the morning. Sure, I won't mention it to anyone.

There was a smile on Mark's face as he put the phone back in his jacket, a grin of satisfaction that he wanted them both to see.

"What did he say?" Taploe asked.

"He wants to meet up. Wants to meet yours truly for a little Sunday breakfast in Hackney. Got a business proposition, apparently."

"Really?"

"Really."

"Well, good for you," Ian said.

"Yes, good for you," Taploe added, and the business with Ben seemed forgotten.

40

The meeting lasted twenty minutes.

"I can learn everything I need to know about a man by the way he behaves at breakfast," Tamarov said, standing in the foyer of his new restaurant wearing Ray-Ban sunglasses, a button-down Tommy Hilfiger cotton shirt, and Armani denim jeans. It was nine o'clock in the morning. "I am a busy man, Mark, a very busy man. We have businesses in Moscow, in London, in Paris, in Belgrade. Later this morning, I fly to Amsterdam to eat only lunch. So if a person is to do business with me, I want to see the color of his eyes in the morning. I want to hear him speak to me. I want to know the truth about him."

It was as if they had never met. Tamarov was suffocating Mark with Russian bluster, the browbeating bullshit of a thug used to getting his own way. They weren't even *eating* breakfast: Tamarov was in too much of a hurry. Had it not been for his duty to Randall, Mark would have made his excuses and caught a cab back to Kentish Town.

"So what business are we exactly *doing* together, Vlad? You didn't mention anything specific on the phone. What kind of thing is it that you have in mind?"

Tamarov put the whole weight of his arm on Mark's back and began walking with him toward the kitchens. "Well, I have been thinking," he said. Right from the start, Mark had the impression that Tamarov was in a tight spot from which he needed rescuing. "I am wondering if you would be interested in a small venture with me?"

"A small venture."

"I am opening up this bar, this restaurant, in less than two weeks and I need somebody to help me out."

Mark looked around him. The restaurant was a shell of scaffolding and fallen plaster. Despite the fact that it was a Sunday, there were workmen everywhere, architects in hard hats, interior designers poring over color charts. As they came into the kitchen Mark could see gas burners and extractor fans still boxed in the center of the room.

"Is Tom not your partner on this?" he asked. "You two have been spending so much time together recently and . . ."

"No, not on this," Tamarov replied firmly. "This is not with Thomas anymore. I cannot trust him as I could trust you."

Mark disguised his astonished reaction to this by slackening off his tie.

"I'm sorry you feel that way."

"Don't be," Tamarov said, removing his arm from Mark's back. "I have been hearing good things about you from Sebastian for so long and now we meet in the club and it occurs to me yesterday that this would be a good partnership between us. I have in mind to open a chain of restaurants. But I am always in six cities at once, always doing business. I need somebody to be a director in the same way that you are looking after Libra."

It didn't feel like a trap. That was what he told Randall afterward. For hours they sat around trying to second-guess Tamarov's motive for making the offer, finally conceding that it had been made in good faith. Kukushkin was expanding into London all the time; Tamarov was the man who had been assigned to make that happen. The Scot he had entrusted to see the restaurant through to completion had either quit at the last minute or failed to come up to scratch. That Mark was Tamarov's choice to take over was both a reflection of his skills as a manager and a particularly expedient coincidence.

"But I work for Seb," he said. "I can't just quit and run this place. I'm not even looking for another job."

Mark wondered if that had been the wrong thing to say. If Randall needed him to get close to Tamarov, this was the perfect opportunity. To refuse might jeopardize the relationship.

"Of course we will offer you equity," Tamarov was saying, wrongly assuming that Mark was stalling over money. "We can discuss arrangements so that you own a portion of the business . . ."

"No, it's not that. It's not that, Vlad." He didn't know which way to go. It occurred to him that Philippe had been ensnared in a similar fashion, headhunted out of Libra. "I just don't understand the sudden offer. Is there something I should know about? Everything seems a bit chaotic."

Tamarov looked offended.

"Chaotic? I assure you all restaurants look like this a few days before they are opening. You know this, Mark, it is normal. Does your club in Moscow seem like it is ready for opening? No. So let me show you our bathrooms. They are completely finished. There is nothing chaotic about this. Nothing."

Both bathrooms were indeed completely finished, a mock-Arab nightmare of black tiles and freestanding crimson lamps. Mark continued to waver and Tamarov felt it necessary to force his point.

"My problem is this," he said, and actually pressed his index finger against the lapel of Mark's jacket, as if retaliating to an insult that had never been landed. "People in your country are concerned. They think that we are all gangsters in the East, they think that it is a mistake to trust us, to let us invest in your country. Perhaps *you* think this, Mark, even though you have been in Moscow, you have been in Petersburg, and you have seen these things at first hand. But let me tell you something, as your friend but also as somebody who knows about how work must be conducted. If you were a Russian, you *too* would be a gangster." He let the observation settle on Mark, digging out the pause. "You would have no choice. What does this word 'mafia' *mean*, anyway? Does it mean violence? Does it mean that we are criminals? Of course not, and who is to judge? You think that a mafia did not exist before Mr. Gorbachev, before Yeltsin? You think that the Soviet system was not in itself an organized crime? This is naïve. At least now the wealth is in the control of the people."

"Spoken like a true communist," Mark said. Tamarov did not react to the joke.

"The difference today is that the people must now *fight* for this wealth. A clever Russian, a Latvian, a Georgian, understands that today's world is about sinking or swimming. If I am to survive, if I am to put food on the table for my wife, for my children, it is necessary to *fight*. Not with guns, not with violence, but with the mind." Tamarov tapped the side of his head to indicate where his mind might be located. Mark knew for sure that he did not have a wife, nor any children for whom he had to put food on the table, but he let it go. "I am in competition with other men," Tamarov said. "If I make a deal, I make the best deal for myself and for my clients. Does this make me a bad man? Does it?"

Mark didn't answer the question, though he conceded that Tamarov was at least right about destiny. In Moscow, he had been obliged to authorize and pay perhaps thirty or forty backhanders just to get the club up and running. It was a question of perspective; in London a businessman had the luxury of morality.

"So this place is being financed by Mr. Kukushkin?" he asked. "Is that what you're telling me?"

Tamarov physically withdrew from the question. Stepping aside from Mark, he turned and walked back in the direction of the foyer, his voice assuming the lawyer's cloak.

"I represent Mr. Kukushkin's interests," he said. "Mr. Kukushkin has many investments."

Mark followed him and said, "Right. I see."

"Thomas works with Mr. Kukushkin in Moscow. Sebastian has met him on many occasions. Are you seeing this as a problem?"

"Of course not."

"Then good."

Tamarov stood beside a pile of plastic-wrapped chairs and flattened a hand against the crust of his gelled hair. "Look, I do not need a decision now." He started to lean against a column of chairs. It rocked dangerously. "Everything for the completion of the restaurant is already under way." In the street outside, Juris Duchev leaned on the horn of Tamarov's Mercedes, preparing to drive him out to Heathrow. "I have to leave now to catch a flight to Holland.

Why don't we meet for dinner tomorrow? The St. Martin's Lane Hotel?"

"Sounds good," Mark said. But he wondered if he had blown his chance. He had tried not to reject the offer out of hand, but Tamarov now seemed angry. He could surely find someone else to manage and run a restaurant. Then where would Mark be? Most probably their paths would never cross again.

"I just need twenty-four hours to think things over," he said. Tamarov was signaling to the car. "It could be that the timing is right for this. It could be that I could find myself interested."

"Then I am glad to hear it." Out on the street, Duchev was holding the car door open. He did not acknowledge Mark. "I will call you. And then we will meet on Monday."

"Which is when you want my answer," Mark said.

"Which is when I want your answer."

41

In the beginning, Roth had telephoned Alice at least once every two days. After their first lunch together, he had called three times in a single afternoon and sent flowers that raised eyebrows at the *Evening Standard.* Each time, he found a fresh reason for getting in touch: to chat about Ben or Mark; to discuss the latest developments on the new restaurant in Kensington; to give Alice the telephone number of a friend whose first novel might make the subject of a decent piece on the features page. All in all, she had met him for lunch three times and for dinner twice before they had slept together for the first time at his house in Pimlico. There had also been cocktails at the Hempel with some of his political contacts in the government, one of whom had later furnished Alice with a decent diary story.

She had always flirted with men of consequence, had done so since her teens. There was something about the buzz of flattery, the empowering thrill of constant male attention. But only once before—in the very earliest stages of her relationship with Ben—had Alice toyed with the idea of an infidelity, and succumbed to a one-night stand. Usually the moral justification for her behavior lay in keeping men at arm's length: sex, after all, changed everything. It was best just to keep them ticking over, best just to enjoy them as a game. And then Roth had come along and ruined everything. Roth had come along and humiliated her.

That afternoon at the hotel, just a few minutes before she was due to leave, he had told Alice how uncomfortable he was with "the concept of adultery," how bad he felt for "cuckolding Ben." Maybe it was best if they just "cooled off" for a little while; maybe it was best if it just ended. At that moment—less than an hour after Roth had been inside her—Alice had seen him for what he was, and glimpsed her own stupidity. An argument had ensued in which she had accused him of using her, of treating her like a whore. What made it worse was that Roth had refused to retaliate: he understood why she was so upset, he understood that the timing was bad. But in a few days she would come to realize that this was the best decision for everyone. "This is a time when you should be with Ben," he had told her, and Alice had even wondered if he was hinting at blackmail.

Work was harder now. She thought that people knew about what had happened. Roth's friends, the contacts he had so willingly given up and whom she had so gleefully cultivated, stopped calling. She was certain her reputation had been permanently damaged by their association. And for what? The sex hadn't even been all that good. All the way through it Alice had been comparing Roth with Ben and wondering what the hell she was doing. But there had been such excitement in the seduction, such novelty, and the affair had provided the perfect distraction to all Ben's grief and torpor.

She was terrified of losing the marriage. Ben's life was her entire structure: his loyalty, his friends, his love. Without that, Alice was nothing, a hack with no friends, and single on the wrong side of thirty. She started to worry about her looks, about her career. In those first days, the insecurity was like an illness.

She called Ben all the time, wasn't even aware that she was doing it. Just to talk to him, just to hear his voice. Alice needed to know that there was still somebody out there who found her attractive, somebody whom she could still rely on as a friend.

She missed the call to her mobile from Michelle Peterson at Customs and Excise. It was three o'clock on Monday afternoon. A bustle of male subs and journalists had gathered near her desk, discussing layout and trying to catch her eye. Were they laughing at her, or had nothing really changed? That was one of the things she had liked about Sebastian: there was nothing sleazy about him, nothing furtive or sly. He had been predatory in a way that most men would never understand.

Michelle left a text message and when Alice connected to the switchboard in Portsmouth she made a point of saying: "Customs and Excise?" in a voice loud enough to be heard by the news editor, who was standing just five or six feet away from her desk. She wanted him to think that she was engaged on a story more edifying than hemlines or hairstyles.

"I've just had a message from Michelle Peterson," she told the receptionist. "Could I speak to her, please?"

She had to wait while the call was connected. To her delight, the news editor honored her with a smile, the first good thing to happen in days. Then she heard Michelle's voice on the line, anxious and close to a whisper.

"Als?"

"Shell?"

"Call my mobile, will you? But give me a minute to get outside."

Alice waited and dialed back, the news editor now replaced by a young work-experience boy from public school looking ineffectual near the watercooler.

"Hello?"

Michelle was outdoors. Alice could hear cars, sky noise. "Can you hear me?" she asked.

"Just about. How's it going?"

"Fine. Fine."

"Listen, I'm talking from the car park. Can't really chat." Alice heard what sounded like the clunk of a van door, a metal sound. "I found out about Leonid Sudoplatov. Somebody using that name entered the UK on the first of December last year. Is that any help to you?"

"I think so." Alice scribbled *Sud. Dec 1st* on a pad. "I'd have to check the dates."

"We have him as a Russian national. Sixty-three years old. Birthday sixth of December 1939. Records say it was a new passport, all the right channels issued eighteen months before. He stayed in the UK for eleven days and then caught a Heathrow flight back to Moscow on the morning of the twelfth. British Airways."

Alice was writing a sequence of notes in shorthand.

She said, "December the twelfth?"

"That's right. That's about all I've got." A seagull squawked in Portsmouth.

"I really, really appreciate it."

It was a godsend. She thought that Ben would be pleased when she told him. She thought that this was exactly what she needed to do in order to make things up to him.

42

She told Ben as soon as she walked in the door. He was slumped on the sofa reading *Archangel*. They no longer kissed when they saw one another; merely an eye contact, a sort of shrug.

"Listen, I talked to Michelle Peterson."

Nothing.

"My friend from university. You remember? The one who works for Customs and Excise."

Ben turned a page.

"A man calling himself Leonid Sudoplatov arrived in London on December the first last year. That's eight days before your father was killed. He left from Heathrow on the morning of the twelfth. And he was Russian. Sixty-three years old."

Now Ben rose from the sofa with the sluggishness of genuine surprise. The novel fell out of his hand. He might have said that it was impossible, that McCreery and Mark had disproved Bone's theory. He might have told Alice to mind her own business and suggested with a look that things had moved on. But Kostov was alive, and his existence made perfect sense.

"Did you tell Mark about this?" Embarrassed by his behavior in the club, Ben was wary of upsetting his brother, of making further mistakes.

"He's not answering his phone," Alice said.

"I always knew that fucker was lying to me."

"Who? Mark?"

"No. Not Mark. McCreery. Jock McCreery. I always knew he was hiding something."

To Ben's surprise, Alice came over and kissed him on the forehead. They both sat down.

"McCreery said the letter was disinformation," she said.

"I know. I know. And I sat in the pub and I listened to him smooth things over and I bought what he was saying, but in the back of my mind I always had this element of doubt. And then, when . . ."

"When what?"

"Nothing." Ben had to check himself. He was about to mention Mark's work for MI5. "McCreery is definitely covering for SIS," he said. "There's something going on."

"Maybe somebody else is using Sudoplatov's identity," Alice suggested, running her hand through his hair. "Is that a possibility?"

"It's a possibility." Ben wondered why she was being so affectionate toward him, so helpful and understanding.

"You don't think that's what's happened?"

"Well, Kostov had his own false identities. Sudoplatov would have belonged to him. Unless somebody was trying to frame a dead man for murder, why would they bother using his passport?"

Alice nodded and looked at the floor. Was she hoping for a reconciliation, for an end to all the silences and the ill feeling? Ben wondered if talking to Michelle had been her way of making things up between them. He wondered if she was tired of his moods and anxiety. He wondered if she had spent the entire afternoon fucking Sebastian Roth.

"How's your piece going?" he asked. "The one about the restaurant?"

Without a flicker, Alice said, "It got spiked."

"Spiked?"

"Yeah. Seb just pulled out all of a sudden and Features said it was a bad idea. Anyway, I hadn't heard from him in ages."

There was a beat of distrust between them, nothing more. Then Alice said, "It was probably a good thing, anyway. I'd looked into Seb's file at work. He's not a particularly pleasant man."

"How's that?" Ben was jealous of Roth and any criticism of him—particularly coming from Alice—was music to his ears.

"When Libra was first starting out," she said, "Seb employed dealers to go into rival clubs and sell pills and trips to customers. Did you know about that? Does Mark know about that?" Ben frowned and shrugged his shoulders. "Then he would tip off the police and get the club closed down. And when journalists have questioned him about this, he's disguised what happened as a moral crusade, denied that he had any part in it."

"Yeah," Ben said. "You notice that about corrupt people. Always the ones pointing the finger. Always someone else to blame."

"That's right." Alice nodded and appeared to warm to her theme. "Roth's so tight, so money conscious, that he won't even have people pouring themselves a glass of water in the toilets at Libra. You go in there with an empty bottle of Evian, security have instructions to confiscate. You've got to buy water at the bar, just like everything else. No matter that there are dealers authorized by Libra on the sly selling pills to dehydrated punters who are already forty quid out of pocket just for coming in. The only thing Seb really cares about is the Libra share price. I wouldn't have felt comfortable writing a piece about someone like that."

"Exactly," Ben said. "And you think a guy like that, a man with his contacts, his leverage, doesn't know a thousand journalists who could have written a puff piece about a restaurant opening? It was all a game. He was trying to get you into bed."

Alice managed to make her embarrassment resemble modesty.

"Don't be silly," she said.

"I'm serious. I've talked to Mark about it. The concept of adultery, of stealing someone's wife, it's meaningless to him. He sees it as *competition*."

Alice took a cigarette out of her bag and was pleased that her hand did not shake as she lit it.

"Well, I don't know . . ."

"It's funny." Ben looked relieved. "I thought you fancied him. I thought you two had a bit of a crush."

The sentence died away in his mouth, a moment of frankness that he had not intended.

"*Fancied* him?" Alice made a face of appalled disgust, like a child swallowing medicine. "He's revolting. How could you think that?"

A great wave of relief, of confidence-boosting pleasure, swept through Ben's body. He smiled.

"Just a hunch," he said. "Just a paranoia."

Again, Alice ran her hand through his hair. They kissed now, the sweet forgiveness, and Ben felt the skin on her back, reaching for the soft exquisite warmth of her stomach. For the first time in days he was at peace. "We should do something about Michelle," he said, galvanized and relieved. Alice looked taken aback as he rose from the sofa and lit a cigarette.

"We should," she said instinctively. "She told me Sudoplatov was using a new passport, issued in the last couple of years. If he was in the KGB, he'd still have contacts in the Russian government, in the mafia, people who could get him passports, lines of credit, information."

Ben inhaled deeply.

"Then we should try to get in touch with Bone," he said, aware that he was slipping back into a role for which his temperament was ill suited. "Would you know how to do that?"

"Sure," Alice said.

"I haven't got a contact address for him, and I gave fucking McCreery my only copy of the letter. I don't remember the number of the P.O. Box. There's probably no way of finding him."

"Of course there is." Alice stood and took his hand in hers. "We'll find him on the Internet. Let me get a glass of wine and we'll go upstairs."

Ben was technologically backward; he barely knew how to switch on Alice's computer. In her study—a small, windowless cupboard on the same floor as their bedroom—he stood behind her as she opened Internet Explorer.

"What are you doing?" he asked. He had his hand on the back of her neck and was stroking her hair. The prospect of tracking down Bone seemed secondary to the knowledge that they would very soon be in bed together.

"We just find Google and type in the name of the town. What was it? Where did the letter come from?"

"What's Google?"

"Are you *serious*? Where did the letter come from?"

"Cornish. New Hampshire," Ben said. "Somewhere in New England."

The connection was fast. Within three seconds, a screen had appeared, saying: NEW HAMPSHIRE ONLINE. NH CITY GUIDES.

"Now we find the phone number. Then we call the local post office and say that it's an emergency."

"Is that what you do at work? Lie and make stuff up?"

Alice didn't reply. Ben could feel the light heave of her shoulders, the gradual uncurling of her spine as she breathed.

"Welcome to New Hampshire," she said, reading aloud from the screen in a cod American accent. "What do you want to know about? Local restaurants? Ski conditions? *Where do you wanna go today?*"

Another screen appeared, a long list of cities and towns. Alice scrolled through them and clicked: CORNISH. "So we just look here," she said, another page loading.

"Legal services. Libraries. Fire Departments . . ."

"Post Offices!" Ben exclaimed, pointing at the bottom of the screen.

Alice smiled, muttered "Bloody artists," and clicked the icon. There was a single Post Office listed for Cornish. She wrote down the telephone number on the back of a gas bill and shut off the connection.

"Do you want me to call them?"

"Yeah, you do it," Ben said. "You lie better than me. You're a journalist."

Alice seemed to take this as a compliment. There was a phone beside the computer. She dialed the number.

"They're five hours behind," she murmured as the number connected. "It's about two in the afternoon. Hello?"

A woman at the Post Office had picked up. She said, "Post Office, good afternoon. How may I help you?"

Alice curled a loop of hair behind her ear and touched Ben's arm. He pressed his ear close to the phone in order to hear what was being said.

"I'm trying to get in touch with one of your customers. He has a P.O. Box registered at this address. A Mr. Robert Bone. My name is Alice Keen. I'm calling from London." The woman took an unusually long time to respond.

Ben heard her cough and say, "Could you repeat that name for me, please?"

"Yes, it's a Mr. Robert Bone. He sent a letter to my husband here in London, but there was no return address." Alice made her accent sound polished, more upper-class. "We need to get in touch with him as a matter of urgency."

Another pause. Then, "May I ask if you're a family member?"

At first, neither of them understood the significance of the question.

Alice said, "I'm sorry?"

"It's just that we've had a lot of inquiries recently about Mr. Bone from the United Kingdom."

"No, no, I'm not a family member. Neither of us is."

Ben was frowning. He took the telephone from Alice's hand and said, "Hello?"

More silence. He wondered if the woman had left her desk to look for more information. Then Ben heard movement on the line, a different voice, a man.

"Hello, miss?"

"No, this is Benjamin Keen. You were just talking to my wife . . ."

"Yes, sir. That's right. To your wife. I understand that she was looking for Bob?"

"That's right. I don't know if your colleague explained, but we're calling from London and—"

"I'm sorry to have to tell you this, sir, but we've had a shooting here. Almost three weeks ago now. Bob was killed out at his house. You didn't hear about it? Did nobody think to let you know?"

43

From time to time, Stephen Taploe would lie to his agents, present a more optimistic view of an operation than was realistically the case. He did it to maintain their trust. He did it to keep them onside. Running a joe was a delicate art and he had been taught long ago that it was acceptable to manipulate the truth if an officer had one eye on the long-term gain.

So Taploe had lied to Mark about Timothy Lander. He hadn't asked SIS to track him down because MI5 had done so themselves two weeks before, using phone records obtained from Divisar. In fact he had never wanted SIS to play any role in the Kukushkin investigation, for fear that he would lose control of the case, and out of a more personally motivated concern that they would discover that Christopher Keen had been an agent for MI6. Keen's dealings with the Swiss bank had also provided a convenient smoke screen which Taploe had used to lure Mark into cooperation; there was no evidence at all that Kukushkin or any other syndicate had funds lodged in Lausanne. Furthermore, in the cab Taploe had failed to disclose his intention to recruit Juris Duchev; Mark's suggestion that he try to do so had been merely a coincidence. For seven weeks, Service analysts had been weighing up the risks of running the Latvian. On Sunday, Taploe had made his pitch.

The team had Duchev's routine down pat. He was up at six every morning, usually switched on the television in the sitting room of his flat, cursed in his native tongue as he took a shower, then rang his daughter in Jelgava to catch her before she went off to work. Between five past and ten past seven he would walk fifty meters to a greasy spoon down the road and find a seat in the window. It turned out that Duchev had a fondness for British breakfasts. Thelma, who had run the café for fifteen years, knew him on sight and knew his order: plenty of black pudding, a heap of baked beans, two sunny-side fried eggs, at least three pork sausages, several rashers of bacon, and a pair of pip-oozing fried tomatoes. Duchev ate it all up, wiping his plate clean day after day with margarine-smeared pieces of toast. "You better get to him quick, boss," Ian had joked. "We're not careful, he'll be dead from a heart attack before he's any use to us."

Taploe had waited in the café from 6:45 on Sunday morning, flicking through the dreck and betrayals of the *News of the World*. Duchev appeared half an hour later, washing his breakfast down with three cups of Thelma's indifferent and scalding coffee. Ian had the van outside—just for observation—but it had proved surprisingly easy to strike up conversation and to take Duchev for a walk around Shepherd's Bush and to let him know that he was being watched around the clock and that he would find himself doing time unless he gave Her Majesty's government his full cooperation. Taploe knew all about the land in Andalusia, you see—a last-minute bonus from Mark—and all about the Bosnian prostitute in Park West Place that Duchev was banging and beating up behind Tamarov's back. Taploe didn't let on about Macklin, of course, nor profess any knowledge of the Libra conspiracy. It was enough to imply that his days as a criminal underling were numbered. He was offered a generous cash sum in return for his cooperation—and advised him to keep his mouth shut.

Forty-eight hours later, the timing of Taploe's pitch would form the subject of intense discussions at both Thames House and Vauxhall Cross. Why, for instance, had Taploe risked alerting a senior figure in the Kukushkin organization to a law enforcement presence without a cast-iron guarantee that Duchev would turn? Why, furthermore, had he attempted to recruit the Latvian just as Mark was cementing his relationship with Tamarov on Monday night? Hauled before a gray-faced committee of his superiors, Taploe would later be asked to account for every minute of the weekend, beginning with the journey by cab he had taken with Mark and Ian on Saturday morning, and ending with the events of Monday night. Time and again he insisted that every precaution had been taken. Tamarov had confirmed the venue for the dinner as the St. Martin's Lane Hotel on no fewer than three separate occasions. The position of his reserved table had been established and steps taken to secure that specific area of the restaurant for sound. A separate table, occupied by Service personnel, had also been reserved for observation. Mark had agreed to travel to the meeting by car and to have his own vehicle wired on the understanding that he would offer the Russian a lift at the end of the evening and attempt to start a conversation about Macklin. Ian Boyle had been assigned to tail the vehicle from Mark's flat in Torriano Avenue. Little of this made any impression on the members of the panel, who sensed blood and seemed determined to bring Taploe down. Something of an I-dotting, T-crossing bureaucrat himself, it nevertheless occurred to Taploe that something reductive in human nature emerged within the context of institutions. Normally sympathetic, sound-minded colleagues appeared suddenly to revel in his misfortune. It was as if his peers derived as much satisfaction from the suffering and collapse of one of their own as they would from the successful arrest and conviction of a hardened criminal. Either development, after all, could be termed progress, of one kind or another.

44

Ben worked it out inside ten minutes.

Robert Bone had been dead for three weeks. The CIA, alerted to the murder, had obtained access to Bone's house in New Hampshire and found a copy of his letter to Ben on a PC or word processor. SIS had been alerted immediately and the link to Keen's death established. Teams—perhaps from Special Branch—were then dispatched to obtain the original version of the letter from Elgin Crescent and the second copy posted to Mark's flat in Torriano Avenue. That was why Mark had never received the letter; that was why the original had gone missing from the shoebox in the studio. SIS had then instructed McCreery to convince Ben that Bone's theory about Kostov was a deception spun by the Americans. The meeting at the British Museum had been engineered: McCreery had waited until Ben was alone and then coolly plied him with Guinness and lies. SIS were covering up, trying to disguise the fact that a renegade KGB officer was killing its former associates and employees. McCreery had known all along who was responsible for his friend's murder, yet he had concealed the truth to protect the reputation of British Intelligence.

What Ben could not work out, however, was any link between Kostov and Kukushkin. Nor was it clear what Bone had done to trigger such an act of vengeance. Ben assumed that the CIA had also been involved in Mischa's recruitment, but it was a question to which he felt he would never know the answer. It was possible that Bone's death was simply a coincidence, a random act of American violence visited upon the wrong man. Not for the first time, Ben felt weighed down by ignorance, embarrassed both by his slender grasp of the facts and by the ease with which McCreery had duped him.

Toward nine o'clock, out of simple expedience, he decided to tell Alice about his brother's work for MI5. At first her reaction to the news was measured and sanguine. Sitting by an open window in the kitchen, a draught of winter air goose-pimpling her skin, Alice listened very quietly as Ben documented the extent of Macklin's involvement with Russian organized crime and seemed pleased that Roth would almost certainly suffer as a consequence of it.

"He knows nothing about this," she said, with a conviction that annoyed Ben. "When he finds out, he's going to go crazy."

Ben asked her how she could be so sure, and she barely skipped a beat.

"Just from talking to him. I get the impression Macklin pretty much runs Libra nowadays. Seb's too busy with other projects."

"What kind of other projects?"

"Well, the restaurant I was writing about, for a start."

"But Macklin's involved in that too."

"Only in a legal capacity. Tom's just a partner."

They sat in the kitchen over a supper of takeaway pizza and flat bottled Coke. Ben enjoyed the process of knitting things together, of finding their structure and shape. At one point he put his elbows on the table and seemed to draw an idea out of the air.

"You should *write* about this," he said, "about all the shit that Libra are up to. You should write about Kostov, about the whole fucking thing. That's what they fear. That's what SIS will stop at nothing to prevent. It might really help your career."

Alice only shrugged in response and moved uncomfortably in her chair, as if something were digging into her back.

"Something just occurred to me," she said. "SIS can't know anything about this. They can't know about Kukushkin's involvement with Libra. And Randall probably has no idea that Kostov is going around killing MI6 officers."

"Explain."

Alice started kneading the flesh in the palm of her hand, as if it would somehow help her to think.

"It's simple. If McCreery knew what Macklin was up to, if he was aware that Kukushkin was laundering money through Libra, he could have blamed your father's murder on the Russian mafia. That's the obvious line MI6 would have taken."

"But what about Bone's letter?"

"That's just what I'm saying. When you were talking to McCreery in the pub, why didn't he tell you about Macklin's links to the mob? That would have been the perfect response to the Kostov story. It would have taken you right off the scent. But instead, he blames a diving instructor in the Cayman Islands and some random private bank in Lausanne."

Ben was nodding, searching for a flaw in the theory. "And Randall?"

"Same thing." Alice stood up. "Randall doesn't know about Kostov. And he's never even heard of Mischa. McCreery's people are keeping this to themselves. The last thing SIS want is MI5 laughing at them. They must be going crazy trying to track Kostov down."

Ben was amazed by the simplicity of it. "You're right," he said. "And Mark wasn't going to say anything to Randall because he didn't believe Bone's letter, especially when he heard what McCreery thought about it. He thought the whole Kostov thing was bullshit."

"Precisely." Alice walked into the sitting room, looking for cigarettes. "We have to tell your brother," she said.

"He's not returning my calls. I already tried three times."

"Then leave him another message. The sooner he finds out about this, the better."

45

But Mark was already on his way to the St. Martin's Lane Hotel, steadfast in his refusal to speak to Ben. It had been a mistake to involve his brother in his work for MI5. Drawn at last into something more complicated than the application of paint to a canvas, Ben had quickly waded way out of his depth.

Mark's attitude seemed justified when he listened to the tone of Ben's first telephone message just after six o'clock. He was walking in the door from Libra and ignored the call when he noticed its origin as Elgin Crescent. The subsequent message, played aloud into the sitting room, was a rushed and word-swallowing garble about "fucking Jock" and "Sudoplatov" and it angered Mark that Ben had carelessly mentioned their names on a landline. Two hours later, after sending no fewer than three text messages urging Mark to "CALL ME," Ben telephoned again, but Mark was shaving in the bathroom with the radio on and the news of Bone's death passed him by.

He regretted his confession in the garden; everything had been simpler before Ben's inexpert participation.

Prior to Wednesday, Mark had thought of his work for Randall as a private, dignified tribute to his father's memory, and he was annoyed with himself for having lacked the courage to continue that task in secret. At least tonight he had the opportunity to meet Tamarov alone and to develop their relationship free of Ben's interference.

Taploe had made his final contact at seven thirty to ensure that Mark was set. As had been the case on Sunday, he again avoided mentioning that Ian would be tailing Mark's car to the meeting, and had said nothing about the Watchers who would be positioned across from Tamarov's table in the St. Martin's Lane Hotel. This was standard operational procedure: he didn't want Mark second-guessing the position of MI5 staff while the meeting was in progress.

"Rest assured we'll be keeping a close eye on you all the way in," he said. "Just go where Tamarov takes you, don't try to rush anything along. It's important that you appear amenable without seeming eager or greedy. Remember, he sees you as essential to Kukushkin's long-term success. Accept his offer of a job, but ask the right questions about control and hierarchy. Tell him you need a break after what has happened to your father and that Roth will understand your situation."

At ten past eight, Mark picked out his favorite Hayward suit and then, as a conscious expression of his duty to Keen, a pale blue Brooks Brothers shirt that had belonged to his father. It fitted perfectly, tailored as if for the same two bodies. In a further moment of conscious sentiment, Mark then selected a pair of silver cuff links that his mother had given him as a twenty-first birthday present. He had fifty minutes to reach the hotel for the nine o'clock appointment, and time for a beer in the sitting room before walking to the car. There was no sense in being rushed.

He was turning on the television when Tamarov contacted his mobile. Glancing at the display, Mark felt a thud of worry that he was calling to cancel the dinner. Muting the TV, he put his drink on the floor and said, "Vladimir?"

"Yes, Mark, hello."

"Is everything all right?"

"A change of plan, my friend. A change of plan." His voice was jovial and easygoing; it was hard to picture the expression on his face. "I meant to call before but I have been very busy with work. I am sorry." It sounded as though the Russian were calling from a deserted building; there was an echo of open space. "Perhaps we can meet for dinner an hour later. I have altered our reservation. This is appropriate?"

Mark smiled at the mistaken idiom and said, "Yeah, no problem."

"But I am thinking I should introduce you to Christina at the restaurant before we meet for dinner. I am standing with her now."

"Christina?"

"She would be your assistant in Hackney. It is not possible for her to come to the West End because she is working here. Do you remember where to come?"

"Sure." It did not cross Mark's mind that he should tell Randall about the change in circumstance. *Just go where Tamarov takes you. Don't try to rush anything along.* Besides, Christina might be pretty.

"You will come by cab?" Tamarov asked. It didn't sound as though he cared about the answer. "By car?"

"Car, probably," Mark replied, and used the excuse that Randall had given him. "Stops me drinking too much."

Tamarov laughed enormously.

"Then this is easy for you. The traffic is not so bad. Avoid King's Cross with the roadworks and breakdowns. I came through Highbury Islington and got here in ten minutes. Just avoid the one-way system near the restaurant."

"You were speeding, Vladimir?" Mark joked, trying to match his breezy mood.

"Not me," Tamarov replied. "Juris. The Latvian, he drives like a maniac."

46

Torriano Avenue curves steeply uphill, left to right, but Ian Boyle had a good view of the street from his position in the Southern Electric van. He saw Mark emerge from the house at 20:25, wearing a black coat and carrying a mobile phone. It was like catching sight of an old friend in the distance: the easy, sloping walk, the way Mark's head bobbed from side to side as if swayed by thought or music. On a typical London evening in late winter, indistinct of color and temperature, locals drifted into the corner shop at the foot of the hill and emerged with flimsy green plastic bags filled with cans and milk and videos. A very faint mist was visible in the glow of the streetlights as Ian dialed Taploe's number.

"Yes?"

"Boss. He's leaving now. Getting into the car."

"Good. Contact me again if anything changes. I'm just sitting here waiting at my desk."

Ian started the engine as Mark started his. Sounds inaudible to one another, just two vehicles leaving the street. He let Mark reach the top of the avenue before pulling out and followed the black Saab as it slipped into a stream of cars heading south along Brecknock Road.

Ian had been listening to Jazz FM while he waited and he turned up the volume on a Billie Holiday cover of "Summertime," humming the tune in the shunting traffic. The job was so routine he drove almost on autopilot, keeping the van a hundred meters back from the target, separated by three, sometimes four other cars. He knew Mark to be a decent driver, quick and liable to switch lanes smoothly in the quest for space. One time, ages ago now, back when Taploe had his suspicions, he had been tailing Mark from Heathrow and lost him at the Hogarth roundabout, just disappeared into the Chiswick streets never to be seen again. Ian thought the same thing was about to happen when he saw the Saab make an unexpected turn off York Way, the two-lane north–south artery feeding traffic into King's Cross. He was sitting high up in the van and had a decent view of Mark's car as it steered left toward Islington.

"Where you going, mate?" he muttered to himself, and had to accelerate through a changing amber to stay on Mark's tail.

They were on Market Road now, not the route Ian would have taken to the West End but maybe Blindside knew a shortcut, a trick. After all, there were roadworks in King's Cross until April 2047, so maybe he was doing them both a favor. Still they kept heading east, crossing Caledonian Road, then directly into the heart of Islington. "What's he up to?" Ian said again, shutting off the radio to concentrate. That was when Taploe put the call through to his mobile. "Boss?"

"Ian?"

"What's going on? I'm tailing Blindside to the hotel but it's arse about face. He's on his way east, taking me into Highbury."

"There's some confusion," Taploe said.

Ian was speaking hands-free, a microphone clipped to the sun visor above the wheel.

"What kind of confusion?"

Taploe took a while to respond. "Katy has just handed me some intel. We think Tamarov may have changed the meeting. We think he may be en route to Heathrow."

"*Heathrow?*"

"It's not confirmed yet. Where's Blindside?"

"Like I said. Going east. I'm on . . ." Ian had to look for a street sign. "St. Paul's Road. Nowhere near Covent Garden, in other words. Maybe he's got errands to run."

Again Taploe waited before responding. It sounded as if the boss was holding four conversations simultaneously.

"That's not the case," Taploe said eventually. "We had a tap on a call Tamarov made half an hour ago. He told Blindside he was with the Latvian in Hackney, at the new restaurant. Asked him to get there prior to the meeting at St. Martin's Lane. Then someone else phoned the hotel and changed their reservation to ten o'clock."

"So what's the problem?" Ian asked. "Why Heathrow?"

"The problem is, we traced the first call to Paddington Station. Got it to within sixty feet."

"And where is he now?"

"Still trying to establish that. A conversation took place immediately after Tamarov had spoken to Blindside. In Russian, the phone moving west."

"He was talking to our friend?"

"To our friend." Taploe cleared his throat, a noise that sounded like nerves. "He's not in Hackney. We think Duchev may be on his way to Helsinki. Michael lost him at five. Again it's not confirmed.

I'm trying to obtain a translation of the conversation. Of the transcript. These things take time."

Up ahead, Ian saw Mark's Saab, black as a silhouette, swing fast into the right-hand lane of Ball's Pond Road, as if preparing to make a turn south. A pretty girl was jaywalking through the traffic and he thought he saw her smile in Mark's direction. In his rearview mirror two motorcycles, fifty feet back, were crawling single file in the narrow gap between cars.

Taploe, his voice now pinched with stress, said, "I think we should get Blindside out of there. Tell him the meeting is off."

"You sure about that, boss?"

A beat.

"I'm sure about that."

Taploe didn't sound it. He was relying on technology, a satellite hunch, on little more than a feeling that something was wrong. Up ahead, Mark indicated on the green light and Ian followed him.

"Can you see the Saab?" Taploe asked. He sounded demoralized and Ian felt for him: if Duchev had done a runner twenty-four hours after the boss had tried to pitch him, there'd be hell to pay.

"He's making a right-hander," he said. Then a white Fiat Punto stalled in front of Ian's van and the lights were changing back. One of the motorcyclists passed Ian's window, frog-walking his machine. Ian leaned on the horn. There was a second passenger, leather clad in black, riding pillion on the back of the bike. They buzzed past the Punto and ran the red light.

"Fuck," Ian said and hit the horn again. Both the bike and the Saab were no longer visible around the corner. He wondered where the second motorcycle had gone. It was the training, the intuition. One of the motorcycles was missing.

"What's going on?" Taploe's voice rose on the question. "Get to him, Ian. He's not answering his mobile. Get Blindside back to Kentish Town."

"I'm trying, boss," he said. "I'm trying. Somebody stalled in front of the van."

Ian noticed exhaust fumes emerging from the tailpipe of the Punto and looked up to see the back of a green Range Rover edging slowly around the corner. *Good*, he thought, *there's traffic on the other side, something to hold Mark up*. Then he saw the missing bike, two feet back in the passenger-side mirror, long female hair dropping below the helmet. Speaking to Taploe in his office, he said, "I think everything's OK, boss. I think everything's OK."

Mark had been listening to demo tapes all the way from Torriano Avenue: new tracks from Danny Tenaglia, and a set by a French DJ he'd never heard of who was looking for a gig in London. He had turned the music up high as a reaction against the microphones installed in his car. The volume allowed him to maintain his privacy. Mark was shutting out the spooks.

Without thinking, he had thrown his mobile phone into the back of the Saab, an awkward arm-twist and stretch behind his seat. As a consequence, he spent most of the journey wondering if the constant stream of voice calls and text messages was important Libra business or yet more attempts by his brother to get in touch. Mark was aware, too, that Randall might be trying to make contact, but he was committed to acting alone tonight, without interference or advice from his controller. He felt that things had worked best in the past when he had been left to his own devices; when you introduced a third party, it seemed, the business of spying became altogether more complicated.

On Ball's Pond Road, he opened an *A to Z* and realized that he would have to make an immediate right-hand turn at the next junction to avoid the one-way system on the approach to the restaurant. Flicking out an indicator, Mark pulled the Saab quickly into an adjacent lane, catching the eye of a pretty young girl who was weaving on foot across the traffic. She smiled at him and he grinned back, making the turn at speed. Somebody behind him blasted their horn: the noise was loud and relentless and it smothered the first and second rings of another call on his phone. Steering with his right hand, Mark stretched into the back seat and began padding around for the mobile, hitting papers, freebie T-shirts, a map, cans and bottles. He could not find the phone without looking.

"Where are you?" he muttered, his bicep starting to ache. Then the traffic came to a halt and he was able to twist right round in his seat. The phone was buried in his coat and Mark wrenched it out of the folds, seeing "Rand" on the readout in black.

"Hello?"

A motorbike pulled up parallel to the driver's door, its engine a soothing pulse. The first shot, fired by the passenger riding pillion, obliterated the window of the Saab and passed three inches behind Mark's neck.

Taploe said, "Mark?"

The sound he could hear from the room in Thames House was at first indistinguishable from squelch or static. Then he heard traffic noise, and the blast of a distant horn.

The shooter could see clearly now, watching Mark turn dazed in his seat, looking up at the bike and reaching for the handle of the door. His hair and his clothes were covered in glass, shards like roughened diamonds that bit deep into his skin. The second shot killed Mark outright, a sound Taploe heard as a sustained scream because a woman had stepped out of a nearby shop and was approaching the Saab from the pavement. The bike moved off immediately, up to forty miles per hour inside five seconds and gone before Ian could see it. Alerted by the first shot, he had come around the corner on foot, and it was just as if the world had ceased to move on a switch.

47

Taploe's colleagues gave him a lot of credit for volunteering to break the news to Ben; that was a brave thing to do in the circumstances, a grim task he might easily have delegated to someone junior on the team. Taking three Special Branch officers to Elgin Crescent, he put Alice and Ben in a vehicle en route to a Kensington safe house, where he informed them of Mark's death. He thought Ben had recognized his face from the night of Keen's murder, but perhaps the shock of the news deflected any suspicions he might have had. Watching his reaction, Taploe was reminded of Tamarov's remark in the club on Friday night—*they were screaming, like animals on the floor*—and he was glad that Alice seemed to provide some comfort to her husband, a wife's consoling touch. It looked as though things had improved between them since the end of her affair with Roth. God knows he would need her now. God knows Ben would not want to be alone.

Juris Duchev made it to Moscow from Helsinki, but Customs stopped Tamarov at Heathrow checking on to a late Aeroflot flight with an unidentified woman who would later be released without charge. The translation of his conversation with Duchev came through shortly after midnight, but was lost until morning in the panic and confusion of events. It appeared that the Russians had had no concerns or worries about MI5 surveillance until Taploe had mentioned the land in Andalusia to Duchev in his pitch on Sunday morning. The Latvian had told only one person about his secret plans to retire. That one person just happened to be Mark Keen.

At first they couldn't find Philippe d'Erlanger. He was not at the restaurant in Covent Garden, nor sleeping at his flat in Tottenham Court Road. The Belgian was eventually discovered back at the lap-dancing club in Finchley, tucked into a darkened corner with Ayesha giggling softly in his ear. Accompanied outside by two officers, he was taken swiftly into custody and visited at dawn by Paul Quinn.

Macklin had flown to New York on Libra business on Sunday, and when Taploe heard that he had received a telephone call from Roth and then fled immediately to Grand Cayman, he thought that at last he had conclusive proof of Roth's involvement. The call had been logged at 15:47 local time, ten minutes before the shooting in London. How else could Roth have known that Mark was about to be killed? How else could he have been in a position to tip off Macklin that the game was up? But this was to prove the final irony of the Kukushkin case, the one random element that neither Taploe nor Quinn could ever have anticipated. It bore the stamp of SIS. It was the revelation of Elizabeth Dulong.

48

She came to Thames House at midday on Tuesday, accompanied by Jock McCreery and an attitude of barely suppressed hostility. Quinn had returned from interviewing d'Erlanger and was drinking tea with Taploe in his office on the third floor. Neither man had slept for thirty hours.

"Can I help you?" Taploe said when Dulong entered without knocking. He recognized McCreery instantly as Keen's friend from SIS.

"This room's too small, too public," Dulong announced. "We have a very serious problem. Can you take us somewhere more private?"

She, too, had been awake all night, coming to terms with the fact that senior employees at the company belonging to one of her most valuable intelligence assets had been under MI5 surveillance for almost a year. There were simple reasons why Taploe had never been able to pin anything on Sebastian Roth, and why Macklin had been given such free rein at Libra. In a windowless conference room in the basement of Thames House, Dulong explained that Roth had been an SIS agent for three years.

If Taploe's reaction to the revelation was at first one of numb resignation, Quinn almost exploded.

"Why the fuck weren't we told?" he said.

"Why the fuck didn't you ask?" McCreery replied bluntly.

That exchange set the tone of the three-hour meeting, a period characterized by long, embarrassed silences, the unmistakable sound of careers on the skids, of buck-passing and the covering of backs. When Quinn had recovered enough to ask his first question, he directed it at McCreery.

"How did you find out that we were investigating Libra?"

"Audio surveillance," McCreery told him wearily. "A conversation between Benjamin and Alice last night. That was when we put two and two together."

Quinn, slumped heavily in a chair like a man who had over-eaten, looked stunned.

"*Audio surveillance?*" he said. "Why was Elgin Crescent being bugged?"

McCreery coughed nervously and made an unnecessary fuss of straightening a set of papers in front of him. He was seated opposite Quinn at the far end of a long wooden table in the conference room, his walking stick leaning against the wall.

"The property was under audio surveillance because of a letter Benjamin received from a retired CIA agent who was murdered recently in New Hampshire."

It took a further forty-five minutes for McCreery to brief Taploe and Quinn about Robert Bone. Tired after working eighteen-hour days for almost a month without cease, his account of the Kostov operation was matter-of-fact to the point of bloodlessness. The men from MI5 listened in awed silence to the litany of SIS deceits: from Bill Taylor, a subordinate of McCreery's, issuing instructions to a Tracy Frakes for the theft of Bone's letters from Elgin Crescent and Torriano Avenue; to McCreery himself engineering a meeting with Ben at the British Museum, at which he had lied about Keen's work in Afghanistan and misleadingly blamed the CIA for Mischa's recruitment. Taploe and Quinn's proper astonishment, however, was reserved for the story of McCreery's entirely fictitious son, Dan, and his difficult wife, Bella, invented apparently as a means of gaining Ben's empathy and trust.

"That was a quality touch," Quinn said, with heavy sarcasm. "Really first-rate, mate, really classy. What was that about, eh? Showing Ben we're all human? Implying he'd been wrong about his dad? Jock's children don't really understand their parents so Christopher's didn't as well? What was the thinking behind it? Share your wisdom and experience with the rest of the class."

"Can we get just back to the subject?" Dulong said, before McCreery had a chance to retaliate. He looked genuinely angry at being spoken to in such a manner by a man half his age.

"Of course we can," Taploe said. His approach was conciliatory, because he had nothing left to lose. "So what happened with Macklin? We heard this morning that Roth tipped him off."

"He's in Grand Cayman," Dulong replied, stumbling on another bit of awkward news. She was at the angle of the table, just a few feet from McCreery, a white polystyrene cup of water lying untouched at her right hand. "And it wasn't a tip-off," she said. "Sebastian just flew off the handle."

Standing by the door, Taploe spoke in a voice that was barely audible.

"Come again?"

"I said, Sebastian flew off the handle." Dulong's voice was clipped and authoritative, the faint Lothian accent becoming increasingly pronounced with stress. She smoothed out the sleeves of her white blouse as Quinn stared at her, shaking his head in disbelief. "I telephoned Sebastian last night as soon as I learned of your investigation. I wanted to arrange an emergency meeting with him, to discuss the best way to proceed . . ."

". . . and Roth then called Macklin straightaway," Quinn said contemptuously, arms folded into a visible reproach.

"Against his better judgment. And against my strict instructions."

"And how long did you say you've been running him?" Taploe asked.

"About three years." Dulong was fighting for a way out. "A long time before you started to have your suspicions about Libra, in any event. Roth has been doing some very important work for us on the Russian government. His government contacts in London are also first-rate. It's important that you both realize he brings in pedigree CX on a vast range of subjects."

Quinn stirred. "And you're—what—here to tell us how determined you are to keep him on board, to keep that sort of information rolling into the Cross?"

He could see it happening, even if Taploe could not, could already sense what they had come for. The fix. The deal. All the hard work on Kukushkin lost for the sake of a source and a few careers.

"That is certainly one of my aims," Dulong conceded.

A long silence ensued. The trepidation of a game of cards. Then Taploe moved forward, emerging from the corner of the room as if from within his own shadow.

"So what are SIS saying?" he asked. His manner was oddly deferential for one who held the FCO in such high contempt. "What is the exact purpose of this meeting?"

McCreery answered on Dulong's behalf.

"We're saying that it won't have escaped your attention that Sebastian Roth is an immensely well-connected young man." As he spoke he tapped a Biro on the surface of the table, as if to reinforce his point. "He has friends in high places. His father, for example, is a Tory peer who sits in the Lords . . ."

"Who Roth never speaks to," Quinn said quickly.

McCreery dropped the pen.

"Do you think that I might be able to finish?" There was a military sting to the question. "I was nevertheless going to say that there are a number of people, Elizabeth included, who would prefer it if Roth were not exposed, which would inevitably happen if your inquiries into Libra and Kukushkin ever entered into the public realm."

Taploe breathed very deeply.

"I don't understand how Roth can be so invaluable to you," he said. "After all, he's not even aware of what's going on in his own backyard." The observation was almost apologetic. "How can Elizabeth trust an agent who alerts a suspect against her own specific instructions?"

"Sebastian's a strong character, a hothead," Dulong replied.

Quinn laughed undisguisedly.

"What's funny?"

"A *hothead*? A *strong character*?"

"Yes—a strong character who makes split-second decisions and acts on instinct." Dulong had to raise her voice. "Usually that quality is a great asset to us. It is illustrative of how hard Sebastian has been working for SIS that he has allowed Thomas to assume a greater responsibility over the running of Libra. He trusted him, of course, with unfortunate consequences."

Briefly Dulong looked flustered. Quinn was getting under her skin.

"That's what you'd call it, would you? Unfortunate consequences?"

McCreery stood up and appeared to wince at a stab of pain in his legs.

"Look," he said, "we're all here today to try to sort this thing out. We're all of us here today attempting to resolve this little dilemma."

But Quinn did not back down.

"That's what we're here for, is it, Jock? Is that the line you're peddling?" Quinn was the youngest person in the room, yet he would not allow his relative lack of experience to count against him: on the contrary, he felt professionally and intellectually obliged to question MI6 every step of the way. "I'll tell you what I think you're here for. I think you're here for cover-up. I think you're here to make sure we take the heat for what's happened. I think you're here to make sure that nobody steals your pension."

"I am merely stating," McCreery said, coming down hard on the consonants, "our desire to go about this in a civilized fashion." He was leaning on the table. "Stephen, I'm sure you would concur."

"Of course," Taploe replied, "of course," and flashed Quinn a look of disquiet. "Let's just hear them out, Paul, eh? Let's just at least do that."

Dulong seized on this.

"I may as well tell you that Jock and I came here directly from a meeting at the Cross. Seeing as you've brought it up, the consensus is that Libra should remain untouched. Thomas Macklin cannot be prosecuted."

"Here we go," Quinn muttered under his breath. "Here we go."

"In these unfortunate circumstances, Macklin must be allowed to remain in Grand Cayman." Dulong continued as if he had not spoken. "We wouldn't ask the authorities there to make an arrest. Equally, if and when he returns to the UK, the Crown cannot prosecute for money laundering. Sebastian's role would inevitably emerge."

"Fucking bullshit," Quinn shouted, flinging a fist out into the room. Everyone turned to face him. "That is an absolute load of fucking bullshit and you . . ."

"It is not . . ."

But he could shout louder than Dulong.

". . . you know as well as I do that the only reason you're prepared to protect Macklin is to conceal the fact that a former KGB agent slipped out of Moscow and murdered two Western intelligence officers before anybody knew what was going on."

McCreery stood in a bid for control. Quinn's idealism needed to be snuffed out quickly or the plan would unravel.

"We cannot deny that we are anxious to keep Kostov's movements under wraps," he conceded. "That much is true." Slowly, he limped toward the door. "But this has an impact on the Security Service just as much as it affects our side. Imagine how difficult it will become to recruit agents if potential targets think British Intelligence cannot protect them. Would you fancy going back to Ireland, to Paris, to Frankfurt, with the Kostov scandal hanging in the air? *Would* you?"

"I've never been to Frankfurt," Quinn said flatly, because he could not resist the joke. "I'm a lawyer, mate. I'm paid to work in

London. I'm employed by the Home Office to help track down and prosecute the kind of people you're talking about setting free."

"So we're just going to let Macklin go?" Taploe asked, as if the revelation were still dawning on him and did not yet seem scandalous. "What about Tamarov?"

"I'm afraid we would also condone Tamarov's release." Dulong did not dare look at Quinn. "He would not be permitted to return to the United Kingdom, although any established organized crime networks would of course be dismantled. But prosecution is out of the question. Ditto Juris Duchev. Now nobody's saying that's the ideal solution but . . ."

"Too fucking right it's not the ideal solution." Quinn pressed himself up from the table and walked toward McCreery. He knew that his appearance worked against him—his weight, his sweat—but he still held out the faint hope that his arguments would carry the day. "Tamarov has a UK right of residency. How are you going to take that away from him?"

"Look," Dulong countered, "this has come from very high up . . ."

"What, *God* doesn't want Tamarov arrested? Did He tell you that in person, or just send a courier?"

Nobody laughed.

"It's not all bad news," Dulong said stiffly. "Macklin won't be coming home. He'll think the Russians know about the double dip and assume he's a marked man in London. At our earlier meeting, my colleagues also discussed the possibility of asking the Cayman authorities to implement a Mareva injunction on Macklin's accounts."

"What's a Mareva injunction?" Taploe asked, as a phone rang in an office across the hall.

"It means they're going to try and freeze Macklin's assets," Quinn explained quietly.

"That is correct." Dulong straightened her skirt. "So you can see that it's not as if he's got away scot-free."

"Well, that's assuming the Cayman courts agree," Quinn said, swallowing a glass of water in three loud gulps. He sat down. "Any foreign authority would need conclusive evidence linking Macklin to the Pentagon accounts and to the criminal activity in London."

"But we *have* evidence, Paul," Taploe said. "More than enough, in fact."

"Course we do," Quinn tried. "But will Elizabeth and her merry men be sharing it with their new pals down in the Caribbean? Somehow I doubt it."

Dulong caught McCreery's eye and he dug her out of a tight spot.

"You needn't have any concerns about that, Paul," he said, collecting his stick from the wall. "The boys in Cayman are pretty keen nowadays to be seen to be cleaning up their act. They'll comply, believe me."

"And then wonder why we haven't asked to have Macklin extradited."

"Well, let's worry about that one later, shall we?" Quinn collapsed into a slouch. This was self-evidently a fait accompli. He wished, not for the first time in his career, that he were ten or fifteen years older, not just the bright, straight-talking Cockney whose views were eventually expendable.

"Macklin would also be disbarred from practicing law in the UK," Dulong said, almost as if she were trying to cheer him up.

"He won't be able to gain registration with any foreign law society or enjoy rights of audience in a foreign court."

Wearily, Quinn contested even that assertion.

"Not true," he said. "Macklin was dual-qualified. He's a member of the Florida Bar. Did a degree in Miami nine years ago."

This was a revelation too far for McCreery and Dulong, both of whom looked stumped.

"Then we'll just have to have a word with our American friends, try and sort something out," McCreery offered. He kept a straight face while saying it.

"And what happens to Libra Moscow?" Taploe asked, as if it was pointless to dwell on the frank impossibility of Macklin's or Tamarov's arrest. Better just to wrap things up and try to salvage his career.

"Well, that was one of the things Sebastian and I talked about this morning," Dulong said gratefully.

"Roth's in London?" Taploe asked.

"That's correct." She took a plastic clip out of her bag and used it to pin up her hair. "At this stage, he thinks the club will most probably be franchised to a local entrepreneur in Moscow. Gradually, Libra will sever ties. He's going to stay in London for the foreseeable future and take hands-on control of the London operation. There may even be a stock-market float."

"I see, I see." Taploe smiled, sickening Quinn with the speed of his compliance. A queasy mood of settled business had suddenly pervaded the room.

"And Kostov?" he said. Quinn had noticed they had left the Russian out.

McCreery tapped his walking stick on the carpet.

"Well, there at least there's some good news. While we've been sitting here our colleagues should have finalized plans for Kostov's extradition."

Quinn stirred.

"How does that work?"

"Very simply." McCreery clasped his hands together and produced a punchy smile. "Kostov has been tracked to one of Kukushkin's properties. He's been under surveillance for several days."

Taploe was confused.

"He was working for Viktor Kukushkin?"

"Not exactly. Dimitri does some very occasional work for the organization, but only as a favor to keep him in rubles. Kukushkin and Kostov are old friends, you see, from school and university. Grew up in the same Moscow suburb. Twenty years ago, Kukushkin was a big player in the Party machine so, like a lot of ex-KGB, Kostov was able to maintain some very strong links with organized crime. He was farmed out to Byelorussia after the Mischa fiasco, but Kukushkin kept an eye on him. And when he started to benefit from Gorbachev's reforms, he brought him back into the fold, found him somewhere to live, that sort of thing."

Taploe stretched. "What sort of work does Kostov do for him?" He might have been inquiring after the time.

"As I said, very little. We don't really know much beyond the fact that Kukushkin has always looked after him. Some instruction, perhaps. The odd tip-off. A lot of Kostov's breed worked euphemistically as 'consultants' of one kind or another, though it's unlikely he would have been all that effective. Kukushkin was heavily involved in strong-arming government ministers into transferring state money to privatized brokerage houses in the early days of Yeltsin. We're fairly sure Kostov helped out on that. He was always best when operating as a bit of a thug . . ."

". . . and eventually he came across Keen's name because of his work for Divisar?" Taploe said.

"Almost certainly," Dulong replied. "Not that Kukushkin knew anything about it."

Quinn sensed they were concealing something, and challenged them.

"You said Kostov was under surveillance."

"That is correct."

"Who from? Moscow law enforcement?"

Dulong bought herself some time by wiping her nose on a small white handkerchief concealed in her bag. McCreery looked uncertainly at the floor and knocked his wedding ring against the table. Quinn realized he had found the lie. Their eyes had gone.

"Come on, out with it. Who's watching him?"

"*We* are." McCreery spat the confession as if it had been taken under duress. "SIS are watching the apartment block."

"He's not under police arrest?"

"No."

And thus the full picture emerged. All loose ends tied.

Quinn's mouth slackened in disbelief as he recognized that McCreery's little problem had been resolved with a grim sleight of hand.

"Fuckin' hell," he whispered. "Fuckin' hell. Six have talked to Kukushkin, haven't they? You've struck a fucking deal."

Dulong balled the handkerchief under the sleeve of her blouse and indicated to McCreery that she would be prepared to answer the question.

"We have channels in Moscow," she said. "The quid pro quo involves Kostov's handover . . ."

But Quinn did not let her finish.

"In return for what?"

"In return for the conditions we have already outlined. Prosecution immunity for Tamarov, d'Erlanger, Macklin, and Duchev. Total withdrawal of UK operations. Surely the latter is of some comfort to the Service after all your hard work?"

Taploe stepped between Quinn and Dulong as if he felt a professional obligation to speak on behalf of MI5. Quinn looked up at his pale, exhausted features—a man failed now, surely beyond redemption—and felt that his whole future would depend on Taploe's response. If he caved in to the SIS plan, he would quit; if he showed some semblance of disgust, they could at least walk away with a moral advantage. Taploe briefly touched his moustache.

"I have to say first and foremost that I don't admire what has happened here today." This seemed encouragingly unequivocal. "To negotiate with criminals, to strike deals with members of a recognized organized crime syndicate makes me feel very uncomfortable. Very uncomfortable indeed." Quinn inched forward. Perhaps it was going to be OK; perhaps there were standards after all. "Nevertheless, I can understand why such a decision has been taken and, although I do not condone it, I recognize that, at the very least, the Kukushkin organization cannot now, at least in the medium to long term, flourish on the UK mainland . . ."

For a large man Quinn stood with surprising speed, his hands raised up as if to block out Taploe's charade. Twisting to gather his notes, he folded them under one arm and moved toward the door.

"Paul? Where are you going?" Taploe asked.

"Into the private sector."

"What?"

There were shadows of black sweat under his arms.

"You really think Kukushkin is just going to hand Kostov over, friend or no friend? You really think he'll keep his side of the bargain, let him get to court?"

The tone of the question was at once mocking and profoundly serious.

"That's the quid pro quo," Dulong answered uncertainly.

"You don't believe us?" McCreery said. "You still remain skeptical?"

Quinn shook his head.

"Oh, it's not that I don't believe you, Jock. It's not that I don't believe you."

"What, then?"

He was stepping through the door.

"It's the thing I knew would happen." He was muttering the words, almost to himself. "The thing I feared. The compromise."

"Paul?" Taploe said again.

Quinn looked up. His face might have been that of a man who has been informed of a tragedy: washed-out, shocked, then suddenly indignant.

"Yeah? What is it, Stephen? What is it you're going to say?" He was in the corridor now, eyes accusing them, looking back as if on a lost innocence. "You think I got into this business to listen to what you just said?"

"You have to understand that . . ."

But Quinn had walked away. Dulong, McCreery, and Taploe were left staring out into an empty corridor. After a time, McCreery said, "Temper, temper," and Dulong had the nerve to smile. Taploe, however, felt a greater sense of shame than he had ever experienced at any point in his career.

"So it's settled, then?" McCreery said.

"It's settled," Taploe replied, after a long delay. His voice was very low.

"And you, Elizabeth?"

"Settled," said Dulong.

"Good. Then we move on. I'm not sure I want to spend another moment of my life worrying about Dimitri bloody Kostov."

SPRING

49

The Russian is sitting alone on the back seat of a brand-new Audi A4. Smooth, cushioned upholstery, a smell of leather and artificial pine. It is dusk in the suburbs of Moscow, banks of low white clouds bringing late spring snow to the capital. Through the back window of the vehicle, nineteen storeys up, he can make out the balcony of the flat where he has lived for the past eleven days, his latest refuge in a long line of hotel rooms and apartments. The flat, belonging to an associate of Viktor Kukushkin, has a single window looking out on to five gray, deserted breeze-block towers, each of them defaced with structure cracks and graffiti. Kostov is not going to miss that view. He is looking forward to the house in the country.

Three hundred meters from the car, across a flat expanse of buckled concrete randomly interrupted by weeds, two young boys are playing football against a white brick wall. It is below freezing and the light is failing all the time, but their eyes must have adjusted to the pre-dark gloom because the yellow ball cracks regularly against the wall. If he strains for it, Kostov can hear the rubber contact of their shoes against the asphalt, voices echoing among the buildings, the sudden gasps and shouts.

He adjusts his position in the back seat and leans on a large canvas bag containing most of his clothes and possessions. A man of sixty-three with his whole life in the back seat of a car. Kostov grimaces at the thought. There are aches in every part of his body—in the back of his head, along the sciatic nerves of his thigh, behind his knees—and the temperature inside the vehicle only makes this worse. This is not the cold of London or New England; it is the bone chill of Russia under snow. He raps on the window and urges the driver inside.

Leaning on the roof, Juris Duchev finishes his telephone call and steps into the car, bringing with him an odor of sweat and impatience. Like Kostov, he is also wearing a black winter coat and thick gloves, one of which he removes in order to light a cigarette.

"You want one, Dimitri?" he asks in Russian, turning to the back seat.

"Not for me," Kostov replies. "Not for me. Just turn on the fucking engine. Get some heat in here."

The smoke now deep in his lungs, Duchev turns the key in the ignition and the engine hums into life. Fans pump blasts of cold air into the car through vents in the dashboard and floor.

"Fucking freezing," Kostov complains.

"Just give it time," he is quietly told.

Do they know? Have they found out about Keen and Bone? Kostov lives with this persistent doubt, the paranoia of imminent discovery. He watches the eyes of Kukushkin's people all the time for the tell of sudden betrayal. For days, he has suspected SIS of following him around town, two skinny foreigners with the look of British diplomats. Somebody, someday, will put two and two together. Some-

body, someday, will find the link between Kostov and Christopher Keen.

"I thought you lived in London, Juris?" he asks. "How come you're back in Moscow?"

"I just came home," Duchev replies. "Just came home for new business."

Duchev loathes Kostov, despises him. A so-called friend of Viktor whose vengeance has ruined London. He takes his old friend for apartments and money and gives him only trouble in return. Reversing the Audi in the narrow road, he heads for the highway and actually looks forward to the night ahead. The phone call merely confirmed that all the arrangements are in place, the plan to foil the British and to end Dimitri's lies. Kostov is not being handed over to SIS. Kostov is being taken out to the woods.

"Where are we going?" he asks, lolling tiredly on the back seat like a fat, unexercised dog. "Viktor told me I was going to his house in the country."

"I have a job beyond Sheremetjevo," Duchev explains. "A package needs collecting. Then we'll go to the village, Dimitri. Then you can see your new home."

Driving at fifty miles an hour through blinding April snow, Duchev can track the SIS tail in the Audi's rearview mirror. A Volkswagen with St. Petersburg plates that has been following Kostov for days. This is his only problem. This is what he has to lose. But right on time, just as the phone call had promised, the strobe of a police vehicle punches through the night, sixty meters behind the Volkswagen and closing all the time. Good, Duchev thinks, Pasha doing what he has been paid to do. Above the roar of the road he can hear the siren and watches with pleasure as the Volkswagen is pulled to the edge of the motorway. Imagine the swearing in that car right now. Imagine the fat load of trouble those British spies are going to get into just as soon as they get back to the embassy.

And from now on it is easy: Kostov even falls asleep in the back. For an hour Duchev drives in silence, deep into the black night south of Moscow. At eight o'clock he spots the turnoff into the woods. There are no other vehicles behind or in front of him and he turns the Audi without indicating onto a single-track road running east into the forest.

"Where are we going?" Kostov asks, muttering from the depths of his sleep.

"Package," Duchev intones, "package," and reaches for the handle of the gun.

He parks and switches off the engine in a clearing half a mile along the road, surrounded on all sides by high, broad pines. Nobody in sight. Nothing but snow. Then, blinding in the darkness, the sudden momentary flash of Tamarov's headlights, a signal hidden discreetly ahead among a thick clump of trees.

Kostov, dreaming of Mischa, is never conscious of the shot. A single bullet to the head, and then perpetual sleep. He is stripped of himself, of his teeth and fingers, while Tamarov soaks the vehicle in petrol. Within five minutes the brand-new Audi and Kostov and his canvas bag are ablaze in a brilliant column of fire that flares and heats the trees. The Russians are already on their way home. Now they can go back to business.

ACKNOWLEDGMENTS

The American writer referred to in chapter 38 is Paul Auster; Vladimir Tamarov quotes from Auster's book *The Invention of Solitude* (Faber & Faber, 1989). I am also indebted to the following authors and their works:

Inside the Soviet Army in Afghanistan by Alexander Alexiev (RAND, 1988); *9-11* by Noam Chomsky (Seven Stories Press, 2001); *Comrade Criminal: Russia's New Mafiya* by Stephen Handelman (Yale University Press, 1995); *Holy War, Unholy Victory: Eyewitness to the CIA's Secret War in Afghanistan* by Kurt Lohbeck (Regnery Gateway, 1993); *Lenin's Tomb* (Vintage, 1994) and *Resurrection: The Struggle for a New Russia* (Picador, 1997), both by David Remnick; *The Laundrymen* by Jeffrey Robinson (Simon & Schuster, 1998); *UK Eyes Alpha* by Mark Urban (Faber & Faber, 1996); and *The Third Secret* by Nigel West (HarperCollins, 2001). Rajan Datar's 2001 film for the BBC's *The Money Programme, Big Business Beats*, was also very helpful.

C.C.
Madrid, January 2003